Other books published by the same author include:

Novel
   The Time to Live (Ward Lock 1959)

Educational Books
As L. G. Humphrys
   Wonders of Life series, Books 1–4 (Blackie & Son 1959–64)
   Life is Exciting (Blackie & Son 1959)
   Science is Exciting (Blackie & Son 1966)
   Science Through Experience series, Books 1–4 (Blond Educational Books 1969–70)
   Your Body at Work (Basil Blackwell's Learning library 1963)
   Weather in Britain (Basil Blackwell's Learning library 1966)
   Men Learn to Fly (Basil Blackwell's Learning library 1966)
   Drinks (Basil Blackwell's Learning library 1971)
   Men Travel in Space (Basil Blackwell's Learning library 1971)
   Glass and Glassmaking (Basil Blackwell's Learning library 1963)
   Tools (Basil Blackwell's Learning library 1975)
   Machines (Basil Blackwell's Learning library 1976)
   Motion and Power (Holmes McDougall 1977)

Science Fiction
As Vektis Brack
   Odyssey in Space (Tit-Bits Science Fiction Library 1953)
   The "X" People (Tit-Bits Science Fiction Library 1953)
   Castaway in Space (Tit-Bits Science Fiction Library 1953)

As Bruno G. Condray
   The Dissentizens (Tit-Bits Science Fiction Library 1954)
   Exile from Jupiter (Tit-Bits Science Fiction Library 1955)
   The Outer Beyond (Tit-Bits Science Fiction Library 1955)

The Wild Knight

Geoffrey Humphrys

Blenheim Press Limited
St Albans

First published in 2008 by
Blenheim Press Ltd
Codicote Innovation Centre
St Albans Road
Codicote
Herts SG4 8WH

ISBN 978-1-906302-09-2

Typeset by TW Typesetting, Plymouth, Devon

Printed and bound by CPI Antony Rowe, Eastbourne

To my wife Jeanette

for her superlative secretarial work
always

ONE

The rebel curs had murdered his father, their sovereign lord to be honoured, served and obeyed – King James III of Scotland.

Squatted on the window seat of a Stirling Castle ante-room, Prince James strained forward to distinguish the words of voices issuing from a guardroom below; two roughneck traitors were discussing the battle in devil-may-care, soldierly manner.

'Ay, the King fled the field of Sauchieburn with my lord Gray close on his heels,' said a gruff Highland voice. 'The King's forces were outnumbered, and when our archers and spearmen gained the advantage, Jamie quitted. He never was a fighting man. Scotland wouldna' be in the state it is, had his sword arm been half as strong as his talk.'

Young James gripped tightly at the embrasure ledge, knuckles gleaming, teeth clenched together in rising anger, ears straining for every word, yet his whole body trembling, trembling, trembling.

'Where did he make for?' asked the other soldier.

'They say he reached Milton and rested.'

'Is that where he spoke to the lass at the well?'

'Ay,' came the chuckled reply. 'Up he gets and tells the lass that in the morning he was her king.'

His companion joined him in coarse, mocking laughter. 'And the lass went to fetch him a priest?'

'That's what she said she'd do, but she fetched no friar,' chortled the soldier. 'My lord Gray's men were after Jamie like a pack of yelping hounds. One of them puts on a priest's robe over his armour and goes to the King, who asks to be shriven. The only shrift he got was a sword through his innards.'

Flesh afire, the young prince's face glowed like a burning log with charred edges as he shuddered with rage. Suddenly everything within him exploded and he beat at the latticed windows until glass shattered down upon the startled soldiers. As they raised the alarm, his voice filled with resonance as he shouted down to them, 'You misbegotten, traitorous curs! What an end for a king. By God's holy name, I'll make you all suffer for this day's treachery.'

He struggled to apply a tight rein on his temper, and as he stared at his cut and bleeding hands, his brain flashed the searing realisation that the rebel noblemen who had set him up as their nominal leader had all along intended killing his father. Dastardly Lord Gray was one of the instigators and, from what he had just heard, probably the chief architect of the plot to kill.

James screwed his eyes up tight and bit on his teeth as he recalled Lord Gray coming to him. Typical of his traitorous ways, he must have come straight from the battlefield, chainmail smeared with tufts of grass and earth, a smirk of evil satisfaction across his saturnine face as he reported, 'His Grace your father is dead, killed honourably in a battle beyond his control.'

He had stared at the nobleman nonplussed, incapable of articulating adequate words, conscious only of rising tears. Shocked beyond comprehension he had been unable to hold the tears back, let them flow like a bairn, allowing Gray to retreat in contemptuous triumph. That was when he should have displayed kingly strength and smashed a strong clenched fist into the traitor's loose, lecherous mouth, as he had once seen his enraged father strike a knight full in the face and send blood from his rotten teeth dribbling down his chin.

Killed honourably in battle! The murderous swine! They called themselves noblemen; yet they acted like whore-begat scum. He slumped down on the window seat. They had murdered his father, slaughtered him in cold blood, made mockery of his kingship and annihilated him.

So in the glorious summer of June 1488, the King of Scotland had been fiendishly put to the sword by traitors, and his son had sanctioned the killing. Ay, sanctioned it by his failure to detect the first signs of storm-brewing treachery. These were the soul-destroying facts that would be written into the history of his beloved land. Could he ever overcome the shame of it?

The finality of death suddenly pierced through him as a dagger thrust. He would never see his father again. Never again. Never. Never. Each negation impinged deeply upon his body, heart and soul.

What would his dear mother have said of this tangled web of political intrigue? Mercifully, perhaps by Almighty God's design, she had not lived to see it, so the shame was solely his own. But the rebel noblemen had forgotten one important fact. They would soon have to crown him

King James 1V of Scotland, then learn to their cost that even though only sixteen years of age and a minor, his future life would be devoted to making sure there was nothing nominal about his leadership. Those craven whelps were his subjects and he intended to master them or die in the attempt.

Large brown eyes that glowed almost black flashed downhill over isolated carse land to the Ochil Hills. A shaft of sunlight split the clouds erupting from a peak-dominated skyline and shone on the river, brightening it to the radiance of burnished silver, scything like a giant sword through the heather-covered hummocks of his birthright land. It was now territory pillaged for him by malcontents, their hands stained by his father's blood. He, a royal Prince, had sanctioned its execution. Is that what the people of Scotland would think?

The verminous band of rebels would present the facts in that manner, masking their own guilt by pointing accusative fingers at him.

Privately his own conscience accepted the guilt and, in doing so, learnt the first major lesson of kingship – there could be no excuse for weakness. In future he must control the tempest raging within him and cultivate strength – strength of heart, mind, body and soul – and channel his entire self into strength of policy and kingship.

Memories continued rasping raw across his mind: history repeating itself. This castle, once the strongest in the realm, his father's birthplace. He too had succeeded to the throne as a minor – the same situation now thrust upon himself. Those pox-ridden soldiers had called his father weak; they would soon learn that from this day the new king would gather strength of body, strength of mind and strength of kingship. They and the whole of Scotland, Europe and the world would have a different person to reckon with – a king with power at his command, not a puppet in the hands of swinebred, rapacious rebels. If nothing else, he could thank his father for teaching him that need.

The heavy door of the ante-room swung creakingly open as Archibald Douglas, Earl of Angus, flounced in red-faced and fuming. 'What ails thee? Why all the clatter?' he demanded, staring at the broken windows.

James sprang at him and grabbed the collar of his tunic. 'Is that the way to address your King?' he flashed.

The burly Angus looked down at him with twisted-feature surprise, then effortlessly eased him away and sat on the wooden coffer beside the shattered windows. 'I hear Gray has reported the events of the day,' he said. 'That numbskull never knows when to keep quiet.'

3

Angus then swung his sword to the back of his blue and gold-quartered tunic and looked hard at the young king. 'You canna be squeamish in battle, Your Grace. You should have learnt that from your knightly training. Strength is the only standard in battle, and that your father lacked.'

James stood staring at him wildly, his whole body trembling with indignation as he tried to infuse strength into it.

'Well, sit you down now before you burst your breeches,' advised Angus, almost paternally.

James sat upright on the window seat, facing Angus resolutely, his young smooth face contrasting sharply with the gnarled features of the nobleman. 'There are orders for my father's funeral that I want carried out. He will be buried beside my dearest sweet mother at Cambuskenneth and Masses said for her and for his soul.'

'Your wishes will be respected, Your Grace.'

'That they will, now and always,' fired James, his eyes pinpointed black with determination. 'Even though only sixteen years of age, I am now the King of Scotland. Let nobody forget it, not even the Earl of Angus. Nor will he sanction my detention in these closed quarters any longer. I was closeted here before on the orders of the King of Scotland, my father. Now I am the King, and from this day, I give the orders.'

'And I am your Councillor, Your Grace, not your gaoler,' replied Angus, rubbing thoughtfully at his broad jaw. 'You'll be needed to preside over the Council, to appoint the chief officers necessary to maintain the welfare of the kingdom.'

James glanced at the blood congealing on his hands, then looked up quickly. 'That's right. I'll preside over everything, and ask for advice only when I think I need it. You've given me much to think about, my lord. I'll see that strength is the standard by which I rule, have no fear over that!'

Angus's uncertain smile revealed his bad teeth. 'Fitting words for a king,' he said. 'But I soon hope to bring you a visitor. I hear that Your Grace has found Mistress Marion Boyd pleasurably fair.'

The expression on the young King's face softened and brought a gleam to his eyes, as he momentarily considered one of the more satisfying possibilities of kingship. During his brief periods of freedom he had dallied with Lady Margaret Drummond on the banks of the Tay at Stobshall, even written the song 'Tay's Bank' for her. But that was sweet and innocent child's play; now he was a king and had the choice of any woman who pleased him. 'Marion Boyd is a pretty lass,' he murmured.

'It would be an honour for her to bed with the King, would it not, my lord?'

'Indeed, it would, Your Grace,' encouraged Angus. He rose, saying, 'Now I'll go and see that fitting apartments are made ready for Your Grace. When I return all will be to your satisfaction.'

'Then speed your return, Angus, for I am not prepared to bide here while you consult with rebels, but you can tell them all that their future is now firmly in my hands.'

As Angus walked along the stone corridors a knowing smile seeped into his expression. The lad would be far less observant if occupied with the delights of sporting with a woman, and since the idea came from his own mind, he no doubt had the capacity. There had been gossip about an association with one of Drummond's lasses that should have whetted his appetite for female flesh more than the half-marriages to English infants his father had sought to arrange.

Angus fingered his genitals as he walked, thinking of the body that occasionally warmed and enlivened his bed. Lady Jane Kennedy had a lust for uniting flesh as strong as any man, and when aroused, she became as demanding and consuming as fire itself. Her tantalising body had fired him too, but not often enough. That was her secret; even after rousing passions to the utmost peak, she never relinquished control, so that each time she had to be won again, and acceptance was always on her terms, inspiring the desire for more of her pulsating delights.

When Angus left, James returned to the window seat and sat by the broken windows, breathing in the air deeply through his nose, filling his lungs. His thoughts were tumultuous, but one indisputable certainty shone through all the trauma – he was now King of Scotland; neither Angus nor Gray had raised any trace of demur. But the inner exhilaration he felt was tarnished by his awareness that he ought to be better prepared for kingship.

He wriggled for comfort on the window seat, thinking of his father and the strangeness of their relationship, pondering why it should be so. He knew only what his mother had told him. How he wished she could be with him now, to kneel at her feet, as he had done as a child, rest his head in the haven of her lap, feel her hands soft upon his neck and smell the scent of rosemary in her gown. She was the only person he had ever been able to fully trust and so totally relax in her company.

How different with his father, who had seemingly distrusted him from the moment he was born. This evidently due to the report of some

God-denied astrologer who, because of the peculiar position of certain planets, prophesied that the infant Prince would cause his death or dethronement. So the seed of estrangement was sown whilst in his cradle and it remained a barrier between them throughout his father's life.

The Archbishop of St. Andrews, another ardent follower of the celestial sciences, added to his father's fear, interpreting a dream as a mystical warning that 'the royal lion of Scotland, in course of time would be torn by his whelps'.

Because of these mystic omens, perhaps, his father fortified Stirling castle and confined him in it with his mother, under the care of the treacherous castellan, Shaw of Sauchie. Even when protected by his mother, captivity rankled, and it became intolerable after she died. Release by the plotting noblemen came as a blessing from God. He spent most of the time among the delicious groves of Stobeshall with Lady Margaret Drummond, his childhood sweetheart. His father then for a short time must have felt that his freedom constituted no threat to the realm of Scotland.

How wrong his father had been! How wrong he had been! Both of them had been ensnared between the camps of two internecine factions, ready to split the kingdom to the point of civil war, if it suited their purpose, one group fawning over the King's favours, the other resenting to the soul any reward bestowed outside their interest.

Snarling at their empty-handedness, the insurgents had installed him as the figurehead leader of their militia. Blinded by his eagerness to display his horsemanship and accomplishment at arms, he had regarded it all as part of the political manoeuvring that always surrounds a throne. But he should have recognised that only loyalty to the King could benefit Scotland. Now it was too late. The rebels had once again confined him to this fortress, and were at this moment probably scheming ways in which they could rule rather than be ruled.

Now, as he had told Angus, the future of them all was in his hands. But he had no-one in whom he could confide, whom he could look to for advice or even trust. Even so, with Almighty God's help, he would outwit their chicanery and hopefully bring honour and prosperity back to Scotland.

That night in the lofty hall, James sat at the top table, deliberately apart from those who tried to placate him. The sounds of rough hilarity and heavy drinking reverberated from the walls as nobles and knights raised their voices in song and jubilation. They thought they were celebrating a victory, but he had a shock for them. When they were least expecting it, James stood and struck hard at the wooden table with the flat blade of a broadsword. The loud metallic crack penetrated their noise and all eyes flashed to its source. They saw a pale-faced youth with red-gold hair standing resolutely before them. His statuesque figure stunned them to silence.

When he spoke it was in a clear determined voice, the inner passion of his feelings inspiring confidence. 'I know not what you are celebrating tonight,' he rapped out. 'But I hope it is not the evil deeds of this day on which my royal father, your King, was murdered.'

He paused, so that they could absorb the full impact of his accusation. Then he went on, 'For my part in his ignominious death, I shall wear an iron penance belt for the rest of my life. During that life as your King, let no man here ever talk to me of valour on this accursed day.'

He stood resolutely facing them, his nigrescent eyes holding them spellbound. Even so there were several seasoned campaigners who felt a twinge of apprehension at the sight of this slip of a lad addressing the whole assembly with the ferocity of a mountain cat. But when he left, the roistering started up again and continued throughout the night.

On his Coronation Day, James stood at the west door of the Abbey of Scone with Angus at his side. He had issued orders that there should be no traditional colour; all must wear black as a mark of respect for his father. He had feared the countryfolk might blame him for the inglorious end to a long reign marred by ill-chosen favouritism, but as he gazed at the assembled crowd and waved to them, they cheered from good strong throats.

'The people receive me well, Angus,' he remarked.

'No doubt about that, Your Grace.'

'And your Douglas men look well. I've noted their spears gleaming in the sunlight all along the route.'

Angus beamed. 'Those spears are always ready to serve Your Grace in whatever you command.'

James nodded with satisfaction. He neither trusted nor even liked Angus, who could influence his own kin whichever way he pleased. But with the Scottish folk it was different. They had turned out in great array as the sun of the last week in June cast dazzling highlights and long shadows upon the surrounding hills.

7

Patrick Hepburn moved to his other side. 'All are pleased to see you, Your Grace,' he remarked. 'Such numbers would never have mustered for anyone else.'

'I hope you're right, Patrick, for our future depends upon their allegiance.'

As he spoke he surveyed the scene in detail, the honest upturned faces tanned by their outdoor labours, acclaiming him it seemed with hearts full of rejoicing. They stood beneath the shade of thick-girthed oaks and elms, sun-drenched leaves hanging motionless in air so dry and still that every horse hoof raised a lingering puff of dust. Many men were stripped to the waist, muscular arms folded across deep chests; lasses wore kirtles, their breasts as firm as early-formed fruit.

Watching them as they stood before the traditional crowning place of Scottish kings, James felt purpose and resolve steadying his inner trembling. He turned to enter the Abbey, flanked on each side by Douglas men, with those who had plotted the rebellion forming up behind him. 'Stay close to me, Patrick, for I feel very much alone,' he said to the man already promised the Earl's belt forfeited by Sir John Ramsay, formerly one of his father's favourites.

'That I will, Your Grace. Now, and always.'

He looked and sounded genuine, but this could be due to his expectancy of being created Earl of Bothwell.

'I shall need such loyalty, so I hope you stay of the same heart, and many others like you. Though some around me now inspire little confidence.'

Patrick faced him and smiled reassuringly, handsome features firm and friendly. Yet it could be false, thought the young king.

He moved forward to the altar and the nobility of Scotland focused their eyes upon him. They were human, yet beyond the touch of kindred feeling, for he stood alone, totally isolated by kingship. Cut off from the cheering people outside, he again felt nervous and vulnerable. Officers of State stood within touching distance, faces masked by such blandness that he could detect neither loyalty nor treachery. Even the Archbishop of St. Andrews, vestments rich in colour against the mourning black of the Court, appeared more a potential enemy than a servant of Almighty God. At any moment a cloak could open and a dagger thrust transform him into a writhing heap of all too human flesh and blood. That was how his father had been betrayed, with those responsible fixing their gaze upon their new King as he sat on the traditional Coronation throne.

He repeated the solemn oaths and listened to the hopeful prayers, then two thousand choirboy voices boomed cannon-like through the Abbey, resounding against its ancient timbers. The weight of the crown rested heavy upon his head as he heard the acclamation of his subjects. Was it loyal response? How could he tell? He looked at the future Earl of Bothwell, relaxed and again smiling encouragement, seemingly support-ive, but –? That was the trouble, there were question marks hanging over all these followers, perhaps only feigning to appear loyal in public.

Angus kept close at hand, chipped granite features as unpredictable as a necromancer's black magic. Angus the murderer; slayer of the Earl of Mar, another of his father's one-time favourites. Angus, prominent in the recent rebellion, now his official guardian. Angus, known as Bell-the-Cat, the Great Earl, who had intrigued with England against his own King. What would Angus guard him against if it meant personal gain to leave him unguarded? The Douglas men could just as well line the way to the scaffold.

He noticed Angus nod to a tall, gracefully proud lady among the rows of black-gowned noblewomen flanking one side of the Abbey. The object of the Earl's attention had raven-black hair bound in pearl fillets, the upper roundness of her breasts gleaming white above the square neckline of black velvet, her wide-set compelling eyes following the Earl's approach to the throne to pledge his loyalty.

They came forward one by one, making the pledges that were his birthright, one traitor following another, and not a trace of conscience. But this was the object of the great assembly – to swear allegiance to their King. That included them all, even Angus's leman, on whom his gaze kept fixing, in spite of a conscious effort to avoid doing so. There was something about her that stirred him strangely, and when their eyes met he had the feeling that she too felt an empathic awareness. Yet he could not remember seeing her before, did not even know her name. By the time the pledges were finished he would have wagered that she was as conscious of him as he of her. As soon as he could speak to Patrick Hepburn he nodded in her direction and asked, 'Who is that lady?'

'You don't know Lady Jane Kennedy, Your Grace?' he queried, with obvious surprise. 'She's a rare beauty, one Angus prides and seeks to keep solely to himself.'

She was obviously aware of the King's inquiry, for she turned haughtily so that they could only see her back. Even that had a commanding uprightness about it, enabling her to be easily picked out from all others.

Now it was time to move out of the Abbey. James stepped forward, so the procession could assemble behind him. A sea of faces surged up from each side of the aisle as he walked slowly to the west door. As the doors were flung open, the Douglas men in red tunics smartly re-formed the guard on each side.

At first sight of him the crowd burst into spontaneous cheering. James stood assimilating it, almost trying to breathe it in, to convince himself it was true loyalty, the true regard of a people for a king. Yet he knew it was not so. As a person they knew nothing of him, the day was just an excuse for celebration. Yet he felt ready to pledge himself to their service, knowing that in the final analysis, his success as a king would be judged on what he did for those who now roared to give them a thirst for the free ale to be distributed.

Patrick Hepburn came close behind him. 'The honours are being carried out with great respect, Your Grace. The people of Scotland greet you with devotion in their hearts.'

'I should like to think so,' he replied, trying to embrace them all with his waving acknowledgements. 'I want this day to pass without any demonstration of dissent, a day upon which we can look back as the beginning of a new greatness for Scotland.'

'It can be as you say, Your Grace, in spite of what Angus fears. The people are for you, if not for him.'

'We have all sinned, Patrick, and must not forget it. Our only justification will be to prove that it was for the benefit of the whole realm. That is my true oath of kingship, and I shall demand a similar oath from any man who aspires to counsel me as King of Scotland.' Determination tinged every word as his thoughts crystallised concerning the duties imposed by the crown so recently placed upon his head. The infidelity of those around him provided an adequate reminder of how quickly the scene could change. It happened to his father and, indeed, to the king of all kings – acclaimed on Palm Sunday, then five days later the mob yelled to have him crucified.

Mindful of his destiny, James walked steadily down the steps and mounted his chestnut horse. The cheers rose to a unified crescendo. The feeling of warmth emanating from them almost brought tears to his eyes. These were not plotters and sycophants. Already excited groups started to dance, preparing for the celebrations and bonfires to be lit at nightfall. These were his subjects, seemingly pleased to see him crowned, but their respect and affection could only be maintained by deeds. A feeling of confidence stiffened his back as he rode fully stretched upright, more eager to impress with his manliness than the richness of his jewels sparkling in the sunlight.

As the cheers rang out again and again, so his mind scanned the tasks ahead. First, the stain of Sauchieburn must be removed, and with it the jealousy and enmity which had been its root cause. He wanted Scotland to be great, recognised by Europe and the rest of the world as a country ruled by a powerful and purposeful king. This meant unifying the noblemen in their service to the Crown, making them accept a fair distribution of administrative power and stopping the currying for royal favours. This was his challenge, nothing must sway him from it, making them accept him as the final arbiter in ruling the kingdom.

Before the cheering crowds he sensed that if his policies were seen to be fair these hearty Scots would support him. Again, knowledge that their destinies were linked with his brought a lump to his throat. Then in spite of these portentous thoughts, the sight of so many women smiling and waving to him evoked the tantalising image of the elegant-figured, proud-faced lady who seemed to have some particular allegiance to Angus. That was something to investigate on a personal level, for already he deemed her to be a worthy bedmate for a king.

This thought kept recurring throughout the Coronation revelries that followed. Yet although he looked for her in every gathering, no opportunity of meeting Lady Jane Kennedy occurred. He learnt with displeasure that she had returned to the lands of Angus in Forfar. But that was certainly not the end of her.

As each day of his reign followed another, James made the achievement and display of personal and kingly strength the driving force of his life. He started to grow a beard and insisted upon attending the audits of the Exchequer, travelling on the justiciary circuits and presiding in Parliament – not to the liking of Angus.

'You have able Councillors, Your Grace,' he protested during one stormy interview. 'Time enough for you to bother about affairs of State when you come of age.'

'By which time the kingdom could no longer be mine,' James snapped.

'You don't trust your Councillors?' flashed Angus.

'A king can trust no man, my lord. That's why every day I practise horsemanship and feats of arms, challenging only those from whom I can learn more.' He rose from the Council Chamber throne chair, indicating the outline of the penance belt beneath his green and gold outer robe.

'I've worn this since my father's obsequies. Apart from private memories, it serves as a reminder that a king must be sparing in his trust.'

Angus tried to avoid the alert brown eyes that now no longer flinched before him. 'You do well to be cautious, Your Grace,' he grudgingly admitted.

'God's wounds, you're right, Angus!' exclaimed James, with a loud laugh. 'And how quickly you change your tune. But no more of it now, we have to journey to Leith to welcome my uncle Junker from Denmark, land of my beloved mother's birth.'

A troubled frown contracted Angus's cumbrous brow. Events were not going well for him. His influence during the King's short minority had already diminished, but he could not check the decline without adequate support. Hepburn as Lord High Admiral, Home as Lord High Chamberlain and Campbell of Argyll as Chancellor, each were receiving generous grants of land in return for unconditional loyalty.

The young King too increased in confidence every day, already stronger in character than his father and ominously, he kept making inquiries about Jane Kennedy. Could it be that she held the key to the future of the Earl of Angus? If so, he knew from experience how unpredictable she could be, for beneath the screen of unquestionable beauty lurked a keen and scheming mind. She was quite capable of exploiting the King's interest for her own elevation, even if it meant the exclusion of her liege Lord.

TWO

Leith was in gay mood when James arrived, roads to the harbour bedecked with fluttering bunting and flags, local folk jostling each other for a good view of their sovereign and his foreign royal visitor.

James rode with the newly created Earl of Bothwell, again uplifted by the cheers of greeting. The green and red tunics of the guard gleamed in the sunlight, the skirl of traditional music enlivening the gentle breeze, and where the sea and sky met in a delicate comparison of blueness on the horizon, the white sails of Danish ships glistened as symbols of maritime strength.

'My uncle visits us in fine ships, Patrick,' observed James, his eyes brightening as they distinguished the Oldenburg crests on the approaching sails.

'They make an impressive sight, Your Grace.'

'A sight we must see more of in Scotland,' emphasised James, reining his horse to a halt. 'Good ships are a sign of power, both in war and trade. As my Lord High Admiral, it is certainly something to occupy your thoughts.'

Bothwell glanced at him sidelong. Like Angus, he too realised that in the past few weeks the King had aged in years, replacing callow youth with an inscrutability that made it difficult to judge the true intent of seemingly casual remarks. 'The building of ships is a costly business, Your Grace,' he countered.

'Then we'll have to raise the levies, for Scotland can never be truly great without ships. I have a great attraction to the sea, Patrick, so I'll question my uncle Junker closely about his ships.'

The crowds cheered as they saw the King dismount and step lithely into the red and gold barge to go out and welcome his guests. Several officers of State climbed more warily aboard, their resplendent robes providing the first display of full colour of the new reign. James had ordered mourning robes to be discarded for this special occasion. He set the example himself, with an under-robe of black velvet covered with cloth of gold trimmed with ermine. His over-robe was girded at the waist by a jewelled belt, surmounted by a jewelled collar to cover the shoulders. On his head he wore a black velvet bonnet turned up and fixed at the right side with a jewelled brooch and pendant pearl. Today he had wanted to look fully a king, not the fair wee lad many folk expected to see.

The Count of Oldenburg came ashore with all the ceremonial due to visiting royalty. A sudden gust of wind blew up a swirl of dust from the surrounding countryside. It caused confusion among ladies of the Count's party. One in particular seemed to be in trouble and James despatched a page to seek the reason.

Lucan Fairfax, his recently-chosen fair-haired page, was anxious to please and quickly returned to his master. 'Dust has blown in the eyes of one of the waiting ladies and it bides there, Your Grace,' he explained.

'And we have no physician with us,' said James, turning apologetically to his uncle. 'But to make good the deficiency, I'll tend the lady myself.'

The blustering, bewhiskered Count objected. 'Eet ees nothing, Your Grace,' he puffed. 'She can be attended by one of the women.'

'My esteemed uncle cannot have heard of my ability to cure ills. I'll attend to the lady right away.' He turned to the page to stem further objections. 'Have her taken to one of the pavilions. Tell her the King of Scotland won't allow her eyes to remain blinded to the beauty of his kingdom.'

The gangling page bowed, unable to conceal the look of astonishment on his boyish face. He remained standing before the King, blue eyes widening, wondering if it were a jest.

'Move yourself and do as I say, churl!' James roared at him. But suppressed humour burst through his words.

The lad scampered away with the speed of a deer alerted to danger. James followed and found the lady in a state of fluttering confusion. One glance made his impulse worthwhile. Young and amply curved, her skin glowed with the delicacy of a sun-blushed peach, and her long red hair in silver cauls framed an exquisitely gentle face. 'Have no fear, lady,' he comforted, as she dropped into a low nervous curtsey. 'There is no cause for alarm.'

As he put one hand on her cheek and eased the lid of the affected eye with the other, he felt her tremble and awareness of her femininity surged through him. It was the same ineffable softness as his mother, yet different, so different. He lingered over the treatment deliberately, thrilling at the smooth warmth of her skin, his touch instinctively tender.

'Has the pain eased, lady?' he asked.

Embarrassment at their proximity shone in her green-tinged eyes and dappled her features with extra colour. She nodded, too overwhelmed for speech, her lady companions having retreated in awe. He moved his hand from her cheek to rest it on her waist beneath a green, silver-patterned cloak.

'You are very fair, sweet lady,' he whispered, eyes twinkling with gaiety. She was the first woman beyond his Court whom he had closely encountered since becoming King. It suddenly became important to impress her with his manliness and the protection he could offer.

'Your Grace ees most kind,' she murmured.

'To one so mighty fair I could be even more kind,' he assured her, sensing the brief gleam of coquetry in her expression. 'After supper I shall see if my healing has had lasting effect.'

'Eet ees already better, Your Grace.' She smiled and they exchanged glances far more expressive than words.

He pressed her hand. 'We can make sure after supper. The beauty of such eyes must not be jeopardised through lack of sufficient care.'

She curtsied with practised elegance, upraising her eyes in a flash of femininity he found enchanting. He let her see his pleasure, then bowed and strode off, determined to arrange an after-supper meeting.

The procession formed up and moved off in splendour. The Earl of Bothwell watched the King, aware of his thoughtful expression, apprehensive that he might be thinking more about ships.

Towards the end of the revelry of musicians, jesters and mummers, following the feasting in the Great Hall of Holyroodhouse, James slipped away to his private chamber and immediately despatched his page to fetch the Danish lady whom, owing to tactful inquiries, he could now name as Guelinda. She was still with him after the Hall had been cleared, the floor laid with new rushes, and all including the lowliest servants gone to their beds.

James awoke with the first chink of dawn, for they had slept on his uncurtained day bed. At once he became aware of the warm, naked body curled in deep slumber beside him. He caressed her into wakefulness, and she drew him close, explored his body with soft, manipulative hands, then once again submitted completely to his desire.

When he finally released her a new sense of vitality coursed triumphantly though him, a guarantee of his manliness. He leapt from the bed and glanced at the rising sun casting saffron rays upon the grey light, heralding that soon the last traces of night would melt into the fresh golden brilliance of a late August morning. He drew on a long silk gown and stood over the bed, amused and emotionally touched by Guelinda's serene face. His heart beat with gratitude, so much so that he bent and kissed her tenderly. 'You served me well, lady,' he whispered. 'Bestowed delights upon me that a lifetime of women can never efface.'

She sat up, drawing the bed wraps over her full, round breasts. 'Your Grace has a capacity for love. You could bring delight to many ladies.'

'But I'll never forget the first, sweet Guelinda,' he said, then strode about the chamber picking up hastily discarded garments. He felt exhilarated, possessed with a fiery strength ready to be unleashed. 'As for you, if you look back in your old age and reflect on what you have not done, you can always say that you made a man of the King of Scotland.'

'That I shall do, Your Grace,' she murmured, with a quiet but firm conviction which thrilled him further.

He laughed out loud. 'But now you'd better return to your quarters. I'll call my page to lead you.'

Opening the door, James found Lucan Fairfax asleep on a straw pallet across the doorway. He roused him, then returned to the chamber. 'Today I'll take your master hunting, Guelinda,' he cried out. 'And by God's nails, I've never felt more like it in my life. This morning I could ride the fiercest horse in Christendom.'

Guelinda pulled on her crumpled emerald green gown. Her red hair hung loose over her shoulders as she turned to him and smiled. He noticed the state of her gown and made a mental note to have many ells of the richest cloth sent to her. He took hold of her hands and squeezed them in appreciation. He kissed her once again, then bellowed for the page.

After she left, he threw off his gown and, convinced of his manhood, pranced naked to the gard-robe singing loudly, savouring Guelinda's prophecy that he would bring delight to many ladies.

When he emerged dripping wet, he saw the page tidying his discarded clothes. On the spur of the moment he said, 'Lucan, when I take our royal guest hunting this forenoon, you can accompany us. I want to see if you are as good a horseman as your father boasts.'

Lucan's eyes lit up with inner delight. 'Thank you, Your Grace. I shall try to have never ridden better.'

So much had happened to him in the past few days that Lucan still found it hard to accept how dramatically his whole life had suddenly changed. A farrier at the castle, his father had recommended a special horse to the King who, when he returned from riding it, found father and son together in the stables. During the talk, his father embarrassingly revealed to the King that he and Lucan were born on the same day. This seemed to interest the King. 'Since we share the same star courses, your son Lucan and I ought to be closer associated,' he had said.

This idle remark ended the matter as far as Lucan was concerned, but two days later the King summoned him to his private chamber. 'I hear that you were taught to read and write by a Dominican friar and took well to it,' he said.

'The holy friar was a good teacher, Your Grace.'

That the King had bothered to inquire about him surprised Lucan. He stood steady as the King's large brown eyes surveyed him deeply, but with obvious friendly intent. At last the King said, 'Would you like to serve me more closely as my personal page?'

'If Your Grace wishes it, I would be greatly honoured.'

'Then I do wish it, lad,' said the King decisively, clapping his hand on Lucan's shoulder. 'Born on the same day, I feel our future ought to be linked together. The good friar who tutored you agrees with me.'

When Lucan told his mother, who worked in the castle laundry, she nearly burst with a combination of pride and shock. Now he was to go hunting with the King, and already, come what may, he felt happy to serve his royal master for the rest of his life.

Whilst the Count of Oldenburg remained in Scotland, Guelinda frequently had more than her eyes examined by the young King. James rewarded her handsomely with jewels and fine cloth for his physical experimenting, and when he complimented her one morning on her lovemaking ability, she surprisingly replied, 'There's another in the Danish party who seeks Your Grace's favours.'

'Who is that?' queried James, fondling her rounded naked body.

'My lady Dana, the Count's love daughter. I think she ees most – what you say, jealous of my veesits to Your Grace. Every time she want to know what we do.'

'Have you told her?'

'I have told her that Your Grace ees a much loving man.'

James beamed and smoothed his hand across the exquisite warm silkiness of her upraised buttock. 'Did that please her?'

Guelinda stretched and pulled a coverlet over herself, then looked at him with troubled eyes. 'She has ordered me to help her gain Your Grace's favour.'

'Has she, my sweet one? And what do you think of that?'

'She could make much trouble for me,' Guelinda replied, with obvious concern.

'So you want me to see her?'

'Eet would help me, Your Grace.'

James rose from the bed and laughed. 'Then I shall see her, Guelinda, for your sake. You can make the arrangements yourself, then she'll have no reason to cause you trouble.'

Guelinda blushed, then looked at him with gratitude and said, 'Your Grace ees most good.'

That night after supper Lady Dana, the Count's love child, came to his private chamber. She was a tall, willowy blonde with a more graceful than exciting body. But it amused James to compare her sporting ability with that of a countrywoman. He found them both pleasing in their different ways, so throughout the autumnal mists and rain of the ensuing days, the Count and his advisers supplied him with information about ships. At night James could take his pick of two Danish ladies. It bolstered his manhood confidence in that he seemed able to satisfy them both. Angus pried into the comings and goings of the Danish women with some satisfaction. Temporarily the young King was diverted from the interest shown in Jane Kennedy. Angus had risked summoning her to Court, hoping that seeing the King's dalliances might influence her against any schemes of her own. Although he watched for developments with vulpine vigilance he reached no conclusions.

The King noticed Jane's attendance at Court, Angus had no doubt about that. But Jane gave no evidence of responding to the royal glances with any noticeable encouragement. Although some consolation it meant little, for Angus knew of Jane's ability to stir the appetite of any man, if she so desired. He also knew that since her awareness of the King's attraction he had not once enticed her into his own bed. It riled him to think that Jane, in her own inimitable way, had adopted the role of lady in waiting.

The Danish party finally left Scotland towards the end of the year when snow covered the hills. Soon afterwards, Angus arranged with the Earl of Huntly to invite Marion Boyd to Huntly Mansion during a hunting visit by the King.

On the day of his arrival, James saw Marion sitting alone in one of Huntly's abundantly-stocked plant houses on the east side of the mansion. Recognising her immediately, he stood on the outside of the glass and appraised her in a new light. This was the lass he had desired before his initiation with Guelinda, then Dana. Was she still so desirable? Petite and slender, the wintry sun shone through the glass on her long fair hair as she gazed upon the array of Huntly's greenery. No question about her being a beauty, for she possessed a virginal aura, like a representation of the Madonna.

Obviously Mistress Marion had been invited here for a purpose, possibly by Angus. Momentarily it aroused his curiosity to find out. He could approach by a side glass door. If he moved quietly she might not hear him. He went forward stealthily; the door opened without a sound, but she immediately became aware of a presence and looked up with alarm.

'May the King of Scotland share your resting place, mistress?' he asked, in a soft voice.

She rose quickly, colour dappling her cheeks as she curtsied with hurried confusion. 'I would be most honoured, Your Grace. The greenery is truly remarkable for this time of the year.'

'Yes, Huntly enjoys his reputation of being a wizard with plants,' he said, stretching out his hands and raising her to her dainty feet. 'But not one of the rich leaves or buds can compare with the radiance of your fair countenance, Marion.'

Her innocent face registered surprise. 'You know my name, Your Grace?'

'I certainly do,' he confirmed, motioning her to sit again on the smooth wooden seat. Helping her, he noticed the fading and needlework repairs on her red brocade gown which nonetheless gave a pleasing glow to her white skin. In spite of her nervousness she gave him an impression of tranquility and calm, the contrast he needed between the asperities of hunting and striving for greater strength of arms. The Danish women had delighted him physically, but in no way else. Here was a Scottish lass, with whom he could have much in common, and who in his leisure moments could temper the fires of kingship which he must keep burning within him. With her he could momentarily forget the cares of State and relax in the warmth of her femininity. The vision appealed to him, so he sat down gently beside her saying, 'I first gazed upon your fairness when you were in Perth with your father a few months ago.' He took off his blue bonnet and fingered its golden tassel. 'I marvelled at your beauty then, but you're even more fair at the closeness I now enjoy.'

'I remember the time, Your Grace, but –' She broke off, too self-conscious for words.

'But what, Marion?'

She smiled nervously, displaying perfect white teeth. 'You seemed such a boy then, Your Grace. You are greatly changed.'

This pleased him and he laughed outright as he stroked his fledgling beard. 'The trials of my birthright have hastened growth, both in kingship and manhood, for now I have a man's capacity for love.'

'Your Grace!'

Her virginal expression of shock and the fluttering of her long lashes delighted him. He moved a little nearer and lightly put his hands on her lap. 'You need not be afraid, Marion. I've thought of you often, only duties of State have kept me from you.'

'Your Grace, you flatter me unduly. This chance meeting appears more and more as a dream.'

He moved closer, reaching for her hands, but she secreted them in the wide sleeves of her gown. Smiling reassuringly he said, 'Marion, this is neither a dream nor any chance meeting. The Earl of Huntly received orders to invite you here, and I've rearranged the affairs of Scotland to enjoy your company.'

'Now you're making fun of me,' she suggested.

'Do you doubt your King, Marion?' he queried roguishly.

'No, Your Grace, but –' her tiny hands emerged and twisted together, her clear blue eyes flooded with alarm.

James arrested the hands, then held them with gentle firmness. 'Would you then refuse his love?'

'What command have I of his love?'

'Full command, Marion. Would I have arranged this meeting otherwise? I've admired you since you first curtsied before me in Perthshire. You're the one who first opened my eyes to the appreciation of a woman's true beauty.'

'Your Grace, I don't know what to say.'

'Then don't say anything.' He cupped her chin in his hand, eased her face to his and kissed her lips.

She moved away as one of the cauls of her hair slipped and hung across her bare shoulder.

James disentangled the scarlet thread, kissed her shoulder and puckered its flesh between his lips, then dropped the caul into her lap. 'All you need say, Marion, is that you won't refuse me.'

'But, Your Grace, only a short while ago I heard Lord Drummond talking of embassies abroad seeking a wife for you.'

'That is so, my Councillors want me wed. They send embassies to Rome, Spain, France and all Europe. They seek a wife who will best serve Scotland's future affairs.' His voice lowered as he continued, 'I have to marry to further Scotland's interests, but I can't love in like manner. If I must marry a foreigner for the good of my kingdom, surely you'll not deny my heart, Marion?'

'But what Your Grace suggests is a mortal sin.'

'Such love as I've had for you since Perth can never be sinful,' he assured her.

'Your Grace . . . Your Grace, again I don't know what to say. I am only a simple soul, inexperienced in the ways of Court.'

'If you have any love for your King, Marion, don't remain deaf to his pleas.'

She looked him full in the face for several seconds, awed and uncertain. 'What you've said, Your Grace, thrills me greatly, but at the same time frightens me.'

He encircled her in his arms and held his face close to hers, whispering, 'You need have no fear, Marion, if you put your trust in me.'

'What do you want me to do?'

'Love me as completely as I want to love you, sweetest lady of my realm,' he replied, brushing his lips against her ear.

She gripped tight at his arm and he sensed her apprehension. He continued gently kissing and fondling her hands. When he again sought her lips she responded without demur, so he quickly outlined his plan. 'Tomorrow, I will have you returned to your father. Tell him the King will see him properly cared for. Two of my body knights will ride with you, then conduct you to Stirling castle. There Lady Lindsay will receive you as my honoured guest. You can have all you desire, Marion, and I'll come to you as often as I am able.'

'Your Grace!' she whispered, but he silenced all further objections by kissing her lips until she finally agreed.

Sitting with his face against the soft sheen of her cheek, he felt a different sense of achievement from that experienced with Guelinda and Dana. They had given their bodies almost as part of Court procedure when visiting foreign royalty. But he had genuinely wooed Marion into agreement, and the acquisition of a leman would be yet another mark of his growing manhood. With Marion at Stirling he could escape from the

21

bickering and conniving of his Councillors, as they sat in judgement over the terms of marriage treaties. She would be his life beyond the throne, the felicity his subjects accepted as a natural right, yet denied a king because every phase of his life had a bargaining power. With Marion he could be himself, and let his Council haggle over who should be his politically suitable Queen. The idea warmed through him, the thought of a repose in which he would be a king, but need not constantly act as one.

Once she was established at Stirling, James made regular visits to Marion, who soon devoted herself to him entirely, learning to love him, yet content to remain beyond the Court. He derived intense satisfaction from these visits, and when Marion became pregnant it provided further evidence of his manhood. But the first child was a girl, and although he tried to hide it, Marion sensed his bitter disappointment.

During her time at Stirling, Marion's position gave rise to much gossip among the servants. Even the lowly serving wenches were aware of the embassies sent abroad to secure a marriage allegiance. They sniggered behind her back as they discussed these overtures within her hearing with malicious glee. Of course, they were jealous, she told herself. They knew that at Stirling she commanded James, denying any chance of them earning a grant of land or a bright jewel as a reward for bedding with the King. But their snippets of conversation so disturbed her that she decided to tackle James on these matters on his next visit, even though he repeatedly said that he came to her to escape the sordid marriage wrangling and be at peace. She understood this, but it seemed there was now so much speculation that he could not blame her for trying to seek some assurance concerning her own position.

When they were in bed after their initial lovemaking, Marion whispered, 'James, I hear so much about the negotiations for your marriage that I can't help feeling distressed.'

'What have you heard?' he asked, holding her in the crook of his arm.

Surprised at his calm response on the subject which could so easily cast him into a rage, she went on, 'That a daughter has recently been born to the King of England.'

He laughed scornfully. 'And that Angus considers my marriage to that infant would be to Scotland's advantage? Will I ever silence that old fool?'

'I've also heard that the child's grandmother, the Countess of Richmond, favours the match,' Marion countered.

James snorted angrily as he moved his arm away. 'Since when has the King of Scotland been subject to the whims of the King of England's mother?' he snapped.

'Don't be angry with me, James,' pleaded Marion soothingly. 'I'm here so much on my own. I hear so much gossip. Only you can tell me the real truth.'

'That is so,' he admitted with an understanding which again surprised her, but of which she wanted to take advantage.

She snuggled close to him, felt with joy his arms again encircle her protectively. She loved him with every fibre of her being; he had become her whole life. Yet she knew that legitimate marriage to him was out of the question. One day he would marry a foreign princess, but when he came to her it did not matter; she could be happy in their physical closeness. He had only just made love to her, thrilled her body until it burst inwardly with the ecstasy of his penetration. The fruits of love were not yet dry on her limbs, so why was she tormenting herself? 'Tell me all that is happening, James,' she whispered into the darkness.

She felt the grip of his right hand tighten round her breast momentarily, then he relaxed with a sigh and shifted into a more comfortable position, still keeping her close to him.

'How could my marriage to a bairn affect us, sweet Marion?' he asked reassuringly. 'Such is the nonsense of my royal birth. As a mere boy I was promised to two English brides; nothing came of either. Don't worry about it, so far all the embassies abroad have returned home with nothing to offer. You can be sure that whoever my Council bargain for me to marry, it will be solely for political reasons and can make no difference to us.'

His hands began to explore her, and as she warmed to his caresses, her fears gradually subsided. It was not long before she was receiving him into her again and she held him with all the physical manipulation in her power. The fire of her love increased to such an extent that she experienced a single impossible desire, that they could remain fused together like this forever.

The following morning brought news of Lord Forbes raising a rebellion in the north and James scattered all before him as he prepared to leave for battle.

'Must you go, James?' Marion pleaded.

'Of course, I must go,' he thundered. 'That treacherous cur has been stirring up old antipathies all over Scotland, raising an army carrying the supposed bloody shirt of my father as its battle standard. He's undoing all that I'm trying to achieve in uniting Scotland together, so that Europe can recognise us as a powerful nation with policies of its own. This is another test of my kingship, and by God I'll grind any rebel mob into the dirt, until they yell for mercy.'

Marion knew it was futile to raise further objections. This was the part of him over which she had no influence – the power-craving and warfaring king, concerned only for his country. She ran to one of the upper towers to watch him gallop off into the unknown distance.

It was Easter before James returned, riding at the head of part of his army. As soon as he reached the castle gate he gave orders for his men to be drilled and given archery practice for as long as they stayed. The bearded sergeant-at-arms who received the orders had obviously felt the lash of the King's tongue, which did not augur well for those who were to be under his instruction.

Later James reclined on a long chair in the sunniest solar of the upper court. Marion sat at his feet, resting against him, pregnant and lazily content at being with him once again, humming melodically. Looking up at him she realised that he was dozing and smoothed her hand over his brow. 'You're tired, James.'

'Yes,' he said sleepily. 'The effect of pounding those churlish rebels to disarray.'

He suddenly jerked upright, eyes ablaze with anger. 'I wish to God I could put an end to their treachery, but they fled like vermin before hounds. I would have followed them, but tomorrow I must return to Edinburgh to receive the Spanish ambassadors.'

She waited for his anger to cool, knowing that it would quickly, for he never bore grudges very long. Every time he came to her he looked bigger, thicker set and more handsome. 'You drive yourself too hard, my sweet lord, and take too many risks,' she ventured.

'A king must take risks, Marion, particularly when he's plagued by rebels.'

'But couldn't your loyal nobles pursue the rebels?'

'Loyal nobles, who are they?' he queried, with a bitter laugh. 'I don't know who are my friends or enemies. Alexander Home has concluded a peace treaty with England, but you can be sure that I have no friends in England either.'

'Lord Drummond is your friend, James. A true and trusted friend.'

'He does well, but advises drawing in my reins when instinct spurs me on.'

'He has the wisdom of age, my lord.'

'That he has, my sweeting, and we shall see which of us prevails, for I am determined to run these trouble-making scullions to ground.' He turned to her with mouth tight and grim, revealing that part of him she could never possess, the real king, willing to protect his kingdom against any threat. 'Lennox and Lyle are still rampaging in the west and Forbes in the north, but I'll cast them out to the four winds, even if it's the last thing I accomplish.'

Once again the inner tension relaxed and his expression changed completely as he said, 'In the meantime, Marion, let us forget warfaring and think only of love.'

She leaned against his loose blue doublet, but the sudden thought of losing him caused her body to stiffen in his arms.

'What's wrong with you, my love?' he asked, with concern.

She avoided his anxious eyes and stared at the ledge of the oriel window decorated with twigs bearing long tasselled catkins. 'Tomorrow you meet the Spanish ambassadors.'

'That's nothing for you to worry about, sweetness.'

Her pale complexioned face felt very hot, eyes on the verge of tears. 'Are you sure, James? Aren't they coming to discuss a marriage treaty?'

'Yes, they are, but they bring nothing to tempt me or my Councillors. They come from England, where they've been negotiating a marriage treaty between the English heir and Princess Katharine of Aragon. They're offering a match solely to try and prevent me renewing my alliance with France. But I'll treat them with equal guile, for they offer only the Infanta of Spain, who is already betrothed. No doubt Henry of England has told them that I'll not be content with one of Ferdinand's many royal bastards.' He laughed out loud, momentarily carried away by political chicanery, forgetting she had borne him one child and carried another of the same designation. 'God's bones, it seems the whole of Europe sees me as the husband of a bairn. Marion, you should know that an infant –' He broke off, for she drew away quickly and he realised his blunder. 'My sweeting, don't alarm yourself,' he whispered soothingly. 'The marriages of kings are sordid affairs for Councillors. Let's leave the bickering to them.'

He tried to embrace her, but she resisted, saying, 'What we are doing is wrong in the eyes of God, James.'

'Has your Confessor told you so?' His voice rasped with the same anger as when speaking of traitors.

'No, but only because his living depends upon you.'

His eyes dilated, then he spoke with incisive softness: another characteristic she knew well, deliberately keeping control of himself. He could do so for only a limited period, then temper burst out in a torrent. 'That's not the way to speak of a man of God,' he charged, with a tight smile.

Realising the futility of argument, and having no wish to disturb him further, she gradually succumbed to his tenderness and assurances. But when he left in the morning, she felt a strong presentiment that she would not stay much longer at Stirling, knowing that her removal could be arranged as easily as her installation: the penalty of being the mother of royal bastards!

Contrary to her expectations, James returned after she had presented him with another bastard, this time a son. He was delighted and treated her solicitously. When he made love to her she was aware of the vitality coursing through his strong body. She did her utmost to match it, although not anxious to bear him another child so soon. Twice he brought her to the peak of fulfilment, then lay with her and related his successes with glistening-eyed fervour.

'I told you that I'd overcome those traitors, Marion,' he enthused. 'I burst into their stronghold at Duchar, then again at Crookston, scattering them as I said, but not before my sword dipped into enough blood to make them sorry that they'd betrayed the King of Scotland. I made sure several of them would never have another chance.'

Marion trembled inwardly at the fierceness of his whole mission, knowing the fury he could unleash and his desperate desire to prove himself a true warrior. Yet she also knew how gentle his hands could be on her body. 'As I've said, James, you take too many risks.'

'That's the penalty of being a king. I intend to rule by example and show that I fear no man.'

'I wish for your sake it need not be necessary.'

'But it is necessary, Marion. That's why I went on to Dumbarton, where the Earl of Argyll was besieging the castle held by Lord Forbes and the Earl of Lennox. We found out that Lennox had gone to the highlands seeking reinforcements, then one of my advance groups brought a deserter from Dumbarton into our camp. I put both my hands round his throat and threatened to squeeze out his eyes and tongue if he failed to reveal their defences. When he did speak I took him with us, having promised to split him into two pieces with my sword if he had told a word of a lie.'

It was not the sort of talk Marion enjoyed, but something she had learnt to endure. So often he had told her that she was the only one in his kingdom to whom he could speak freely. It was the lifeline to which she clung. 'Did he speak the truth, James?'

'Yes, he did, my sweeting, and I roused my men to such a pitch that when we stormed into the castle blood flowed like water sweeping down the hills. My sword was covered in it up to the hilt. No wonder they surrendered. My soldiers would not have left a manjack of them alive had I not called them off.'

'What of the Spanish ambassadors, James, how did you fare with them?' asked Marion, to change the subject.

He laughed out loud. 'I kept them guessing, my love, and do you know what, they presented me with a Spanish sword and dagger. I must show them to you, both jewelled and finely wrought: trophies of my increasing skill as a diplomat, as well as a soldier.'

She smiled at his confidence. 'Then everything is in order, my lord?'

He fondled her hair, a cynical smile twisting his mouth as he said, 'A king and his kingdom are seldom all in order, but events are turning the right way. I am gradually winning more supporters, so have fewer enemies than my father. We have reason to celebrate, Marion. I'll soon be going to Edinburgh and you can join me there.'

'I'd sooner stay here and wait for you, James.'

'I can't keep closeting myself here at Stirling, you know that. There are affairs of State that I must attend.' He looked at her with a tender smile. 'Besides, it will do you good to have a change. It's many months since you were last at Court.'

She rested her head against his bare chest and sighed. 'All right, James, if it will please you. But I don't welcome your courtiers making remarks behind my back.'

He cupped her face in his hands and smiled reassuringly. 'They'll feel the point of my sword if I hear them, but don't concern yourself, my sweeting. The women are jealous of your beauty, and the men would rather have you in their beds.'

'More likely the women would sooner have you in their beds,' she murmured ruefully.

He laughed out in high spirits, and reaching forward, scooped her up naked from the bed and danced round with her in his arms, singing loudly. Then he laid her back on the bed, gently easing her into a position that he could once again enjoy her body. Sensing it could be the last time, in spite of what had been said, Marion held him close to her for as long as she was able.

THREE

Early in the new King's reign, the Earl of Angus realised that his attempts to gain control of Scotland's affairs had failed. Receiving scant courtesy from the King and seeing other Councillors flourish, the head of the Douglas family renewed his tenuous links with England.

Given leave of absence from Court, he sought to inveigle Lady Jane Kennedy into accompanying him to his castle at Tantallon. In this too he failed, so finally went alone, expecting a messenger from England any day. Fortuitously Thomas Bladden arrived that night and Angus had him ushered immediately to his candlelit bedchamber.

'Well, Bladden, what news do you bring?' demanded Angus, sitting upon a bearskin bed cover, his dark eyes knit together in a heavy frown.

'I've ridden hard from my master, Sir John Ramsay,' gasped the squire, loosening his thick cote-hardie. 'Four days in the saddle, my lord.'

'Ay,' grunted Angus. 'I'll see you have wine and victuals and a good night's rest, but first your news.'

'Sir John has a commission from King Henry of England, charging him to deliver King James and the Duke of Ross, his brother, into the hands of the English,' said the squire, an evil smile spreading over his swarthy countenance.

'And my part in the affair?' queried Angus.

'To do all in your power to ensure the smooth execution of Sir John's commission, my lord Angus.'

'On what terms?'

The squire's smile broadened. 'Once the King and his brother are out of Scotland, the Earl of Angus can dictate his own terms. I am instructed to say that he will not find the King of England ungenerous.'

Angus rose from the bed, his purply face thunderous as he kicked the rushes about his feet. 'Patrick Hepburn, the one who buckled on your master's belt, has governance of the Duke of Ross. No attempt would succeed without his aid, particularly with the King's brother.'

Thomas Bladden listened to the cold air moaning through the castle embattlements during the ensuing silence. Angus stood at the window staring out into the darkness, brow furrowed over a tormented mind.

'King Henry presses for the King at least,' put in the squire. 'If that will ease the difficulty, my lord.'

'I doubt it,' snarled Angus. 'Not much goes on in Scotland these days without the King or Bothwell being aware of it.'

'Then perhaps the Earl of Bothwell could be tempted to seek more power?'

Angus turned on him angrily. 'That's my master's suggestion,' the squire cried out, retreating to the door.

'Ay, it would be,' agreed Angus, huge fists bunched. 'It's common knowledge he went snivelling to the English King with his troubles. Doubtless he thinks all Scottish nobles are as treacherous as himself.'

'That I can't answer, my lord. But Sir John doesn't complain of the treatment he received from King Henry.'

The prominent veins in the Earl's legs bulged through his thin hose as his restless feet thudded at the stone floor. 'The miser of England is not likely to be generous enough for a Douglas,' he said, with narrowing eyes. 'Or a Hepburn, judging from the grants Bothwell has lapped up recently.'

'In England it's thought that you, my lord, might be the best person to approach the Earl of Bothwell.'

Angus bellowed out madly. 'So that my neck hangs for treason,' he snapped, again advancing towards Bladden menacingly.

The squire cowered further towards the door, body twisted with a shoulder misshapen from the blow of a battle-club received in a border skirmish. 'These words are put to my lips, my lord. They're not of my making.'

'Lucky for you I know it,' flashed Angus. 'Otherwise, I'd cut out your liver and throw it to my hounds.'

He looked as if he meant it, and the squire squirmed before the florid face made fiendish by the flickering shadows of the candles. 'What shall I tell my master?' asked Bladden hesitantly. 'Shall I carry a letter?'

'Not from me, Bladden, for the same reason you carried no written word to me.'

'I warned my master that such would be your reaction, my lord.'

'Then you warned aright, Bladden. Now fill your innards with hot ale and Scotch beef, then get to your bed.' He bellowed for a page, and when he appeared, gave him instructions for attending the squire.

Before Bladden left, Angus said, 'I'll be returning to Edinburgh tomorrow. Perhaps be gone before you wake. Tell your master I'll look into what he suggests and send a messenger should any possibility develop.'

The squire bowed respectfully, then, with his strange lopsided walk, followed the page to the kitchens.

The snail pace progress of affairs of State and Council negotiations, together with the slimy unction that attended them, irked James as he fretted to make swift wide-ranging decisions. Previously, when completely frustrated, a hard ride to Marion at Stirling had exhilarated him. Now she was pregnant again, and so docile and lacking in understanding that she no longer provided enjoyment for either body or mind.

He stood at a window high in Edinburgh castle, overlooking the sprawling city, thoughts fragmentary and scattered. It would soon be Yule again, the trees against the skyline a tangle of scarecrow limbs, the sky a cauldron of dark clouds soon to boil over and further saturate the already sodden countryside. Looking down from this high crag, his gaze swept over mounting striations of black rock into which clumps of tussocky grass had become embedded. Here he kicked his heels whilst his Councillors yapped like bitches about to whelp. They twisted their tongues round every word of each proposal, and finished dribbling out nothing upon which he could act decisively. This they called diplomacy, and he was forced to accept their blather, for he could look to no totally-committed royalist faction for true, self-denying support.

There were a few individuals upon whom he felt it safe to rely – Lucan Fairfax, Patrick Panther his secretary – but among the Council, only Patrick Hepburn could be regarded as a friend. Most of the others had at some time been enemies of the Crown, and he kept this unwelcome fact uppermost in his mind when dealing with State affairs. It helped temper his self-recognised rashness with caution, but did not prevent the current lack of progress stabbing at him like a physical pain. But what else could he do?

He had pardoned Lennox and Forbes, although he would sooner have massacred them with their rabble of malcontents. Another crisis could easily sway their flimsy loyalty. Argyll and Huntly served him well in the Western Isles, but would they remain steadfast if they could gain by deserting the royal standard? Every way he turned there were hints of possible treachery, the latest being murmurings of a plot to deliver him and his brother Jay, the Duke of Ross, into the hands of Henry of England. It seemed there was no end to Scottish infamy, and these were his own subjects.

Sir Andrew Wood of Largo stood out as a lone figure among all his recent negotiations. This imposing, tall, lean man with the clear blue eyes of a sailor had greeted him with unquestionable loyalty. They were at his shipyard at Leith and the grey-haired sea captain embraced him as if he were his own son. 'I would willingly have given my life for your father, and I'll do the same for you, lad,' he said, his familiarity ringing with sincerity.

'I remember the first time I met you, Sir Andrew, you were so handsome and majestic that I momentarily mistook you for my father.'

'That you did, lad, and it brought tears to my eyes. Such a weak young lad surrounded by demons.'

'You speak your mind freely, Sir Andrew.'

'That I do, and always will. Your royal father knew it, that's why he tried to escape to one of my ships when those blood-thirsting rebels pursued him after Sauchieburn. That was when we first met each other, during that unholy search.'

James nodded, recalling the incident with sharp pain: how the searchers had dragged him along with them, then cast him back into Stirling castle whilst they completed their bloody misdeeds.

Sir Andrew sensed his feelings. 'Murderers, cold-blooded murderers, the lot of them!' he exclaimed, with a disgust that etched his finely-chiselled features. 'But it will do them no good. You're now King of Scotland, and I know your problems.' He banged at his chest. 'In here is a Scottish heart, Your Grace, one upon which you can rely. One that will never be swayed by anything English.'

'Then we have a deal in common, Sir Andrew.'

'We also have a love of Scotland in common. That's why I'm building ships and constructing our defences. Give me the chance of smashing the English Navy and you'll not find me wanting. I can assure you of that, both for your sake, and for that of your father.'

'Then we must hope our time will come, Sir Andrew, for we are of the same heart.'

They went on to talk of ships and sea defences in a way which made James recognise that Sir Andrew Wood was a man who truly loved his country, a true Scot of granite breed, who stood out as a glittering jewel among a beach of dark pebbles. He even felt proud to be familiarly called 'lad' by such a man.

James now stood strumming his fingers on the dark wood window-ledge, restless, biting contemplatively at the coarse whiskers of his lower lip. When would he be able to take advantage of Sir Andrew's fighting qualities and strike a decisive blow at England?

Mercifully, relief from his agitation came when Patrick Panther, a slippery eel of a man in tight black cleric gown, came to inform him that the Lord High Chamberlain had returned from Coldstream, and would wait for him in his Royal Presence Chamber.

Alexander Home rose as James entered, then without preamble gave a swift and incisive account of his truce negotiations with England.

James listened attentively, then said, 'At the moment, my lord, it is not to Scotland's advantage to conclude a long truce with England.'

Home's gravity lengthened the network of deep lines on his thin face. 'I gained the impression that King Henry is anxious for peace, Your Grace.'

'Then he has strange ways of negotiating for it,' replied James, moving to a round table and arching his fingers on its waxed top, as his dark brown eyes bored into the elder statesman.

'Your Grace has intelligence unknown to me?' queried Home.

'That King Henry is plotting to secure possession of my own person, as well as that of my royal brother, the Duke of Ross.'

Home looked shocked as his mouth loosened from its tight line. 'From what source does this information come? I know nothing of it.'

'Do you not, my lord? Then that's all the better for you. But others in Scotland are well aware of King Henry's scheming.'

'Can you name those others, Your Grace?'

'I have my suspicions, and in time will gather proof. That achievement will be a sorry day for those who would conspire against their King.'

James stared hard at him, intending that his eyes should reinforce his words. He had no cause for suspecting Home of any involvement, but neither could he be absolutely sure of his innocence. This was the perfidy that cankered all his dealings. Noting Home's discomfort he went on, 'So King Henry offers me his infant daughter as a bride. Does he seriously consider that sufficient inducement for a lasting peace? Scotland and England could have destroyed each other before I had a chance to bed with her.'

'In England they consider King Henry anxious for peace with Scotland, Your Grace.'

'Only because he probably knows of Sir Andrew Wood's successes and does not relish him tweaking the tails of his English ships. I warrant

Henry will be quick to ratify our short term proposal if we put sufficient strength behind it.'

Home remained glumly silent.

'I've other plans afoot, my lord,' James continued, relishing the Chamberlain's confusion. 'Just as the monarchs of Castile and Aragon keep me dangling for a suitable bride, so I'll wibble-wabble Henry of England over a term of truce.'

'I must warn Your Grace, there could be bloody consequences if you bait him too far.'

James banged the table vehemently with his clenched first. 'Then let there be bloody consequences,' he flared. 'My sword is as keen as Henry's, and in a short while my ships will be better too.'

The two men stared at each other in a silent battle of conflicting opinions. Alexander Home, grandson of the now aged first Baron of Home, who had been brought up to appreciate all the finer points of political expediency, was not impressed by the King's youthful show of bravado. 'Impetuous action is ill-advised, Your Grace. The north of England has been strengthened by the appointment of Thomas Howard, Earl of Surrey, as lieutenant-general.'

'Then it would seem most likely that we will have imminent dealings with my lord Surrey.'

'He is a valiant soldier who fights without mercy for the Crown of England. Having already put down one insurrection for King Henry, he's now entrusted with the care of the borders,' warned Home. As he spoke the corners of his mouth tightened with annoyance at the King's failure to understand this new threat to Scotland's security.

'Have no fear, we'll not underestimate my lord Surrey when the time comes,' said James. 'Now, Alexander, you've devoted much time on my service in England, so I give you leave to spend Yule with your family. I'll summon you when we receive King Henry's ratification.'

Home bowed respectfully. 'You are most generous, Your Grace.'

'You can give my felicities to your good lady. When one of my embassies does eventually secure me a wife, I'll come to Fastcastle to learn how to produce sons.'

Home's face relaxed into a smile for the first time. 'You could not come to a better place for such instruction,' he confirmed with obvious pride, then turned towards the double gilt doors, made his final bow, and departed.

The young King was growing fast and had spirit, he thought as he made his way along the draughty stairways of the castle. According to gossip, his visits to Stirling had ceased and Mistress Boyd returned to her father with considerable grants of land for service to the Crown. The same informer related how at Perth he had stumbled accidentally upon the King closeted in an attic with a lodgekeeper's daughter. Whilst he searched for the lodgekeeper, the plump-breasted lass emerged with her gown split down the front and the white flesh of her neck reddened with teeth marks, for which subsequent payments and ells of cloth were ledgered in the name of Mistress Fraser at Perth.

Yule passed with a bleak, icy spell which almost froze Edinburgh to a standstill. A howling wind rampaged through the castle battlements and none ventured from the crackling log fires until necessity demanded it. Out in the city the alehouses sold their ale piping hot; fires burned in the streets to thaw the icebound tracks of cart wheels and horses' hooves. Shops were boarded up and picketed outside, the extreme cold having driven the hungry to desperation. All suffered; not even the richest fur-lined robe kept out the raw cold, but it prevented its owner from dying of exposure, as happened to so many with nothing to wear other than threadbare doublets.

Lucan Fairfax wakened his master one morning and immediately made an urgent request. 'Your Grace, can I have permission to visit my grandparents today?'

'Today, Lucan? Where are they?' asked the King, rubbing the sleep from his eyes.

'Like so many others, trapped in a cottage west of the castle, without sustenance. My parents are anxious for them.'

James leapt from his bed. 'I'm anxious for them too, Lucan, and for any other of my subjects in similar peril. Not only do I grant you leave, Lucan, but I'll accompany you with soldiers from the castle. We'll carry provisions and rescue all we can. Those close at hand can be fed and warmed in the castle kitchens.'

They set off in a blizzard, fighting their way through snow-laden streets, distributing alms freely, escorting those who could be moved back to the castle, among which were Lucan's grandparents. The King himself helped carry Lucan's grandmother part of the way, and when he delivered her to the safekeeping of her daughter in the castle quarters, the old lady kissed his hand and said, 'Almighty God will bless you for such goodness, Your Grace.'

Her appreciation was repeated again and again during the ensuing days, when the young figure of the King striding through the snow, face as red as his beard and dark brown eyes agleam with purpose, became a familiar sight. He continued when others flagged, refused to admit defeat even if it meant putting his own life at risk, and even though many perished before relief came, his efforts earned him the unstinted regard of the Edinburgh folk. They talked of his rescue ventures in endearing terms long after the thaw set in. This was the only reward James sought – that the people of Scotland knew he cared for them far more than for the gaggle of noblemen who plagued him with their duplicity.

King Henry's ratification of the short term truce came to Edinburgh with the return of spring sunshine, causing the woodland eruption of yellow celandine stars and golden coltsfoot buttons on pink-scaled stems, much to the delight of herbalists who used the first plant for curing warts and the other for making cough potions.

As James anticipated, England's response came more speedily than usual. He summoned Home and received him in the Council Chamber with Bothwell, Huntly and Sir Andrew Wood in attendance.

James tossed the rolled paper across the table to his Lord High Chamberlain, a hint of amusement in the curl of his lips. 'Did I not say there would be no great delay, my lord?'

Home's grey-blue eyes scanned the document. 'Then it confirms what I said about King Henry's desire for peace.'

'Or what I said about his fear of Sir Andrew's ships,' countered James, with a laugh.

A frown now puckered Bothwell's normally smooth featured face. 'King Henry has had a rude lesson in making the English pay for a war,' he observed. 'Nonetheless, he's not been slow to crush all who've risen against him, whether he desires peace or not.'

'Bothwell's right,' put in Home; then fingering the cords of his long jacket, he went on, 'The English King plays a canny game by behaving as if he's still at peace with France, yet making war against her in Brittany. He's no mean diplomat, Your Grace.'

James's eyes narrowed. 'Neither is the King of Scotland, with your help, my lords,' he declared. 'True, Henry's defeated those who have tilted for his crown, but he still has the French situation to resolve.'

Huntly nodded thoughtfully. With his thick-set, broad-shouldered body hunched in a large crimson robe and incongruously small head jutting forward, he resembled an overgrown monkey. Even so, he commanded respect as the King's representative throughout the all-important Highlands. 'It would seem wise to await developments, Your

Grace,' he suggested. 'As yet nothing's been settled about your marriage, so there's no need to embarrass relations with Spain by completely refusing a peace with England.'

'You can question Bothwell on the subject of my marriage,' snapped James. 'He's spent the past year trying to negotiate a match.'

The sudden flashing of all eyes towards him ruffled Bothwell's usual calm. He gestured with his hands, but before he could offer excuses, a household page entered the chamber and spoke with the King.

A self-satisfied smile creased James's firm lips. 'You can send him in,' he said aloud.

Without delay, a fair-haired youth dressed in a green and silver tunic emblazoned with the Tudor rose entered to pay punctilious respects. James took the scroll he presented, read it, then tossed it across to Home saying, 'King Henry grows impatient for my ratification of the truce terms.'

Home finished reading the letter and received the King's curt nod to pass it round the table.

'You may refresh yourself, then return to your royal master,' said James to the messenger. 'Tell him that the King of Scotland and his Councillors have not yet reached their decision. We will send it when we've concluded our deliberation.'

The messenger bowed low with a flourish of his plumed bonnet and departed.

'Well?' queried James, glancing round the long table. 'It seems that King Henry's anxious to keep peace with Scotland, for fear of what might develop in France.'

'That appears to be the way of it, Your Grace,' agreed Home. 'And since we're also interested in the resolution of the English foreign policy, perhaps it would satisfy our interests by agreeing to a truce of but one year.'

'But you, my lord, have already agreed to a five-year term,' James reminded him, a mischievous glint in his eyes.

The thin face of the nobleman blanched. 'Only subject to Your Grace's ratification,' he put in defensively. 'The situation has changed.'

'Indeed, it has, my lords,' fired James, eyes brightening excitedly. 'During yesterday's forenoon I received letters from Ireland. They came from the Earls of Desmond and Kildare, who speak of one who could oust Henry Tudor from the throne of England.'

Bothwell stopped in the process of raising a goblet of wine to his lips. 'The one who claims to be Prince Richard, Duke of York?' he queried.

'The very same, Patrick,' confirmed James, his earlier criticism forgotten. 'Now, Alexander, tell us what you know of him.'

Home's gaunt figure leaned forward in earnest. 'The so-called Duke landed at Cork last year, Your Grace. I had word of it through the English representatives at the truce negotiations. They vowed him an impostor.'

'Of course, they would,' said the King. 'But while he is in Ireland, trying to muster support to press his claims, he has now appealed to me for help.'

'Does Your Grace feel disposed to grant it?' asked Huntly. The political magnitude and implications of such a move had caused him to sit upright and straighten his shoulders. He clearly recognised the young King's astuteness in withholding such information until this crucial moment.

James sat with his hands moving in and out of the wide sleeves of his blue outer robe, smiling confidently, enjoying the suddenly aroused suspense. 'This is not an occasion for a rash decision, my lords, but I'm keenly interested. Would it not be of purpose to Scotland to have an English King who owed his crown to Scottish support?'

'A situation rich with possibilities, Your Grace,' agreed Huntly, with a knowing smile.

'Exactly,' chuckled James. 'Which makes it advisable for us to accept my lord Home's suggestion to prolong the truce only until the end of the year.'

Sir Andrew Wood, who had remained listening silently for so long, straightened up impressively in his chair.

'Well, Sir Andrew?' queried James, always pleased to hear his considered views.

'We should overhaul our ships in the interim,' suggested the sailor.

'And build as many more as possible,' declared James.

'Ay, if the exchequer will provide the resources, Your Grace,' Sir Andrew reminded him.

James nodded. 'There's work for us all in the next few months, my lords. Patrick, as warden of the east and middle marches this involves you on land as well as water. Alexander, you are warden of the west marches. The pair of you must organise regular wapenshaws, which I shall have Parliament authorise. Men must be mustered and trained in archery. I want as many trained bowmen in the field as can be found in Scotland, and the mustering must be speeded up, so that an army can be brought together in the shortest possible time. Is that clear, my lords?'

They each nodded their assent in turn.

James picked up a silver salver of comfits on the table. 'Then my lords, we can adjourn.' He crammed a handful of comfits into his mouth and leaned back expansively, watching them depart, roguishly aware that he had given them much to think about, and at the same time, impressed them with his political ability.

At last there was action afoot, work to be done, a special mission for a king – promoting his country to greatness. In this he could absorb himself completely, and start disproving the astrologer's prediction concerning the unfavourable position of the planets at his birth. Before this year of 1495 ended, every astrologer in the land might have reason to regret those rash words.

In the midst of preparing for sudden war to take advantage of England possibly becoming embroiled with France, a letter arrived from the Earl of Kildare.

James summoned Lord Home and received him in his private chamber at the Palace of Holyroodhouse.

Home wore black robes, mourning his greatly respected grandfather, whom he had succeeded as the second Baron of Home. 'Bad news, Your Grace?' he queried, with a frown of concern.

James flung the letter on to a small carved table in disgust.

Home read it quickly and the tension of his features eased. 'This is not bad news, Your Grace.'

The King's mouth quirked with irritation. 'If I could establish a hold on England through a king whose cause I supported, there would be no limits to the demands I could make. I was itching for quick action and have scoured the kingdom urging all haste to be ready for war. Now Prince Richard has gone to France, so all my plans are delayed.'

A smile flecked Home's tight lips. 'A delay we can use to advantage,' he pointed out. 'The Duke of York's doubtless trying to secure allies.'

'Then we must hope he succeeds. For my part, my patience is at breaking point. Events move far too slowly, my lord. I want to jab them with a sharp lance to provide the initial impetus.' He stood and walked to the grilled window. 'I think I'll go to Castle Campbell for some hunting with Argyll. He's a lively wit, and wherever his yellow and black arms flutter one can be assured of good cheer. Archibald finds entertainment in wine and women, and I feel in sore need of the solace of either, but preferably both.'

Home smiled tolerantly, his keen brain enumerating the factors involved in the fresh development. 'This reopens the question of the truce with England, Your Grace. The present treaty expires next month.'

'Then we will have to renew it.'

'For as short a term as possible?' suggested Home, with a wry smile.

James turned from the window and nodded. 'That is our agreed policy. You, my lord, will lead the commission.' He clapped his hands together in exasperation and began pacing the rush-strewn floor. 'God's nails, no more affairs of State, Alexander, they addle my nerves. Tonight we'll have a masque at the palace. Tomorrow I'll go to Castle Campbell, then my lord Drummond has invited me to his castle. I must do something to relieve the suspense of waiting. If I rely on my embassies I'll die a bachelor, and God alone knows when Prince Richard will bring the English cauldron to the boil.'

'Events might well stir with the suddenness of a squall, Your Grace. There's no need to be impetuous.'

James swung towards him with a swirl of his blue fur-trimmed robe. 'Save your sagacity for your sons,' he snapped, then quickly controlled his temper and added, 'Now leave me, for I fear I'm easily deranged this day.'

Home departed and James called for food. When brought and laid out on the table, he pecked at it, then with a bellow of impatience, pushed it away, kicked the table over and strode into the stables to bully a groom into saddling a horse. He would gallop alone and sweat out some of his surplus energy before the masque. Scotland needed a Queen and an heir to the throne, yet he was wasting his seed on Court trollops.

FOUR

In the Great Hall of Stirling Castle, six hundred courtiers sat down to supper in the happy atmosphere that usually preceded a masque. Beneath the magnificent hammer beams, the hum and buzz of chatter went on ceaselessly as the gathering fed from huge haunches of venison, roasted ducks, peacocks covered with thick sauces, boars' heads, boiled capons, jellied eggs, baskets of raisins and strawberries dancing in wine. Musicians strummed their harps and lutes, minstrels sang louder and louder, knights and squires washed down their food and whetted their appetites for gaiety with Gascon wine, Scotch ale and flagons of mead.

James sat at the top table on the royal dais with his senior ministers and their wives. When the eating finished, he rose and the whole assembly shuffled awkwardly to its feet. He nodded to his confessor who intoned a prayer in Latin. The 'Amen' spluttered late from several mouths after the main response.

A group of house carls swept into immediate action, pushing back eating tables and trestles to prepare space for the masque. As they scurried feverishly, the impatient courtiers were meant to be diverted by a band of mummers performing a violent ballad of treachery and murder, but few other than the players showed much interest.

During these activities James caught sight of a figure that alerted his attention like a lightning flash. With a quick nod he summoned Lucan Fairfax. 'I think I've seen Lady Kennedy. Find out where she is and how I can go straight to her when I wish.'

Lucan hesitated, his fresh boyish face troubled.

'Stop dithering, and do my bidding,' snapped James angrily.

It appeared that Lucan had wanted to say something, but aware of his master's mood, changed his mind and scampered away.

James looked around, observing the rising excitement as the ladies slipped away into hiding places to don a variety of elaborately decorated masks. The ballad completed, the sound of music and the voices of

41

gleemen reverberated from the timbered roof to every corner of the Hall. He noticed several masked ladies grouping together, so that he could choose his partner for the first dance from them. He cared not which he took, for he now had a singular objective. Tonight he would make Lady Kennedy take notice of her King.

He approached the group of masked women simperingly waiting for him. He extended his hand to one about his own height, with a fair complexion highlighted by a black mask. 'Lady, let us lead the dance.'

She curtsied deeply, looking up at him and smilingly revealing perfect white teeth. 'I'm most honoured, Your Grace.'

As he took her to the floor he noticed how she turned back to glance at the other women, a coquettish victory smirk. But he was only interested in her as a partner for one dance, not as a person. He whirled her around with such fervour that she had neither the time nor the breath to speak, then with perspiration on his brow and still unheeding of her personal qualities, led her back to the group and thanked her. Again she curtsied in a flurry of smiles and feminine wriggles, but he went straight back to his chair of State, aware that he was leaving a pair of amply revealed gleaming white breasts whose owner would dearly have loved him to have led her off to one of the alcoves to fondle them. This she no doubt hoped would have gained her passage to his bed, with the possibility of a rich reward if she pleased him.

Mopping his brow he gazed around at the figures swirling around the lantern-lit Hall. He could see neither Lady Kennedy nor Lucan. There were many with young firm breasts like his dancing partner, their upper curves tantalisingly revealed by low square necklines of brocade, taffeta and velvet, the lower curves given eye-catching appeal with fur trim-mings, jewels and exquisite embroidery. But where was Lucan?

He deliberately avoided conversation with his top table guests, wanting no conversation of State matters. Instead, as he searched for sight of Lucan, he noted how the ladies' head-dresses reflected the fluctuations of fashion – from the high steeple-crowned hats embellished with flowing colourful silks to the gable-pointed hoods stiffened and edged with fur and jewel-work. To divert his impatience he picked out the wives of his Councillors, amusing himself by imagining how they treated their lords in bed. This soon palled, for he reached no conclusions to make him envious. Then his glance came upon the tall, graceful beauty standing apart from a group of dancers twirling in a frenzied dervish of laughter and enthusiasm.

Even though masked he recognised her at once – the ebony blackness of the hair, unmistakable proud bearing, slightly raised tilt of the head, challengingly arrogant. Now there was a perfect dancing partner for a king, and one he would not disappoint in any desire for fondling. At that moment Lucan appeared at his side. 'What news of Lady Kennedy?' he demanded.

'She's here, Your Grace.'

'I can see that, lad. By all that's holy I can.' He noted his page's grimacing and twitching. 'What else, lad? You're acting like a sucking pig on a spit. What's wrong with you?'

Lucan ventured no explanation.

'Have I to choke words out of you?' flared James. 'What mischief are you withholding?'

'None of my making, Your Grace.'

'Then what's the cause of you hopping from one foot to the other. Have you St. Vitus dance? Come, lad, speak! What have you found out about Lady Kennedy?'

Lucan knelt beside the chair of State, almost in supplication. 'She saw me skirting around her party and beckoned me.'

'To what purpose?'

'She asked if you'd sent me to spy on her.'

'To spy on her at my Court?'

'I said words to that effect, Your Grace.'

'And how did she reply?'

'That unless you wished to summon her as King on affairs of State, she was otherwise engaged this night.'

James clenched his fists and banged them on the sides of his chair. 'God's bones, Lucan, what did you say to that?'

'I ... I ... told her that ... that I would tell Your Grace,' he stammered nervously. 'What ... what else could I say?'

'You could have called her a worthless trollop, you could have cut her tongue out, or smashed a lighted lantern over her head,' thundered James, temper rising so that those around him glanced his way questioningly. 'I tell you what, lad. Go to my bedchamber and see that it's ready to receive a wench. I'll have Lady Kennedy there tonight even if I have to drag her there by the strands of her black mane of hair.'

When Lucan remained beside him he grated out. 'Do what I say, churl! Before I make you suffer for that trollop's impudence.'

Lucan rose quickly and went, but not to the King's bedchamber. He considered he could best serve his master by being out of sight, but close at hand for what troubles might develop.

Slowly James gained control of his temper, realising that he could not outwit such a woman if blinded solely by physical lust. She was obviously aware of his attraction to have summoned Lucan, who wore the royal insignia on his jupon. She had been aware of his glances in the past, but not responded by making any approach of her own as most women at Court would have done. The one he had danced with, for instance, he could have whisked her off and her clouts would have been up and around her neck before he was ready for her. What made Jane Kennedy think that she was so different?

Once again she came into his view. His eyes cleared of burning rage as he watched every detail of the activity around her. In spite of entreaties to join a nearby spirited group, she remained apart, black gown embellished with gold embroidery accentuating every line of her femininity. Two wine-befuddled knights tried to entice her into their company. He saw the determination register on her mouth before she uttered some remark with obvious imperiousness. Drunk as they were, the two knights recoiled, retiring with expressions so cowed that she could have been a witch incanting the vilest imprecation.

After considering his next move, James suddenly rose and much to her surprise joined the Countess Bothwell in the dance, this being the easiest and least conspicuous way across the Hall. Achieving his purpose, he handed the Countess to a nearby nobleman and dodged round the fringe of the dancers.

He calmed the tempest raging within him, then approached Jane from behind one of the fluted stone pillars separating the Hall from the alcoved window embrasures. 'My lady Kennedy does not wish to join the dancing?' he queried, in controlled tones.

Startled momentarily, she soon regained her composure and curtsied in a manner which conveyed scant respect.

'I trust I did not disturb you, Lady Jane.'

Her haughty look returned and he could see her eyes glinting through her lavish mask. 'I'm not easily disturbed, Your Grace,' she replied, in a husky feminine voice. 'But this is a masque. I didn't wish the sanctity of my disguise to be so soon stripped away.'

She undid the strings of her mask, revealing fascinating blue-green eyes.

Even his anger at her insolence could not mar her striking appearance. 'I did not wish to intrude, lady. Though I have no regrets, for such beauty should not be concealed behind a mask.'

She half-turned from him almost contemptuously, ignoring his presence and continuing to watch the dancers with a bemused smile on her deep red lips.

The scraping of fiddles, the strumming of lutes and the bawdy voices of the revellers no longer sounded as merriment to his ears. There was a rasp in his voice as he said, 'If we sit out in one of the embrasures I can have refreshments served to us.'

'I have supped my fill, Your Grace,' she returned coldly.

'Surely you'll not deny your King the pleasure of your company?' He ground the words out through a pounding desire to make her yield to him.

Her black eyebrows arched expressively. 'You'll have to command me as King to force me to obey.'

Never before had he felt so inclined to strike a lady. He tried to face her without flinching, but failed. With difficulty he said, 'Then it is my command, lady.'

'Then I hope you'll regard it as the limit of your command of my person, Your Grace.'

Smarting with resentment, he led her from open gaze through the screens and heavy drapes shielding the embrasures from the Hall. He indicated the red brocade window seat and she sat gazing pointedly out of the grilled window at the full moon illuminating the indigo sky.

'You have not been at Court for a long time, my lady Kennedy. I did not even know that you would be attending this masque,' said James placatingly, still anxious to make an impression.

'I knew nothing of it until I arrived after noon.'

'You came from Forfarshire?'

She inclined her head in agreement.

'From the Earl of Angus?'

Her regular white teeth flashed as she said, 'His lands are in Forfarshire.'

The thought of old Angus pawing this beauty and slobbering over her with his bad breath and rotting teeth disgusted him. 'And his bed, lady, so I'm told.'

'My lord Angus is closeted at Tantallon with his physicians, I know nothing of his bed, but he retains my loyalty as my liege lord. I returned to Court to visit my father at his wish.'

'Then you obey the wish of a traitor and not your King?'

'I know of no traitor.' Her eyes turned their full fire upon him.

'I speak of Angus. No doubt you know that he's been in league with England to depose me from my throne.'

'No man would accuse him of that treachery to his face,' countered Jane. 'It would cost him his life.'

James beckoned a page to bring wine. His lips quivered with unleashed temper, but he eventually forced a smile, saying, 'Let us not argue over Angus, Jane. He's a brave soldier and may yet serve to please his King.'

She started to speak, but he halted her by upraising his hands. 'Shall we talk of you and your father?' he went on. 'I had not realised that he holds such humble office. He could be easily elevated.'

Once again her eyes fixed on him as she said, 'I have no doubt of that, but my father's not an ambitious man. He's of an age when he'll soon be requesting to retire from Court. I need work in no bed to advance him. You seem much occupied with bedding from all accounts, Your Grace. But even if you think that as King you can command the use of my body, let me emphasise that only a real man can ever win the full enjoyment of it.'

No courtier, man or woman, had ever dared to speak to him with such disrespect, not even Lord Gray at the height of his arrogance after Sauchieburn. 'Lady Kennedy, you forget you're speaking to your King. I could banish you from my kingdom for such impudence.'

Her eyes glinted with fire and purpose, then the firm line of her lips relaxed as she feigned great shock. 'I merely demonstrate my loyalty to my father and my liege lord. I thought a King would regard loyalty as highly desirable.'

'Trollop, you know not what loyalty means!' He jumped up and took a warning step towards her.

Jane rose too and stood her ground, face defiantly raised, almost tempting him to strike her. Her voice penetrated incisively as she said, 'But I know in which bed I choose to stay.'

James bellowed out so loudly that it caused a scuffle from the other side of the screens. He heard women giggling and men whispering, chuckling or guffawing according to how much they had drunk. His face felt hot and bloated, more so because he knew that Jane Kennedy had bested him and was fully aware of the fact.

Confidence sounded in her voice, as with the fleetness of an accomplished dancer, she drew away from him and said, 'Have I your permission to withdraw, Your Grace?' The words were correct, but her tone and manner waspishly supercilious.

James again moved towards her, seeing only the composed superior smile, hating it, a mere slender thread of control preventing him from cuffing it from her face. 'You have not, lady, for I'll leave before you. But the mischief you've caused tonight is something the family of Kennedy could have cause to remember for a long time.'

He stood motionless before her, hoping the warning might yet prompt contrition. When it did not, he spun round sharply to withdraw, but collided with the incoming page and sent goblets of wine cascading to the floor. A group of dancers skirting the grey stone walls towards the shadows of the windows observed his clumsy exit. They stopped their swaying steps and burst out laughing, but once recognition seeped through their merriment, quickly hid their faces in the folds of their robes to escape the fury in the young King's face.

James pushed through the revellers, heedless of eyes following his head-down progress across the Hall. Some speculations were made, but most courtiers were either too drunk or too preoccupied with their own dalliances to care what ailed the King. Those who sensed trouble with a lady took solace from the fact that their own partners were more obliging.

Jane watched his departure with a tight-lipped smile. She had achieved her purpose and felt sure that the young King would not forget her. It remained to be seen how he responded to the affront. If he proved himself a man, he might not find her lacking in the art of being a woman.

In his bedchamber, James kicked the rushes all over the floor, jerked savagely at the restricting cords and buttons of his clothes, then stripped to the waist and pounded a frustrated tattoo with clenched fists upon the royal arms of Scotland embroidered on the bedcover. Jane Kennedy had thwarted him without effort. Now he would have to find some way of making her grovel for a pardon, for he could no longer find true satisfaction in tumbling trollops.

This latest encounter made him desire her more than ever. Not only his whole mind, but every fibre of his being lusted for the possession of her flesh. It was so burning a passion that until he conquered her, he would go on wanting her and wanting her, again, and again, and again. She herself had said that as King he could command, but in the light of what had happened it would be a sign of weakness to issue any such command. He had to prove himself merely as a man to fully enjoy her.

But she was worth winning, and win her he would, no matter how much it cost him.

Slowly reason stilled his febrile mind and he parted the herb-sweetened sheets to relax his naked body in their smoothness. But sleep eluded him as the image of Jane Kennedy constantly recurred, magnifying into a symbol of success beyond his grasp.

By God, he would make her suffer for treating him like a whore-mongering soldier! Yet even as these thoughts coursed through his despondency he recognised the insincerity of them. More than anything in the world at this moment he wanted Jane Kennedy; failure to make headway with her typified the lack of fulfilment which seemed destined to blight his reign. But why? Where was he going wrong? Could it be that the astrologers who had influenced his father were right?

Always some circumstance or person fell short of expectation; nothing reached a complete and satisfying fruition. The bickering amongst the Council about a suitable marriage; the promise of the Duke of York temporarily dimmed by political manoeuvring; and now Jane Kennedy openly flouting his kingship, intimating that as a seducer of trollops he had no place in the bed of a lady of distinction. When he finally slept, Jane's face floated disembodied through his dreams.

The same image barbed when he reluctantly prolonged the truce with England, then visited Castle Drummond where he again met with Lady Margaret, formerly one of his mother's maidens of honour, whose girlish charms had attracted him as a boy. She had grown into a glittering woman, fair-haired and fair complexioned, a broadish face with large frank blue eyes that shone like jewels but also possessed a twinkle of impishness. She was young and joyful, vivacious and laughter-loving.

Walking with her in the walled gardens on the first afternoon, James immediately warmed to her exhilarating presence. She had skipped happily ahead of him to inspect a clump of magnificently blossoming rose bushes. He caught up with her as she handled one of the deep red flower heads. 'It's good to be with you again, Meg. You don't know how I've suffered since becoming King.'

She laughed, displaying a splendid show of teeth and a full-lipped luscious mouth. Catching hold of his hand spontaneously she said, 'I've heard of your troubles from my father. What a wild and impetuous young man you've become. He's likened you unto an unsaddled colt. But now you're my King,' she added with mock seriousness, skipping away from him to make an exaggerated curtsey. He took hold of her lively body and instantly thrilled at its touch. There was something pure and fresh and vital about her. It was as if they had never been parted. He held her close to him. 'Sweet Meg, it's good to have your company again,' he repeated. 'My dear mother was so fond of you, and having you near me takes me back to the only happy time I've ever had in my whole life.'

'Poor Jamie.' Her eyes twinkled. 'I can imagine you trying so hard to be a grand and imposing king.'

Inwardly he knew she was laughing at him, but in a manner which gave no offence. He felt conscious only of an empathy, a bond which sprang from their childhood association. Here he could forget the humiliation of his dealings with Jane Kennedy, for Margaret possessed a natural exhilaration of womanhood which required no artifice. 'I am a grand and imposing king,' he said, matching her devilment with mock pomposity.

'Who wishes to put fear of the Almighty into English hearts,' she went on.

'Who has put fear of the Almighty into English hearts,' he responded. 'For they don't know what I intend. Only yesterday I prolonged our truce. Now they suspect I have other plans, but are not sure what they might be.'

'My father has mentioned a so-called Prince Richard.'

'Has he told you of the possibilities of the same Prince enabling me to further Scottish interests?'

'As a little boy you were always a schemer. I can imagine how your mind is working,'

They walked on together across the lush grass with hands linked and James felt uplifted by her spontaneity and closeness. She could be so effortlessly cheering, yet through it came the evidence that she had inherited much of her father's wisdom, and with it a sense of history and destiny. 'You were always the one who detected my craftiest scheming,' he reminded her.

'Perhaps Jamie was not so clever then as he is now.'

'I think that highly likely,' he confirmed, with feeling.

'But my father also tells me of the risks you take, Jamie. You should not take risks unnecessarily.'

'Perhaps I still need your guidance, Meg.' As he said it, sudden realisation sprang to his mind, that her family had provided Scotland with a Queen. Could it be that in spite of all the negotiating for a marriage with a foreign princess he was now enjoying the company of the future Queen of Scotland?

She ran off and he chased after her, catching her and once again holding her close, becoming more aware of the curves of her lovely body and his instinctive appreciation of the effect she had on him.

That night they danced together in perfect unison, their bodies moving as one with the music. Beforehand they had cantered hard across the countryside, with Margaret displaying her love of horses and her ability to ride them. She was graceful in all she did, and James found himself marvelling at the way she had rid his mind of all the problems which had weighed so heavily upon him when arriving at Castle Drummond.

So it continued for the next three days, until on the third night they left the Hall together and James guided her along the castle corridors with his arm lightly round her waist. At the door of her bedchamber he said, 'Meg, the past days have been the happiest of my whole life.'

'I'm glad you've enjoyed them, Jamie,' she replied, looking at him in the light of the lantern beside her door.

It was she who clung to him, held herself firm against him, so that he could feel her body trembling.

'Meg, sweet Meg,' he murmured.

They stood locked in a tight embrace, silent, as if both absorbing the full import of the fact that they were now man and woman, not boy and girl.

'Jamie, do you want to come into my bedchamber?' she almost whispered.

'Do you want me to, Meg?'

'Yes, yes, I'm sure I do,' she replied, clinging hard to him. 'But I'm not practised in the ways of men. I only know that my body is making demands I've not known before. It must be because of you.'

He pushed upon the door and led her in. Again they clung together, then Margaret drew away and sat on her bed. 'Jamie, there has never been another,' she said nervously.

He knelt beside her and fondled beneath her robe, but it was she who first began to remove her clothes. He helped her and when she was naked in his arms, felt her perceptibly tremble. 'Have no fears, Meg.'

'Jamie, Jamie,' she whispered.

He disrobed quickly and lay beside her. What followed had a touch of magic about it, an inevitability. Above all, it was a mutual desire, for at no stage had he actively sought this intimacy. As he caressed her deliciously smooth flesh she instinctively moved to receive him, yet he could feel her pounding heart and the occasional tremor of alarm. When they finally joined together as one it was the ultimate expression of supreme happiness. Fully aware of her initial pangs of modesty, it required no effort for him to be more tender than he had ever been; his heart, mind, body and soul dictated it. At last he had achieved complete and utter satisfaction.

The next few days were idyllic, tinctured with all the charm of childhood sweetheart innocence blossoming into adult appreciation of the mental and physical joy of being in love. James had no doubt that he was totally in love with her and she with him.

Drawn back to Edinburgh by the developing situation with England, he left Castle Drummond secure in the knowledge that Jane Kennedy no longer held any sway over him, for he now had plans to make Margaret his Queen. Even so, he was not blind to the internal complications which could arise from him marrying a Scot. So all the possibilities throbbing through his head had to remain within himself, shared with no-one, not even Margaret herself.

As soon as James reached Edinburgh castle he summoned Bothwell to his private chamber to be greeted with, 'You look mighty well, Your Grace. I don't think I've ever seen you look more happy.'

'I don't think I have ever been more happy,' he confided.

Pleasing as this was, Bothwell's immediate observance of the happiness that glowed within him made it necessary to delay what he had intended to discuss. He had not expected the change in himself to be so noticeably obvious. Now he judged it as foolhardy even to trust Patrick Hepburn by asking what he thought of him marrying a Scottish lady. Patrick would immediately guess the identity of whom he had in mind and the reason behind the inquiry.

'Your stay at Castle Drummond has done you good. Drummond must have entertained you well,' observed Bothwell.

'That he did,' responded James. 'So I return fresh and ready for affairs of State. What news have you of the marriage negotiations?' This was to put Bothwell off the scent of associating his happiness with the company of Lady Margaret Drummond. Inwardly, he congratulated himself on the quick reversal of intention. Patrick would have drawn the right conclusion at once.

'It seems our embassies abroad make little progress, Your Grace. There's much talk, but nothing in the way of hard and firm promises.'

Bothwell's crestfallen manner pleased James. How easily he could have revealed too much. 'Then what of Prince Richard? What news of him?'

'There are developments, Your Grace.'

James indicated a chair. 'Then sit down and tell me about them. I hope they augur well, for already I feel my good temper ebbing away.'

Bothwell sat and crossed his hose-clad legs easily, thinking the change in the young King quite remarkable. Something at Castle Drummond had obviously affected him. Could it be Lady Margaret Drummond? With keen intelligent eyes he watched James, closely weighing his words, waiting for a slip of the tongue. Although he thought he enjoyed the King's confidence, at Court one could never be sure. So much went on behind one's back, those jealous of any status or privilege always ready to bring about a downfall. He too had heard about Angus, a dangerous man to cross. He had warned the King many times, as well as the Duke of Ross, now in his care. But he had said nothing to either of them about the alleged overtures with England. As custodian of the King's brother he had remained on guard, aware that positive action against Angus required absolute proof.

'You're thoughtful, Patrick,' charged James. 'I hope you're not thinking of words to keep me in good humour.'

Bothwell smiled. 'Nothing but the truth is helpful to our cause, Your Grace.'

'I wish all my Councillors thought the same.'

'Each must act according to his own conscience.'

'True, but that's difficult for those who have no conscience. Now, Patrick, tell me what happens beyond this Court.'

Bothwell met his probing gaze without qualm. 'I have had news from various embassies, Your Grace. There are those in Europe not willing to give the so-called Prince Richard the credence with which you have favoured him.'

James slowly straightened up in his chair, eyes never leaving Bothwell's urbane features. 'Do you question that judgement, Patrick?' he asked.

'My mind remains open, Your Grace. To date I'm not convinced of the truth either way. As I have said all along, we must be cautious before committing ourselves too far.'

Banging the small table before him, James cried out, 'God's nails, Patrick, spare me more caution! It's all I hear from the lot of you. If Scotland could prosper on caution we'd be the most prosperous nation in the whole world.'

'Without it we could easily lose all our bargaining power, Your Grace.'

'Then what of Prince Richard?'

'After signing the treaty of Etaples with England, Charles of France dismissed him as an impostor.'

'At King Henry's behest?'

Bothwell nodded. 'The Prince then went to the Duchess of Burgundy, who seemingly accepted him as a bona fide nephew and pressed his claims to other Continental monarchs.'

'She would not do that without reason,' observed James thoughtfully. 'Have you sought the reasons?'

'I have been into the matter most thoroughly, Your Grace.'

James nodded approvingly. 'Go on.'

'The Duchess is eager for the return of the revenues granted her by King Edward IV of England and stopped by King Henry.'

James thumped the table again. 'I imagined something like that. Then what, Patrick?'

'King Henry displayed his annoyance by prohibiting trade with the Netherlands and recalling his Merchant Adventurers from Antwerp to Calais.'

'Ho! Ho! So Henry doesn't like the developments?'

'There are more, Your Grace, causing unrest in England.'

'Anything of which we can take advantage?'

When Bothwell hesitated, James quipped sarcastically, 'With due caution, of course, my lord.'

Bothwell smiled at the friendly jibe, warming to the young King with every new dealing, realising the enormities of his position and the haunting uncertainties that must plague him. 'The apprentices and merchant house servants in London broke out in revolt, resenting the lack of trade which could cause the loss of their livelihood. It required troops to put them down, such was the violence.'

James nodded, fingers scraping at his beard, eyes alight with interest.

'Even more significant, Your Grace, the Lancastrian King Henry must be much concerned about possible dethronement,' Bothwell continued. 'Evidently several prominent Englishmen have recently lost their heads for suspected Yorkist sympathies, among them none other than Sir William Stanley, Lord Chamberlain of England and brother of the King's stepfather.'

James whistled expressively, eyes flashing with excitement. 'And who knows of all this, Patrick?'

'None other than yourself, Your Grace. As you commanded, I've had all messengers from England report to me personally, then disclose their intelligence in private.'

'That's the way it must remain whenever I am absent. You've done well, Patrick. I should like to think that you're one of my Councillors whom I can trust,' said James, staring at him challengingly.

He noted that Bothwell did not flinch as he replied, 'I should like to think that you do trust me, Your Grace. To my knowledge I've never done anything to betray your trust.'

James acknowledged his remarks thoughtfully. His fingers pranced actively on the table, analysing the import of what he had been told, considering the next step, weighing how far he could reveal the working of his mind. 'Yet not all my Councillors have my confidence, you know that, Patrick. Situations and circumstances beyond Scotland develop in their own way and beyond my control, but I must still be concerned about persons within my own realm whom I can't trust. You are aware of the plot to secure the possession of the Duke of Ross and my own person?'

Bothwell nodded noncommittally.

'You know the prime mover in the plot?' pressed James.

'I have my suspicious, Your Grace.'

'And you have my brother's activities under constant surveillance?'

'A double guard on his every move, Your Grace.'

'Against whom?' James laughed at the alarm that flashed into Bothwell's eyes and the concern that drained away his easy manner. 'The Earl of Bothwell is cautious,' he added.

'Suspicions are one thing, proof another, Your Grace.'

Straightening in his high-backed chair, together with the relaxing of his taut features, gave Bothwell the impression that the King had reached a decision. It came as no surprise when he said, 'Then what would you think of my deciding to bring the Earl of Angus back to Court and reinstate him as Chancellor of the Kingdom? Between these four walls you can speak your mind freely, Patrick. We're not in Council.'

The urbane expression returned to Bothwell's face and he too relaxed as a smile of appreciation flickered across his firm mouth. He rubbed the side of his nose as he said, 'I should assume that Your Grace has discovered that Angus had a proposition put to him, but for the moment decided not to enter into treachery with England. As a reward, you have decided to reinstate him to office, so that you can keep closer watch on his future activities.'

James jumped to his feet and clapped his hands resoundingly. 'Capital, capital, Patrick! I think you read my mind as well as myself.'

As Bothwell stood, James came round the table and embraced him warmly. 'Today we're of one accord, Patrick,' he said. 'I perhaps detect that in the Earl of Bothwell I've not only a keen and observant supporter, but also a friend.'

Bothwell was visibly touched by this demonstration of trust. He had to swallow a lump in his throat before he could say, 'Your Grace's royal person is very dear to me, because it's the embodiment of my love for Scotland.'

James clapped him on the shoulder enthusiastically. 'Spoken like a true knight, Sir Patrick. Now you'd better be about your business and find me a wife, but keep in your heart all we've said. In that way any enemies we have will be mutual enemies.'

'On that too you have my knightly oath, Your Grace. My destiny is yours for the commanding.'

Again James embraced him. There were traces of tears in both their eyes when they parted.

The next few weeks passed in a whirl of activity. Between receiving messengers from England with the Earl of Bothwell, James rode with Lucan to Castle Drummond. He had him escort Margaret to Stirling and superintend her installation into the castle. She agreed without question, also recognised that he had to go off and organise regular wapenschaws throughout the kingdom to expedite the mustering of men.

Lucan returned full of admiration for the gracious Lady Margaret, who treated him as a friend of the King rather than his servant. He reported how she had swept into Stirling castle and started to organise its household as if she were Queen. This delighted James at a time when the slowness of progress in mustering an army drove him into a frenzy of effort. Not one of his potential battle commanders escaped the lash of his criticism at their tardiness.

Even so, now standing looking out at Edinburgh from his favourite spot in David's Tower, he at last felt some satisfaction. He had once again ratified a truce agreement with England, but as a result of his own zeal the whole of Scotland was preparing for war. With a touch of irony he had made it known that the truce with England was brought about upon the advice of the reinstated Earl of Angus.

The fair-headed Lucan Fairfax came into view as he climbed the winding stone steps to the top of the tower. There was a spring in Lucan's step and a gleam on his chubby red face, so that against the stone pockmarked by the ravages of time and growth of lichens and mosses, he shone as a beacon of young life and hope. James had promised him that if the campaign against England developed, he could accompany him for the first time as his battle body squire. As a result, Lucan was as eager for the fray as his master. He leapt up the last three steps and bounded into the tower's observation garret.

'Save some of your energy for battle, Lucan. You might need it,' quipped James, with a smile

Lucan's royal coat of arms doublet rose and fell with his heavy breathing. 'Those steps are good training for me, Your Grace. Perhaps that's why you have me going up and down them so often.'

'You'll be kicked down them next time if you take so long giving your news. What brings you here this time?'

'A message from Lady Jane Kennedy, renewing her plea to see you privately.'

'Did she say why?'

'To thank you for your kindness to her liege lord the Earl of Angus.'

James laughed out raucously. 'Is that all?'

'All she would confess to me, Your Grace. But again she pressed the urgency of her request for the audience you've so far not granted, stating that it would be to Your Grace's advantage.'

'I can well imagine,' said James, recalling the humiliation of his last encounter. 'You can tell her that I made a poor choice of my Chancellor if he needs such as her to speak for him. You can add that the King of Scotland has too much to do to satisfy her whims.'

Lucan bowed. 'That I will, Your Grace,' he said enthusiastically. 'But she'll not like it, and will no doubt give me a further message to bring up those steps again.'

James took no exception at his familiarity. They were growing into manhood together and their relationship was based upon a close understanding of each other's position. In Lucan he had a devoted servant, but he liked the lad personally as if he were his own brother. 'Then you can tell her that I've given you orders that on no account are you to return to me through her choosing. Now get you gone, lad, there is much, much I have to sort out if we are to achieve our aim. You want to go to England, don't you?'

'At your side I would venture into the valley of Hell, Your Grace.'

'Tell Lady Kennedy that's where she can go, but not at my side.'

'That I will, Your Grace,' Lucan responded, with obvious pleasure. 'If only to see the expression on her proud face.'

He went off and James watched him bounding down the steps until their spiral took him out of sight. As dusk fell over the city he watched the lights from the surrounding homesteads flicker to life. Starlight flooded the sky in a rush, then the stars began to appear individually against the clear indigo background. He continued staring at them defiantly. Now he needed no astrologer to read his courses, like his father. Those stars out there had tainted his short existence in the world, but he had formulated a plan for his own destiny. It was as if the sky had opened all the way to heaven and revealed divine inspiration. A battle had to be won, but he had devised a way of making Margaret his Queen, a plan that would thwart all the political wrangling of his Council. At the moment he must keep it all locked within himself until he received one vital piece of information from England. But at last he could visualise a clear objective in which both man and king could be fulfilled.

Love for Margaret now made him impervious to the likes of Jane Kennedy, and when he had executed all in his mind, his Council would no longer keep braying for him to marry Henry of England's six-year-old child. But by supporting the Yorkist cause and marching with its scion into England and crowning him Richard IV, Margaret Drummond could be acclaimed Queen of Scotland and it would be King James IV of Scotland who would dictate the terms in both countries. He finally descended from the tower and went to his bedchamber. Lucan was in the ante-room. 'What of Lady Kennedy?' asked James.

Lucan pulled a mock wry face. 'Sore aggrieved, Your Grace. Her eyes flashed like those of a witch, and her lips clamped together as tight as a musket block.'

'Had she further messages?'

'She had, but I repeated your order.'

'Then what did her face look like?'

'I didn't wait to see, Your Grace. But there was enough hell about it to speed me away from her. If she had carried a sword, she would probably have run me through.'

James laughed. 'Well, bed you down now, Lucan. If a messenger from England arrives I want to be awakened at once, you understand?'

Lucan nodded and smiled. James knew he had no further cause to worry about the messenger being seen by anyone else.

Both Lucan and his master had risen from their beds before the messenger did arrive. After receiving the scroll James yelled out in delight. He came dashing into the ante-room. 'Lucan, see this lad is victualled and cared for, then have our horses saddled so that we can ride to Stirling straight away.'

'Good news, Your Grace?' asked Lucan, brushing at his tousled fair hair.

'The best we could wish for, Lucan. 'Twill not be long before we journey to England in battle array.'

Lucan whooped exuberantly at the thought of achieving his ambition to serve the King on the battlefield. He grabbed the messenger and rushed him off, whilst James stood absorbed by the full import of the confirmation that Prince Richard was on his way to Scotland.

After a hurried breakfast, two young riders galloped out of Edinburgh on fresh horses. They raced each other all the way to Stirling, with the fervour of leading a battle charge across the English border.

FIVE

Upon arrival at Stirling, James despatched Lucan with a series of orders that made the squire's head reel, then with cape and red hair flowing, the king dashed along corridors and up steps until he burst in upon Margaret in a sun-filled oriel with needlework around her feet.

'Margaret, my sweeting. How do you fare at Stirling?'

She jumped to her feet immediately, and as his hands smoothed over the curves of her body, he pressed his lips hungrily upon her receptive cool lips.

'Now that you're here, James, my happiness is complete.'

Her blue eyes sparkled with love, strengthening all the resolve which had crystallised into finality during the ride to Stirling. 'I have wonderful news for you, Meg. Wonderful, wonderful news! Prince Richard is on his way to Scotland!'

'Already, Jamie? This is a quick change of course.'

He noticed the trace of alarm which momentarily dulled her happiness. 'Yes, and I've already sent messengers to him. We shall receive him here at Stirling, and I intend to make his official welcome to Scotland an occasion such as has not been seen for many years. Come, my love, there's much for us to do before our royal guest arrives. Cast away that embroidery, there'll be no lonely minutes to fill in during the next few days.'

'You've ridden from Edinburgh, Jamie?'

'That I have and outstripped Lucan at every race along the way.'

'I don't envy Lucan if he's tried to keep pace with you in your present mood.'

James laughed exuberantly. 'Lucan does well, and none could be keener for his baptism to battle.'

Margaret held him firmly. 'The King of Scotland looks as if he's been dragged through a bramble patch,' she remonstrated smilingly. 'Before you do anything else, you need to refresh yourself, change your clothes and eat.'

'That I will, for I'm famished. Then we'll tour this historic castle together and set it in readiness for the glory of Scotland. There's much to do, my love.'

She submitted to more of his hugging, then made him listen to the practicalities of the situation. He accepted her directions good-humouredly, but was like a horse fretting for a gallop until they began their inspection of the castle.

When they entered the empty Great Hall he slipped his arm round the waist of her green velvet gown and flourished his free arm over the scene with pride. 'This, my sweeting, is the finest example of secular Gothic architecture in the land. At least, that's what my brother Jay says. Look at these high walls, the trumpet gallery, the open timber roof and the raised dais on which we will sit with Prince Richard. There's no finer place in Scotland for the entertainment of our royal visitor.'

Margaret clutched the arm of his red tunic. 'Are you sure he is a royal visitor?' she asked.

'As sure as I need to be, my darling.'

She squeezed tight on his arm. 'I hope you're not risking too much on his flimsy promise.'

'Meg, don't start advising caution,' he warned. 'I hear too much of it from my Councillors.'

'I'm only cautious for your sake, loved one.'

'Then leave me to calculate the risk, Meg.' He moved her forward, saying, 'Perched on its massive rocks Stirling has been Scotland's main fortress for nearly three hundred years, and several times been in the hands of the English. It is the perfect setting for me to plan a campaign that will oust the King of England from his throne, and so strengthen Scottish influence across the border.'

Sensing her concern from her silence he momentarily felt inclined to confess the whole of his plan, but he moved her out of the Hall, judging it best to keep his ultimate aim to himself. She might inadvertently let something slip to her father, who was best kept in ignorance at this stage.

They walked hand in hand to the south side of the castle and looked out on the now sunlit field of Bannockburn. Again he appreciated her sense of history when she asked, 'Isn't that the field where Robert Bruce triumphed over King Edward IV and the English?'

'That it is, Meg,' he responded enthusiastically. 'Look how the sun shines upon it, what a glorious omen.' He gripped her hand tight and led her to another parapet. 'Look down there at the solidity of the mass of rock on which we stand, and across there is the Old Bridge where William Wallace defeated the English. Mark my words, Meg, beside you stands another Scottish leader who'll rout the English. Henry VII won his crown at Bosworth, but has been insecure on the throne ever since. I feel it in my bones that once again the time has come for Scotland to gain ascendancy in the centuries-old struggle against England. Look at Ben Lomond out there, the sun sparkling on its peak to confirm my words.'

Margaret snuggled against him to shield herself from the cooling breeze. Her surface shivers had penetrated inwards. She had known him since a boy and had a good idea of what he was planning. She loved him with all her heart and would support his every move. But if what she imagined were true, she knew the opposition it would give rise to in Council. There were stormy times ahead, but for the present, the preparation required was enough to offset morbid thoughts concerning the future.

Two days later Prince Richard and his party arrived. All was ready for them, and after the brief welcoming ceremonies, the whole assembly took their places for the afternoon tournament staged in the visitor's honour.

James rode up to the loge under which Margaret sat with Prince Richard, together with the Earl and Countess of Bothwell. Her heart beat with excitement as he leaned forward to her and said, 'Your scarf, my love. I want all to know that I ride for none other than Lady Margaret Drummond.'

With visor raised his eyes radiated with love. She removed the scarf emblazoned with the family sleuth-hound badge and kissed it. Handing it to him at arm's length she said, 'Be careful, my lord. Use all the skill at your command.'

'That I will, Meg, for I'll make a good tilt at Huntly.' He too kissed the scarf and fixed it to his helmet in true chivalric style. 'This emblem will carry me through to victory.'

Again Margaret experienced a chill of foreboding. He was willing to tilt against all odds, for Huntly was an acknowledged jousting hero and she knew that for all his practice, James had yet to gain a victory over the resourceful Earl. 'Jamie, for my sake, be careful!' she whispered to herself.

He had ridden away, his red and gold colours flapping in the breeze as he went to the preparation tent prior to entering the lists for the general mêlée. Everywhere was ablaze with the blue and tawny Yorkist colours and white rose emblems, but Margaret's eyes were fixed on the jousting field, wishing that this part of the celebrations were over.

As soon as the knights were assembled on the field she picked out James by the plume in his helmet. He led a body of knights against those headed by the Earl of Huntly. Each pass across the field sent her eyes darting from one unsaddled rider to another, but the King remained in his saddle, as did Huntly. Then she picked out James again and Huntly on the other side. She gripped at the wooden rail in front of her as the two riders charged towards each other, the thunder of horses' hooves seeming to beat straight through to her heart. Both men had their lances poised. As they crossed Margaret leapt to her feet and cried out in anguish. The cheers that followed confirmed that the young King had unhelmeted Huntly and by doing so tipped the marshal's tally in his side's favour.

Margaret sat down, self-conscious about her display of concern.

Bothwell, who had watched her intently, smiled at her reassuringly, but her heart continued to pound as the knights quit the field. All were now cheering the King, and he stood in his stirrups acknowledging that he had gained his first victory over Huntly. Margaret felt that she alone would know how much this would please him. She also knew that what she had endured was a true measure of her love for the victor, although it would have made no difference had he been the loser.

She became dully aware of Bothwell standing beside her chair, following her gaze as James rode off the field acknowledging the cheers with jaunty waves of his hand. 'The King fought with great skill, my lady. It will please him greatly to have bested such a jousting champion as Huntly.'

Margaret looked up at the smiling face with sincere brown eyes, 'Then you know him well, my lord.'

Bothwell inclined his dark-haired head in agreement, then looked deep into her eyes in a kindly way. In that instant, without any words spoken, an understanding became apparent between them. This was now a triangle. She felt sure that James would not have confided the intent of his plan to Bothwell without first apprising her. She felt equally sure that like herself, Bothwell was not only aware of the reason for his scheming, but that his victory on the jousting field would make him all the more determined.

Bothwell's tall figure covered them from the view of their guests, and he leaned over to gently touch her hand. She recognised it as a gesture of friendship and smiled her gratitude. She rose and turned to his wife. 'My concern for the King has made me neglect my duties as hostess. Thank you, my lady, for entertaining our guests. Now we must look out for the return of the King. Any moment he's likely to come riding like a strong wind to greet us.'

The Countess laughed and they all joined in conversation until James came riding up, helmet under his arm, red hair flowing in the breeze that cooled the sweat-flecked sides of his horse. He handed Margaret her scarf and said, 'It was all in your honour, my sweet lady.'

Her face radiated happiness as she replied, 'You performed like a great and mighty king, Your Grace. I'm proud that you carried my talisman in such a victory.'

All joined in the congratulations and James's smile shone as bright as his chainmail in the sunlight. Seated on his horse, huge against the turquoise sky sprinkled with tiny puffs of white cloud, Margaret had never seen him look more handsome. Truly this was the man she loved.

'Patrick, help my lady Margaret see to our royal guest,' James said to Bothwell. 'My horse needs rubbing down and I too need to wash off the grime of a goodly conflict.'

He looked hard at Prince Richard, then trotted off to the tents, again waving jauntily to all who acknowledged him.

Many eyes gazed at the King sitting on the royal dais that night with Lady Margaret Drummond at his side. They looked a handsome couple with the great stone fireplace behind them and the imposing oriel windows flanking each side of the royal table. Margaret realised that the King's overt devotion to her must be setting tongues wagging, but James was in buoyant mood, impervious to the inevitable gossip and speculation of his Court.

She imagined that there would be some accusing of her, or at least her father, of scheming to raise her to the throne of Scotland. But such was not her wish. She was in love with a man; the fact that he happened to be a king was of secondary consideration. Even so, she knew enough of the political scene to realise the implications of her love. A time of reckoning would have to come, when she would either have to accept becoming Queen or, for internal political reasons, renounce her love.

James drew her attention to Prince Richard, surrounded by a group of ladies on the floor of the Hall. 'Well, Meg. What do you think of him?'

She detected the trace of a frown on his otherwise happy face, as they watched the Prince demonstrating new dancing steps from the Continent to the laughing, colourfully-gowned ladies. 'He seems most charming, so gay and chivalrous.'

'Yes, he carries himself well in the dance,' James said.

'But you have doubts about him on the battlefield?' she queried.

'I did not say that.'

She put her hand over his. 'You don't have to, Jamie. I saw your look when you rode up to the loge after the joust. You were wondering then how he would have accounted himself on the field.'

'God's bones, are you a witch? It seems you can read my mind no matter what I do or say.'

'That's because I love you, Jamie, and have only your welfare at heart.'

He looked at her and squeezed her hand, but the frown had triumphed over the smiles. 'Henry of England is doing all in his power to brand Richard an impostor, but his credentials satisfy me, and he faced a barrage of questions from my lord Councillors without flinching. I am prepared to stake my crown on his being whom he purports.'

Margaret now felt a constriction of her own happy mood. 'Then we must pray that you are right, Jamie,' she whispered.

Seeing the flicker of apprehension dim her fair-skinned radiance, he turned to face her with a scrape of his chair among the scented floor rushes. He held both her hands within the fall of the full sleeves of her crimson gown. 'My own future is so wrapped in his that I refuse to contemplate failure,' he admitted. 'It is our future too, Meg.'

Margaret averted her eyes from the assembly being amused by the antics of a court jester. This was the first time he had linked her with Prince Richard, but she required no explanation. 'Many still press for your marriage to Princess Margaret of England,' she warned, meeting his earnest gaze.

'Many in England and Spain, but the eyes of Europe will turn to Scotland with greater respect now, for I'll not forsake Prince Richard until his cause is won.'

With a tender smile she returned the pressure of his hand. 'If it can be done, you will do it, Jamie,' she said, once again looking deep into his intense dark brown eyes.

In a flash he cast away his foreboding as he marvelled that their childhood romping could have blossomed into such vital love. 'That I will, as long as you believe in me, Meg, my love. So come now, let us join the Prince in the dance. We must not be outdated by his new fancy steps.'

Many observers remarked that they had never seen the King look so happy, as he and Lady Margaret moved to the music as one. Passing the Prince, James patted him on the back heartily. 'Tonight, Your Highness, my court is joyful in your honour,' he declared. 'But we shall come to a more significant purpose before this month is out.'

The flashing smile acknowledgement came from a weak mouth, thought James, studying him closely, but he had a well set chin and eyes bright with resolution. There should be little trouble in finding a Court lady to marry him, for he must have a Scottish bride to perpetuate his union with Scotland. At that moment, James's eyes lighted on Lady Catherine Gordon and he let out a whoop of triumph.

'What is it, Jamie?' asked Margaret, smiling up at him.

He brushed his lips tenderly across her brow and whispered, 'I've found a bride for Prince Richard.'

'Surely not so soon?' A hint of sadness suffused her eyes, but her mouth immediately dispelled it with a laugh that highlighted the dimples on each side of her chin. 'Give him time to look around for himself.'

James fingered the ruby fillets in her fair hair. 'No need, my darling, when such an admirable match springs straight to mind. Lady Catherine has great beauty, and she and Richard will make a handsome pair. I'll present her to him myself.'

There was no point in trying to restrain him. Ever since telling her of the possibility of the Prince's coming, James had concentrated every fibre of his being on controlling each move and strategy. Tirelessly, he entered every venture with a new determination to gain his way: whether a joust in the lists, inspection of the castle, a visit to the justice ayres or receiving a foreign ambassador. It seemed he had centred everything on this questionable Yorkist scion.

'But what of Lady Catherine?' asked Margaret.

He laughed. 'It won't distress her to wed such a promising husband, particularly if she has my blessing.'

'And her father?'

'Huntly will be as proud as a peacock to have his daughter the Queen of England. It will be just recompense for my defeating him this afternoon.'

She suspected that neither the Earl, his daughter, nor the Prince would have much option. James would manoeuvre them to his master design, his pattern for the future; his inspiration from the skies, as he liked to think of it. She alone perhaps realised that his display of supreme self-confidence acted as a cover for inner doubts. Although this afternoon the Earl of Bothwell gave indication that he too knew the King well. She knew from family experience that unanimity was hard enough to achieve in Scotland. When England was involved too, there was always the likelihood of sudden and unexpected reversals.

Lady Catherine appeared sufficiently blushing and impressed when presented to the Prince; and not in a position to disapprove the whims of his host, the smiling Prince accepted all with the gracious ease of a practised courtier. He soon led Lady Catherine to one of the window alcoves, screened from the Hall by thick wine-red drapes patterned with the royal arms.

James watched their departure and drew Margaret's attention to it. 'There they go like two turtledoves. I knew it, they make a most natural match. We must have them wed early in the New Year.' He suddenly broke off, for across the Hall he noticed Jane Kennedy. She attracted men like a flame drew prowling moths, for there were at least six laughing males around her.

Margaret followed his gaze, noticing the sudden change of expression in his eyes and the conscious, self-discipline tightening of his lips. Little happened at a King's Court that escaped all prying eyes, and when secrets were discovered, they either became common gossip or were whispered behind the hand, according to the rank of those engaged in the scandal-mongering. Through whispers not sufficiently hushed, she knew of Jane Kennedy's earlier treatment of the King, and guessed the effect of being denied would have on him. The expression on his face now provided adequate confirmation. 'Lady Jane Kennedy is celebrating her birthday, Jamie,' she said, acting on impulse, 'will you not wish her well?'

He turned to her in a moment of searching hesitation, then said, 'Yes, I will.'

As he moved round the Hall, one of the men toasting Jane saw his approach and obviously warned the rest. All turned to him, but Jane remained unruffled as she rose from her specially garlanded birthday chair and curtsied.

'I did not know that you were born under the sign of Scorpio, Lady Kennedy,' he said, staring hard at her. 'I offer my felicitations on your birthday.'

Again she curtsied, smiling inscrutably. 'I'm honoured, Your Grace. I was not aware that you were so well acquainted with the zodiac signs.'

His eyes absorbed her indisputable beauty in a black gown with gold tippets stretching the length of the sleeves; a black and gold steeple-crowned head-dress added to her impressive height and dignity.

'As a Mars subject I'm prepared to meet the future as I've dealt with the past,' she declared.

One of the noblemen noticed the King's sharp intake of breath before he replied, 'Mars may well have its full fling in the future, lady. But you should learn to make the most of your opportunities; sometimes chance knocks but once.'

He rejoined Margaret on the dais, conscious of the puzzled glances of Jane's attendants. In this encounter he had given as good as received, but her presence disturbed him. There was something strangely unpredictable about Jane Kennedy, something which at its worst could pose a threat to the high stakes for which he now gambled.

Margaret immediately sensed his concern, a woman's appraisal of the effect of another woman upon a man. She sensed too that the score between them was not settled, but she redirected his attentions by saying, 'Jamie, look at the Duke of Ross. He doesn't appear to be joining in the merrymaking.'

James glanced across at the pallid face of his younger brother, who had drawn the Earl of Bothwell away from the gaiety. 'Jay has more taste for learning than merrymaking,' he said, with a wry smile. 'But he's a handsome lad, and according to his tutors, has a keen brain. Maybe one day I'll send him abroad to widen his learning. At the moment, he's well served by Patrick's company.'

'And who's that glancing evilly at them?' asked Margaret, indicating a sharp featured man pressed against a stone corbel. His dark, deep set eyes were fixed in clearly discernible enmity upon the Earl of Bothwell.

'That's Sir John Ramsay, newly returned from England,' said James. 'Patrick wears the Earl's belt he forfeited for the error of his ways.'

'He looks as if he'd like to snatch it back,' observed Margaret, with a perceptible shudder.

James pressed her hand to stem her fears. 'Perhaps he would, if he dared. But he returned to Scotland, not finding England or King Henry much to his liking.'

As a line of serving men passed them, James snatched a venison patty sprinkled with cinnamon from a heaped platter. He took a mouthful and smacked his lips with approval.

'I wouldn't trust him, Jamie,' warned Margaret.

'Who?' queried James, still chewing.

'Sir John Ramsay.'

James finished his mouthful. 'He'll get over the loss of his belt and perhaps serve Scotland the better for it.' He still held the remains of the patty in his hand, but not wishing to finish it, tossed it at the table beneath the dais. It struck a burly squire on the side of the face.

The squire leapt to his feet and swung round angrily, then learning the King was the culprit, changed his expression and bowed as if he had received a benefice. The moment the King turned from him he flaked the pastry, and taking deliberate aim, showered the fragments into the bosom of a laundry lass on the adjoining table. Her companions tittered as she tried to extricate the crumbs. Shrieks of laughter followed when the squire went across and offered pawing assistance.

When Lord Home came to the top table, James made a remark about his recent pilgrimage to Canterbury. With a sly smile on his serious face, the Lord High Chamberlain referred to King Henry's graciousness in granting him a safe conduct during the journey. James too appreciated the joke. He then looked for Prince Richard and, not seeing him, beckoned Lucan Fairfax. 'Where's our royal guest?' he asked.

A smile twitched the squire's lips. 'He took Lady Catherine Gordon out into the pleasance, Your Grace.'

'Did he, the sprightly young cock?' Smiling again, James turned to Margaret. 'And you accused me of hurrying him.'

Margaret laughed, then clinging to his arm said, 'You were right, Jamie, they are admirably matched.'

Although mocking him, her eyes twinkled with laughter as he drew nearer, saying, 'Come, my sweeting, we'll leave the company to their revels.'

With the departure of the King, many of the knights and squires went off in quest of ladies requiring an escort to their quarters. Others lingered in the Hall, voices grew louder, the music more strident, and the dancing more promiscuous than graceful.

Later, as she lay in bed in the King's arms, Margaret whispered, 'Jamie, do you seriously think it possible for Prince Richard to gain the English throne?'

He held her firm, warm body tight against him. 'He'll not fail through our lack of trying,' he said, with conviction. 'Scottish hearts are with him, and our weapon arms are strong.'

'And if he succeeds?' she asked.

James blew out the candles in the silver candlesticks on the bedside coffer. 'Then you shall be my Queen, sweet Margaret. That I promise you,' he murmured, into the smooth hollow of her neck.

At last he had put his thoughts into words. It was no revelation to her, and she felt sure the Earl of Bothwell had surmised similarly. But even as she responded to his caressing she wondered if his hopes would ever become reality. She knew her father would welcome her sharing James's throne. For herself she loved the man more than the king, but loving the one made her appreciate that the man could not be separated from the king. This indivisibility strewed the passage of the future with so many imponderable factors – the challenging gleam of Jane Kennedy's blue-green eyes, the saturnine glances of Sir John Ramsay, the noticeable absence of the true warrior in Prince Richard himself.

SIX

Preparations for Yule were made at Linlithgow Palace, Margaret herself arranging the crib after the fashion of the St. Francis famous representation at Greccio. The Great Hall was decorated with huge clumps of glistening dark green holly with berries the colour of blood, and garlands of ivy, yew and other evergreens; the carollers sang *Gloria in Excelsis Deo* with resounding reverence.

After Midnight Mass the revelry began, but Margaret was aware of an underlying tension-charged expectancy throughout the Court. As she danced with James she saw his probing glances at Prince Richard's light-footed dancing. She knew from discussion with her father that many in Scotland were already doubting the Prince's capability of striking a resounding blow at the 'auld enemy'. Her father too had stressed that the coming events would severely test the young King. It seemed that after the way he had quelled sporadic groups of rebels none doubted his courage, but the more experienced campaigners knew that waging war against England required astute generalship, as well as strength of armament.

Although she followed her partner's footsteps with practised lightness, her heart was not in the dance. Her head ached and she longed to be alone with James in the quietness of their bedchamber. It was the only time they could talk to each other freely, not only as lovers, but also of the thoughts activated by each day's events.

She felt him brushing her hair with his lips and smiled up at him. 'What are you thinking, Jamie?'

'That you're the fairest of all gathered here. Also that you're the one with heavy thoughts. I can feel them buzzing through your head.'

'Yes, and with pain. I should like to withdraw as soon as possible.'

He was instantly solicitous. 'Do you need a physician, Meg?'

She laughed. 'No, it's not that kind of pain, but my head is throbbing with so many doubts. I feel more like talking to you than dancing, Jamie, but we can't talk properly here.'

His warm brown eyes looked at her with concern and she felt the increased pressure of his hands in hers. 'We'll leave as soon as we can,' he promised.

This assurance helped her through the remaining ceremonies, but she was not completely at rest until snuggled in his arms in their canopied bed.

'Now, what is it that's troubling you, my sweeting?' he asked tenderly. 'Let me cast aside your doubts.'

Margaret smiled to herself. She knew he would try to set her mind at rest, and ultimately she would go through the charade of letting him think that he had. But recently she had found it more and more difficult to share his high hopes. This was chiefly because she could not accept Prince Richard as a genuine claimant to the English throne. She had tried, but there was something about his person that did not ring true, a lacking of the confidence that came from true royal blood. It appeared to her that he had neither the strength of character nor the birthright resolve to press his own claim, so was relying upon someone else to do it for him.

'Soon we shall be heralding in 1496 as an auspicious year, Jamie, but are you sure that Prince Richard is deserving of your support?'

James cleared his throat and she sensed the irritation in his voice as he replied, 'I've accepted his credentials, just as the Duchess of Burgundy and many Princes of Europe have done.'

'Have you considered that they could be wrong?'

He propped himself on one elbow, looking at her quizzically. 'If they're wrong, then so am I. But I stand by my judgement.'

'But is it good judgement, Jamie?'

'What do you mean? Only through him can I hope to make you my Queen.'

'That's what I mean, your personal wishes could be obscuring your political judgement.'

He held her with the gentle firmness which never failed to thrill her. Into her hair he whispered, 'Perhaps, but the sooner it's settled the better.' He eased her away slightly as he added, 'That's why I must leave you tomorrow.'

'So soon?' she queried.

'The summonses for a levy were issued long before Yule. I didn't tell you before, so that you wouldn't count the days. Now the time has come and I am needed at Castle Campbell for the musters from my lands in Knapdale.'

'Then you'll not return quickly?'

He fondled her hair as he said, 'Scotland must be prepared for our future, Meg. There's much for me to do.'

'So you won't be with me at my confinement?' Tears quickly gathered in her eyes.

He changed his position and cradled her in his arms. 'If it can be arranged I'll travel the length and breadth of my kingdom. But I make no promises, for it is vital that we strike when the moment is opportune. In any case, I will have your mother brought to Stirling to attend you.'

Saddened by the inevitability of his departure Margaret shook her head. 'I don't want her to leave the family on my account. If you can't be with me, then I'll return to Castle Drummond.'

He remained silent for a few moments, clinging to her tightly, trying to draw from her the resolve to succeed. 'Perhaps that would be best,' he admitted, at last. 'You should not have chosen a king to love, Meg, for his affairs can't be halted even by the birth of his child.'

'As long as I have his love, I'll not complain,' she murmured, as fear chilled right through her in spite of his body warmth.

When Margaret returned to her family, James arranged for work to be started at Stirling on a royal palace on the west side of the lower court. He wanted to change the character of the castle, so that apart from being a fortress it could also serve as a royal residence. He had plans for an elegant building in the French style to be built round the court known as the Lion's Den. It would be a royal retreat for Margaret and himself after she became his Queen.

Having made this provision for their future, he busied himself up and down the country mustering men for training and generally advancing preparations for an invasion into England. Sir Andrew Wood co-operated with unceasing vigour and gained the valuable assistance of the three seafaring Barton brothers.

Spring was beginning to sprinkle colour over heath and moorland when Don Pedro de Ayala, the Spanish ambassador, arrived at Stirling and requested a private audience. With builders and masons in occupation, and Margaret in the care of her family, James now found the castle chillingly desolate. In spite of the duplicity of earlier Spanish embassies he decided to see Ayala – a tall, distinguished looking man with flashing dark eyes and black pointed beard, who bowed without unction when announced to the King in his Presence Chamber.

72

'So, Your Excellency, the King of Spain has more proposals for my marriage, I take it,' greeted James, with a tight smile.

The Spaniard smiled pleasantly 'That is so, Your Grace. But I'm instructed to state that my master cannot offer the Infanta of Spain.'

'Neither could your predecessors, yet they did.'

'An unfortunate circumstance my royal master much regrets, Your Grace.'

James snapped his fingers irritably. 'As right he should, but now, Excellency, what are your new proposals?'

Ayala glanced at the colourful tapestries around the walls, then said, 'My proposals have been presented to Your Grace already by the King of England's embassies.'

'You mean Princess Margaret Tudor?'

Ayala nodded. 'My master believes that such a union would promote peace between England and Scotland.'

'No doubt it would, but has your master considered who is the present honoured guest at my Court?'

'That is uppermost in his thoughts, Your Grace.'

James clenched tight at the arms of his throne chair. 'And I suppose like King Henry he insists on the surrender of my guest as a condition of the marriage?'

The ambassador avoided the King's intent gaze as he replied, 'That is so, Your Grace.'

James glared at him fiercely; even his hair and beard seemed to bristle. 'That is not so, Excellency,' he snapped. 'For I will not be bound by conditions imposed by your master or the King of England. Neither will I dishonour my guest to suit their purposes. King Henry has joined the Holy League to keep France out of Spain, so your master thinks the English Princess will relieve Henry of the burden of Prince Richard, making it more ready for himself to co-operate on the Continent, is that not the truth of the matter?'

Ayala held the edges of his gold embroidered red cloak. 'I am instructed to remind Your Grace of a truce made with England.'

'You may inform your King that in Scotland we have not forgotten it. We are also aware of the change of circumstances since concluding the truce.'

The ambassador offered no further comment, but stood respectfully awaiting the King's next move.

'I'll communicate your proposals to my Councillors,' said James pensively. 'Then we'll talk again after they have considered your offer. In the meantime, Excellency, you are invited to the best hospitality my disrupted Court can offer. The Chamberlain will attend to your needs.'

They parted as two men who clearly held respect for each other.

In the ensuing weeks as harebell blue, hawkweed yellow and purple heather spread in profusion over the countryside, James received other ambassadors. Roderick de Lalaing came from Flanders, pressing him to abandon Prince Richard's cause – a sudden change of attitude, for the Prince had originally emerged from Flanders. But the Netherlands were sorely tried by King Henry's trade embargo and pressed for better relations with England. Not surprisingly, the ambassador refused James's invitation to discuss his proposals with Prince Richard himself.

The French envoy, Alexander Monypenney, Sieur de Concressault, also visited Stirling and offered one hundred thousand crowns for the surrender of Prince Richard, whom his Government also had once recognised.

'And what would France do with Prince Richard, the rightful Duke of York?' James retorted.

The whiplash response to well-prepared pleas startled the Frenchman. 'That . . . that intelligence has not been conveyed to me as part of my instructions, Your Grace.'

'Then I'll tell you,' fired James. 'Hand him over to the English King.'

Concressault's opening air of confidence wavered as James systemati-cally stripped the veils off his pretence. With difficulty, he finally said, 'I shall convey the feelings of Your Grace to my master.'

'Do that, and tell him both my Council and myself are tired of considering his many double-edged proposals,' snapped James finally. He dismissed him, then made a special visit to view the new working in the castle, prior to taking a progress report to Margaret.

As the Frenchman left the Presence Chamber and made his way down the winding stone steps to the courtyard, he saw a lurking figure against the wall. As he approached warily the stranger asked, 'How did the French proposals fair, Your Excellency?'

The Frenchman's hand flashed to his sword.

'Please, Excellency, don't be hasty,' said the interloper, as the outer grille of the window reflected its close mesh pattern across his swarthy face. 'My name is Sir John Ramsay. I, too, serve His Grace the King of England.'

Concressault looked puzzled and doubtful. 'I have discovered import-ant information,' Ramsay went on. 'It comes straight from the lips of John Meautis, King Henry's French secretary.'

'Then speak it, Sir.'

Ramsay drew away from the window. 'Not here, Excellency, these stout walls have ears. My position is one of delicacy.'

'Or treachery!' fired the Frenchman. 'But tell me what you know.'

'Better we meet beyond hearing,' cautioned Ramsay. 'Go to the postern gate in the north bailey and pass through as if seeking a view from the uppermost crag. I'll follow if you pass unnoticed.'

The warm sunshine blazed on the solid stone of the castle walls, but beyond the sheltered courtyard a keen wind swept across the rocky precipice. Concressault held his thick blue cloak tight as it began to billow and flap. Below the crag-scarred hill, the sun lit up the countryside's purple-splashed abundance of heather.

As Sir John Ramsay approached him the Frenchman moved towards the thick-set unprepossessing figure. 'I hope I'm not here merely to be buffeted by the wind,' he greeted him. 'I find Scotland a cold and draughty country, even when the sun shines. Now, Sir, your information.'

'It is our mutual concern, Excellency,' said Ramsay, walking on toward the dark face of the formidable crag. 'Its success depends upon your giving away no secret of the origin of what I impart.'

The Frenchman followed, his smooth features wrinkled distastefully. 'You have my word on that account.'

'It will be the only way to serve your country,' Ramsay emphasised, his shifty eyes glinting with a hint of menace.

Impatience added further colour to the Frenchman's wind-flushed cheeks. 'Speak your purpose,' he rasped.

'It concerns the so-called Duke of York, whom your countrymen once received with full honour. The English King's secretary informed me that his master has documentary proof that he's an impostor, the son of a burgess of Tournai.'

The Frenchman's diplomatic training enabled him to conceal his surprise. 'I'll see this information is conveyed to the right sources,' he promised.

'Remembering that the source of its origin was John Meautis,' put in Ramsay slyly. He added by way of explanation, 'My position is difficult, Excellency. Such negotiations as I perform are fraught with danger.'

Concressault nodded. 'Nor are they likely to regain your Earl's belt, Sir John. But I understand, revenge has its sweetness.'

'That is so, and a body must live,' said Ramsay emphatically.

The look he received from the French envoy as they strode back to the castle was one of denial rather than agreement.

In early September, Ramsay managed to secure attendance at a meeting of the Council. Here he learned that if the invasion of England proved successful, King Richard the Fourth would restore Berwick to Scotland, grant seven sheriffdoms to Scottish control and pay fifty thousand marks. This intelligence he sent to King Henry as a mark of his active work on his behalf.

At a final Council meeting, James tempestuously took the initiative by sweeping aside all plans for his marriage to the English Princess. He outlined the proposals, counter-proposals and double-dealing of the various ambassadors, then with the strength of his summing up on the duplicity of foreign governments, swayed the indecisive Councillors into agreeing to strike for Prince Richard without delay. Flushed with success, he committed himself by summoning his troops to meet him on the borders at Ellemkirk on September the fifteenth.

The date now set for the supreme test of his sovereignty and manhood, James rode to Castle Drummond to bid farewell to Margaret. When she heard the full spate of his biased account, concern etched her glowingly healthy features and doubt radiated from her clear blue eyes. 'James, it troubles me deeply that you're prepared to leave Scotland on such a dubious venture,' she confessed, with concern. 'I've talked it all over with my father. Although he would not admit it to you, he doubts the wisdom of placing so high a stake on the head of Prince Richard.'

They were alone in a private chamber brightened by a display of red and pink roses. James knelt at her feet, both his hands encompassing hers, his face touchingly earnest. 'Have no fear, sweet one. I shall return in triumph. As far as I am able, I have covered every possibility to make this campaign successful. This is why I've been away so long planning every move, why you've seen so little of me, and why I must return to Edinburgh straight away, before my lips are dry from your welcoming kisses. When I go to the border I take with me the future King of England.'

Although she tried desperately to appear cheerful, she could not dismiss the chilling thought that this could be the last time she would see him alive.

He sensed her feelings and guessed her fears, so gently released her clasping hands and kissed them. He raised her to her feet saying, 'Mark my words, Meg. When I return it will be to make you Queen of Scotland.'

Margaret crossed herself. 'All I seek is your love for the rest of my life.'

He kissed her full red mouth, held her tight for a few heart-thudding moments, then led her to the courtyard. 'You will have all my love and a throne, sweet Meg, for I promise by all that's holy I shall not fail. When I return triumphant, there will be nothing my Council dare deny me. So, dearest heart, be of good cheer, everything is set for an outcome capable of stirring the hearts of all Scotland and achieving our most cherished desire.'

The groom stood ready with his shining black horse. The Earl of Bothwell, already mounted, waited to ride back to Edinburgh with him, having pledged himself to fight for the cause dear to the King's heart, even though he too believed it to be politically suspect.

James took the horse and leapt to the saddle without using the stirrups, an action which brought a tolerant smile to the face of Lord Drummond watching from a window overlooking the courtyard.

Anxiety etched Margaret's face as she looked up at Bothwell and called out, 'Take good care of him, my lord!'

'Don't worry, lady, we have a long ride to the border,' replied Bothwell, smiling sympathetically. 'Time enough for His Grace to temper his present exuberance.'

James waved until clear of the courtyard, but once out in the open countryside quickly spurred his horse. Although Margaret rushed back to a high window of the castle, she only saw two distant riders disappearing over a brae in a cloud of dust.

On September the twelfth, when a bright early autumn sun lit up the open fields with the swaying heads of purple spear-plume thistles and yellow hawkweed, James reviewed his artillery at Restalrig. The leaves of the trees were beginning to change colour, but as he surveyed the natural scene he knew the stillness to be deceptive. In the trees, among the plants and in the soil there existed a vast world of teeming life, an army of predators each awaiting the chance to feed on their prey before they became the prey of another. He likened it to his adherence to Prince Richard's cause, a host of different circumstances drawn together for one all-pervading purpose.

Two days later, still planning the advance stage by stage, he led the march to Haddington. After pitching camp, he called his commanders together and they worked out a strategy for engaging the English enemy. On September the twentieth, they crossed the tufted grass of the Lammermuir Hills and burst upon English soil with a thunderous roar of galloping hooves and whooping voices, ready to crush all before them.

The English borderers offered only token resistance in the face of the first Scottish onrush. James, in chain mail and glinting helmet, halted his destrier and surveyed the closed doors and barred windows of the first English hamlet they encountered. He raised his sword for silence, but the muttering among the troops indicated that they were already thinking of loot.

'King Richard's proclamation cannot be read to people who cringe behind barricades,' yelled James. 'Light torches and fire the thatch over their heads. We'll smoke them out into the open or roast them alive.'

Although clad in the full armour of a fighting man, Prince Richard's pale complexion and trembling mouth betrayed his agitation at this sudden turn of events. He tried to intervene, but James spurred his horse and rode among his men, goading them to more spirited efforts. As the fires spread, so the English came out prepared to fight. A minor holocaust seemed likely to ensue, but before blood lust took control of the Scots, James ordered his commanders to withdraw their men.

A tense stillness was eventually achieved, a reluctant truce, for the borderers on both sides were accustomed to barbaric warfare and each faction had past debts to settle. James rode to the Prince. 'Let the proclamation be read!' he shouted. His petulant Stuart mouth was set firm, the glare of his large brown eyes defied contradiction.

The Prince noticeably hesitated, then, glancing round at the scene of momentarily arrested conflict, gave the order to his herald.

Amid the acrid smoke and crackling of flames, King Richard IV of England was proclaimed and unanimously received with derisive laughter from the English. Not a single volunteer came forward to acclaim him or accept the monetary awards offered for service to his cause. Indeed, fresh fighting broke out, and James, incensed almost beyond control, pitched into it with the intensity of a demon.

The unaccepted king tried to call a halt, but had as much hope of stopping an avalanche of snow from a mountain as the impassioned Scots swept him aside. Led by their own fighting King, they destroyed all that could be laid to waste, looted anything of value and dark-stained the light brown earth with the blood of any who tried to stop them.

James surveyed the pillage with satisfaction. 'See there, Richard!' he yelled, sweeping his arm over the scene of destruction. 'Such is the way we'll serve those who refuse to muster to your cause. Now let us march on.'

The Prince's thin lips quivered. 'We cannot continue in this manner, Your Grace. I have no wish for any more bloody murder on my account.'

James held his champing horse with difficulty, for the beast seemed as crazy as its rider. 'Why so?' he roared, thinking of Margaret waiting for news of him at Castle Drummond and his promises to make her his Queen.

The two men's eyes met, but Prince Richard did not flinch from the murderous gleam fixed upon him. 'This is not the way to convince my people that I am their true king,' he declared steadily. 'I cannot butcher my way to London. I'll have no more blood of my subjects shed this day, no more of their property devastated.'

With a loud neigh James's horse rose up on its hind legs. The struggle to control it provided a momentary outlet for James's mounting rage. 'You concern yourself over much about those who seem scant of interest on your account,' he snapped.

'The time is not opportune for our purpose,' replied the Prince. 'I'll recross the Tweed and retire to Coldstream.'

'You do that if you lack spunk and already feel sick at the sight of blood,' flashed James. He redrew his sword and brandished it with vigour. 'But we go on to make you King, even if we have to bring back your crown and clamp it on your cowardly pate.'

The Scottish commanders exchanged startled glances. Few had seen the King in such a savage mood. Bothwell watched anxiously, prepared to intervene as Prince Richard tried to withdraw with dignity, for it looked as if the King might smite him down. The danger passed, James's own royal dignity arresting his sword arm, but only until Richard's party quitted. He then ordered the army to march and seek fresh encounter with the enemy.

The devil-crazed Scottish horde required no urging. They moved off on foot and horse, lust for blood in their hearts and the acrid tang of smoke in their nostrils. They constantly recharged themselves with both as they pillaged their way along the Northumbrian border.

That night, after pitching camp, the Earl of Bothwell, the Duke of Ross and Lord Home jointly consulted with the King in his tent. At first he would not listen to their warnings, repeatedly shouting in their faces, 'I am in command! We march on! We march on, I tell you!'

He stamped around the tent like a maniac. 'Any of you who wish to withdraw can follow Prince Richard. But I shall lead my army on.'

It was his brother Jay's quiet measured words that eventually simmered him to reason. 'You're leading a wild and undisciplined mob, Jamie, incapable of achieving anything honourable. Remember how such troops turned on our royal father and murdered him.'

These words spoken from the heart of an intelligent man penetrated through the King's hysteria. Pensively he recognised that Jay was right. He had no need to observe the approving nods of Bothwell and Home. Nonetheless it rankled to be proved wrong, particularly by his younger brother who made no pretensions of being a fighting man.

Bothwell broke the heavy silence. 'Prince Richard's withdrawn, Your Grace. It leaves no reason for going southwards to further a cause seemingly he can no longer stomach.'

The King's tigerish eyes flashed at him and he expected another tirade. Instead, James stood motionless, forcing control upon himself, recalling Margaret's fears about the Prince. All his hopes for the future now seemed as devastated as some of the hamlets through which his army had passed.

Home took the opportunity to make his views known. 'I've lived all my life on the borders, Your Grace. My family has more scores to settle in England than any other Scottish family, but my considered opinion is that it would be folly to venture further south on this occasion.'

James looked into the faces of each of them, seeing no condemnation, merely a willingness to give advice. But he saw his own impetuosity as the reason for their mutual agreement. The reckless purge of the border terrain which he had instigated had so scattered his ranks that he was now insufficiently organised for a major campaign. He had defeated himself by his own lack of generalship – the realisation almost brought tears of frustration to his eyes. They were interrupted by Huntly bursting into the tent. 'Your Grace, a messenger has just arrived stating that a large English force under Sir George Neville is on its way to engage us. We're in no fit state to honour Scotland if we stay here.'

All their eyes flashed on James, but none conveyed the accusation he felt within himself. At last he spoke. 'Prepare to retreat at the first light of dawn, my lords,' he conceded

The relief which showed on their faces changed to alarm when the following morning, seething with anger, the King gave his troops freedom to despoil everything in their path until reaching Scottish soil again. This time he did not ride at their head. He was going home as a defeated general, thoroughly discredited by his own bad leadership, crestfallen and bereft of any future plans.

Back at Edinburgh, James continued to smart with resentment, particularly at the wild folly of his own command. With nothing but failure to report, feeling bruised, uncouth and savage, he could not bring himself to face Margaret. The campaign had besmirched him mentally and in reputation. Margaret would hear of his safe return, that was all she would care about. But he had promised her so much, leaving her as a confident, all-conquering king and returning an unsuccessful barbarian.

How could he go to her and admit an ignominious defeat, bad judgement of spunkless Richard and the irresponsibility of his own command?

The pivot of his plans shattered, he needed time to readjust himself, to raise another army against England and a potent reason for convincing his Council of its necessity.

That night, in the Hall of Edinburgh Castle, Jane Kennedy walked conspicuously across the view from the top table. James followed her movements with eyes glinting a fire compounded of hatred and desire. This was the proud lass who had refused to yield to him, mastered him with her sharp tongue. A new resentment began to foment, demanding possession of her as some form of recompense. The thought kept jabbing at his troubled mind, gradually outweighing all other considerations. Tonight, at least, he would conquer Jane Kennedy, bend that proud body to his will.

Mind fixed upon one objective he summoned Lucan Fairfax. 'Tell Lady Kennedy that I would like to see her in my private chamber,' he said, with soft spoken determination. 'Approach her yourself and make my royal wishes known to her. Nobody else is to know of your commission.' He looked hard at the squire, then smiled grimly as he added, 'You know the price you'll pay for failure.'

Lucan bowed, anxious to please after prejudicing his position as the King's body squire during the recent campaign. 'I'll not fail, Your Grace,' he promised.

'Good!' James nodded with approval. 'Take her up the courtyard stairway and see that we're not disturbed until our business is completed, no matter how long it takes. You understand, lad?'

'Perfectly, Your Grace.'

'Then get about your duty. Impress upon Lady Kennedy that it's the King's wish you carry.'

Lucan, again clad in blue and silver Court livery, slipped away noiselessly. The King had reminded him of what failure would mean, yet this was another mission which caused him misgivings. But his feelings counted for nothing. Of course, he knew that, and should have kept his tongue still when on the campaign in England, after refusing to fire the thatch over the heads of English villagers. When ordered to follow the King on this mission, he had instinctively cried, 'Why, Your Grace, this is not war? My old grandparents live in such a homestead just beyond Edinburgh.'

'Then you'd better join up with the Prince,' the King fired at him. 'Seems your opinions suit his mind better than mine.'

Of course, he followed the King, keeping at his side, yet not throwing any burning brands. The King had berated him soundly that night, threatening that his first battle campaign could be his last.

Now there was more mischief afoot. He had assumed that the King would go to Lady Margaret at Castle Drummond, a sweet and beautiful lady worthy of a king. His knowledge of their situation had set him reckoning that the King was seeking a way to marry her. Now, instead, he obviously intended bedding with Lady Jane Kennedy who, for no reason, treated servants like dirt. But his sole desire was to serve the King, to fight with him against the English and, if necessary, give his life to protect his royal master. Nonetheless, he had no heart for what he was now about. It would not be his way of treating Lady Margaret. He knew the King, however, and in his present mood, he was just as likely to dismiss him if he failed.

James took a final look at the assembly, then avoiding Bothwell's puzzled gaze, rose and left the Hall, not wishing to hear any more about the failure of the campaign or the wailing over the pusillanimous Prince.

He strode briskly across the small courtyard, passed the gatehouse of the upper bailey, then went up the stone steps where Lady Kennedy would be led. He went through a small anteroom containing his hunting and riding equipment into a private chamber with a wide fireplace and shuttered windows.

Inwardly coiled with frustration he flung his red cloak across the upholstered settle, kicked some life into the smouldering fire and tossed on a fresh log. He lit the candles in the silver candlesticks and set them on an exquisitely carved round table. After their initial spluttering, they glowed with a gentle lambency which lit up the vivid colours of a Bannockburn tapestry stretching the full length of one wall.

He looked around, restless, desiring solitude yet irritated by a sense of loneliness; isolated, set apart from the comforts and consolations his subjects took for granted. He pulled the settle closer to the fire, then placed a large stool alongside it. He sat on the stool and gazed into the kindling flames, but could not rest for long. To employ himself he sprinkled herbs from a decorated pomander on to the fire, filling his lungs with their fragrance. But this soon sickened him and he slumped across the wide settle, slipping deeper and deeper into a mental pit of despair. His whole body yearned for action, violent action to smother the pangs of his troubled mind. A knight could carry off a recalcitrant wench bodily and it would be laughed at as a joke. If the King acted in the same way the scandal would spread throughout the Court.

As he waited, he cursed and wished the damnation of hell upon Prince Richard. Then he thought of Margaret, lovingly awaiting him. He loved her, no doubt of that, and because of it would make her his Queen; but she could not tame the raging beast within him tonight; merely being with her would emphasise the failure he so desperately wanted to forget. Tonight every part of him craved for a triumph over a humiliating adversity of the past, a physical demand personified by Jane Kennedy, the woman who had refused her King. She had to be made to yield.

Would Lucan be skilful or persistent enough to persuade her to come? After his timidity across the border he had to prove himself obedient without question, and Jane too ought to be responsible enough not to jeopardise her own and her father's position at Court by openly flouting his wishes. Yet there was no woman in Scotland more unpredictable; this was her chief attraction tonight. Before his thoughts reached a fresh peak of frustration footsteps sounded from outside, Lucan treading heavily to announce his approach. James rose, straining to distinguish sounds, heart quickening as he picked out the accompanying lighter tread.

He gazed fixedly at the door, and it suddenly swung open, revealing Jane, shrouded in a dark blue hooded cloak, the fire and candlelight immediately flickering upon her fresh, cool beauty. This sight made all the torment of waiting worthwhile. He moved to her, assisted in removing her cloak. 'Jane, you came,' he whispered.

'Your squire was devilish persistent, Your Grace,' she said avoiding the urgency of his eyes. 'He pleaded as if his head were at stake.'

James smiled sardonically. 'Perhaps it was, for I don't know what I might have done had you not come.'

'Your compaign with Prince Richard did not go well, so I am informed,' she said, surveying the chamber with almost insolent appraisal.

He noted her splendid purple gown trimmed with ermine and, more particularly, the smooth-limbed grace of her movements. He detected a certain affinity in her expression, the hostility of their previous encounters no longer present, a feeling furthered by the fact that she had come without coercion. 'A temporary setback only, yet it rankles to the very dregs of my soul,' he admitted.

She allowed him to lead her to the stool and he sat behind her on the settle. When his hands moved with caressing softness over her shoulders, she turned to him, eyes scintillating with puckish gaiety. 'You look troubled, Your Grace. I noticed it in the Hall.'

'Then you felt my gaze upon you?'

'Your eyes were like flaming torches looking for moths to devour.'

'And you came because of it?'

She smiled, the firelight enhancing its effect. 'Because I was commanded,' she mocked.

Her playfulness stimulated him, encouraged frankness, sure now that she would not spit at him with the fury of a mountain cat. 'It was not as a king that I called you, Jane.'

'I know,' she said, turning to fully face him, her long-fingered hands resting on his knees. 'And I came not to a king, but to an ambitious man suffering misery because his plans have gone awry. I, too, lead my life by plans, Your Grace. Perhaps that's why I know I can bring you consolation.'

His hands moved to the inside of her wide sleeves, gently advancing up her arms until he touched the warm, resilient firmness of her breasts. As he did so their eyes met and he knew then he had not mistaken her look of affinity. 'Jane, beautiful Jane, surely tonight you'll not deny me,' he murmured, caressing his cheek against her soft skin.

Her lips slightly parted, but she eased him away until their eyes met again. 'Not so long as you remember that I also have plans, Your Grace.'

As he felt her body relaxing he began to part her clothes. 'You shall have all you desire, Jane.' Words no longer had any meaning; both their hands were active, seeking to uncover the focal point of their desire, her lust for him as great as his for her as they wrestled among each other's clothing.

Soon they were both completely naked on the animal skin rug in front of the fire, and he felt her thighs wriggling provocatively in anticipation of receiving him. The gratification of his entry into her was so intense that it momentarily and obliviously solved all his problems, so much so that the aftermath of the first ecstatic release provided the stimulus to arouse the second.

That night Jane Kennedy taught her King things he had never known about a woman's body, the most enlightening revelation being that its passion could be as strong and as demanding as that of any man. She stirred him again and again, her bucking body matching his every thrust, as with teeth clenched and sometimes sunk into him, her desire for release was as urgent as his own. No woman had ever served him with such vigour or provided such delight. She let him explore every crevice of her body and he revelled in it.

The thrill of this new and vital experience brushed aside all the recriminations of campaign failure. He had justified himself as a man in gaining her total submission as a woman for the full enjoyment of her body, and from her lustful cavorting he reckoned she had gained no small measure of delight from his manhood.

During the ensuing days at Edinburgh, James remained entranced by Lady Jane. Stimulating new peaks of sensation at each fresh encounter, she kept him in complete subjection with her lovemaking variations. She proved herself not averse to mounting him and matching thrust for thrust until their bodies melted into each other with the sheer rapture of total and mutual gratification. Once ecstatically experienced, he could not resist joining with her again and again, for every time she left him it was with the promise of yet further ecstasy to come.

In spite of her irresistible attraction and the engrossing physicality they shared together, each aftermath brought the realisation that he did not and could not love her as he loved Margaret. With Jane it was union of mind and body, but with Margaret heart and soul were added. But what he had shared with Jane could never be forgotten. She had raised him from the depths of despair, infused fresh manliness into him and with it new resolves for happiness of the most lasting nature.

Neither did he fail to perceive that the fiery passion and animal grace of Jane's body were controlled by an intelligent and all too human mind. Her parting reminder that she had personal plans gave hint that eventually his sanction would be sought for some furtherment of her future.

SEVEN

On the day of Jane Kennedy's departure from Edinburgh, James heard from England that King Henry had received a subsidy from his Council for war in the north. This provided the change of policy he needed, incentive for further action. He called an immediate Council meeting, and although bleary-eyed from restricted sleep, spoke with masterful authority from his throne chair. 'If a Scottish army doesn't cross the border to show its preparedness, the English are almost certain to invade Scotland,' he informed the assembly. 'This being so, my lords, this Council must today sanction the issuing of notices to sheriffs for the mustering of men for another campaign.'

There were many questioning glances from one Councillor to another, but James silenced any objection by stating, 'I shall regard any opposition to my commands as tantamount to treason. So I take it our business is finished, and as there's much for each of you to do, I detain you no longer.'

Although alarm flooded many faces, no single voice gave utterance to what several felt. Leaving many troubled minds behind him, James set off for Castle Drummond. Again he had a plan to offer as hope for Margaret.

Once clear of the city he spurred his grey charger to a fast gallop, still tingling from the excitement of his apparent victory over the stupefied Council. Covering the hoof-indented tracks across the undulant country-side, however, his mood changed. Remorse began to creep over him as with each stride he became more unsure of Margaret's welcome.

Without doubt the yap of the Court would have reached her. What he had done was bad enough. What the tongues of women would make of it would be unquestionably worse. Was there anything he could say which would convincingly excuse his faithless conduct? Would she understand if he told her the truth? What in fact was the truth? Could he now assure her of anything after the all too easy thwarting of his earlier plans?

Eventually he stopped, tethered his horse to a tree and sat on a fallen tree trunk, staring disconsolately at the individual blades of grass between his feet. Reaching no conclusions and finding no allegory, he raised his eyes to the sky. A tiny hummock of sun-tipped cumulus cloud rose from the lofty horizon of fir trees, climbed slowly, then spread out like a mushroom cap at the top, until it burst and sent a handful of white searching fingers across the sky. This serial movement stirred him into once again mounting his horse. One thing was certain, he now had to face up to Margaret and convince her of his penitence. It did not help to know that without expressing it, Lucan disapproved of his conduct. That was why he had been left at Edinburgh.

Arriving at Castle Drummond without warning caused courtyard servants to scurry like disturbed ants as they recognised him as the King, then finally to conduct him to Margaret's apartment.

Her joy at seeing him did not completely conceal the look of reproach in her tender blue eyes. 'Jamie, you have been away so long,' she whispered, as he embraced her.

'My sweet, you've heard of the disgrace I suffered at Prince Richard's hands; our gallant adventurer turned out to be a milksop.'

'So my father told me,' she said, with pained emphasis. 'But that's what I feared all along.'

'I know, like Patrick and the whole of my Council, you advised caution. But these days no King can rule effectively without being prepared to take a sword in his hand.'

'My fear is that sometimes you are too ready with the sword.'

He drew her nearer. 'Perhaps that is right, my dearest love, but to make you my Queen I'd fight the whole of Christendom, if necessary.'

She eased herself away to hide rising tears, gulping as she said, 'Jamie, do you still love me?'

He rested a hand beneath her chin, turning her face to his gaze. He kissed her lips and held her tight. Her closeness and sweetness engulfed him. This was real love, not the bestial lust he had shared with Jane Kennedy. He regretted every moment of absence now causing her so much disquiet. 'My heart is yours, purest Meg, my darling,' he murmured, into the side of her head. 'It will never be another's as long as I live.'

A frown puckered her face and her lips pursed to speak, but she changed her mind and sighed.

'Meg, do you doubt me?' he asked fiercely.

'All I ask is for you not to deceive me if you wish to seek another Scottish bride.'

'Why do you talk of deception?' Rising anger tinged his voice.

Two natural puffs of colour inflamed her cheeks as she struggled for words to reprimand him. 'Euphemie, my sister, is home from Court after suffering badly in marriage. She's embittered against men and has confirmed what I've heard whispered among the servants. I find it humiliating, Jamie.'

He held her shoulder firmly. 'What are you talking about?'

'You know what I'm talking about,' she flashed, her face lined with wretchedness. 'I'm grateful for the joy your love has brought me, but I know that you're the King and cannot always obey your heart. You only have to say that all is ended. I have no ambitions for myself.'

'Don't speak like that, please,' he implored, realising the depth of her resentment. 'Jane Kennedy is no rival of yours. True, she shared my bed, but what campaigning soldier has not whored his way to forgetfulness after miserable defeat?'

Her misty blue eyes widened in their demand for explanation. 'Then it was not out of love that you sought her?'

He laughed contemptuously. 'She knows of lust, but not of love, Meg. Only with you can I be my true self, knowing that the man's more important than the king. I command no words powerful enough to describe what that means to me. By all that's holy I swear that you're the only woman who touches my heart!' He held both her hands, looking at her fully, trying to let her see what he felt must be reflected in his face, for it came from within him and he meant every word.

Love dagger-pierced by doubt once again stifled Margaret's words.

'Truly, my sweet, my heart is yours, no matter who fills my bed or to whom my Councillors plight me in marriage,' James went on. 'You're the brightest jewel in the realm of Scotland, and were it wholly in my power, you, my loved one, would already be my Queen.'

'All I want is your love, my dear sweet lord.' A smile returned to her wan face and she stretched up to kiss him saying, 'Jamie, more than anything in the world I want to believe you. The depth of my hurt only indicates the depth of my love for you. I've been wretched waiting for you to return, wondering if in fact you would ever come again.'

'Never doubt that, Meg. I will always return to you. By my life's blood, I swear it!'

'And you will now stay with me, so that we can enjoy our infant daughter together?'

He sighed heavily. 'I wish it could be so, dearest one. But the only way I can make you my Queen is by the sword. Letters are going out to the sheriffs for more musters and I must personally see that they're carried out properly.'

Disappointment once again brought anxious lines to her rounded mouth. 'But, Jamie, you've been away so long.'

'I know. I know.'

'Surely, you can stay with me tonight at least?'

He held her close to him. 'If you want me to, of course.'

She made him feel even more contrite by replying, 'I always want you with me, whether in victory or defeat.'

Swallowing hard he said, 'Sweet Meg, I don't deserve such love, but I'll return as quickly as possible with plans for a real victory this time. Only in this way can there be full purpose to our life together.'

She noticed how failure had tempered his buoyant confidence. She kissed his head, his lips, his cheeks and his closed eyes, and accepted with gratitude that he was with her again.

When he returned to Edinburgh next morning, James busied himself with necessary State matters prior to his departure from the capital. He also learned that Jane Kennedy was back at Court. They came face to face after supper that night, but James only exchanged ridiculously polite greetings with her before retiring to his bedchamber alone.

Jane watched him go and smiled confidently. She guessed why, having come straight from Castle Drummond, he wanted to try and avoid her. It was only temporary control on his part and she felt confident that her time would come again. Few men were capable of not returning for more of the nights they had shared together. She had kept old Angus at her beck and call for long enough with the memory of far less intimate occasions. If the King intended marrying a Scot it would not be Margaret Drummond, she thought to herself.

Lucan Fairfax also had thoughts that night. It pleased him that Lady Kennedy had been shunned by the King, but more so that upon returning from Castle Drummond, his master had informed him that he would be accompanying him on the tour of the kingdom as his body squire. He greeted the news with surprised relief, having fully expected to be relegated to some menial work in the castle and perhaps never again serving the King personally.

James first went to the lands of Lord Home, where he found his castle greatly strengthened, feudal lieges mustered and the Baron's eldest son eager to be at arms.

In a small chamber studded with the relics of border skirmishes they discussed the situation. 'The longer we delay, Your Grace, the longer we give the English time to prepare,' declared young Home.

No father and son could have been less alike in appearance – the son diminutive in stature, full-faced, barrel-chested and thick-set; the father tall and thin, with angular features.

James smiled. 'I wish all my nobles were in the same state of readiness I find here. I could march tomorrow if your example had been followed.'

The older man wagged his head tolerantly. 'The English also prepare, Your Grace,' he pointed out. 'Since he became Bishop of Durham, Dr Fox has been fortifying Norham castle and the border defences.'

'Which means we must strengthen Scotland's defences before we march, my lord.'

Lord Home nodded. 'That's essential, Your Grace. There's much to fear in the surprises a soldier of the Earl of Surrey's calibre can spring. I'm told he and Bishop Fox are in close league.'

'Then we should raise hell to cleave that league,' put in young Home.

'Well spoken, Alexander,' praised James.

Home turned to his son with pride. 'You have yet to learn caution, Alex,' he warned. 'The business of war starts long before the army is given orders to march.'

'Agreed, but I admire the lad's spirit,' observed James. 'You're lucky to have a castle so well breached with sons. Your lady Nicola served you well.'

When James arrived at Dunbar to inspect Sir Andrew Wood's fortifications, he heard more about King Henry fortifying the English border and moving troops northwards. Time was running short, yet Scotland's progress towards war lacked the urgency he was desperately trying to infuse into it.

The need became more pressing with the news that impatient of delay, the English had crossed the border to commence hostilities. Lord Home's readiness enabled him to defeat them at Duns. Their retreat gave a little extra time for James to rouse his subjects to greater efforts, and a few days later he arrived hopefully at Melrose to meet his artillery and the feudal levy. His spirits plunged as he reviewed the men and their cannons. Bothwell rode at his side as they inspected the lines. The sun warmed their chain mail and a light breeze fluttered the battle standards.

Azure blueness filled the sky, but James's brow darkened at the size of the turn-out.

'There are not enough bodies, Patrick,' he complained bitterly. 'More summonses must be sent out. Remember how ill we fared last time owing to the size of the approaching English army.'

The Duke of Ross came forward, then held his charger in check as the trio wheeled at the end of the line of red-coated archers. 'And we know how the English have been mustering rapidly in the north.' He spoke in a dull, matter of fact, manner, ready to support his kingly brother, but with no real conviction for the cause.

James nodded and spurred his horse up a slight rise, then looked down upon the whole army, shaking his head disconsolately.

Frustration and foreboding sank sharp killing teeth into his hopes of striking invincibly and claiming a decisive victory. 'I've coined the Great Chain to equip this expedition with guns, and Mons Meg is the biggest ever, the largest and most powerful cannon in Europe,' he informed his two companions. 'But in men we are lacking, yet we can not delay much longer. The summonses must go out for a meeting at Lauder. Then we can cross the border and let the Devil claim those who belong to him.'

The Duke of Ross sensed the desperation in these words; to him it made the war even more futile. He did not know that James was thinking of Margaret and his daughter, issuing orders to ensure that if next time Margaret bore him a son, he would be born in wedlock to become the future King of Scotland.

Before the muster, James received a messenger from England. Evidently Cornishmen had risen in objection to the raising of taxes for the English army in the north. James immediately called his battle commanders to Melrose Castle. 'My lords, King Henry has diverted part of his army mustered for service in Scotland to subdue malcontents in the south of England,' he informed them. 'This is without doubt our opportunity to strike.'

A babble of speculation broke out at the announcement. James allowed it scope for a while, then banged the table top with the flat of his sword. 'As a result of this development, my lords, we will muster as planned, then straight away, regardless of any deficiencies, march to make an attack on Norham castle.'

Swift glances of uncertainty flashed across the table. Bothwell used his privileged position to say, 'Norham has been strongly fortified by Bishop Fox, Your Grace.'

James's eyes blazed at him. 'So I've been informed, which means that our artillery will have to batter much harder. That's the purpose of cannons like Mons Meg, to crumble strong fortifications.'

This riposte silenced the others, who sensed that nothing would dissuade the King.

The order to advance on Norham was given beneath a red raw early morning sky at the end of July. The artillery had been dragged laboriously into position, crushing down the plumes of thistles and teasels which had recently forced their prickly heads through the matted grass. Between the intermittent bursts of cannon fire, the delicate petals of crimson poppies wavered on upright stalks, then were pounded to the ground as the sound of thundering hooves echoed across the fields, when first the King, then the Earl of Bothwell, Lord Home and Lord Hamilton led assaults upon the castle. But each wave received an eruption of penetrating fire that scattered their formations and made withdrawal the sole means of survival.

The village folk and their cattle had been strategically withdrawn from the countryside, but every able man called in to protect the defences, and it soon became apparent to James that the castle could be captured only by a long siege. Once again, because victory meant so much to him, he had underestimated the enemy by ordering a premature attack. Once again, he should have listened to those who had advised caution.

He glanced across the field at a messenger spurring a flagging horse towards him. He watched as the tottering animal lurched forward. Little more than a lance-length away, the horse sank to the ground in a tangle of dust-covered legs, then gurgled its last breath with blood spurting from its mouth. The messenger extricated himself and staggered towards the King.

'What news do you bring?' asked James. 'I hope its urgency warrants your treatment of that horse.'

'Bad news, Your Grace, grievous bad,' gasped the messenger, loosening his blue cloak and paying obeisance at the same time. 'The Earl of Surrey advances rapidly with ten thousand men. He's supported by a fleet carrying another ten thousand.'

Alarm suffused the faces of the nobles gathered round the King. Lord Home's angular nose twitched as he said, 'My lord Surrey has a reputation for marching fast, Your Grace.'

'And for claiming the utmost vengeance,' put in Bothwell.

High in the sky, a flock of starlings banked and headed northwards. James followed their progress until they became a single black speck in the distance, his thoughts winging with them to Castle Drummond, where Margaret and his daughter awaited him. If he failed again they would remain his leman and bastard child instead of Queen and royal Princess. Every instinct prompted him to stay and fight, even if it meant death. But he was King of Scotland and had no heir other than his brother, a young man whose love of learning transcended that of kingship and soldiering, whose accession could result in internal strife and an ignoble end similar to that of their father.

Cold reason slowly wormed its way into the fever of his thoughts. He turned to his commanders, eyes dark and pitted with misery, arms limp at his sides. 'So 'tis another campaign from which we retreat,' he whispered, then without another word, walked to his battle tent. Inside he slumped on the rough bed; eyes near to tears, his plans a funeral pyre around him. When he finally stirred to full awareness he had resolved other issues. Prince Richard could no longer be sheltered in Scotland. He would not surrender him to any ambassador, but allow him to go free and press his claims elsewhere, though the milksop deserved harsher treatment.

So the retreat to Ayton began, with the Earl of Surrey so hot on their heels that he made a retaliatory raid on Ayton castle. He also challenged James to single combat, but the Scottish Council were unanimously opposed to acceptance of the challenge. Utterly dispirited, unsure of his next move but certain he must offer Margaret some recompense, he took the Council's advice. There was no other practical alternative, and it looked as if he might soon be seeking his Council's support for what it would initially consider an impossible issue.

James went straight to Castle Drummond, but found nothing to revive his low spirits. Margaret and her sister were engrossed with the infant girl; her father kept urging caution concerning England, and outside there were damp, clinging mists and drizzling rain. It came as a relief to return to Edinburgh and receive Don Pedro de Ayala again. Aware that this would entail more negotiations concerning marriage to Henry's daughter, he left Margaret with her family.

As expected, Ayala came to discuss a truce between Scotland and England, this time a seven-year term, its good faith sealed by agreement to marry Margaret Tudor. Still without any definitive plan of action, James had to provisionally agree to Bishop Fox arranging a treaty. Respecting the Spanish ambassador's perception, James sensed that he would be sceptical of too ready an acceptance, so he acted out a delaying charade with the skill of an experienced negotiator, but the deception disheartened him even more.

At the height of this wavering indecision, Jane Kennedy returned to Court. No matter how he tried to avoid her she kept appearing wherever he went, as persistent as a shadow – tempting, taunting, gradually undermining his resolve. Finally, she surprised him by gaining entry to his private chamber, then, enfeebled by the seeming hopelessness of developing events, he could not resist the all-absorbing diversions she offered. The barrier broken, nothing could be gained by denying himself the receptivity of her bewitching flesh. So he lost himself within her scheming ambit; also lost all sense of purpose, again his future temporarily laid to waste on the battlefields of defeat.

True realisation of his sexual immersion came with the news of a border skirmish at Norham, violating the recently ratified truce. James emerged from the bedchamber with different passions aroused. Such a breach of good faith demanded instant action, and he ordered Lucan Fairfax to fetch Lord Home.

When Home arrived he found the King stalking his presence chamber. 'Well, my lord, what news?' flashed James, voice high-pitched with rage. 'What further indignities am I to suffer at the hands of the English?'

The Lord High Chamberlain, recognising the King's fractiousness, made over-punctilious obeisance to allow himself time to think. He knew the King sought any excuse to avoid concluding the marriage treaty with England. 'I've not yet received all details, Your Grace,' said Home, his tall, spare body stiff and awkward. 'It seems that garrison troops at Norham mistook a group of Scots for spies and made an assault on them.'

James stamped round the long table, fists clenched and face contorted with fury. 'Are all my subjects to be treated as spies? Can they not wander abroad without being assaulted by the English at every turn?'

'I'm given to understand that the Scots were imprudent, Your Grace.'

James arrested his agitated pacing and faced his minister with wildly dilated eyes. 'Given to understand by the English no doubt. And you, like Bothwell, favouring a union with England, accept their point of view before that of your King.'

The bland expression of tolerance on Home's face changed. His right hand clutched at the revers of his short coat, fingernails dug into the fur and knuckles whitened as he considered his words before uttering them.

'Neither the Earl of Bothwell nor I have any wish to offend Your Grace. Neither have we sided with anybody against Your Grace. Our advice is based on what we think best for Scotland. We would be failing in our duty if we did not express our opinions, even though they be not popular. As regards this present breach of the truce, I've already registered a strong protest in your name to Bishop Fox.'

'That's not good enough. The protest must be registered to King Henry without delay. I demand instant redress.'

'Very well, Your Grace. I'll send another messenger to express the depth of your feelings.'

'Do that, and see that he has fast horses, for I'll not rest until I hear King Henry's reply.'

The sunlight cast the latticed shadows of the outside grille of the window across the table; the same rays lit up the dust caused by the King's restless feet among the floor rushes. The Lord High Chamberlain hesitated, then braced himself and said, 'Would it be politic to suggest that you are willing to commence negotiations for your marriage, Your Grace?'

'There'll be no talk of marriage until this affair is settled,' fired James. 'Our objection will most likely result in a visit from Bishop Fox. I'll make my own overture to him regarding the marriage, if I obtain satisfactory redress.'

Home bowed, recalling that the Council continued pressing for the marriage with Princess Margaret Tudor, this being the easiest way of avoiding a disastrous war with England. But the King pigheadedly conceded nothing, other than the dismissal of Prince Richard, finally realising that neither the Council, nobles, nor Scottish troops were prepared to man another campaign on his behalf.

Meanwhile, the King remained as tight as a clam regarding his personal attachments. All the Court knew that Margaret Drummond had presented him with a natural daughter. On the other hand, many were aware that Jane Kennedy shared his bed, much to the displeasure of Angus, who, by speaking his mind, had again lost all favour at Court.

Home requested his leave, judging it inopportune to argue further. He had no wish to be packed off to his lands in disgrace like Angus, for he reckoned that Scotland would need his family experience in handling further negotiations with England.

James sat for a moment in sober thought, particularly about the grants recently bestowed upon Jane Kennedy, then in a sudden outburst of activity leapt up, yelled for Lucan to have horses saddled and rode at a demon-inspired pace to Castle Drummond.

Margaret was sitting embroidering with her sister Euphemie when she heard the King's arrival announced. She moved to the door joyfully, but her sister laid a restraining hand on the full sleeve of her blue velvet gown. 'Wait, Margaret!' she exclaimed, eyes strange and hard.

'Euphemie, don't look at me with such a fierce expression,' protested Margaret. 'I must greet His Grace the King.'

Euphemie's grip tightened. 'Let Father greet him. You demean yourself showing such devotion when he treats you so shamefully. He's not been here for weeks, and all that while Jane Kennedy has warmed his bed.'

'Euphemie, let me go!' cried Margaret, frightened by her sister's uncharacteristic violent attitude.

'Don't you see that he'll soon be casting you aside like any other leman?' urged Euphemie

'That's not true,' flashed Margaret.

'Of course it is, and I've heard you sobbing at night fit to die because of it,' pressed Euphemie, with more tenderness. She rose and put her arms round Margaret's shoulders. 'My darling, he's not worthy of one so sweet. He'll never make you his Queen.'

'All I want is his heart. I have no wish to scheme for a crown.'

'Then I pity you,' snapped Euphemie, turning away.

Distressed by her sister's melancholy, Margaret went to her side. 'You've had misfortune in your marriage, Euphemie. You and Lord Fleming think too much ill of each other. I love the King, and I'm sure that he loves me.'

Euphemie laughed scornfully. 'And he shows it by sharing his bed with any woman willing to offer him a night's sport. Lord Fleming is cast in the same die.'

'Yours was a mistaken match, Euphemie. You must not allow it to blight your whole life –' She broke off, for unheralded the King burst into the solar and became ensnared by the drape hanging across the door. It swept his plumed bonnet from his head and tangled between his hose-clad legs.

'Meg, my sweet one,' he laughed, wrenching himself free from the entanglements and stretching out his arms. 'Your father told me I should find you here, so I dismissed the servants. I fear I didn't make a graceful entry.'

He embraced her warmly, then glanced at Euphemie.

She looked at him with icy distaste. 'You need not dismiss me, Your Grace,' she said, with a scant curtsey. 'I'll go of my own accord, by choice.'

James glanced questioningly at Margaret, as Euphemie swished from the solar with head held high.

'She negotiates the door and its drapes with more grace than I could muster,' James admitted. 'But her eyes were plunging dagger points into me up to the hilt, why is that?'

'A bad marriage has addled her mind, but I don't share her feelings. It's a long time since you were here, Jamie.' Her voice became a whisper as she snuggled close to him. 'You're much thinner, are your affairs still so troubled?'

'If the Devil himself had meddled with them he could not have done worse. But tell me about yourself, dearest one, and our sweet child.' He broke off, sensing the strained atmosphere and afraid of it developing into something crucial. Holding her silently at arm's length he eventually said, 'My physicians give me good account of your health and the progress of our loved one.'

'The physicians know nothing of the working of my heart, Jamie.'

He dropped on one knee in front of her, taking both her hands in a tight, entreating grasp. 'Meg, what's troubling you?'

Tears welled up in her eyes, 'I hear so many rumours. Even my own kinsmen return from Court with news I am loath to hear.'

'I know, my flesh is weak and my troubles many. I try to lose myself in company I would not otherwise keep,' James confessed.

'Jane Kennedy?' she queried

He nodded. 'I can't deny it. Yet I swear there is no love in my bedding her.'

Margaret picked up her needlework to avoid his troubled eyes.

With a quick, impulsive movement he swept it aside, so that cloth and threads were flung across the floor. 'Meg, before leaving Edinburgh I made up my mind, in defiance of the Council, we will be wed.'

Her face flooded with shocked surprise, a tic twitched at the right side of her mouth, her eyes widened in a stare of incredulity. 'But, Jamie, you know that is impossible.'

'Impossible! What do you mean impossible? Am I not the King of Scotland?'

'Of course, you are, my love. So you know better than I that you can not marry without the agreement of your Council.'

He slumped down on a chair and reached for her hands. 'God's bones, Meg, I haven't the freedom of the commonest churl! I love you! I want to marry you. Surely that's good enough reason for the Council?'

She leaned forward towards him. 'Jamie, don't torment yourself. You said just now that you are the King. That being so, you must be prepared to accept a marriage that will benefit Scotland.'

'But how will my marrying you disadvantage Scotland?' he protested.

'You know the answer to that question, Jamie. If you marry against the will of the Council it will split the ranks of the powerful noblemen. There will be those prepared to support you, but others will oppose our marriage. It could well lead to civil war, create the situation which led to your father's undoing, sow the seeds for another Sauchieburn.'

His eyes glazed with misery, but he held tight to her hands. 'You speak with your father's tongue,' he said. 'You have obviously discussed it with him.'

'I speak from my own heart too, Jamie. Do you think I didn't realise all this from the moment I fell in love with you? My body craved for yours, we came together and as a result I've borne you a child. Even so, I realised that we were living for the moment. I have no ambition to be your Queen, but every fibre of my being wants to accept you as my husband.'

'And that's how it shall be, Meg. By all that's holy, it will! I am the King! I shall marry whom I choose! The Council can raise their objection in hell!'

'Jamie, you speak rashly.'

He leaned over and kissed her brow. 'No, my love, with considered thought, it would not be politic at this time to apply for a dispensation from His Holiness the Pope, but I have a priest's assurance that our relationship is not within the prohibited degrees. This means that we can be man and wife in the eyes of Holy Mother the Church. That's all that matters.'

'That's not all that matters, Jamie, and you know it.'

She met his gaze, saw the concern in his eyes.

'Perhaps,' he whispered. 'Nonetheless, we shall be wed.'

'But how?' she again queried.

His eyes suddenly glowed with fresh resolve. 'In secret at first, until I've settled with England. The important thing is that we will be married. I've made up my mind on it. Nothing is going to sway me!'

She sighed and looked at him with an expression full of tender love. 'Jamie, you have admitted that your affairs are troubled; this could only make them worse.'

'No doubt it will, my beautiful one. This is why we must keep it closely concealed until the time's opportune to obtain the dispensation, then declare you my Queen.' He stood and raised her into his arms, and held her tight as he nuzzled his face into the fragrance of her hair. 'This way you will be my legal wife, my proof to you that I love you as none other.'

She reached up and fondled his red hair saying, 'That's poetic talk, Jamie, for you know your Council can marry you to someone you've never seen. But, my dear sweet lord, although I want you as my husband more than anything in the world, I beseech you not to prejudice Scotland or any part of your kingdom for my sake. Think hard before you make any decision. Neither the Council nor the clergy will approve what you are considering; they only want you to marry the English Princess Margaret.'

He smiled wryly, stroking his hand down her back. 'There's much I shall have to settle, Meg, but I'll do it some way or other. Matters of State are one thing, but this is my private life, and I have only one, just like everybody else. I have made up my mind what I want, and as King of this realm I am determined to gain my way. But I appreciate all you have said, particularly about Sauchieburn. That's why it would be folly to declare my intentions, why none but your closest family must know of the marriage.'

'Then it is not a proper marriage, so why involve yourself in so much trouble?'

'It will be a proper marriage to us, that's what really matters, nothing else. We will be circumspect and face the problems as they arise.'

He sat her down on the chair and knelt before her saying, 'Now do you feel assured of my love, Meg?'

'Yes, Jamie, I do,' she admitted, cradling his head in her lap. 'But I wish there were some other way, and I want you to be absolutely sure.'

He looked up at her earnestly. 'I am sure of my love for you, Meg. That's the only certain thing in my life at the moment.'

She clung to him, unable to restrain her tears in spite of her happiness. 'Then I will support anything you decide, my love. So will the whole house of Drummond.' She eased him away, and with a quick change of mood added, 'Now you must come and see our bonny Margaret. She favours her father in looks.'

Leaving threads scattered over the solar floor, they left with arms entwined round each other, oblivious to the glances of castle servants and the whispering that started as soon as they passed. If the couple had been overheard the whispers could quickly spread through the length and breadth of the kingdom, with the possibility of dethronement or death on the battlefield being the price the King might have to pay.

The marriage took place under a heavy veil of secrecy, not even all the Drummond family fully aware of it. After the clandestine ceremony James stayed at Castle Drummond until he attended Parliament at the end of the month. He then returned with Lord Drummond, after an early snowfall had thawed. The horses sunk into the mud up to their fetlocks and throughout the journey a keen wind howled around them, disarraying their storm bonnets and thick cloaks.

William, one of Drummond's sons, came out to meet them when, wet and bedraggled, they finally reached the courtyard. The tall, silver-haired nobleman dismounted with laboured slowness and his son rushed forward to assist him. 'God's nails, lad, the cold has eaten into my bones! Send a page to have hot ale made ready.'

James joined them, stamping his feet vigorously. 'Well, my lord, I'll not be sorry to test the warmth of your fire on this foul night. I hope it is as warm as your hospitality has been.'

'Then let us hasten to it. Will, attend to the grooms, His Grace and I are near to perishing.'

Lord Drummond led the way to his apartments, sending servants scuttling in all directions on a series of tasks for their comfort. James entered a small, cosy chamber still stamping his feet and flapping his arms. He tossed his sodden mud-flecked cloak and bonnet aside, then walked to the fire of heaped logs crackling in the red stone hearth.

Drummond followed his example, and they toasted their hands and buttocks until a spit boy came in with three kitchen men carrying dishes of beef and bannock. 'You've no objection to eating here, Your Grace?' queried Drummond, rubbing his fingers and pulling wry faces.

'At this moment I'd be content to eat in the stables. But you look pained, my lord. What's troubling you?'

'Chilblains, the heat in here has set them prickling.'

James laughed. 'I know a remedy for chilblains, you must try it.'

'Gladly,' replied Drummond, rubbing at his chafed fingers.

'It's a simple cure,' said James. He examined the affected fingers and nodded. 'A poultice of borax mixed with the natural water of swine will give quick relief. Send a servant for the ingredients and I will apply the cure myself.'

'Swine water?' gasped Drummond incredulously. 'I doubt if my pigs will pass water to suit my convenience.'

'Then charge your swineherd to give them drink until they do,' replied James, with a smile.

Drummond gave the necessary order to a servant who looked as dumbfounded as his master. 'Go then, man!' he snapped. 'And tell them in the kitchen to hurry with the mulled ale. His Grace and I have icicles stuck to our gullets.'

A frenzy of activity over the spit and from the kitchen resulted in food and ale being set upon the small table in front of the fire. The two men sat facing each other, eating ravenously of the thick, juicy meat and swilling down each mouthful with draughts of steaming ale.

The requisites for the poultice arrived in due time, and Lord Drummond recalled hearing about the young King's predilection for dabbling in physic, but had thought it only gossip. A story was told of how he had persuaded Angus to let him extract one of his bad teeth, with disastrous results on the tooth and the nobleman.

Drummond also suffered the embarrassment of being treated by the King. He even professed a relief not truly felt, realising that by so doing he enhanced the King's reputation as a physician, possibly in the same way as others to escape further treatment.

Ostensibly relieved, Drummond leaned back in his chair and loosened his belt. 'Before we join the ladies, Your Grace, there is something I think you should know.'

'Go ahead, my lord.'

'It concerns Sir John Ramsay,' said Drummond, glancing from beneath the shadow of his grey bushy eyebrows. 'I saw you speaking in earnest with him in the Council Chamber.'

'Yes, he brought news of my brother in Rome. You know the Duke of Ross is there to have his appointment to the see of St. Andrews confirmed by His Holiness the Pope.'

Drummond nodded.

'Evidently the new bishop has been received with favour by the Romans,' James continued, with fraternal pride.

'That is good news, Your Grace, nonetheless the bearer of it is not to my liking. Neither am I alone in being worried by your receiving Ramsay back to favour. It worries Margaret too in her new position. She asked me to speak of it.'

James pressed the fingertips of both hands together and smiled.

'Margaret need not fret, my lord. There's little harm in Ramsay now. He is anxious to make amends for past wrongs and keep me in touch with the changes of the English scene. There might be some circumstance I can turn to good advantage.'

'But can you trust him, Your Grace? He's also served King Henry.'

'The very reason I accepted his return, my lord, for I think he might serve Scotland the better because of it. King Henry has a whole army of spies and agents, but as in all things he treats them niggardly and Ramsay rues his service. Have no fear, my lord, I shall pursue the right course for achieving our purpose.'

James guessed him to be thinking of how his daughter could be proclaimed Queen of Scotland. Not surprisingly, at Parliament, Drummond's voice had not risen in the general clamouring for the match with the Princess Royal of England.

The doubt of the bride's father clearly registered on his face. 'Then don't disclose any confidences until Ramsay has well proved his change of coat. It was he who gave details of the terms under which you supported the so-called Prince Richard of York.'

'That is so,' agreed James, with a smile. 'But do you know why? Because I admitted him to the Council Chamber. I wanted that information carried to England. You can rely upon my judgement, my lord.'

In the perilous position he was now placed, Drummond certainly hoped so, but his features remained troubled as he said, 'Then with your leave, I'll seek my lady Drummond.'

'And I'll go and quieten Margaret's fears,' said James.

He found her waiting for him in the bedchamber. 'I'd almost given up hope of receiving you,' she greeted him, with a mock pout of her well-curved lips.

She was clad in a black silk robe embroidered with the rich colours of extravagant Chinese platters. It had come from Andrew Barton, one of the many mementoes which enabled James to overlook the sea captain's piratical exploits. He sat on the bed, cupped his hands beneath her breasts, sensuously delighting in the body warmth though the silk. 'You must blame your father, my love. He was particularly loquacious tonight, after I had tended his chilblains.'

The account of the treatment so amused Margaret that she laughed out merrily, her opal blue eyes sparkling with love, fair hair hanging lustrously unrestrained down her back. James held her so close that she gasped for breath. 'Jamie!' she protested, easing herself away. 'What did my father say?'

He cradled her in his arms, parted the robe and darted kisses all over her revealed breasts.

'Jamie! Jamie! Jamie!' she laughingly protested again, wriggling free. She sat up and adjusted the robe. 'Did he mention Sir John Ramsay?'

'He did, but why are you so concerned about Ramsay?'

'I feel sure that he seeks to cause you harm.'

He parted the robe again, but with less playful intent, pensive. 'Then forget your fears. I've set him up with his roots in Edinburgh again because he could form a vital link in my hope for our future.'

'In what way?' she asked earnestly.

He sighed and lay back against the head rest, his left arm round her shoulders, although now deep in thought. 'I don't rightly know, since our milksop pretender has been captured and confessed to his origins. But the fact that he aroused so much support in Cornwall suggests the strength of dormant Yorkist sympathies still exists, so while the Earl of Warwick remains alive, Henry cannot feel completely safe on his throne. That's why I have Ramsay back in my service and encourage the prior of Moray to retain his benefice in England. In this way I can keep in touch with any development likely to aid our cause. At the moment the Council want peace with England at any price, and you know, Meg, that it would be unwise at this stage to impose a marriage of my own choice against the will of so many powerful noblemen.'

'All this because we love each other,' she murmured.

He read the sadness in her eyes, only moments ago so gay and full of laughter when hearing about the treatment of her father's chilblains. It is the penalty of being born a king,' he sighed. 'As I told you, I'm not as free as the commonest churl. God's bones, it sets my blood aboiling at times! But I'll find a way, Meg, that I promise you.'

He felt her shiver with apprehension, so he drew her down into the bed to banish her fears in lovemaking. But afterwards, with the candles extinguished, they both lay in the dark, each conscious of the other's contemplation of the possible immensities of their future.

EIGHT

Returning to Edinburgh for another session of Parliament, James found Jane Kennedy in attendance at Court. He guessed she had been awaiting his arrival, and through several informants learned that since last seeing her, she had spurned an offer of marriage from the Earl of Angus and given birth to a son. When she requested an audience through Lucan, he refused to see her, then dismissing his squire told him threateningly not to come again on Lady Kennedy's behalf. It was an order Lucan received with delight.

Having eluded her after supper, James sat in his private chamber, staring vacant-eyed at the fire, reflecting on the tribulations of the past months. His marriage to Margaret had brought only inner satisfaction, but the preservation of the secret irked them both. They now had to be doubly careful in all they said or did in the company of others. If anything, the internal situation had developed in a way that revelation of the true circumstances would exacerbate their political effect. Every ploy to test the effects of declaring Margaret as Queen had produced adverse responses.

As he sat in sorrowful contemplation of all this, his eyes were rimmed with pouchy darkness, body slack and dejected, attitude morose, and he was aware of the violent fits of temper which made all who attended him cower in fright. Unable to make headway and forced to quieten the yap of his Council, he had ratified a lifelong treaty with Henry of England, and that cunning scoundrel now demanded conclusion of the marriage arrangements with the Princess Royal of England.

During the past year James had stalled for time, issued hollow promises, ranted in Council, tried to placate Margaret and escape her English namesake, all the time hoping for some contingency he could turn to advantage. Nothing remotely helpful emerged; an imposture of the Earl of Warwick had been detected and Ralph Wilford hanged. Now the *bona fide* Earl of Warwick had gone to the block after being imprisoned in the Tower of London for fourteen years, another chance of dethroning Henry lost. The confessed Perkin Warbeck had suffered a similar fate: a grim prospect for the bogus Prince Richard who had not relished the sight of blood.

The turn of the century had come and gone, and with it the hope of a miracle. The first day of the year 1500 was as lacking in hopeful developments as the last day of the old century. It brought no revelation or relief, and James now accepted there was no rational reason why it should have done. As before, each day followed the other, worsening his plight, so that even with Margaret at Castle Drummond, he had succumbed to Jane Kennedy at times of acute distress, hating and despising himself afterwards. He was thinking that this folly would mean further cost to the royal finances when a knock sounded on the door, and the castle chamberlain entered requesting an audience for Lady Jane Kennedy.

James leapt at the tall, blue-coated figure and grabbed him fiercely by the throat. 'Tell her to go to hell,' he snarled.

The small, round eyes of the chamberlain almost popped from his white face as James squeezed insensitively hard. At last he controlled himself, recognised the half-wit's fright and released him. The poor wretch scampered to the door just as Lucan burst in. 'Your Grace, I've just found out that Lady Kennedy wheedled round this old fool to approach you. I tried to head him off, but she acted as a decoy for him to get away.'

Lucan was blazing with anger in his own right and had his hand on a dagger. James had never seen his body squire in such a passion. Perhaps seeing it in another made him realise that Jane would find a way into his chamber and take him by surprise as before, or get the better of somebody, perhaps at a time not to his advantage. Better to see her now and dictate his own terms.

'Take your hand off that blade, Lucan,' he said sharply. 'I've decided to see Lady Kennedy.'

The chamberlain and Lucan stared at him in disbelief, but before either could react Lady Jane herself suddenly appeared standing in the open doorway, her eyes as bright and hard as jewels. She waited for the servants to be dismissed, then advanced forward saying, 'You observe me well, Your Grace. What I have to say requires your immediate attention.'

James met her insolent gaze. 'What do you want, milady?'

She walked round the table slowly, then with studied nonchalance drew a chair beside him. 'Assurance, James.'

'Assurance of what?'

'That my son shall be provided for by his royal father.'

'Are you sure that your son has a royal father?'

'Yes, my lord, most positive.' Her eyes flashed with a devilish glint as she added, 'So are many other bodies whose evidence cannot be denied.'

'It shall not be. The King does not disown his kin, even if they be bastard.'

Jane leaned forward, breasts straining at the bodice of her gown as she took a slow intake of breath and exhaled it. 'Yet the King could make his kin legitimate, if he so chose,' she whispered.

He banged the table so hard that the candlesticks jumped and the flames spluttered. 'Lady, you forget yourself too readily,' he snapped.

She moved even closer. 'Well, my lord?'

'I'm not free to choose my bride like any country lad. The Council presses for my marriage to the Princess Royal of England.'

'Yes, but I know how you guile your Council, James.'

A thin smile flickered across his lips. 'It's fortunate for me, lady, that such discernment as yours is not pitted against me in the Council Chamber.'

'It's there, but the threat of attainder prevents it being mouthed.'

'Then my Councillors show more good sense than my lady Kennedy.'

'I've nothing to lose, but everything to gain,' she countered.

He faced her determinedly and said with cutting emphasis, 'Your son can't gain you a crown, Jane, if that's what you seek.'

She recoiled as if struck, face flushed, mouth visibly trembling, momentarily out of control. It took conscious effort to regain her composure, as through shock-pinched features and bloodless lips she said, 'So your heart is set on Margaret Drummond.'

'Where my heart lies is none of your concern,' he replied, leaping to his feet with rising temper. 'You'll not lack, lady. But by God, you'll never share my throne!'

'Perhaps not, whilst Margaret Drummond lives,' she spat out contemptuously.

'Go, lady, before I forget myself. If you were a man I might have despatched you at the point of a sword.'

Although pregnant once again she rose gracefully, and like a flower opening its petals to the sun, seemed to reabsorb all the elegance which had momentarily drained from her. She smiled in the manner that could be both alluring and tantalising. 'You, James, have had sufficient evidence of my not being a man.'

The remark broke the spell of hostility between them. His voice lost its acerbity as he said, 'Go, Jane, I'll see you again, after the child is born.' He watched her withdraw, too morose for dalliance, and after she left he drank malmsey until it drugged him into a besotted sleep.

The summer brought news of further ill omen. The Pope had granted a dispensation to King Henry for the marriage of his daughter to seal the peace treaty between England and Scotland. Events were closing in on James. He knew that the traditional enmities were still smouldering among his noblemen and could be inflamed by the slightest indiscretion on his part. Jane Kennedy's warning about the duplicity of the Council, no doubt based on information gleaned from Angus, provided sufficient confirmation.

He watched the rain beating upon the shuttered windows of his chamber, hearing it send trickling messages from gutters to projecting ledges. He closed his eyes and thought of his secret wife, who had never once complained of the enforced concealment. She provided the only sanity in a welter of bickering and bargaining; the one person who loved him for himself, his faults and foibles, his extravagant promises that had no real foundation and so eventually came to nothing.

A molten pot of low-lying cloud hung over the city. James sighed as he caught sight of his clavichord in the far corner of the chamber. The last time he played it was to compose a ballad for Margaret. How her eyes sparkled when he rode specially to Castle Drummond to sing it to her, and how many times since with their mutual love of music and literature, she had soothed his vilest peaks of frustration.

Even thinking of her calmed him and he picked up the clavichord, strumming it idly. Snatches of tune began to blend harmoniously and his nimble fingers manipulated the strings with more purpose. A liveried page entered and James glanced up but continued playing. The red-faced lad looked embarrassed, but obviously preferred a music-playing master to one distraught with temper. At last James set aside the instrument and turned inquiringly to the page.

The lad spoke with the rich, clear accent of the Highlands. 'The prior of Moray requests an audience, Your Grace. He brings fresh news from England.'

James sighed wearily. Andrew Forman would be primed with more importunings from King Henry, more requests for plenipotentiaries to conclude the marriage treaty. Would he ever silence this interminable wrangling for a bride he had no wish to wed, yet dared not openly refuse?

Detecting signs of rising temper, the page started to back away to be sure of escape.

'I'll see him here,' James commanded. This was kingship, receiving sycophantic advisers who continually tried to impose their will upon him without incurring his displeasure.

The door opened and the squire ushered in the prior, wearing many of the rich trimmings acquired in England. Bland-faced, he bowed low to the King.

'Well, Andrew, what news do you bring?' asked James, with a familiarity that brought a flush of delight to the prior's fleshy face.

'I've received a messenger from England, Your Grace. King Henry is anxious that his commissioners now here in Scotland return with a definite proposal regarding the marriage to Princess Margaret.'

'I'm not a serf that jumps to the command of Henry of England,' snapped James.

The prior's face quickly blanched and he hurriedly explained that he was the bearer of the news, not the sender of it.

'Yet sweet are your mouthings for the match, if my reports from England are aright,' fired James, eyeing him closely.

'Your entire Council is agreed that the match would benefit Scotland,' declared the cleric, with a show of spirit.

'Yes, and perhaps they are right,' James admitted. 'But I'll not be forced into acceptance of any of their proposals, certainly not in a time limit stipulated by King Henry.'

'As you wish, Your Grace,' muttered the prior, thinking of the empty promises made in England to secure his benefice from the Rutherford heiress, who he hoped would soon be more generous to him through marriage to his brother.

James glanced at the rotund figure in clerical black adorned with rich ermine and jewels. He did not blame the prior for looking after his own interests, particularly when serving Scotland ably. But he could go too far. 'It most certainly will be as I wish, and don't forget it. It would be foolish to lose the living of Moray by over-pressing King Henry's desires.'

The prior's well-fed face quivered with anxiety. 'My loyalty is ever to Your Grace's person and to Almighty God,' he put in quickly.

'A worthy combination,' approved James, smiling faintly.

Alone again, he realised that with his Council and the English commissioners now in session over the planning of his life, he would be best out of Edinburgh. If he stayed he might be tempted to send some of the English Commissioners fleeing for the border with the marks of the flat of his sword on their backsides. Inwardly, he felt as tense as when Prince Richard refused to continue the advance into England, but now there were no border hamlets to burn. He would go to Castle Drummond, stay with Margaret for as long as he could, glory in being wedded to her, watch from a distance, remain alert for any chance development that could be exploited.

Autumn withered the summer blooms, swathing the countryside in glorious shades of yellows, browns and reds before the leaves fell. As winds grew stronger, the colours were stripped away and the bare limbs of deciduous trees stood out in scrawny contrast to the sentinel evergreens. Yule went by, then Hogmanay, with events closing tighter round the King of Scotland. All in England were ready for his marriage to their Princess Royal, unaware of his attachment to another Margaret. Then James made his decision; he could delay no longer. He would send for dispensation from His Holiness the Pope, and when it was promulgated, openly declare Lady Margaret Drummond his Queen, and their daughter the Princess Royal of Scotland.

After reaching this conclusion he journeyed to see the Earl of Argyll, deeming it politic to be apart from Margaret until hearing from Rome. It was also necessary to ascertain as far as possible upon whom he could rely for support in the event of a rebellion.

His arrival at Castle Campbell created immediate speculative interest. All knew the position regarding the English marriage, many guessed who was the father of Jane Kennedy's son, yet Lady Margaret Drummond commanded more attention of the King than any other subject. It was an explosive situation, and the King had a reputation for making recklessly hasty decisions. That night they watched as he entered into the dancing and merrymaking with the fanatical zest of a man trying desperately to deny himself time to think.

On the following day James rode out to the Argyll coastline, surveying its watery aspect where the sea had risen over the centuries, flooding river valleys and creating a series of narrow inlets and headlands. He rode with Lucan Fairfax, revelling in the scenic splendour of his kingdom, determined to maintain control of it with the woman he loved as Queen. They rode hard across the headlands, then paddled their horses through the shallow waters of the inlets.

James returned feeling physically refreshed from the release of pent-up energies and purged mentally too, for his communion with the water-washed landscapes seemed to confirm the rightness of his chosen course. As he joined Argyll talking to a group of ladies in the castle grounds, a liveried page came forward, bowed with trembling reverence, then whispered earnestly in the Earl's ear.

Noticing the glances towards him, James called out, 'What secrets are these, Archibald, that they must be whispered before the ladies?'

'Nothing, Your Grace,' gasped Argyll. But the pallor of his face denied the words, and as he listened to the page his mouth sagged open with shock.

Unaccustomed to seeing Argyll struck speechless, James moved towards him. 'Does this news concern me?' he demanded.

'It does, Your Grace,' murmured Argyll. 'But let me confirm it from its originating source.' He turned to Lucan Fairfax and added, 'A messenger's come from Castle Drummond; go with my page and bring him to your master.'

James glared at Argyll with widening eyes. 'Is this news of Lady Margaret Drummond?'

Argyll nodded.

'Has harm befallen her?'

'I am afraid so, Your Grace.'

'What harm?'

The Earl indicated Lucan approaching hurriedly, dragging with him a short, thick-set messenger bearing the Drummond sleuth hound badge.

James rushed forward and grabbed the man, who immediately sank to his knees, eyes dilated and fearful, mouth quivering. 'Get to your feet, master, and speak,' rapped James. 'What news do you bring?'

'Grievous bad news, Your Grace,' replied the messenger, cowering away as he rose.

'Then speak it!' roared James.

The man retreated further, anticipating the King's reaction and fearful that he might suffer for the news he carried. 'It's Lady Margaret, Your Grace, she is dead,' he gabbled, then made as if to run.

Argyll grabbed him and held him fast as James gasped in incredulous amazement.

An immediate silence fell upon the gathered people, like the sudden arresting of a summer's ballad drama. The sun shone warm and pleasant from the sky, but each human form froze as if turned to ice on the carpet of lush green grass. At last, James murmured, 'Dead?'

The messenger nodded.

'There's no doubt of it?' queried James.

'No doubt, Your Grace. God rest her soul!'

The onlookers were surprised at the King's calmness, but his glazed eyes and quivering features indicated the inner tumult. 'What harm came to her?' James pressed.

'It struck her and her two sisters alike, Your Grace,' replied the messenger, tentatively.

'Euphemie and Sibbie?'

'The same, Your Grace, and all three perished.'

'All three!' James passed his hand across his brow. His head pounded with two words. 'Margaret dead' 'Margaret dead' 'Margaret dead'. 'How did it happen?' he gasped.

'They were poisoned, Your Grace. It's thought that their breakfast was tainted, for the three sisters ate of it together,' explained the messenger.

'Then the food must have been tainted by some hand within the castle.'

'Ay, Your Grace, inquiries are being made. But the house of Drummond is deeply distressed this day.'

'As well it might be,' muttered James. He stood in a daze for several seconds before adding, 'When you've been refreshed return with my condolences to my lord and lady Drummond. Tell them that the foul murderer will be found if I have to scour the whole of my kingdom. Lucan, attend to him, find out all you can.'

James turned to Argyll, whose humour-loving face looked all the more tragic because of its unusual pained expression. 'Archibald, make my excuses to your guests. I don't want to see anyone other than Lucan.'

Argyll held his arm sympathetically. 'How can I express the grief we all feel for you, Your Grace?'

James clung tight to him as he whispered, 'It is the greatest misfortune of my life.'

Argyll led him away, and with the sensitivity of the born clown, his eyes were brimmed with tears. Lucan guided the distracted messenger to the castle kitchen, talking to him earnestly.

In his chamber, James threw himself across a daybed. Sorrow ate like a virulent pain into his flesh, went deeper into his bones as full awareness penetrated the initial disbelief. He bit tight at his lips to control the flood of multi-pronged thoughts coursing through him – one moment sickening grief, the next wonder at who could have perpetrated such evil, then a burning demand for vengeance. Utterly distraught, he let out a wail of despair, rolled over on his stomach and sobbed with the nerve-racked hopelessness of a man defeated by impossible odds.

As his tears dried and transient thoughts began to spark again, one realisation crystallised into a hard knot of mental and physical pain – with Margaret dead all hopes of personal happiness had gone for ever.

At last he stood up, flexed the stiffness from his muscles and started pacing the oak-raftered room. A rap of a dagger handle clattered on the door, an agreed signal with Lucan. 'Enter,' he called out, moving towards the door, eager to start inquiries.

The tall, fresh-faced squire look surprised to see him upright and resolute.

'Well, Lucan, what have you found out?'

'Nothing other than a babble of words without much meaning and a growing brood of rumour.'

'Is there any doubt about what we've been told?'

'It would seem not, Your Grace.'

'All three sisters were poisoned?'

Lucan nodded sympathetically.

'Are there any suspects mentioned?'

'In no way that I would give tongue to their names.'

James grabbed hold of Lucan's short tunic with both hands, roughly screwing him so close that their faces almost touched.

'But you'll tell me all you've been told, or I'll cut your tongue from its root and stuff it down your gullet.' He released him with a jerk towards a chair. 'So sit down and talk while you still have the power.'

Lucan obeyed, pleased to see the King's spirit. He had recently become accustomed to these temper-inspired but empty threats. He enjoyed a rewarding man to man relationship with his master again, and although he had not been told, he suspected the true bond between the King and Lady Margaret, a woman he himself worshipped as if she were a goddess. 'Castle Drummond is rife with rumour and several implicated, Your Grace,' Lucan informed him.

'I can imagine that, but the poison must have been ministered by a hand within the castle, somebody in the kitchens with access to the food,' James stated, sitting on the bed and unconsciously scraping his toes on the stone floor.

'Sir John Ramsay considers it so. He's ridden to Castle Drummond to press such inquiries, and asked me to inform you that he'll return to you as soon as he finds anything to report.'

'Ramsay, eh? Why should he be so interested?'

'Having only recently been returned to Your Grace's favour, he likely fears his own name could be implicated.'

'Yes,' whispered James, remembering Lord Drummond's and Margaret's opinion of Ramsay. 'Could this be part of King Henry's doing to force his brat upon me?'

Lucan remained diplomatically silent, vowing to himself that the King would have no more willing ally in seeking out the foul murderer. Even so, he knew better than to put forward his own ideas. After all, he could be wrong, but he had never liked or trusted Lady Jane Kennedy.

'I hope for Ramsay's sake that his search proves fruitful. Who else features in the rumours?' pressed James.

'Much talk concerns the ill-will Lord Fleming bore his lady Euphemie, Your Grace.'

'Yes, another ripe possibility, but something he could have devised without making it triple murder.'

'True, Your Grace. I said so –'

James cut him short by further pressing, 'Who else?'

'Old ulcers have been opened concerning the Monivaird church outrage.'

'And is Lady Jane Kennedy's name involved?'

'By several, it would seem.'

'Yes, she had a motive stronger than any yet mentioned,' murmured James, walking to the small grilled window overlooking the castle grounds as he remembered her remark at their last meeting. 'By God, if this is her doing I'll have her burnt at the stake!'

Lucan understood the depth of rage in his master's heart. As for himself, he would willingly burn Lady Kennedy at the stake if charged to do so. Yet sleeping on a pallet across the door of the King's chamber on occasions, he deduced that if Lady Kennedy was capable of being party to such a crime, then she also had the intelligence to cover all traces of implication. Again he waited in silence.

James turned to him. 'My head's awhirl with thoughts and my heart turned to granite with grief. Leave me, Lucan. Have a messenger go to Hailes and bring back my lord Bothwell. Now I'll see none other than Sir John Ramsay, and bring him the moment he appears.'

'Your Grace is assured of my obedient service,' pledged Lucan; in an attempt to console he added, 'If this fiend can be found, we'll find him.'

'Or her,' added James, vehemently.

Lucan withdrew, determined as much as the King to investigate Lady Jane Kennedy's possible implication. In this respect he was better placed than the King to go through the servants' quarters and pick up titbits of gossip.

When Sir John Ramsay returned later in the day, he brought no fresh information to explain the tragedy. The three sisters were not in the habit of breakfasting together, so it looked as if the tainted food had not been intended for the three. It remained to be discovered which of them had an enemy vicious enough for such cold-blooded murder.

After the interview with Ramsay, James decided to go to Castle Drummond himself. The ride hardened his resolve to find the perpetrators of the crime and it heartened him to see that Lucan was as determined as himself to the same purpose.

Lord Drummond greeted him with a lined face etched by inconsolable sadness, making him appreciate the full severity of a father having three daughters wrenched from his life in such an insidious manner. 'My lord, we understand each other's feelings, but this is time for action, not words,' said James comfortingly, 'but if you are able, I would like you to be with me as I question each and every one of the kitchen servants in turn.'

Drummond nodded, but his eyes were glazed and his mouth sagged loosely.

'If you're with me, I can check on any misrepresentation more easily and with greater speed,' James went on. 'But if you prefer your castellan to be in attendance rather than your grieving self, then I understand.'

Again Drummond nodded, then replied. 'Any help I can give Your Grace in solving this mystery, I'm prepared to give until I drop.'

'Good, then have the kitchen folk assembled and a room prepared for interrogating them individually and in private.'

A light of hope flickered in the bereaved father's eyes as he began issuing orders. It did not take long before the head cook appeared before both his royal and feudal masters. Together the two of them questioned every person who had any connection with the fatal breakfast. Systematically they checked and crosschecked their stories, so that some servants came back and forth into the room several times. At the end of the questioning, they could find no flaw in any testimony given and were no nearer a solution.

Exasperated, James said, 'You return to your lady, my lord. It is my belief that the poisoner could still be hidden within the castle. With your leave, I want to search every corner of it.'

'Do so, Your Grace,' replied Drummond wearily. 'Anyone you require to help is at your immediate command.'

James summoned Lucan. 'Get the castellan to provide a dozen armed reliable men. We are going to search the castle from the highest towers to the depths of the dungeons.'

Lucan went off with alacrity and soon the search started. James led the party of men with a drawn sword, almost fanatically emptying coffers and chests, tearing down drapes, stabbing his sword up chimneys, until, almost berserk with frustration, he finally had to admit defeat. Every hiding place capable of concealing a body had been sword-thrusted, but no trace of any intruder found.

He went to Lord Drummond and reported. 'We have found nothing, my lord, so I'll return to Edinburgh. But I'm taking my daughter with me for safe keeping. Henceforth she shall be known as Lady Margaret, the King's daughter, and watch kept over her day and night.'

As Drummond nodded, James held him by the shoulders and said, 'I am sure our hearts are similarly afflicted, for my own is bursting with the grief of this day. For your lady and yourself it's a triple tragedy for which you have my deepest, deepest sympathy.'

Tears welled into Drummond's eyes and he could no longer articulate words. James held him understandingly. 'I'll send messengers back as soon as I reach Edinburgh. If any clue comes to light, see that I'm informed at once. God be with you, my lord, and have mercy on your dear lost souls. My body squire is arranging for us to take the child; she is all that I have left of the love of my life.'

He too left with tears flecking his tired eyes, determined that once he had ensured his daughter's safety, then he would pursue inquiries further.

Sir John Ramsay came to him at Edinburgh that night. He was the first to learn of the harsh manner in which the King intended seeking out the murderer. Lucan took him to the King's private chamber and James surveyed him with suspicion-filled eyes. 'Well, Ramsay, what have you found out?'

'Nothing further than your own observations, Your Grace. Whoever administered the poison must have been devilishly cunning.'

James indicated him to sit on a high-backed chair, but never took his eyes off him as he moved round to stand in front of him. 'As devilishly cunning as you have been in the past, Ramsay? Both in working for King Henry and among foreign embassies.'

Fear flooded into Ramsay's shifty dark eyes as the King towered above him. 'I work for none other than Your Grace, now that you've so graciously pardoned me for past wrongs.'

'And you know nothing of this dastardly deed?'

'Nothing, Your Grace. I swear it to God.'

James searched his quivering features for any hint of guilt, but accepted that he was not likely to trace it even if it existed. 'Your soul's black enough for anything,' he ground out. 'My lady Margaret, God rest her soul, never trusted you. She is now beyond extracting any truth out of you, but I am not. Before you speak again, measure your words carefully.'

James suddenly flashed out his hands, encircled them round Ramsay's scrawny throat and exerted pressure so that his limp, bony body twisted on the chair. 'Now tell me, have you been approached by anybody in England concerning Lady Margaret's person?'

'No, Your Grace.'

James exerted more pressure. 'By any agency abroad?'

'No, Your Grace,' choked Ramsay. 'Let . . . let God be my witness.'

'Are you telling me the truth?' charged James, pressing words and grip even tighter.

'Yes . . . Yes, I swear it!'

James still held him as he said, 'Then I hope for your sake that you swear aright, for if anything comes to light involving you, Ramsay, I shall tear you apart with my own hands. I swear to that too.' He finally released him adding, 'Your future in Scotland will depend upon how you come out of this affair, so get you gone and find out anything you can for your own benefit.'

Coughing and spluttering, Ramsay made a hasty retreat and James shook his hands as if ridding them of filth, realising how near he had been to choking the life out of him; certain that he would have done so had he detected the slightest trace of guilt.

The following morning he visited Lady Margaret, his daughter, and took her several gifts. She had his reddish hair and her mother's clear blue eyes. She smiled at him so happily that his heart near broke within him.

After breakfast, he summoned Lucan and they set off for Forfar to catch Lady Kennedy by surprise. On the way Lucan announced his intention of circulating among the servants to probe them for anything which might provide a worthwhile lead.

'You thought well of my lady Margaret, Lucan,' James observed, at one of their stopping places.

'Next to my mother, she was the dearest and sweetest lady I've ever known,' Lucan replied.

His obvious sincerity surprised James, 'I could say exactly the same myself,' he whispered.

'Before anything else, Your Grace, we owe it to her memory to bring the fiend who killed her to the justice of a sword point.'

'Then we're of one mind, Lucan, and if I fail through any reason, then I charge you to remember your own words.'

'I'll never forget them, Your Grace, not as long as I live'

They rode on in silence, each occupied by his own thoughts, each hopeful that they were moving towards a solution.

At Tantallon, James was greeted by the lumbering figure of Angus. 'I'm deeply honoured by your visit, Your Grace. All my hospitality is at your service. Had I known you were coming I would have prepared a fitting welcome.'

'Save your blather, Angus,' snapped James. 'I didn't come to see you, or to bring any honour. Is Lady Kennedy here?'

'She is, Your Grace.'

'Then I wish to see her at once, alone. Lead me to where I can talk to her in private.'

Angus hesitated momentarily. 'My business with her will be short, my lord,' James assured him. 'Unless it is to take her away and clap her in a dungeon.'

This remark obviously alerted Angus to the purpose of the visit and he deemed it politic to be silent. James was given the use of a small ante-room beside the west guardroom. Lady Jane was not long in appearing. She waited until the door was closed and they were alone before she said, 'I understand your visit is solely to see me, Your Grace. Yet this room is not your usual style.'

'Sit down, lady,' he said harshly, indicating the window seat. 'And if you value your life don't jest with me. You probably guess the reason for my visit, so prepare your answers well.'

She feigned shock, her eyes flashing with the combination of mischief and aloofness which made them so hard to read. In a plain black velvet dress which made her skin glow the whiter, she looked bewitchingly beautiful. 'You have not asked any questions yet, my lord.'

'You have heard of the happenings at Castle Drummond?'

'I have.'

'Is that all you have to say?'

'I can express my false sympathy, if you wish it.'

He fingered the jewelled belt round his tunic. 'Be careful, my lady, don't drive me too far. Have you been in any way concerned with these misdeeds?'

She looked up at him haughtily as he stood over her. 'Do you take me for a fool?' she snapped. 'Would I admit it, if I had? You can find nothing to implicate me, for the news surprised me as much as it must have surprised yourself. But admittedly our reactions would be different.'

He took hold of her arms roughly, gripping tight through the velvet. 'Do you swear to me, Jane Kennedy, that you have not been involved in any of this evil?'

'James, you're hurting my arms,' she protested.

'Answer me, lady, before I break them in two,' he raged, beginning to shake her to and fro.

'My lord! James! Release me!' she cried out, struggling.

His grip tightened. 'I'll not release you until you've answered every question I have to ask.'

Judging the full magnitude of his fury she ceased trying to break free. Instead, she met his glaring gaze as she said, 'Be sensible, how could I, or any agent of mine, have gained access to the kitchens of Castle Drummond, without providing some clue which by now you would have wrested from somebody or other?'

'Perhaps I have wrested that clue.'

'Then it's false, for my conscience is clear.'

'Yet you seem to know all about the fiendish crime.'

Again she tried to break free, but he held her even tighter. 'No more than the rest of Scotland. Royal news travels fast, James. You know that well enough.'

'The last time I saw you did you not speak of not gaining your way whilst Margaret Drummond was alive?'

Jane now realised her danger. She had roused this man to passion before, but this was different. She judged him capable of killing her within this room and wondered if she ought to scream for help.

'Did you not?' pressed James, shaking her roughly.

'My lord ... my lord, how can I answer you when you shake me like a dog shaking a rat?'

He forced her back against the chair, his grip now vice-like. 'Did you not speak of Margaret Drummond not living?' he repeated.

'Yes, James, I did. But they were empty words of anger,' she gasped, now desperately frightened.

'Words that could well cost you your life, Jane Kennedy, for if I find anything to implicate you, no matter how flimsy, you'll burn on a stake. That I do swear.' He said this with his eyes blazing into her, forcing her against the chair so that its woodwork dug into her flesh through her robe. She had no doubt that at that moment he meant every word he uttered.

'I have said my conscience is clear. Do you think me capable of triple murder? If I had anything to do with this evil, it would have been planned for one, not three.'

'You could well have planned it for one, that the three ate breakfast together was not usual.'

Again she realised her mistake, and the pain inflicted upon her almost brought tears to her eyes. 'James, I swear by all that's holy that neither my hand, nor my mind, had anything to do with what so inflames you.'

He lifted her bodily by the arms, so that their faces almost touched. 'Is that the Gospel truth?'

'The Gospel truth, my lord. May the Holy Mother of God be my witness.'

He dumped her back on the chair, glaring wildly, then said, 'You'll bear the marks of my rough usage for several days. Let them be a reminder of your fate if your testimony proves false.'

Without seeking anyone else, he strode off to the courtyard, where Lucan waited with their horses.

'Have you found out anything, Lucan?'

'Nothing, Your Grace.'

Without further words they mounted and rode away. As soon as they arrived back in Edinburgh James ordered Lucan to ride to Castle Drummond, where Lord Fleming had been commanded to stay. Lucan's orders were to bring him back personally, limp across the saddle, if necessary.

Lucan had obviously given Lord Fleming a rough ride to Edinburgh, for he arrived dishevelled, thin face drawn and small eyes furtive. James gave him no time to collect himself, but sat him in his private chamber and interrogated him immediately.

'Your marriage to Lady Euphemie Drummond turned out not to your liking, my lord Fleming?' he queried.

A visible tremor ran through the nobleman's slight body. He was patently frightened of the King. 'No worse than many other marriages, Your Grace.'

'But it ended in acrimony on both sides?' pressed James.

'I bore Euphemie no ill-will.'

'That is contrary to what I have been told.'

Alarm suffused Fleming's weasel-like features. He was fully aware of the urgency of the royal summons and having been roughly handled once at Castle Drummond in public, reckoned that he might fare worse in private.

James surveyed him with disgust, but held his hand for only one reason. He could not be sure whether Fleming knew of his secret marriage. Euphemie, of course, had known. But the rift between her and her husband had occurred beforehand. Even so, Fleming could still have been told or learnt the truth from Drummond sources. If he possessed the information, then there could be danger in alienating him too readily.

'Well, my lord? You do well to consider your words, for I want nothing but the truth.'

'I understand that my wife didn't approve of my conduct and that she made this generally known at Castle Drummond.'

'And you didn't approve of that?'

Fleming licked at his dry lips, realising the reason behind the question. 'Not to the extent to wish her harm, Your Grace.'

James moved towards him. 'Are you sure of that, Fleming? Remember my sources of information are extensive. I've questioned every servant at Castle Drummond personally. There are several who spoke of heated disagreement between Euphemie and yourself.'

Fleming appeared to be shrinking in the chair, the fear in his eyes like that of a trapped animal. 'I don't deny that we could have been heard shouting at each other,' he admitted. 'But that could be said of many married couples, particularly when another woman was involved.'

'In your case, other women, so I am told.'

'I don't deny that either, Your Grace.'

'Or that Euphemie blighted your reputation to at least one of those women?'

'She had a vicious tongue, as you too must know, for she once told me of an encounter with Your Grace.'

'So she had a tongue you wanted to silence?' charged James, advancing closer.

Fleming raised his sunken body in the chair. 'Not in the way you're suggesting,' he countered, with a brief show of courage. 'I had the greatest respect for Lady Margaret and her sister Sibbie.'

'But you were not to know that on that fateful morning Euphemie would share her breakfast with her two sisters.'

Fleming moved to stand, but James pushed him back on the chair. 'Is there anything else you know other than what you've told me?'

'Nothing, Your Grace.'

'Did you have any hand at all in this murderous affair?'

'None, Your Grace. I swear it.'

'Did you approach any agent concerning silencing your wife's tongue in any way whatsoever?'

Again Fleming tried desperately to display some spirit. 'I find that suggestion offensive to my chivalric honour.'

'Then what do you think of this?' With a quick movement, James reached to the wall stand and withdrew a long thin sword from its scabbard. Before Fleming could move he pressed him back in the chair, then put the sword point on the flesh of his throat. The nobleman's eyes protruded and his small teeth visibly clamped together in a manner which hideously twisted his mouth.

'Is every word you have spoken the absolute truth?' James ground out.

'The . . . the . . . abso . . . absolute truth, Your . . . Your Grace.'

James stood away from him, holding the sword at arm's length, wiggling it so that the point nicked Fleming's thin drawn throat. 'Then mark these words, my lord Fleming. If I ever find any proof that any of your utterances here are false. I shall personally hack the living breath out of your body in any way I choose. Do you understand that?'

Fleming touched at his throat and felt a trickle of blood. 'Per . . . per . . . perfectly, Your Grace.'

'There's nothing you wish to change?'

'Nothing, Your Grace.'

'And you swear by Almighty God that you've told me the whole truth?'

'I swear by . . . by Almighty God and . . . and on my honour as a knight.'

Taking a final look at the craven figure, James lowered the sword and realising the futility of pursuing the interrogation any further snapped, 'I hope you know the meaning of truth, my lord. Now leave me before my doubts get the better of me.'

Alone, James sank into the chair Fleming had so ungraciously occupied, but the nobleman was already out of his thoughts. He was still no nearer a solution to the mystery he had pledged himself to resolve. Even this seemed to be falling into the main pattern of his life, nothing ever coming to a satisfying fruition, always a factor to irk him and deny happiness. He could not see where it was possible to purposefully pursue his inquiries further, but the matter was not over. Solving it, caring for Lady Margaret his daughter and settling with England, now became the main objectives of his life. Perhaps those accursed astronomers were right after all. He was destined never to be a happy man, much less a happy king.

The following morning he commanded that the three sisters be laid to rest before the High Altar of Dunblane Cathedral, the position of the vault marked by three magnificent blue marble stones. He arranged for Masses to be sung daily for Margaret, but none of this deadened the sharp-pointed pain of deep-seated inconsolable loss. Coupled with it was the gnawing frustration that the wickedness of the murders remained unavenged. It seemed that even Almighty God had deserted him.

After the Requiem Mass at Dunblane James paid his respects to Lord and Lady Drummond and their remaining family at the cathedral door. He surveyed the common folk who had gathered for a glimpse of him, and as he did so his eyes welled with tears. The Earl of Bothwell stood behind him on one side, Lucan Fairfax on the other. Although neither had been told, James suspected that both knew the true significance of what he was experiencing. Lucan, in particular, could not hide his grief during the obsequies. He obviously could not have felt stronger had Margaret been of his own family, even his own wife. Observing this made James think how much easier his body squire could have married Margaret and perhaps brought happiness to them both.

'As ever the folk of Scotland come to support you, Your Grace, even in your grief,' whispered Bothwell.

'So I see,' murmured James, looking around the upturned faces of those good folk who acknowledged him as their King, but knew so little of the life of intrigue he was forced to lead. If on their birthday the tiny bodies of Lucan and himself had been put in the wrong creches, he could have been amongst that crowd looking up at Lucan as King. He would never know how perhaps Lucan had thought the same in relation to Lady Margaret Drummond. She was indeed a lady Lucan could have loved and married, and even now could be thinking that had he done so, she would not be lying cold under that blue marble stone.

122

James acknowledged the murmur of sympathy from the crowd with a wave of his hand. As he did so most of the women genuflected and he sensed that they wished him well. The magnitude and full implications suddenly rose and gripped tight at his throat as another searing thought obsessed him. Seeing the manifest sympathy of the people aggravated the thought that had he been stronger, he could have defied his Council and openly declared Margaret as his Queen. At that moment he felt sure that they would have supported him, in spite of any dissension from noblemen.

'Lady Margaret was loved by all who knew her, Your Grace,' observed Lucan.

'None more so than by yourself, Lucan,' said the King.

He was still scanning the crowd, so did not see the suffusion of colour that flooded over Lucan's fair-skinned pinky features. The King's thoughts were now centred on what could have been had he acted more courageously. But it was too late. Margaret was dead and buried, her murderer still at large, another example of his bad leadership. He was the type of general who promised much, but achieved nothing.

These were the thoughts that riddled his mind during the ensuing months. Every morning and every night he made a ritual of seeing his daughter; he would gallop off anywhere to investigate any possible clue likely to reveal her mother's murderer, but he had heart for little else. Neither did he seek any solace from Jane Kennedy. He felt that inwardly he had been turned to stone. Lucan was his constant companion, and of his Council, only Bothwell had any close association with him.

Wisely, the Council left it to Bothwell to revive the King's participation in the negotiations for the marriage match with England. At last the day came when Bothwell considered it opportune to present the King with the draft marriage document He did so in the King's private chamber where he had been such a regular visitor. Laying it on the table he said, 'It is ready for your signature, Your Grace.'

'So, Patrick,' murmured James, glancing at the impressive-looking document, 'It matters not whom I wed now. I might as well please my Councillors.'

'It will be in the interest of peace for our beloved Scotland, Your Grace. I know that is a cause dear to your heart.'

'I fear nothing touches my heart any longer, Patrick. It lies a dead organ within me, as cold as that slab of blue marble at Dunblane.'

'Time will heal the pain, Your Grace,' assured Bothwell, proffering the inkhorn and quill. James hesitated, then tried to scratch away useless memories with bold strokes of the protesting quill point. 'So that settles it, Patrick; while I have grieved, you and my Council have wed me off to England.'

'We've acted only for the good of Scotland, Your Grace.'

'That's right, for the good of Scotland,' muttered James. 'Apart from Lady Margaret, my daughter, there's not much other purpose left in my life. I've not even been able to find that accursed murderer.' He straightened up from the table, dewy-eyed, but determination re-animating his features. 'Say no more of it, Patrick. You go as my ambassador to England, with the Archbishop of Glasgow and the elect Bishop of Moray. You can also represent Scotland at the wedding celebrations of the Prince of Wales to Princess Katherine of Aragon. I leave the arrangements in your hands. Take with you whom you think will give good account of Scotland, and you have the power to contract the marriage *per verba de presenti*. It will be a happy day for you, Patrick. This match has long been your wish, now you can do your bidding without disfavour, but I feel sure you know how much I wish it were another.'

'That may be so, Your Grace. But there are many reasons why you will never regret this union.'

'I hope you are right, for the sake of my Council. You've plagued me long enough for its execution.' James suddenly covered his face with his hands and cried out, 'By all that's holy, I wish that I too had eaten of that foul poison!'

'You have much good life ahead, Your Grace,' consoled Bothwell. 'And Scotland will always remember you for the greatness of this decision.'

James slowly raised his head. 'I have a yearning for the sea, Patrick. When you depart I'll summon Sir Andrew Wood; perhaps the feel of sea spray on my face will wash away the heaviness that torments me. Had it been possible, I would have gone with the two ships we sent to my Uncle Hans of Denmark to aid him against the Swedish rebels.'

Bothwell nodded his dark-haired head understandingly as he blew away the sand over the signature. After rolling the document he patted the King's shoulder with instinctive sympathy, without thought of rank. 'Your Grace is bound to feel restless, but soon there will be much to divert your mind.'

'That is little comfort now.' James stood up and walked to the door with him. Then with a tight smile said, 'God speed your return home, Patrick.'

Alone in the chamber, James went to the window as the sun broke through an overcast sky. He threw open the shutters and inhaled the earthy smell of the countryside. A sudden infusion of life inspired the need of fresh air and the freedom of a wild gallop. He rushed out of the chamber, yelling for his squire to order fast horses.

When Lucan saw his face he knew that he would be hard pressed to keep abreast of his master. He also recognised that the pangs of grief were receding. He too had reconciled himself to the knowledge that life had to go on, even though reminders of the grave regularly occurred to make mortals more keenly aware of their own mortality. But they could not remain in that state, for there was no bridge across the gulf between the life of the living and the unknown life of the dead. Thankfully, the King had emerged from his trauma ready to live again. But he as much as anyone else knew that his master's heart was not in cementing any bond with England either by marriage or any other way. What Lucan did not know, was how his own life would be transformed by the Earl of Bothwell's negotiations in England.

NINE

James soon received information that the Earl of Bothwell, the Archbishop of Glasgow and the Bishop of Moray were in London for the joyous reception of Princess Katharine of Aragon for her marriage to the Prince of Wales. During the comings and goings of messengers he stayed at Edinburgh, watching over his daughter, still vigilant for any evidence which might in the remotest way provide a clue as to the identity of her mother's murderer.

Sir Andrew Wood had promised him a voyage, but more pressing was the finalising of the proxy marriage. As with all matters relating to Henry of England, infinite precision concerning money could not be avoided. Three treaties were being drawn up at the same time, and every clause of the marriage settlement had its conditions. Each one had to be studied in detail to avoid being disadvantaged.

As a result, the treaties were not signed until the following January, then with the signatures barely dry, Bothwell used his granted powers to plight the troth of his sovereign lord, James, King of Scotland. This done, James could let matters rest for the time being. He had until September of the following year before he need claim the bride in which he had no interest other than political expediency.

The exchange of the ratifications were delayed by the sudden death of the Prince of Wales, and it was autumn before Captain Andrew Barton presented himself at Edinburgh Castle.

James received the tall, dark-bearded sailor warmly. Looking into his clear blue eyes he asked, 'What have you in store for me, Captain Andrew?'

Having been briefed by Sir Andrew Wood only to the extent that the King wished to go on a voyage, Captain Barton was unsure of his mission. 'I've a ship at Leith ready to set sail as soon as Your Grace wishes.'

'Will tomorrow's forenoon suit you?' asked the King.

This took Barton by surprise, 'Ay, we could leave on the high tide, but the ship's yet to be fitted to accommodate Your Grace. I doubt if it could be done properly by then.'

James smiled at the sailor's embarrassment. 'Then we'll leave on the high tide, Captain Andrew. I want no special fittings. I shall sail with you as one of your crew. Once aboard your ship you will be the captain. Take me where you please, order me as you please.'

Barton stared at him in open-mouthed astonishment, speechless.

'I repeat, once aboard the ship you will be the captain,' said James, smiling at his dilemma. 'Until then I am the King and you've heard my orders. I seek no privileges or special treatment. I want to sail as an able-bodied seaman.'

'It's a rough life,' ventured Barton.

'That's what I want, the rougher the better. Perhaps I can prove to your men that their King is not a weakling.'

Barton nodded with approval, but still somewhat mystified.

'What would your mission be if I were not sailing with you, Captain?'

'Scouring Scottish waters for pirates, Your Grace.'

'Then that's what we'll do, and if we find any pirates, you can engage them in your normal manner.'

'If that's what Your Grace wishes.'

'Yes, it is, Captain. Send a messenger with the time you want me and I'll come to the harbour unheralded.'

Again Barton stared at him in near disbelief, but when assured, left to prepare his ship for a normal mission.

Good to his word James entered into the spirit of the voyage, insisting on mixing freely with all on board. He joined with the sailors in hoisting and rolling sails, coiling heavy ropes, raising chains, anything which provided a challenge to his strong, lithe body. He soon won the admiration of the entire crew, and the healthy open air life proved to be the right balm for the open wounds of his earlier shattered hopes. At night he sang songs with the crew, delighting in the feel of spray on his face and the broad canopy of the starlit sky at night.

When he was about to leave the crew gathered around him and Captain Barton.

'I've never seen this bunch of roughnecks take so readily to any other man,' said Barton. 'It has been a wonderful experience for them and for me.'

'Even better for me, Captain Andrew,' said James, wringing his hand.

He waved to the crew as he stood at the top of the gangplank. Without any prompting they cheered in unison, with such enthusiasm that James was noticeably touched.

'You need never have any fear of the loyalty of a single manjack of this ship's crew, Your Grace,' Barton assured him.

'Good,' replied James. 'I hope we can all be shipmates again in the future. Perhaps next time we'll find some pirates. But now I must return to my soft life and a child bride.'

'Although I don't envy you, I say God be with you, Your Grace. And remember that anything my brothers and I can do for Scotland and your royal person, we'll do so with all the strength at our command.'

'Start by capturing as many pirates as you can who enter our waters,' said James, moving off down the gangplank.

'That we'll do, won't we, lads?' shouted Barton.

He was answered by another rousing cheer that guaranteed future loyalty. That night many in Edinburgh heard of the King's exploits as a sailor; it added to the high opinion Edinburgh folk already had of him. Many of them remembered how he had braved the blizzard and snows to bring aid to them.

Back at the castle James learned that the Earl of Bothwell had arrived back from England only that afternoon to consult him on recent developments. Bothwell would not have travelled himself without there being some urgency, so he was seen at once. After telling him of his invigorating experience at sea, James asked, 'What brings you back to Scotland, Patrick?'

They were seated comfortably in the King's private chamber, drinking malmsey together. 'I thought I ought to report to you personally, Your Grace. The death of Queen Elizabeth, your contracted bride's mother, has had remarkable repercussions. King Henry has now lost an heir and his wife since our negotiations started in earnest.'

James nodded, mind actively sifting the possibilities. 'The chief one being that the Princess Royal of England is now closer to accession to the English throne,' he observed.

'Which is causing concern in many English quarters, manoeuvring for power advantage, Your Grace.'

'I can well imagine it, Patrick. Should she succeed to the throne, then I would be well placed for controlling England.'

'That's the reasoning of the objectors, Your Grace.'

'You told me earlier that King Henry argued that in such circum-

128

stances, Scotland being the smaller, it would become an accession to England, not the reverse.'

'That was his reasoning, Your Grace.'

'But these recent deaths have robbed it of much of its potency?'

'That is so, Your Grace. Furthermore, the young Prince Henry, encouraged by his tutor Skelton, has made it publicly known that he is now opposed to his sister becoming Queen of Scotland.'

'Has he, the sprightly young cock,' quipped James, raising his eyebrows.

'He did this before the Court attended by several foreign envoys, much to his royal father's displeasure.'

James whistled. 'Then that whelp needs to be taught a Scottish lesson or two.'

Bothwell added, 'King Henry's suffered further displeasure, for owing to a strong speech by the young Thomas More, the English Parliament has refused to grant a subsidy for your bride's dowry.'

'So King Henry has to dig into his own coffers?'

'For ten thousand pounds,' Patrick informed him.

James laughed. 'That will grieve the old skinflint.'

'Especially as there's talk of a possible restitution of the dowry brought to England by the widowed Princess Katharine,' Patrick added.

Again James chuckled; it was good to know that other kings had their problems. 'So these are sorry times for one so concerned with the acquisition of money?'

Bothwell nodded, face grave, as he said, 'From all reports, he's never forgotten the poverty of his youth in exile.'

'You seem to have some sympathy for him, Patrick.'

'For his past plight, if not for him, Your Grace.'

James leaned back and drained his glass demonstratively. He looked across at his chief councillor and said, 'It seems to me that it is time the King of Scotland made a positive move. You plan returning to England, Patrick?'

'When Your Grace pleases.'

'Then we'll make it tomorrow. I'll sleep on what you've imparted, so that tomorrow I can despatch you with fresh instructions and demands. That voyage has cleared my head. I must claim my bride, whatever Prince Henry thinks. Scotland's future must be settled by my begetting legitimate heirs. You can breakfast with me tomorrow forenoon and I will give you my instructions to take straight back to England.'

Bothwell rose and went to his own quarters, leaving James to ponder on how best he could impose his own stamp on the reported situation. He lost little sleep over it and next morning gave Bothwell precise orders. 'I've decided that I can't wait until the stipulated date for Princess Margaret to be conveyed to my kingdom. You are to inform King Henry that he must make arrangements for her to be brought to Scotland without further delay.'

Patrick smiled at this characteristic rashness. 'That should settle some of the arguments, Your Grace.'

'That's what I reckoned. You stay in England until you are sure the Princess and her entourage are under way. Spare no pain to let them know that any unnecessary delay could adversely affect my interest in the marriage.'

'It will be as you say, Your Grace. I will enjoy this mission far better than some others I've had to England.'

James rose and patted him on the shoulder, recognising that Bothwell appreciated the motive behind his decision. It was Scotland's future that mattered. King Henry would have to sort out the English malcontents the best way he could.

The Earl of Bothwell carried out his mission well, for James soon heard of the getting together of an impressive procession to be headed by none other than the Earl of Surrey himself. So, thought James, he was to meet face to face with the man who had challenged him to single combat, a fearless soldier who neither gave nor expected any quarter in battle. Surrey's name was generally feared among Scottish border troops. They knew him as one who fought loyally for the crown of England, whether its wearer were Yorkist or Lancastrian. Such a meeting was something to look forward to, more a test of his manliness than the necessary attendance on a near-child bride.

News of the approach of the English Princess reached James daily. When she left Berwick he sent her a gift of fresh fruits, then, after she spent the night at the rocky fortress of Fastcastle, despatched another messenger asking her to rest at Dalkeith castle and await his instructions. This put him in the position of the final positive move being of his choosing. He had come to the point of no return. All the past counted for nothing, only the future mattered.

He was marrying for the benefit of Scotland and wanted nothing from an English bride other than that she eventually became a suitable royal mother for a future king. But she had not yet celebrated her fourteenth birthday. Such was the thought he took with him when he finally decided to ride unannounced to Dalkeith for his first glimpse of her, the Princess whose name had been linked with his since her birth; the union of the thistle and the rose, or, in England, the rose and the thistle. It was the long-sought aim of so many Councillors on both sides of the border.

Everyone in the castle at Dalkeith had turned out between the two gateways of the quadrangle to welcome the royal contingent. James timed his arrival so that he rode into the courtyard in the midst of the stabling of the horses of the English procession. He did it deliberately, setting his personal stamp on the proceedings. Surprised stewards and chamberlains were stirred from their planned routines as they first recognised him dressed informally, then had to alert the rest of the castle staff to announce his arrival. It was the last thing they expected.

After several seconds of sweating and fuming by liveried men, the doors of the Great Chamber opened and before him stood the mother of his future sons. She was small, but not daintily so; with long fair hair hung loose as a symbol of her virginity, face childishly pretty above a cloth of gold gown. He paid her full respect with a deep, courteous reverence and noted the dignity of her response.

The tall, commanding figure beside her he recognised by description as the Earl of Surrey, the stature of a soldier, a sardonic twist to his harsh-featured face. James acknowledged him with undisguised friendliness, anticipating that he would have more in common with him than the lass. Even so, he did not neglect his knightly duties to a royal Princess. 'Welcome to the fair land of Scotland, madam,' he greeted.

Again she responded with punctilious correctness, wooden, face unsmiling, inwardly scared no doubt. 'My lord King, I am honoured by your speedy visit,' she replied.

He felt the desire to put her at ease, an adult's natural sympathy for a child's embarrassment. He took her hand, kissed it and smiled reassuringly. 'I could wait no longer to acquaint myself with your fair person,' he explained.

'My wish is to please Your Grace at all times,' she replied. Her smile relieved the tension from her lips, so that her small white teeth flashed attractively.

'I pay the same honour to you, madam,' he responded gallantly.

They conversed inconsequentially until called for supper. He took her by the hand and led her to the silver chalices in which they washed their hands with great solemnity, then they sat at table together. The Earl of Morton's splendidly equipped serving men filled the table with a tempting array of delicacies. James sampled each dish before recommending it to his future Queen.

After supper, the minstrels struck up their music to dancing tempo. He encouraged Margaret to participate in two basse dances accompanied by her aunt, Lady Surrey. She performed well, and when he bade his adieu he kissed her hand and said, 'I have been delighted by your fair company, madam, and the entertainment you have provided.'

Colour flooded to her face and with it an embarrassed childish smile. 'It is I who have been honoured, my lord King,' she almost whispered.

He rode slowly back to Edinburgh, the cool night air fresh on his face after the heat of the day, stars glittering like diamonds set in indigo velvet. Ironically, he had enjoyed the visit in the same manner as when with Lady Margaret, his daughter, a warming effect that came from association with pleasant children. But this Margaret was his bride, not the daughter of the same name presented to him by a mother of the same name, whom he married in secret but failed to make his Queen. Little Lady Margaret Stuart would never be a princess of royal birth now, but the Margaret he had just left would soon be indisputably Queen of Scotland. What did he know of her? That she could dance with light-footed grace and had a natural love of music; a starting point, at least.

In the middle of the night, James awoke to a rough shaking by Lucan. He sat up quickly, pulling a robe de chambre over his bare chest and flinging the bed curtains aside.

'A messenger has arrived from Dalkeith, Your Grace. The stables there have been ablaze with fire.'

'And the Princess?' queried James urgently.

'Safe, Your Grace. The fire was quenched before it spread from the stable.'

'Thank God for that!' exclaimed James, leaping from the bed. 'How is my betrothed and her party?'

'The ladies are sore distressed by the commotion.'

'Ay, they would be. They must be moved from there to Newbattle. Lucan, carry that order to Dalkeith, find out what you can, then return at once with the Earl of Morton.'

Left alone, James's mind immediately returned to the unsolved mystery of his beloved's death. Could this be another attempt to rob him of a queen? If so, it narrowed the field of suspicion. Only Jane Kennedy could have any real motive for trying to burn the unchurched Queen of Scotland in her bed!

Morton arrived incoherent with grief, ageing eyes still watering from the speed of the night ride. James received him in his private chamber, where wine and voides were set out on the table. He invited the Earl to partake and noticed the trembling of his hands. He allowed him time to gather his breath and sip several times from the silver goblet before he said, 'I sent for you, my lord, that I might hear of this unfortunate occurrence from your own lips. In that way calumny and rumour can be avoided. My body squire assures me that the English Princess has come to no harm.'

Morton nodded gratefully. 'That mercifully is so, Your Grace,' he confirmed. 'I went to the royal lady's bedchamber myself, and amid the whisperings of her half-clad, jabbering attendants, assured her that no danger would come to her. The fire was then well under control, and shortly afterwards, totally extinguished.'

Smiling at the mental picture evoked by the Earl's words, James asked, 'How were your commiserations accepted?'

'In a startled manner, Your Grace. The royal lady's eyes were wide and alarmed, like those of a child confronted by an unknown horror. When calmed, she asked how the fire started.'

'How did it start?' pressed James.

Morton took another sip of wine and flexed his stiff legs. 'Due to the carelessness of a young lad in the stables, Your Grace. He left a lantern burning beside a pile of dry straw.'

'And the lad, you know his background?'

'Yes, he's been in my service since birth, his father one of my most reliable grooms.'

'Then you suspect no evil intention?'

'No, Your Grace, though I've made thorough inquiries. There's no evidence to rate it anything other than an unfortunate accident.'

James rose and pulled at his red and gold quartered short jacket. 'Good, but I too shall see the lad. How did you leave my future queen?'

The Earl wrung his bony hands in anguish. 'I craved her forbearance for the unhappy night spent within my walls. But she was grievous upset about the loss of her white palfrey,' said Morton.

'Her palfrey?'

'A gift from her royal father, and the one upon which she learned to ride,' Morton explained. 'But it perished with all the other horses in the stables. We had to sacrifice them to prevent the flames spreading to the castle.'

James nodded understandingly. 'When you return tell her the loss will be well replaced. Are arrangements in hand for her to be moved to Newbattle?'

'They are, Your Grace.'

'Then you can say that I shall attend her there.'

Morton rose and bowed. 'Once again, Your Grace, I offer my humblest apologies,' he said, with an abjection made more pathetic by his advancing years.

James patted his shoulder and smiled. 'If all is as you say, no lasting harm's been done. It would seem you acted with commendable swiftness for the English party's safety, my lord.'

Uplifted by these words, the Earl departed.

James immediately summoned Lucan. 'Did you see this stable lad?' he asked.

'I did, Your Grace.'

'What did you make of him?'

'He seemed an honest enough lad.'

'No evidence of any scheming?'

'I judged it to be nothing but an accident, Your Grace.'

'Did you ask if Lady Kennedy had been near Dalkeith?'

Lucan's clear blue eyes met those of his master and he decided to speak his mind. 'It was my first thought, Your Grace, but it proved a suspicion unfounded.'

'Then perhaps our fears of that concern are without foundation?'

'Perhaps, but it doesn't dispense the need to be careful.'

James accepted the warning with a tight smile, then when Lucan went back to bed decided that his page's loyal service would be rewarded with a knighthood as part of the forthcoming wedding celebrations. This would please him, but not nearly so much as it would excite his mother and father.

Having announced his intention of riding to Newbattle, James left Dalkeith and went by a devious path so that he could again arrive unheralded. He found his future Queen at cards with Lady Surrey, more to pass the time than out of interest, for she quickly threw down the cards and rose to greet him. 'Your Grace, why do you arrive unattended?' she asked, with a frown of suspicion. 'My lord Surrey has ridden out with a party to greet you.'

'I took a fresh path that I might arrive without ceremony. I've heard of your ordeal at Dalkeith and it caused me great concern. Please accept my heartfelt apologies.'

Her eyes bored into him, discerning, no longer childlike, and the cut of her red velvet gown trimmed with gold accentuated the blossoming womanliness of her figure. He saw her as an enigmatic mixture of child and woman, not exactly an oddity, and certainly not without attraction. After furthering his apologies for her disturbed night, the welcoming party returned from their fruitless journey.

James greeted the noblemen with such good cheer that they soon forgot any resentment they might have felt. He paid particular attention to the Earl of Surrey, who confessed that most of the men rode with him to escape the tongues of the ladies, still prattling about the fire.

Minstrels then appeared and an English jester performed a lively set of mumming. James warmly applauded, and when the music struck up again, urged his bride to entertain him with a dance.

He noticed her flush of pleasure, so that when she finished, he applauded the loudest. Inspired by this, she led another dance, this time with Lord Gray. They were followed by many lords and ladies, but James noticed without bias that Margaret's performance possessed an unrivalled fleetness of foot and sense of rhythm.

He served her with wine himself, then played the lute, and afterwards, the clavichord. As he strummed the strings he recognised her innate love of music. It uplifted her, drove away all the petulant suspicion with which she had greeted him.

When he rose to go she looked completely at ease, her earlier white face flushed with the colour of enjoyment, and she allowed him to kiss her, responding in a manner that even suggested more desire than duty. 'My lord, after the trials of last night, your visit today has brought me much comfort,' she confirmed, eyes shining with happy gratitude.

'Thus may it always be, sweet Margaret.' As he spoke a vision of Meg, another sweet Margaret, flashed across his mind. Its effect was like a sudden blow. It had to be absorbed before he could continue normally. This caused a brief hesitation and a slight change of expression, but when he controlled himself he noticed that his bride, if none other, had detected the momentary lapse in his concentration. It made him further aware of her extreme sensitivity to anything just slightly out of the ordinary or unusual. He sensed too that it would be hard to keep secrets from her. He had, in fact, discovered the quality which was to prompt all the women who later served her to name her 'Madam Ferret'.

In that brief instance her reaction made James wonder what she knew of him. No doubt the English envoys to Scotland had taken back ample gossip and rumour. Perhaps she already knew about Margaret Drummond. If she did, nothing could be done about it. He had loved Meg and would never truly love another woman for the rest of his life. If his Queen knew this truth earlier than he had expected her to find out, what difference did it make? It should help rid her young head of any illusions, make her understand the duties of royal birth, how her father had sacrificed her to become Queen of Scotland in the cause of peace. In this role he could have sympathy and respect for her, if not deep and lasting love.

He squeezed both her hands, then bowed and strode away. Although only a brief episode, probably unobserved by others, it left its effects. It was as if the lass had seen the possibility of genuine happiness emerging from filial duty, then in a flash of intuition it disappeared, and with it her smile and the return of the petulant twist to her mouth. A royal drama, enacted by royal principals, which only a royal audience could discern and understand. But he would make her life as tolerable as possible. Her main duty to him would be to produce sons.

Realising Margaret's unenviable plight as a victim of a treaty, James decided that her entry into Edinburgh would be truly memorable, a day upon which she could look back in future years with the pride of being fully recognised as Queen of Scotland. Bothwell had given him the details of Princess Katharine's grand entry into London, and he wanted to show that Scotland could not only equal but surpass any English splendour.

He started the day by sending two palfreys to Dalkeith, compensating for the loss of her favourite. They were equipped in shining new harness and ready to accompany her on the journey to Edinburgh. Soon after her party moved off from the castle along the detailed route, James rode to greet her. He approached at speed, reined in his horse abruptly, bowed with deep reverence, then leapt from the saddle and went to her litter. She looked far more like a woman than a child in a richly-ornamented gable head-dress, cloth of gold gown and black velvet purfle.

'Madam, you look in every way fit to be crowned a queen,' he greeted.

He judged her smile as too set to be natural, but prided himself that his arrangements would appeal to the child in her and thaw out any iciness.

Leaving the litter with a jaunty salute, he leapt on to his horse without using the stirrups, then took his place beside the litter and rode along talking to her gaily, while a gentleman-usher preceded him bearing the unsheathed Sword of State.

Before they entered the city, another gentleman rode out with a fair courser trapped in cloth of gold. James rode up to him, dismounted from his own horse, inspected the courser, then, with another spectacular leap, mounted it and tried its paces. He reined sharply, bade one of the gentlemen ride pillion with him in the manner of a lady, testing the horse's ability to bear his Queen and himself into the city.

He could see Margaret leaning forward in the litter, her confidence growing as he emphasised to all that no efforts for her comfort must be considered too much trouble. After several trial runs he returned and said, 'The courser's unaccustomed to carrying the double load. It will be safer for us to ride on the more gentle palfrey.'

He motioned his attendants to assist her into the pillion position behind him. 'It's only a mile into Edinburgh,' he informed her, after being assured of her readiness. 'But there are many diversions for your entertainment on the way.'

'All has been wondrously devised, and none could be more solicitous than Your Grace,' she approved. Following his example she raised her head high, and again he noted that she needed no prompting to act the role of Queen.

About half a mile from Edinburgh, they reached an expanse of green meadow and stopped beside a newly-erected pavilion. They watched two knights make play with sword and spear in a ballad altercation concerning a lady paramour. He watched Margaret's face out of the corner of his eye, and saw the slight tensing of her lips as she followed the gist of the play.

Vast throngs of people were in evidence as they neared the city. The murmur of their voices rose into the sky and seemed to hover, as if waiting to burst. Leaning back to her he said. 'Watch now, Margaret, as my capital city greets you loyally as its fair queen.'

Colour suffused her face, and as they entered the city gates, the English minstrels sounded their devoir and were answered by the Scottish musicians. The Earl of Bothwell, proud and erect, now bore the Sword of State. A group of Greyfriars came out in procession to greet them, a warden carrying the cross and some ancient holy relics for the King to kiss.

'You first, Margaret,' he insisted, then pointedly rode with his head uncovered as a mark of respect to her.

Across the entry into the city was a gate with two tourelles and a window in their midst. The tourelles contained representations of vested angels, sparkling white, singing with clear, stirring voices. An angel appeared in the middle window, then descended and presented Margaret with the keys of the city. Next came the procession of the College of the parish of St. Giles, a cooling breeze flapping their rich vestments as they carried a relic arm of their saint. The crowd cheered as once again James allowed his Queen to precede him in kissing the holy relic.

James sensed that the people of Edinburgh were undivided in acclaiming both his bride and himself. The same thought had occurred to him when he left Dunblane Cathedral, that if he had defied his Council and married his own choice of bride, the ordinary folk of the country would have accepted the decision. But that chapter of his life was past; this marriage now was for the good of those who cried his name with such warmth.

He held up his hand for silence; courtiers and people alike responded immediately. When all were still, he began to sing the *Te Deum Laudamus* in a rich tenor voice. The ecclesiastics joined with him, then gradually the strain was picked up by the fringe of the multitude thronging the streets; spreading through their ranks and rising to the houses, where lords and ladies, gentlemen and gentlewomen squeezed into every chink of available space. Soon the whole of Edinburgh seemed to be singing with him, and the experience so moved him that tears filled his eyes, the apotheosis of kingship. It took him several seconds to control his surge of emotion, wave to the crowd and receive its tumultuous acclamation, then urge Margaret's obedient palfrey forward.

A cross stood in the middle of the city, and near to it, much to the joy of the milling crowd of men, a fountain cascaded wine for all to drink. The good humour of the crowd bared strong white teeth against sun-tanned cheeks, and bibulous throats were lubricated for more lusty cheering. Nearby a scaffold supported a representation of Paris and the three goddesses, with Mercury, who gave Paris the apple of gold. On the same scaffold, another tableau presented the salutation of Gabriel to the Virgin, the figures white and glittering in the auspicious sunshine. Devices commingling the unicorn and the greyhound, the Stuart and Tudor heraldic beasts, could be seen everywhere, garlanded with the interlacing of thistles and red roses. Buntings, flags and huge banks of flowers splashed colour on every available space. Scotland gave good account of herself, impressing the young Queen and widening the King's smile of approval.

Moving out of town, thunderous voices of welcome came from all sides as they approached the Church of Holyrood. Jay, the King's brother, now the Archbishop of St. Andrews, came out to greet them with many other bishops and abbots, their radiant pontificals filling the scene with an eye-dazzling richness of colour.

James drew up at the entrance to the church and swung from the palfrey lithely. 'I'll lift the lady myself,' he said, waving aside the gathered attendants.

His hands almost spanned her waist as he lifted her with consummate ease, as if she were an infant wrapped in a surfeit of swaddling clothes. He noted the colouring which suffused her face as she became conscious of his nearness; it suggested more adult feelings than those of a child. 'You conduct yourself with true royal dignity, Margaret,' he whispered reassuringly.

Smiling, he led her into the church, where two gold cushions were positioned before the high altar. Another splendid array of colour followed as the noble Earls of Scotland came forward to pay reverence to the new Queen. Afterwards, James guided her through the cloisters to the Great Chamber of the Palace of Holyroodhouse, where a huge gathering of ladies waited to greet her. Glancing around, James saw all the beauty, wit and fashion of his kingdom. Many of the ladies might have superior beauty and intellect compared with his bride; most of them would have more experience in their affairs with men – capable of laughter, gaiety and nocturnal delights. Yet none could match her impeccable royal dignity as she stood alone.

Sensing her isolation, James moved to her side and said, 'Your poise befits the first lady of my realm, Margaret.'

The Bishop of Moray, her guide from England, came forward and presented all the ladies to her by name. James watched with amused interest, again noting how well she faced up to the most critical appraisal.

At the end of the ceremony, he kissed her and said, 'Performed like a true queen, my lady.' He then took her arm and escorted her to an inner chamber where she might rest. Having fulfilled his duty he too felt the need to relax. Although it was quite a strain trying to keep a virgin lass contented, he considered her response to his freely given encouragement amply repaid him. None could fault her so far.

As night descended on the city, the light of bonfires filled the sky with flickering tongues of redness. James watched from the window of his chamber, filled with love for his people, dwelling further on his thoughts of the afternoon, of what might have been but for some unknown murderer who had escaped both his retributive wrath and arbitrary justice.

After supper he danced with Margaret, then almost paternally urged her to retire early so that she would be fresh for the long, tiring rituals of tomorrow. He also retired, but with little personal hope in his heart, activated only by the desire that Scotland should show herself equal to anything that came from England. In spite of his marriage and its concomitant treaties, England remained the traditional 'auld enemy' to him, and he knew that most of his subjects would feel the same.

On the following morning, Lucan, who had not stopped beaming since learning that he was to become a knight, told him of some rumpus which occurred during the night concerning a squire bedding one of the Queen's English attendants. James dismissed it as inconsequential and breakfasted with hungry relish.

He felt quite emotional when Lucan's mother requested to see him, then wished his marriage good fortune and thanked him for the proposed elevation of her son. It was quite an unprecedented interview which caused Lucan considerable embarrassment, for he had tried to usher his mother away.

James mused over the scene as he changed into his wedding robe of white damask flowered with gold. In many ways he envied Lucan his close and uncomplicated family life. But now he had to prepare for the rituals expected of a king.

He had provided Margaret with a gown of the same cloth of gold materials as his own, also presented her with a magnificently jewelled gold crown and a collar of pearls. She came into the church with the Archbishop of York on her right, the Earl of Surrey on her left, the Countess of Surrey bearing her train. They were followed by a long procession of ladies made up of four in a row, two English and two Scottish.

The young bride looked diminutive and pale, but she had learnt a lot from her regal mother, for again her poise and bearing could not be faulted throughout the long ceremonies of the Nuptial Mass. Two prelates advanced towards them and held a Cloth of State over them as they knelt at the altar, the signal for a blast of trumpets to sound out the conclusion of the service.

As James led his now undisputed wife out of the church he saw Lady Jane Kennedy prominent among a group of ladies. Their eyes met for a mere fleeting glance, but they alone could have been aware of all the implications.

The full company did not gather together again until supper in the State Chamber hung with red and blue tapestries representing the history of Troy. The glass of one of the windows had been painted with the arms of Scotland and England bi-parted, the crown interleaved with a thistle and a rose. The Archbishops of St. Andrews and York dined at the royal table with much ceremony.

James noticed his bride's concern at the presence of the rich State bed in the shadowy outer fringe beyond the range of lanterns and candles. He tried to reassure her, serving her with all the dishes before them – boar's head, brawn and gambon. But she pecked at them like an overfed bird, nervous, fluttery, a trapped animal. Throughout the twelve dishes she remained restive, speaking only when spoken to, her alarmed blue eyes flashing furtively to and from the State bed. He felt sorry for her, but indulging such feelings made him feel more sorry for himself, so he talked too much and had his goblet filled too often.

After supper they adjourned to the Great Hall, where he ordered the minstrels to play and sing an epithalium composed in her honour:

'O far, fairest of every fair,
Princess most lovely and preclare,
The loveliest that on life there been,
Welcome in Scotland to be Queen.'

James watched her expression change as a soft medley of voices went on extolling her beauty and fitness to be Queen. At the end of the performance she clapped her small, white hands with delight, calling upon her chamberlain to reward the singers. She sat in a specially installed chair of State at his side, but the Earl of Surrey kept diverting him with talk of battle campaigns and jousting champions. When the company amused themselves with games of Passe-passe, James followed the ramifications with deep-throated guffaws of merriment, but Margaret found the game little to her liking, and became increasingly conscious of the ladies around them giggling and nudging each other.

Every time he looked at his bride, she deliberately concentrated her gaze elsewhere, a game of cat and mouse in progress. They had delayed over long, but in truth he had no more desire to lead her to the State bed than she to accompany him. Custom demanded, however, that the nuptials be concluded in the appropriate manner. So he rose, bowed, then took her hand and led her away, so that none of the Court ladies could smirkingly charge her with having failed in her marital duty.

Ironically, the way took him past Lady Kennedy's smugly supercilious gaze. He could feel her laughing at him, taunting him with the mockery of his royal marriage, that having known her lusty passion he now had to calm a child bride's fears.

In the ensuing days only two events brought any real cheer to James. Lucan Fairfax being created a knight on St. Lawrence's Day, together with forty other men designated as the Queen's knights. Then at the celebrative jousts, Lord Hamilton, his cousin, appeared in such immaculate array that the crowd received him with wild enthusiasm. In the ensuing contests, Lord Hamilton fought a spirited bout with the French knight, Anthony D'Arch de la Bastie. Both men fought with such vigour and determination that horses and men seemed to move together as integral parts of each other. Though neither combination triumphed, each fought with such dexterity that no subsequent bout, either on horse or foot, compared with the first. Gratified by his cousin's exemplary display, James granted him a patent creating him the Earl of Arran.

One disturbing figure lurked ubiquitously throughout the celebrations – Jane Kennedy. Those unforgettable blue-green eyes followed him everywhere, compelling him to be aware of her, mocking, tantalising, flaying him with her scrutiny. His young Queen obviously noticed this interchange of glances, yet this could not be the sole reason for her increasing petulance of manner.

As the English party began to return to their home country she became almost inconsolable with homesickness. The difficulties of the future soon began to evince themselves.

In spite of his patience and consideration she provided ample evidence of her virginity, so much so that he finally lost his temper and told her that his only interest in her body was for it to produce royal sons. Not surprisingly this produced an ocean of wailing tears. Such was the glorious union of the thistle and the rose for which his Council had so assiduously pleaded, which would bring such benefits to Scotland and, as he had suspected all along, would be the bane of the life of its King. Already in August 1503, before he need rightly to have claimed his bride, he was thinking of how best to blunt the thorns of his English rose.

TEN

On the day after the departure of the last of the English party, James summoned the Earls of Bothwell and Argyll into his withdrawing chamber, so that with Patrick Panther recording the details, they could plan a progress to show the Queen some of the beauties of Scotland. Apart from providing the opportunity of seeing the scenic splendour of his kingdom for the first time, he wanted her away from Edinburgh, for already she had started gleaning titbits of information from the palace staff. Tongues wagged freely enough at a royal Court without the spur of ears seeking information.

Above all, she had taken the strongest exception to the presence of Lady Margaret Stuart, the King's daughter. Even in this short time a bitter resentment had developed over the existence of the child, and the protective title by which she was freely known.

Glancing at the chart Panther had left spread on the table with his copious scribblings, James said, 'The Queen seems hard to please, my lords. She has the typically English approach to anything Scottish, that whatever we have there's something better in England. So although we intend showing her some of our lochs, mountains and heather-covered moorland, the Sheriffs of the areas through which we pass must be warned that she needs childish devices to amuse her. Yet she's more like a bitch coursing a hare when it comes to sniffing out my past. This is the child bride you of my Council considered so beneficial to Scotland, but what of me?'

'You must have patience in waiting for the Queen to blossom into full womanhood, Your Grace,' consoled Argyll.

'Patience!' echoed James, with an ironic laugh. 'My reign has been all patience – followed by disappointment. So far I've bedded once with a mournful bairn. What I want to know is, when can she be expected to bear me a son, and what do I do in the meantime?'

Argyll smiled archly, revealing his protruding front teeth. 'Your Grace has many admirers among the ladies of the Court.'

Frowning, James moved to the window, put one foot on the upholstered seat and rested an arm on his knee, looking out intently, as if seeking a solution in the scudding movement of thin clouds intermittently casting light and shadow across the first traces of autumnal colour. Although he loved the countryside, this soon exasperated him in his present mood, for he suddenly turned to the two noblemen. 'The Queen's already intent on thwarting any advances from Court ladies, and this morning complains that a whore-begat squire bedded one of her women, another bairn of thirteen. Surely there was some lusty Scottish wench who could have ridden him better?'

'The Queen's truly bred to her royal station, and I warrant she'll not fail you,' emphasised Bothwell.

Wearily, James returned to the chart-covered table, but they were joined by Sir Lucan Fairfax.

'Well, Lucan, what of this so-called bedding outrage?' asked James.

Lucan carried his knighthood well, its bestowal endearing him closer to his master, as well as elevating his station as the King's closest companion and confidant. There were now several other servants to perform the menial duties, and he had the governance of them all. Only Patrick Panther, the King's secretary, did not have to act through him.

'I have the details now, Your Grace,' said Lucan. 'The man was the Earl of Bothwell's body squire.'

'Ian Tavill?' queried Bothwell.

'The same, my lord,' nodded Lucan. 'Well flushed with wine distributed by His Grace on the eve of the wedding.'

James banged his fist on the table irritably, crinkling the chart. 'So flushed that he couldn't distinguish a half-weaned chit from a willing whore?'

The expression on Lucan's face changed, having expected the incident to be treated as a joke. 'He did not know she was one of the Queen's women, Your Grace. He's been in torment since learning the truth, for the mistress plagued him and not the reverse.'

'Then the wench got what she deserved?'

'It would seem so, Your Grace, and found it not much to her liking, for she leapt from his bed and ran off in the middle of the night.'

'Then there's an end to it,' snapped James, turning to the smiling Bothwell. 'I'll not be plagued by English brats who arouse Scottish passions, then can't stomach the consequences. Cuff him soundly, Patrick, and tell him to keep his eyes on Scottish lasses if he wants to enjoy his sporting. Now, Lucan, to the stables and have horses saddled for us. I've a mind to exercise the charger sent by King Henry of England, now my father-in law, by God! But first tell Panther we've finished with this chart.'

When James returned from an exhilarating canter in which Lucan participated with high-spirited rivalry, he was greeted by the Queen's chamberlain requesting that he visited her apartments. He went at once, bowed respectfully, but remained stern-faced.

'Thank you for answering my call so speedily, my lord King,' said Margaret formally, inviting him to be seated. 'You have received my message concerning Mistress Hampton?'

'Yes, madam, and I have come to end the blather about this lass,' he replied, staring hard at her as she sat before him on a high, draped chair.

'It grieves me to have my English servants so used,' she charged, meeting his gaze with calculated disdain.

'Your servant behaved as a whore and was treated as one, madam.'

This uncompromising retort surprised her. 'Then is the squire not to be punished?'

'The squire is no more to blame than the lass. Yet I have ordered his master to punish him.'

'In what way, my lord? Is he to be banished from Court?'

'For bedding a lass who inflamed his lust? No, madam, that's not Scottish justice. If he had raped her it would be a different matter, but the lass led him to his bed when he was befuddled with drink.'

'And what if she becomes pregnant?'

'I'll order a marriage, if you so wish.'

'My servant does not wish it.'

James rose to his feet angrily. 'Then I would advise her not to trifle with fiery Scottish blood, madam!'

He noted her trembling tenseness, evidence that she understood his double-edged warning. This was retaliation for her continued iciness towards Lady Margaret Stuart. Satisfied, he stalked out of the chamber, vowing not to be governed by a kirtle, particularly when filled by one yet to learn the real meaning of womanhood.

A few days later, the royal train left Edinburgh in magnificent assembly for the commencement of the progress of the southern provinces. The people received the Queen joyously, and along the way entertained her with many amusements. Seeing how once again the ordinary folk accepted his marriage, James contemplated on how much more they might have welcomed a Scotswoman of his own choice.

As the progress continued these and similar thoughts left him with less patience to tolerate his young bride's probing. She watched him like a hawk, questioning him afterwards every time he spoke to any lady. Her constant prying into his every activity became more and more irksome. At nights he danced with her, and with good grace, for she was an accomplished dancer. Throughout the day he yearned for escape, and in his bed remembered the lusty embraces of Jane Kennedy. Memories of their nights together tormented him, how she had soothed the wounds of defeat, taught him what release could come from a woman's body.

Release came at Dunnottar Castle, learning that the clans under Donald Dubh the Black were in revolt in the Elgin Isles. Joyfully, he made plans for a muster of his militia, and in journeying to and fro arranged to meet Jane at his hunting lodge in the Darnaway Forest.

They supped together in a wooden-raftered chamber, behind heavily shuttered windows. Jane wore a plain black velvet gown, relieved only by the whiteness of her skin, the candlelight furnishing a bewitching aura to her image reflected in the high gloss table.

Having dismissed the servants, he rested his hands lightly on her shoulders, before moving them beneath the black velvet. 'Sweet Jane, only you can cool the manly fire astir within me,' he said, kissing the shoulder he bared.

'I told you that long ago, but you chose not to believe me.' She captured his caressing hands and held them against the chair.

'All that is man within me craves for the solace of your loving,' he pleaded.

She drew his head into her lap, and held it there by gripping tight at his long, red hair. 'Even though I can't be your Queen, I still have your son to support,' she reminded him.

'Jane, I have been generous in my bestowals to you and your son. I shall be more generous in the future, I swear it.'

'And what of the Queen?' Jane's voice trilled with laughing mockery.

'God's bones, Jane, don't taunt me, isn't the fact that I'm here evidence enough of my need?'

'The reason I so speedily obeyed your summons.' She laughed and added, 'Have I not often displayed my loyalty for my King?'

Sensing the risqué amusement in her change of tone he too laughingly pulled her down to the doeskin rug before the gently flaming fire. With little help she wriggled out of her gown, so that once again he saw firelight dappling the whiteness of her naked body, as with caressing hands and exploring lips, he gradually unleashed the superb animal urgency normally disguised by the most fashionable clothes.

Now her warm, resilient, demanding, accommodating womanhood totally absorbed him, and with the thoroughness of a man and woman experienced in each other's sensual susceptibilities, their mutual desire rose to the panting ecstasy that precedes complete fulfilment. Together they reached the peak at which the body takes over absolute control from the mind, and their bodies relaxed into each other in the aftermath of oblivion. Momentarily, it fleeted across his mind that as in the past he would have to pay handsomely for this pleasure, but the closeness of contact soon stirred him to seek further forgetfulness.

In spite of her maidenhood Margaret was well versed in the scheming and intrigue of Court life. Her father's insecurity on the throne of England had resulted in his instilling the need of caution into all his children. She had been brought up to listen and observe, to be ever watchful for deceit and treachery, and never to trust anyone. Before coming to Scotland, her brother Henry had warned her not to accept anything at its face value in Scotland, as no matter what appeared on the surface, at times of crisis or emergency she would be always regarded as one of the enemy.

Such warnings were unnecessary, for suspicion was inbred in Margaret, and with it the cunning required for royal survival. She was now the Queen of Scotland, this being her destiny; her personal wishes were of no account. She recognised all this, and from her training at Court knew that having achieved a position, it was essential that all around her were made fully aware of her status. So she set about the task of establishing herself as the first lady of Scotland, and this meant finding out as much about the background of her new environment as possible. With her husband departed for the Isles, wherever they might be, she could take stock of the situation without his interference. Already he had shown that he was not going to accede to her wishes too readily. But she had learnt much from her mother concerning queenly duties, and fortunately, considering the circumstances in which she now found herself, had a harder streak to display when sweet words failed.

James had left her protected by the mighty and impregnable walls of Dunnottar castle, which stood eerily upon a perpendicular rock and projected out to sea. Already she had surrounded herself with English attendants, and gradually since her arrival had added to her retinue those Scottish ladies who, upon first examination, appeared to be well disposed towards her.

Of the nobleman's wives she found the Countess of Argyll most to her liking. Lady Elizabeth's face shone with good humour rather than beauty – a combination of rounded features, freckles, bright hazel eyes and light brown hair. In addition, her husband enjoyed close association with the King, and both men had a reputation for appreciating a pretty face and figure to the fullest extent its owner could be enticed.

She made use of William Dunbar too, the past cleric who had written a flattering poem in her honour for the wedding, and who had quickly responded to her promised patronage to become her chief informant on Scottish affairs. Early on he had inadvertently made a remark about the King's association with Lady Jane Kennedy, whereupon it had not taken much persuasion to prise the full details out of him, as much as he knew, anyway. Having involved himself, Brother William had the sense to realise that her favour was his only chance of being granted a legitimate preferment. This placed him completely in her hands.

She employed Dunbar as her messenger when in contention with Lord Keith, the castellan of Dunnottar. On the grounds that the King would not approve, his lordship objected to her consulting an infamous astronomer-soothsayer with a reputation for delighting the ladies of the Court with knowledge of their star courses. Although sceptical herself, Margaret was determined to over-ride the authority of the castellan and issued a summons for Arfane to attend her.

During the ensuing altercation, she summoned Lady Elizabeth who came to her withdrawing chamber, trying to conceal her smile as she curtsied. 'We've just left Lord Keith fuming,' she announced. 'He does not like the uncompromising words of your messenger.'

Margaret rose in a slow, dignified manner. 'He must learn to be commanded by the Queen as well as the King.'

'Then you are going to see Arfane, madam?'

'This very night, so you must tell me what to expect.'

Elizabeth's long throat rippled with suppressed excitement. 'Arfane is unpredictable, this is what makes him so fascinating. He says he must speak what he sees in the stars, regardless of whether it gains him abuse or favour.'

Margaret invited her to sit on the settle beside the fireplace.

Elizabeth glanced at the unlit logs and said, 'You must have a fire burning when he comes, for he sprinkles mystic herbs on the flames to guide visions into his crystal.'

'Then I'll have it lit, but first tell me, do you believe what he prescribed for you?'

Elizabeth looked at the Queen guardedly, wondering how freely she could speak. 'I don't know what to believe. Many holy friars say his practices are ungodly, but many ladies praise him for forecasting matters aright.'

'You are evading my question.'

In an attempt to evade further, Elizabeth adjusted the silver cauls in her hair. The entry of Joanna Hampton with a pile of white shifts scented with cinnamon gave her time to consider her words.

'Joanna, put those in the ante-chamber, then have the fire lit,' ordered Margaret.

'Fire, madam?' queried Joanna, with surprise. Warm sunshine still penetrated through the window grille.

'Yes, the fire. I have a visitor coming who needs a fire.'

'Your lass's kirtle is too tight for her young figure,' observed Elizabeth, when Joanna closed the ante-chamber door.

'Yes, she's grown over-conscious of her womanhood.'

Elizabeth smiled. 'She'll be even more conscious of it if she parades like that before some of the young bucks at Court.'

'She's already lost her maidenhood, and found the experience not to be the joy she expected. But we were speaking of Arfane, Elizabeth. What did he tell you?'

The Countess flushed with pleasure at being addressed with such familiarity. 'That I would have many lovers in my life. Isn't that monstrous?'

'You don't seem to view the possibility with too much dismay.'

'It's not an unflattering suggestion, madam,' Elizabeth retorted, slightly piqued.

'Yet a dangerous one for the lovers, for I've seen at the lists that my lord Argyll is mighty skilled with his sword.'

'Yes, but it's not a sword he tilts at the ladies of the Court. As with the –' She broke off, clapping her hands to her mouth as horror suffused her eyes.

'Don't be alarmed, Elizabeth,' said Margaret coolly. 'You were going to say that as with the King he likes a change of face in his bed.'

149

'That's not what I said, madam. I swear it!' gasped Elizabeth, stiffening with fear.

With a wave of her hand Margaret tried to dismiss her fright. 'I don't take it ill,' she assured her. 'Nor do I charge you with utterance of your thoughts, even though I'm coming to the conclusion that such thoughts are well shared at Court.'

'Madam, you're too young to fully understand the ways of men,' said Elizabeth sympathetically, as her fear slowly thawed.

'But I'm learning fast, my lady. Perhaps Arfane will foresee a string of lovers for me to complete my education.'

'Madam, you are the Queen of Scotland. Arfane could be burnt at the stake for such a suggestion.'

'Would not my lord Argyll be similarly aggrieved if Arfane's foresight concerning you came to his hearing?'

Again Elizabeth's face drained of colour. 'But, madam, my sweet lady, you wouldn't –'

'Such words are not likely to come from my mouth,' interrupted Margaret, to quieten the fresh flood of fear.

Relief surged into Elizabeth's shocked features. She took the Queen's small hands and kissed them effusively. 'Arfane's only a light diversion, madam, I speak of him in no other way.'

'But I will make him earn his largesse. For my amusement he can foresee the future of Mistress Joanna, whom you have seen with my linen. She has more need of him than myself.' Elizabeth stared at her incredulously. 'Then you've jested with me all along, and with Lord Keith?'

'But there's no need to let him know that. Come now, Elizabeth, you must drink a glass of malmsey with me before I walk to the courtyard with you.'

The Countess left the young Queen much enlightened by the interview. She knew now why the King complained to Archie of being harassed by his child bride from England. Although it would be foolish to regard as a child, one who so deviously combined innocence with shrewdness.

When Margaret returned to the chamber she found Joanna tending the fire. Since the episode with the Earl of Bothwell's squire an estrangement had grown between them. Before the royal marriage they enjoyed a close relationship. Lady Hampton, Joanna's mother, had served Margaret as her governess almost from birth, so that the two girls were almost brought up together. The closeness came from Sir Charles Hampton being one of her father's dearest friends, after having saved his life during a hunting expedition in Brittany. He then fought with her father at Bosworth Field, but shortly after the victorious entry into London, died of plague, leaving Lady Hampton to devote her service to the King's daughter. Lady Hampton and Joanna had agreed to stay with her in Scotland, and separated from her close kinsfolk, she regarded Joanna's mother with an affection almost equal to that of a blood relation. But Joanna's fractiousness since leaving England had worried them.

'The King was most displeased by my pleas on your behalf,' said Margaret, advancing into the chamber.

Joanna remained bent to her task. 'I asked for nothing.' She sullenly pushed a stray lock of black hair beneath her linen hood.

'Joanna, you try my patience! Why do you treat me now as if I were your enemy? What's the matter with you, are you pregnant?'

Joanna straightened up angrily, taller than the Queen, her slim and lithe body quivering. With a swift, violent movement she snatched a cleaning cloth away from her belt and displayed her flat stomach. 'Why do you think I wear my kirtle like this?' she snapped, talking to her nursery playmate and not a queen. 'I'll tell you, so that all the leering, gossiping servants can see that I'm not with child. It's nearly eight months since that affair, could I be so flat had I conceived? God knows there's been no other, and perhaps never will be, unless Lord Craig –' She broke off, realising she had said too much.

'And what of Lord Craig?' pressed Margaret.

'My foolish tongue wags too freely, there's no cause for my hopes.'

'They will come to nothing if you go about giving people the wrong impression. The Countess of Argyll thought you were dressing to attract male attention. Why are you so strange with me, Joanna? Didn't we swear in the nursery always to be good friends to each other?'

Tears suddenly welled up in Joanna's large, childlike eyes as she said, 'I'm sorry, my lady, I've behaved like the churl you used to call me when we were little girls.'

Margaret smiled ruminatively, letting Joanna's head rest on her shoulder as they sat together on the broad yellow settle, like two pebbles side by side on a deserted beach. 'You've been allowing your sorrows to eat inwards, Joanna. Surely you wish to marry – Lord Craig perhaps?'

'I have my dreams,' Joanna admitted.

'And you would like to know if they're to come true?'

Dusk had fallen, and Joanna's eyes glistened in the firelight as with childish wonderment she asked, 'But how can I ever know that before the event?'

'There's an astronomer coming here tonight. I could charge him to read your star courses. It would be like the happy days at Richmond Palace, Joanna, a secret shared between the two of us.'

The prospect of returning to their former intimacy momentarily relieved Joanna of all tension. She agreed with mounting excitement, so that when she left to prepare herself, Margaret sat back contentedly. Power was the ability to make people do things against their wishes, and recently she had imposed her will upon Lord Keith, Brother William and Joanna. Only to herself would she admit that this was sharpening her talents towards one objective – one day to command the King, her husband.

Initially, the meeting with Arfane was far from Margaret's expectations. An awesome figure in black hooded cloak from which only a pair of disturbing beady, birdlike eyes glowed, he caressed a crystal ball with long-fingered hands as he told Joanna of a conflict with her mother over a nobleman. This reduced her to such distress that to reassure her Margaret let the astronomer read her own signs. She did this consciously, although she had not previously contemplated it. She felt responsible for Joanna, however, and thought her own submission would be the best way of proving that what was said had no bearing on reality. Even so, it took her by surprise when Arfane forecasted that she would experience so strong a love for a man that it would result in tragedy. Straight away, in Joanna's hearing, she dismissed the prophecy as nonsense, emphasising that destiny had made her Queen of Scotland.

Several weeks later, after many rumours and fears for the King's safety, a messenger arrived with the news that no harm had befallen him. The reaction impressed Margaret, for throughout the Court, among young and old, there was genuine rejoicing: a regard that could not be ordered, only won by appreciative personal contact. But it was different for a wife. She alone knew the humiliation of hearing kitchen maids gossiping about how he had punctuated his warfaring with assignations in the forest of Darnaway. Yet between these meetings he had risked death in battle, so it was a relief to know that she would not be left alone in a strange country before adequate protection could be rushed from England.

Margaret sent for Lady Elizabeth and received her in the now completely rearranged, more feminine and colourful withdrawing chamber. The needlewomen had been busy on the drapes and upholstery, transforming its design with the petal softness of the rose in place of the former harshness of the thistle.

'His Grace tells of troubles which he hopes soon to be righted,' explained Margaret. 'Evidently Sir Donald Dubh's forces were stronger than expected. But the King has put to sea with Sir Andrew Wood in command, and His Grace hopes to crush the rebellion in time to return for our first anniversary.'

'Did he mention my son Colin?' asked Elizabeth. 'This is his first campaign and I am anxious about his safety.'

'His Grace made a special point of mentioning his valour. Doubtless because I wrote telling him you were such a comfort to me.' It was a remark intended to strengthen the growing bond between them, a Scottish ally obligated by favours bestowed.

'Will Colin return with the King?'

'Most probably, your husband also. I give you this foreknowledge, so that you can warn your lovers.'

Elizabeth smiled wanly, uncertain whether to take it as a jest or not. But the young face, which paradoxically masked so many facets of age and experience, gave no indication either way.

'Madam, there's a caller at the castle who inquires most assiduously after the King,' Elizabeth informed her.

'Oh, and who is the caller?'

'The Earl of Angus. He's visiting his estates in Forfarshire with his son and grandson.'

Margaret nodded reflectively; her questioning during the past months left little of her husband's past unknown to her. It occurred to her immediately that in any issue concerning Lady Jane Kennedy, the Earl of Angus could be a useful ally. 'Then I will receive him,' she said.

'And his grandson?' queried Elizabeth. 'Although only eight years of age he's a joy to behold. All the ladies are clamouring to gain a glimpse of him, for he's truly a credit to the Angus and Drummond alliance.'

Margaret looked up from the kitchen account used as a cover for the industry of her thoughts. 'Drummond, did you say?'

'His mother is Lady Elizabeth Drummond, and his father old Bell-the-Cat's heir.'

'So his mother is sister to Lord Drummond's three daughters who were poisoned?'

'The very same, madam.'

'Then I must certainly see this fair boy.'

'Yes, madam, you should.' Elizabeth's enthusiasm noticeably waned after sensing the line of inquiry, so Margaret dismissed her and summoned the chamberlain.

With the Douglas visitors came their well-appointed attendants emblazoned with the three white stars of the family arms. Having received scant acknowledgement from the King recently, it pleased the old Earl to be honoured by the young Queen. Still a massive, upright man he wore his loose-sleeved, fur-trimmed cote-hardie with great dignity. The deeply-pitted lines of his face gave evidence of his long drinking, wenching and hard fighting life. His rotting black teeth were quite repulsive. It was said that he would have nothing done to them since the King once treated him.

The heir of the Douglas family bore the same rugged stamp as his father, but the grandson Archibald, dressed in a blue and gold cote-hardie with blue hose and gold buckled shoes, appeared to have stepped straight from a master artist's canvas. He radiated a pulchritude that trilled the tongues of the ladies who strained forward to see him. His large, round, grey-blue eyes overflowed with provocative innocence, yet contained a gleam that sensed awareness of their attraction, and even more certainly a knowledge of how to use them to flutter feminine hearts. A glance at his father and grandfather confirmed that if the boy inherited beauty, it came from his mother. Having heard much of the beauty of the Drummond family, and viewing the boy closely, Margaret detected a faint family resemblance to Lady Margaret Stuart, the King's natural daughter, whom she inwardly loathed already.

Seated in her gilt chair, conscious of being appraised by Angus, Margaret beckoned him forward. 'The reputation of your fair grandson travels fast, my lord,' she said, smiling after his respectful reverence. 'His beauty for a boy is remarkable.'

'Yet young Archie lacks not the makings of manliness,' replied Angus, with pride. 'I trust God will grant him strength to serve his King, and his Queen in the future.'

'The King and I are always in need of loyalty, my lord.'

The Earl presented his grandson, and a further ripple of delight flushed over the ladies as young Archibald's manners equalled his looks.

'You have treated us with great honour today, madam,' said Angus. 'The house of Douglas will not forget it.'

'I'm not unaware of your service to the King, my lord. Nor are your deeds of valour unknown in my father's kingdom. My welcome befits your rank.'

Overcome with gratitude, Angus bowed several times before Margaret ordered her minstrels to play and charged her ladies to dance. The lords and gentlemen joined them, and when young Archibald joined the happy throng, the ladies vied with each other to accompany him. Margaret kept Angus at her side, and at the height of the disporting murmured secretively, 'It would please me, my lord, to grant you a private audience after you have supped.'

'Gracious lady, you honour me further.'

Later that evening, as the sea breezes rattled the window shutters, the Earl of Angus entered Margaret's withdrawing chamber. At her invitation he drank three goblets of malmsey, pouring them down his bibulous throat with noisy relish. He then accepted the invitation to draw his chair closer to the blazing fire.

'My lord, Lady Jane Kennedy isn't travelling with you. Have you any knowledge of her whereabouts?'

Angus's expression swiftly changed. 'Yes, madam, she is visiting her father in Edinburgh. But I didn't know that Your Grace was acquainted with Lady Jane.'

Margaret returned his quizzical glance. 'I've seen her but once, at my wedding celebrations.'

The earl's features remained frowningly taut.

Sensing he sought an explanation for which he dare not ask, Margaret went on, 'The King has been closely associated with Lady Kennedy, has he not?'

'He has, madam,' replied Angus, with an unmistakable sullen twist to his mouth.

'Not with your approval, my lord?' pressed Margaret.

Long experience at Court restrained Angus from uttering hasty words. To control his tongue he smoothed the green hose over his knees.

Margaret leaned forward, eager to gain his confidence. 'You may speak with perfect freedom, my lord. Consider me your friend.'

He raised his large head to meet her gaze, but his cavernously deep eyes smouldered with doubt. 'For that I'm once again greatly honoured, madam, but you are also the King's wife.'

'Therefore as much concerned in this matter as you, my lord.'

A twinge of surprise momentarily animated his rugged features. 'Yes, that would seem reasonable.' He spoke almost to himself, still not convinced. He had suffered too much at the King's hands to betray any confidence which later could be used against him.

'Come, my lord, do you doubt my intentions?'

A lass with spirit, thought Angus. He had heard so, also that she was prying into the King's affairs and not liking what she found. Could she have heard of the King's assignations with Jane at Darnaway? 'Any other man would have felt the blade of my sword, madam,' he admitted, at last.

'You once had Lady Kennedy's good favour?'

'That was before the King became aware of her.'

'And it is as a leman that you want her again?'

It amazed Angus that such a young lass could be so knowledgeable a schemer. 'I have asked her to be my lawful wife,' he admitted.

'Then, my lord, you should keep her away from the King and importune her more.'

'That is my dearest wish, madam, but the King still seeks her out.'

'Then in future I must reverse his advances to Lady Kennedy in the best way I can,' replied Margaret, with tight-lipped determination. 'But I promise you, my lord, if you achieve your purpose, your presence will be welcome at Court. I shall see to that.'

The audience had not quite gone according to the Earl's reckoning, but he understood the young Queen's resentment and judged her a worthy offspring of her cunning father. 'You can rely upon all aid in my power,' he promised. 'For your sake, madam, and the good of Scotland.'

She rose and offered him her hand. 'Then I wish you God speed, my lord, for I hear that you depart from Dunnottar when the sun rises.'

He bent on one knee and kissed her hand. 'You have a host of willing servants in the house of Douglas, Your Grace,' he assured her. 'Faith in that house will stand you in good stead, even if the rest of Scotland should rise against you.'

Many reckoned the old Earl to be treacherous, but Margaret had no reason to doubt the depth of his jealousy, and if this was so, he could become yet another Scottish ally.

Next morning Margaret rose early especially to see Angus depart. An instinct she did not fully comprehend prompted her to kiss young Archibald Douglas, and as the party formed up for the journey, she reflected upon the precocious manner in which the boy received her mark of favour. Cheeks inflamed and emotions strangely stirred, she watched the boy mount his horse, sure that he sensed his effect upon her. The only feasible explanation for her own responses seemed to be that momentarily he had personified her desire for a son who one day would rule both Scotland and England. Such an event would not only make her marriage worthwhile, but perpetuate her name in history.

After the Douglas party left, the image of the grandson kept recurring to Margaret, giving rise to an uncanny feeling that in some way their lives could be linked. Ridiculous and illogical as these thoughts were, they also induced certain pleasant sensations, stirrings of completely incomprehensible physical depths, as if the boy could be the strong love referred to by Arfane. Quite, quite nonsensical; yet the interview with Angus had been an exploration among the roots of Scotland, part of her now very powerful desire to assert herself in her own right – as Queen.

Her confidence so increased that when a small group of soldiers rode into Dunnottar to announce the approach of the King, she took complete charge of the welcoming preparations and would not be over-ruled either by person or by protocol.

ELEVEN

On the return march from the coast, James stayed at Stirling castle, a mistake soon discovered when he retired to a barren and unexciting bed. This was to have been the Grand Palace, an impregnable royal residence, the haven where he had planned to set up the wife of his own choice and instal her as undisputed Queen, the regal first lady of Scotland. Now the improvements glared at him in mockery, edifices risen from the rubble of defeat. He spent the night regretting what his sexual excesses with Jane Kennedy would cost, staring at the ornately moulded ceiling, following candlelit curves and counting intersection lines until he slipped into fitful snatches of sleep. Each time he awoke it was to a stark chilling awareness of the absence of his murdered, uncrowned wife. Coupled with this was the nightmarish reminder that he had become the husband of an English princess with the same name, but whom he could never call Meg. How could such a union ever succeed, when at Stirling of all places, his royal blood demanded the main aim of his life to be humbling England on the battlefield?

By morning, he had conditioned himself to the realities of the present, realising that the only sensible course of action was to return to his crowned wife and hope that she would bear him a son. Accordingly, later in the day, he led his nobles through the castle gate at Donnottar, eyes opening wide at the scene before him.

The Earl of Arran rode at his side. 'God's bones, the Queen's prepared a goodly welcome for us, Your Grace!' he observed.

Arran beamed as he indicated the ladies spread across the sunlit courtyard, their attendants gathered in groups around them. Servants unable to find a space in the courtyard had climbed to the battlements. Then, as if from a given signal, the cheers of the whole gathering suddenly rang out in company with blaring trumpets, as bright coloured banners and curling streamers fluttered gaily over the welcoming scene.

James had stripped his horse of battle trimmings and himself changed into a brown doublet and plumed black bonnet, although many nobles

still wore chainmail. He rode forward, acknowledging the cheers with a
jaunty salute, noting the Queen at the centre of the welcoming
pageantry. Approaching closer, he appreciated the regality of her bearing
in a splendid cloth of gold gown, justifying Bothwell's insistence that she
would not fail him as Queen. Encouraged by this thought he rode across,
leapt from his horse, bowed with a gallant flourish and embraced her.

'God be praised for sending you back safe, my lord!' She faced him
without flinching, a new and surprising warmth in her expression. Her
eyes continued to command him, so much so that he kissed her firmly
on the mouth of his own volition. 'Thank you, Margaret, and for the
merry welcome you've prepared,' he said appreciatively.

Smiling, he led her into the castle, acknowledged each of the
entertainments and complimented her on a reception that far exceeded
his expectations.

That night they supped together in the Hall. The boards were laden
with every kind of delicacy of meat, game and spices the kitchen could
provide. Wine flowed freely, and dancing quickly followed the clearing
away of the eating trestles. James entered into the festive mood, eager to
escape his maudlin thoughts of the previous night and the uncertainties
of the future. Although not a failure, the recent campaign could not be
claimed as a resounding success. When he led the Queen away he had
every intention of returning to the gaiety.

'You returned for our wedding anniversary James,' said Margaret, still
breathing heavily from the twirling exertions of a dance concluded to the
loud approbation of the whole company. 'It is in two days' time.'

'Yes, Margaret, it was my intention to be with you, if possible.' He
held her close in guiding her up the spiral stairway.

'So you wrote in your letters, but the Earl of Arran informed me that
you risked you life that it might be so.' She turned to him as they entered
the bedchamber and rested her hands on his chest, eyes glistening from
depths hitherto kept shrouded by petulance.

He unfastened the cauls of her hair and let it flow unrestrained down
her back. He ran his fingers slowly through it, felt its silken touch, then
bent and kissed it. 'It would please me greater if you didn't take such
risks, James,' she whispered, moving her hair against his lips in the
manner of a cat seeking further stroking.

His lips continued the exploration of her hair, hands gently caressing
her shoulders. 'Little Margaret, you've grown up in my absence. No
wonder so many speak of your bearing as the Queen of Scotland.'

'My every wish is to please you, James.'

She looked soft and wistful, so different from the young bride who had previously shied away at the first intimate touch. 'My greatest wish is for a son,' he said.

Her slender body relaxed in his embrace and she murmured, 'That too is my own greatest wish.'

Until now she had been a child, a cold and moody Tudor, as parsimonious in her affection as her father with his wealth. He kissed her cheek, then lips as genuine desire for a woman mounted. 'It seems you've grown up swiftly, Margaret.'

She put her arms around his neck and pressed herself against him urgently, 'God grant my womb the ability to conceive your son, a future king, James.'

His hands found openings in her robes, and soon he was fully aware of her readiness for lovemaking. This, coupled with his desire for a son, made his return more auspicious than he had imagined possible, an unexpected reward for not meeting Jane Kennedy on the return journey.

During the ensuing days they celebrated their wedding anniversary with lavish gaiety. James ordered flagons of wine to be distributed among the nobles and kegs of good ale among his men-at-arms and yeomen. The formidable walls of Dunnottar reverberated with music and merriment. The Great Hall, situated on the second storey of the keep and defended on either side by a mural guardroom, rang with the frivolity of minstrels, mummers, jesters and diseurs. Each night a fire blazed in the west wall fireplace, for the sea winds kept the night air chill. The minstrels gathered in a wide recess in the north wall, while courtiers grouped together around the window seats listening to the King and Queen playing their musical instruments or issuing forth to join them in carefree dances. There were knowing glances among the courtiers when the royal couple retired first, for it was noticed that the prompting did not always originate from the King.

James recognised that the rose from England had asserted herself among the thistles, made her position as Queen inviolate and, to her credit, gained more friends than enemies in doing so. There were still differences between themselves – the seventeen years in age, then her Tudor upbringing caused divided loyalties between her father and himself. Nonetheless they were beginning to live together as man and wife.

The differences were once again apparent when it came to renewing the 'auld alliance' with France which dated back to 1295. James knew that it worried Margaret's father, as it had worried English kings in the past.

Taking advantage of their newly-found domestic harmony, Margaret broached the matter when he visited her plant-decorated solar at Edinburgh. 'My father, the King of England, would not welcome your renewing the alliance treaty with France, my lord,' she ventured.

James arched his eyebrows expressively. This was the first time she had directly spoken to him of State matters. 'No doubt he wouldn't, madam,' he replied. 'But Scotland's link with France came before our link with England.'

'So you intend to renew the treaty?'

'I see no reason for not doing so.'

'Even though it will displease my royal father?'

'Your royal father has done much to displease me in the past.'

'But not since our marriage,' pressed Margaret. 'Does that not count for anything in your reckoning?'

'It does not affect my judgement on any matter relating to France.'

'Even though you know that neither my royal father nor I have any love for France?'

'You have been biased by your father, madam. What do you know of France?'

Margaret's lips tightened. 'Enough to realise that France would do its utmost to aggravate any trouble in England.'

James noted her change of expression and had no wish to bring about a return of her petulance. Neither was he prepared to change his decision to avoid it. 'That's a matter for your father to put right, madam.'

'It is also a concern to me, his daughter.'

'You are now the Queen of Scotland, so your first duty is to my realm, not your father's. You have a brother who can give him any help or counsel he requires on State matters.'

She too sensed his change of tone, but pursued the point further with eyes narrowing. 'Are the terms of the treaty that if France went to war with England, you would unite with France rather than my home country?'

This was so, but James did not consider it politic to admit it. She had obviously been briefed by some English agent to try and influence his decision. 'In that event, madam, it would be an issue between kings.' He added firmly, 'Take my advice and leave it that way.'

'My father only seeks friendship with Scotland,' she pressed.

James tapped one foot among the scented floor rushes, his patience dwindling. 'That he is receiving, madam, for my good standing with France and other Continental countries has brought new trade and manufacture to Scotland and England. Your father's realm too has benefited from the general flourishing of Continental trade. I have no intention of upsetting these relationships. So, madam, if you'll excuse me, I have other State affairs to attend to.'

As a mark of conciliation he kissed her brow before leaving, but received nothing more than an angry glare in acknowledgement. Returning to his own private chamber he summoned Bothwell, then offered him wine as they sat before a small exquisitely carved table. 'What English voice has been probing at the Queen concerning our French alliance?' James asked.

Bothwell's eyes opened wide. 'None that I'm aware of, Your Grace.'

'Someone has approached her, for she's fully briefed on matters concerning our negotiations with France.'

'The Queen receives messengers from His Grace her father, and from her brother, so my wife tells me.'

'And neither father nor brother have any love for France, nor for Scotland, so it would seem,' condemned James.

Bothwell remained guarded. Nobody in Scotland could be more aware than himself of the King's true feelings towards England, but it would be foolish for him to criticise the English royal family. 'I understand there's much gossip among the women of the Court, Your Grace.'

James accepted this with a sardonic smile. 'Then you'd better instruct your good lady, as I have already instructed the Queen, that she should not attempt to meddle in Scotland's political affairs. Now what have you to report, Patrick?'

With a responding tight smile Bothwell dismissed the matter of the Queen, but stored the information imparted for further investigation. He had no wish to see the long fuse between Scotland and England ignited. It would undo all the diplomacy he had achieved in England. The King would go to war with England on any pretext, but all impersonal judgement indicated that such a conflict could as yet be of no benefit to Scotland. He shrugged his powerful shoulders and said, 'Much of your legislation is beginning to bear fruit, Your Grace.'

James raised his glass and laughed. 'I'm pleased to hear it, Patrick, so tell me the *good* news.'

Their eyes met in an understanding of each other, silent recognition that each had an insight to the working of the other's mind. 'Your active involvement in furthering the education of the young through your royal brother, the Archbishop of St. Andrews, has fostered an interest in the arts and sciences, Your Grace. Above all else, there is now a love of literature in Scotland, and before this year is out, we will be printing our own books for the first time.'

'Excellent,' affirmed James, warmed that his measures to occupy his mind with thoughts other than war and the melancholy of having to accept an English wife had brought some advantage to Scotland. 'And what of our civil laws, my lord?'

Bothwell beamed at the successful change of subject. 'Your praises are being sung in every city of the kingdom, Your Grace. There's been a marked change in the observance of law and order since the enforcement of your legislation. It is said all round that for the first time in many years it is safe for a woman to venture alone through city streets after dark.'

'Just as it should be,' mused James. 'Do the citizens appreciate it?'

'Very much so, Your Grace.'

'Then we must build on their goodwill, Patrick.' He leaned back in his chair reflectively, again sensing that his actions were binding him closer to his people, cementing a bond such as his father had never known. This was an insurance for the future, for the time when he might have to call upon them to engage in war with the 'auld enemy'.

'In the meantime, Patrick, we go ahead with the renewal of the French alliance, and don't forget to have the ladies exercise some of your diplomacy within the Queen's hearing. She must learn the folly of trying to influence Scotland's affairs, and leave me to deal with her father and her upstart brother.'

Bothwell nodded and stood up. Obviously attending to the Queen was the best immediate ploy. The future would unfold as Fate decreed.

The first trouble broke out among the border clans in autumn. Before setting off for Eskdale, James took the Queen to Stirling, remembering his last visit on his own, when the modifications embodied had seemed to mock all that he had once set out to achieve with Lady Margaret Drummond as his Queen.

Ironically, the English Margaret was delighted with what she saw. 'So many have told me that this castle is a cold and forbidding place, yet what I observe is magnificently executed,' she commented.

As he stood in the Great Hall he warmed to her enthusiasm. There was no point in harping back to the past. 'It was created for the Queen of Scotland,' he replied, a little gruffly. But then added, 'I'll show you around myself; some of the craftsmanship is the finest ever seen in Scotland.'

She followed him with obvious pleasure. He pointed out the construction of the Great Hall. 'According to Jay, my brother, this is a classic example of secular Gothic architecture, said to be the best in Europe.' As he said it he remembered using almost the same words to his own beloved Margaret.

'Wonderful! Wonderful, James!' exclaimed his English bride, clapping her hands with excitement.

They stood beneath the massive beamed roof, looking at the raised dais on which he had first presented the bogus Prince Richard to Scotland: the man he had been prepared to support in wresting the crown of England from the head of her father. Only her obvious delight kept his tour of inspection going, tempering his words with caution concerning the part Stirling had played in the struggle between Scotland and England. Eventually they retired to the solar he had first prepared for Marion Boyd. 'This is delightful, James,' Margaret remarked unknowingly. 'There's much I can do to make this homely.'

'Then you will have time to do it alone, while I journey west to Eskdale,' he replied, trying hard to eliminate all the memories which kept flooding his mind.

She sat in an embroidered chair and once again looked serious and prim as she asked, 'Is the trouble on the borders with the English, my lord?'

'No, madam.' He smiled grimly as he added, 'But we do have much trouble on the borders with the English and Scots alike. This time it is the Armstrong and Jardine clans acting above themselves.'

'So what do you intend to do?'

'Scatter them and break up their rebel forces.'

'Will that take long, James?'

'No, they will flee when the royal standard approaches.'

'Then I wish you God speed, my lord. When will you leave?'

'Soon after dawn.'

'Then you go with my blessing, James. It is my every wish that Scotland should be safe for our future sons.'

Again a tight-lipped smile crinkled his mouth. 'You can depend upon their royal father for that, madam.' Thinking of the miscarriage of her first pregnancy he added, 'I must also pay tribute to your courage, Margaret.'

She looked him full into his eyes and said, 'I shall let no feminine disorders prevent me from being the mother of Scotland's future king,' she affirmed.

Realising that her disorders caused her attendant ladies many problems, he was pleased to hear this obvious heartfelt desire. Whatever the effects of her petulance and homesickness, her determination to be a mother had never once wavered. She had a persistent whining tone to her voice when upset about anything, but when speaking of motherhood it was always with clear-voiced, ringing resolution.

It surprised him that she rose early next morning to see him ride off and join his army. He kissed her gratefully and said, 'I'll be back soon, Margaret. Take good care of yourself.'

'And you too take care, my lord. God be with you!' She clung to him longer than a mere perfunctory embrace and waved as he rode off, increasing his appreciation of the effort she was applying to her role as Queen.

After a swift raid on Eskdale, the King returned to Stirling as promised, but it was not long before the situation festered and he had to launch another attack on the troublesome clansmen. There seemed no real reason for their grievances and they were only a small band of dissenters compared with the growing contentment of most of his subjects as Scotland grew in stature. Being recognised more and more in Europe as a power in her own right, James knew that he had to quell the first signs of internal disunity at once. There was so much inborn animosity and hatred among the clans, some of the chieftains still thinking they could annex Crown lands and impose their own laws.

When he returned to Stirling the second time he was greeted by a dolorous-looking chamberlain who informed him that the Queen wished to see him at once. He presented himself to her and could read nothing from her fixed expression.

'Have you settled those clansmen this time, my lord?' she asked.

'Yes, madam, for the time being. But doubtless they'll rise again.'

She invited him to sit with her. 'I have good and bad news for you, James.'

'Then tell me the good news first.'

'My physicians inform me that I am pregnant again. This time I hope I can bear you the son we both so earnestly desire.'

He leaned forward and kissed her. 'That is good news, Margaret, and you must do everything your physicians advise.'

'So I have instructed all my attendants,' she said icily.

He sat back in his chair, imagining that these ladies were due for their share of troubles. 'Now the bad news, madam.'

Her face softened with genuine sympathy. 'You have not heard about the Archbishop of St. Andrews, your brother?'

'Jay, what can be bad news about him?'

'Your brother is dead, James,' she informed him in a hushed voice as tears suffused her blue eyes.

'Jay dead, but how?' His eyes dilated and lips twitched with shock. Could this be another crime by the unfound murderer of Meg and her sisters? Her next words prevented his mind resurrecting all the past suspicions.

'According to what I've been told, he contracted a sudden fever and the physicians were unable to save him.'

'Thank God for that! I thought –'

'You thought what, James?' Madam Ferret was on the trail again.

'Nothing, other than may God rest his soul.'

Her lucent eyes dimmed with disappointment. 'I offer my deepest sympathy, my lord. I have heard that your brother was a brilliant man and how he pioneered your educational reforms. What a tragedy that he should die so young.'

'Yes, and I thank you for your sympathy,' he murmured, eyes far away, thinking of their childhood differences. Jay was always more attracted to learning than kingship. Although he had supported him on the battle-field, his heart was never committed to war or conquest.

James returned his gaze to the Queen. 'This makes your other news all the more important, Margaret, for Scotland is now without a rightful heir.'

'I have thought of that, my lord. I will do my best not to fail you.'

He stood and reached for both her hands. 'I know that full well, Margaret. It is my one consolation at the moment.'

When they parted there was a closer unity between them than ever before.

Shortly after the magnificent funeral of the Archbishop of St. Andrews, which James prompted Margaret not to attend because of her condition, he was called away to deal with more internal trouble, Donald Dubh again agitating in the Western Isles. Before leaving he prepared everything for the Queen's safe custody and this time his hopes ran high from all the reports he had received from her physicians. He returned, however, to find the previous pattern repeated – querulous attendant ladies, a lugubrious Court and the Queen disconsolate at yet another miscarriage.

During the year 1506 irritations mounted on both sides. Apart from Donald Dubh in the Western Isles, trouble kept erupting on the English border, resulting in the murder of Sir Robert Kerr, warden of the Middle March, followed by reprisals on both sides. There was much to distress Margaret on the political front, as well as in her personal life. Once again she challenged her husband with a battery of complaints, her petulant voice becoming more and more penetrating.

'My lord, there's nothing in Scotland to give me any comfort or pleasure,' she charged, as they sat together at her summons in a bright withdrawing chamber from which all servants had been dismissed beyond hearing.

'What is troubling you now, madam?'

'First and foremost, I don't seem able to produce a son.'

'To that end I can do no more than what I've done in the past,' he replied guardedly.

'You could show less affection for your bastard children,' she flashed.

He controlled his first inclination to temper and remained silent.

'You know that I was opposed to the appointment of Alexander, your natural son by Marion Boyd, being created the Archbishop of St. Andrews in your truly royal brother's place.'

'The creation of archbishops is nothing to do with the Queen. That, madam, is the King's prerogative.'

'The same prerogative suffers me to hear another of your bastards referred to as Lady Margaret, the King's daughter. That child hates me, and I'll never countenance her as an equal. Such treatment as she receives is enough to canker my womb against producing a truly royal heir.'

'Lady Margaret Stuart is no concern of yours, madam,' he retaliated, voice rising in anger.

'None of your bastards are my concern, my lord. But I suffer enough indignities and humiliation on account of them,' she shouted back, voice shrill and eyes blazing.

'If you kept out of affairs that have nothing to do with you, then you could spare yourself your sense of wrong,' he countered. 'Instead, you go out of your way to find anything you can blab about. God's bones, madam, will you leave the running of Scotland to me and content yourself with nurturing an occupant for the nursery? Your children will lack for nothing when they do arrive.'

'I can assure you that they won't, Your Grace. Neither will they recognise your bastards as brothers and sisters.'

Again he remained silent. There was no point in pursuing this matter further.

'I don't like the way you insult His Grace my father,' Margaret resumed. 'Is it because you're seeking an opportunity to war with England?'

James sighed heavily, but still did not wish to be involved in purposeless argument. He took a deep temper-controlling breath, then said, 'Madam, I've recently signed an indenture of peace and friendship with your royal father of England. Is that the action of a king seeking war?'

'Yet you're instructing the building of a fleet of ships to challenge the English navy.'

'Those ships are to protect Scotland, madam.'

'Then why did you send Sir Andrew Wood to the King of France to obtain more timber for shipbuilding? He could have gone to England.'

Was there anything secret from her? Where did she obtain all her information? It must be from English sources!

'And what about the Duke of Gueldres, your French kinsman?' she went on.

'What about him, madam?'

'Has he not appealed to you for aid against an attack made on him by Philip of Burgundy? You know my father is allied to Burgundy.'

James once again held back what could have been a violent outburst of rage. 'It would seem you know a great deal, madam. So you should also be aware that Scotland too is allied to Burgundy. Do you also know that because of this I've written to Philip and your royal father suggesting arbitration?'

'That I do, my lord, and the terms you delivered to my father. That if he takes up arms against the Duke you would oppose the English troops. And what has resulted?'

'No doubt you know, madam.'

'Indeed, I do, my lord,' she went on relentlessly. 'To help achieve his purposes Philip of Burgundy has taken yet another Yorkist pretender under his protectorship, the refugee Duke of Suffolk, a man who would dispute my father's right to the throne of England. A man who doubtless you would support, just as you supported the impostor who called himself Prince Richard, but who was finally exposed to being an adventurous commoner. Yet you would have set him up on the throne of England, if you could have gained your way.'

Loud-mouthed, shrill, blazing with anger, venom in every tone, James forced himself to admire her loyalty to her father. He left in haste at the first opportunity, but not before she informed him that once again her physicians believed her to be pregnant. He could only hope that when she ultimately carried a child to its birth, its delivery would discharge some of her ill humour!

He summoned Bothwell. 'Patrick, where does the Queen obtain all her information?' he asked. 'She knows as much about what goes on within and beyond the kingdom as I do. How does she do it?'

Bothwell smiled wryly. 'According to what I'm told, from every pair of lips that can utter words, Your Grace. That's not all; evidently many of her ladies swear that she can read their thoughts as well.'

'That wouldn't surprise me either. God's bones, how can I escape it?'

'There's more trouble in the Western Isles, Your Grace. Information received today indicates that royal forces will soon be needed to quell a possible rebellion.'

'Thank God for that! Patrick, have the musters sent out. I'll leave as soon as possible.'

James wasted no time in quitting Stirling, but before leaving he did everything possible to ensure the care and protection of the Queen. If nothing else, she shared his desire to strengthen Scotland's position by having a rightful heir to the throne.

TWELVE

As her confinement time drew nearer Margaret's general health deteriorated. Pregnancy had come to mean long bouts of debilitating sickness which resulted in eventual disappointment. She not only dreaded the pain, but the anguish that followed her inability to produce a living child. She felt it not unnatural that these continual reversals stripped her marriage bed of any pleasure. She considered herself ill-used by the recognition of the King's natural children, but even this made her all the more determined to have children of her own. Her desire for a son remained as potent as that of James. In fact, bearing a son had become an obsession – a mental and physical compulsion compounded of the need to satisfy her womanhood, justify her destiny and increase the marital hold on her husband.

Sir Christopher Garnish, her wizened little secretary, came to her bedside one cold winter's morning, bulging eyes bright with excitement. Aware of the inadvisability of speaking while one of the nurses made the Queen comfortable, his thin frame quivered with the suppressed import of his news.

'Well, Sir Christopher, speak your say before you wriggle out of your robe,' said Margaret, at last. 'Why are you standing there in such a dither?'

'I've news from His Grace the King, madam.' His normal croaking voice squeaked in ecstasy. 'Stornoway castle's been taken and the accursed Donald Dubh the Black in the hands of the royal army. The Earls of Argyll and Huntly are sharing lordship of the Isles and this could be the end of the troubles which have pestered the King. Isn't that joyous news, Your Grace?'

An immediate babble of excitement broke out among the ladies in attendance. 'Silence!' commanded Margaret, putting her hands to her head dramatically. 'My head bubbles with enough sickness without your prattle.'

170

The voices stopped at once, though one or two of the younger ladies pulled wry faces behind the cover of their wide sleeves.

More than three years of marriage, homesickness, the feeling of being an alien, miscarriages and disenchantment with her position had aged Margaret beyond her still tender years. She looked around imperiously, daring any of the ladies to question her word. Satisfied all were suitably cowed she said, 'Yes, joyous news, indeed. But does it mean His Grace will be here for the birth of our child?'

'That will be the wish closest to his heart,' said Sir Christopher, trying to cheer her spirits.

At that moment her chamberlain entered and came forward with as much eagerness as his dour nature could muster. Margaret silenced him with a commanding flourish of her hand, then said to the secretary, 'Send a letter to my lord the King saying that I rejoice at his victory. Also that I've great need of him now that my time draws near.' She sighed and rested back wearily, no longer interested in the sheepish look of the forestalled chamberlain.

The secretary bowed and went to a table in the far corner to fumble with inkhorns and suck at his toothless gums. Margaret called for Lady Hampton. 'His Grace will be flushed with victory. I must complete the joy and provide him with a healthy son. God grant me strength to do it!'

Lady Hampton held her hands with affection. 'I'm sure our Blessed Lord will be heedful of our prayers, Your Grace.'

Margaret looked appealingly at the tall, raven-haired, calm lady, whom she remembered in her early childhood as being so exquisitely beautiful. 'I must be out of bed for the King's return, you know how he despises weakness. Men only want to concern themselves with the pleasures of their sporting, not the pains we have to suffer on account of it.'

'Have no fear, madam,' consoled Lady Hampton. 'The physicians say that the sickness is mending and the child remains lively.'

A gleam of hope lit Margaret's pallid face. 'Yes, it struggles endlessly within me, but what will its struggles be when it is without?'

'His royal father has lessened them with today's glad news.'

'That is so,' admitted the Queen, 'the suppression of this rebellion will strengthen the kingdom for a son.'

Lady Hampton smiled and offered up a silent prayer. Even though she had known the Queen since infancy, and loved her as if she were her own, she often could not tell what fears lurked behind the youthful frown. She remembered Margaret at Richmond Palace as a toddler, strutting about the nursery playing at being the Queen of Scotland. She greatly needed the birth of a healthy son to translate that early imagination into reality.

James returned primed with triumph after the New Year, having marched his victorious troops from the north and received acclaim all along the route. Upon arrival at the castle he hurried straight to Margaret, entering the bedchamber when still thought to be in the courtyard. As a result, he almost collided with a tiring-woman retreating to the garde-robe with a brimming slop bucket, in which a blood-soiled swab buffeted on a surface flecked with expectorated bile. Confusion swept over the scene like a gust of wind, but he speeded the woman's exit by silencing the clucking of the attendants and opening the garde-robe door himself.

The offensive object removed and the ladies having gained their self control, he greeted them with formal ceremony, not without a flicker of a smile, knowing that they would all later feel the rasp of the Queen's tongue. When suffering her sickness nothing right could be done for her, so physicians, nurses, tiring-women, sympathetic attendants, all contributed to the all-pervading wrong. The atmosphere of the bedchamber then alternated between squawks of acrimony from the Queen and the simmering resentment of those under the lash of her flaying words.

Remembering all this, James concluded his salutation and asked the ladies to withdraw. The sweetness of the smiles he received indicated their appreciation of even a brief respite. He kissed Margaret on the forehead, lifted her light body into a chair, raised her feet on to a low stool, then knelt in front of her, smiling his encouragement. 'Now, Margaret, tell me what troubles you.'

She looked at his handsome face, smiling appreciatively at his solicitude. It was easy to understand why women found him so attractive. He had an unerring knack of doing the right thing at the right moment, anticipating feminine mood so that he could encourage or circumvent, and do either with considerable charm. She reached forward and rubbed her hand through his red hair, as usual cut short for his campaigning. 'It's good to have your protection again, James,' she said, with a catch of emotion in her voice.

'Yes, the victory's been won, thus it can be so.' Pride glistened his features, but his eyes were full of sympathy as she told of her sickness and complained about the inept physicians.

He took her hands in his and kissed them, chiefly to check the stream of maladies flowing from her tongue. When she smiled in acknowledgement, he asked earnestly, 'And what of the bairn?'

'Its movements are regular and normal.'

He nodded with satisfaction. 'Then we must pray that it will be a son.'

'And a future king,' she added.

'Is that your wish, Margaret?'

'With all my heart,' she confirmed, squeezing his hands.

He laughed happily, standing and stretching his limbs in exhilaration. 'Then we are truly of one accord,' he said, walking about the chamber. 'I should like the child to be born in Edinburgh. The people of the city would like that too. I have to go to the capital to meet Parliament, so if you feel strong enough, I'll conduct you there myself.'

She moved as if to object, but suddenly checked herself. 'I shall be ready when you desire it, my lord.'

'Good!' He clapped his hands together and puffed out his chest. 'Tonight, sweet lady, we sup in State. The high steward tells me that my people are arriving from all parts of the kingdom to celebrate the end of the rebellion in the Western Isles.'

Margaret sighed and passed her hand across her brow. 'I could not celebrate with you tonight, my lord, not without endangering our unborn child. I know the signs, James. My stomach is queasy and my head throbs like the continual beat of a drum. You will have to crave my pardon of your victorious assembly, so that I can compose myself for the journey to come.'

He patted her hand solicitously. 'It shall be as you wish. Have your secretary write a victory message and I'll read it to the gathering myself.'

He urged her to take care of herself, then summoned her ladies, and with a deep bow which hid the quirking of his lips, informed them that he was leaving the Queen to their loving care. One bright pair of hazel eyes tried to attract his special attention, but he knew better than to arouse his wife's suspicions in her own bedchamber.

The roistering began early in the Hall that evening. Every board that could be found had been set up, laden with the choicest dishes three kitchens could provide. In spite of the continued border skirmishes and a letter sent to the Queen's father containing a veiled hint of war if England supported the Burgundians, James felt well satisfied with the outcome of the campaign. Several nobles glanced at him and smiled, pointed him out to their ladies. Although now clad in a cloth of gold robe sparkling with jewels, they still recognised him as the furious chain-mailed horseman who had led them with such risk and daring.

The Earl of Argyll sat on one side of him, Bothwell on the other. Towards the end of the meal, James rose and held up his hands. Slowly the raucousness of merriment ebbed to complete silence. His voice ringing resonantly through the lofty Hall, he read the Queen's message, laughing good-humouredly when it produced the thunderous acclaim of hundreds of well-lubricated male throats. 'It seems the Queen is mighty popular among my troops, Patrick,' he said, sitting down and turning to Bothwell.

'Isn't she producing you an heir, Your Grace?' replied Bothwell, smiling complacently.

'As I said she would if you gave her time,' burst in Argyll, already showing signs of having drunk too freely.

'Yes, you did, Archibald,' agreed James, slapping him heavily on the back, which, coming as it did, at the outset of a wine-induced eructation, almost brought tears to his eyes.

James left the servers to right him and turned to Bothwell. 'The Queen befits her station very well, that I'll grant you.'

Smiling again Argyll butted in saying, 'She's truly a Queen according to my good Countess, who seems very much in her favour. Indeed, she has spoken of nothing else but the Queen's maladies since I returned.'

'And you would have her talk of other things, Archibald?' queried James, winking at Bothwell.

'I don't care for women's talk at the best of times, Your Grace,' Argyll went on, his prominent teeth making his grin all the more lascivious. 'Many a good lass has spoilt my sporting by mouthing overmuch.' He emptied his goblet and yelled for more wine, a true scion of the drinking and wenching Argylls.

'And where is your lady Elizabeth?' queried James. 'Why is she not with us tonight?'

'She attends the Queen, Your Grace But if your royal wife robs my marital bed this night, then by God's nails I'll find another to fill it!'

'In which case you should not drink more wine, Archibald,' warned Bothwell. 'Else you'll have no life in you for your purpose.'

Argyll raised his goblet with a flourish which spilled half its contents. 'Nonsense, Patrick, I look to this much-prized vintage of Malvasia to fire manhood into my veins.'

Face flushed and black hair awry, it looked reasonably certain that Argyll would be incapable long before the end of the festivities. This soldier-like banter made James reflect on his own bed being occupied by some pretty diversion. After all, the company celebrated his victory. He wiped his lips with a handkerchief and brushed his beard with his cuff. His eyes fleeted round the Hall, from fair head to dark head, taking note of flashing smiles, glinting teeth, well-formed lips, graceful shoulders or the firmness of some lady's breasts, but none responded to his gaze. At one time there had been no shortage of lasses ready to serve him; now it seemed the Queen had intimidated them all.

His ruminations were suddenly interrupted by recognising the unmistakable gnarled features of the powerful, lumbering Earl of Angus, clad in an outer robe emblazoned with the Douglas white stars. Maybe Jane had accompanied him?

Lords and ladies were now disporting themselves in the dance. James rose, dismissing Bothwell by saying, 'You'd better dance with your lady Janet, my lord.'

Following the King's gaze, Sir Lucan moved to his side, sensing trouble. James laughed at him and said, 'God's bones, Lucan, can't you find yourself a lass?'

'I await your orders, Your Grace.'

'Then find a lass with a loving disposition,' quipped James, eyes raking through the Douglas followers. He watched Angus retire into a window recess, then, when the dancing was at its height, skirted round the assembly unobserved.

Those with Angus backed away when the King entered the recess. The old Earl's features quivered noticeably, but he bowed with commendable dignity. 'Your Grace pays me honour by singling me out from so many guests.'

'It is not your company I seek, Angus.'

The Earl's vein-knotted right hand gripped at his outer robe to restrain it from the sword. 'I'm disappointed, Your Grace. You know the house of Douglas is always ready to do the King's service.'

'Where's Lady Kennedy?' fired the King

'I took leave of her in Forfar before coming to give praise for Your Grace's victory.' Triumph radiated from his deep-socketed eyes as he added, 'Lady Jane knew of my mission, but these days Forfar pleases her more than Darnaway.'

The King's own right hand twitched for action. 'You're an old fool to think you can satisfy such a woman,' he rasped, then turned sharply and brushed all from his path as he strode through the Hall to an empty bedchamber.

* * *

After elaborate preparations for the Queen's welfare, the royal party moved off to Edinburgh. Margaret reclined in a litter drawn by two reliable chestnut horses. James rode beside her, with Lady Hampton and Joanna on palfreys close behind.

Weary of the slow pace he leaned forward into the litter. 'Margaret, I'm going to ride ahead to make sure the way is clear.'

Her face had a white deathly pallor. 'Don't stray far, my lord, for I fear that at any moment I shall need your support.'

He turned to Lady Hampton. 'The Queen looks ill, my lady. Is there anything else we can do for her comfort?'

'Nothing other than reach the Palace of Holyroodhouse as soon as possible, Your Grace.'

'I'm riding up front to try and speed the way ahead. If you need me, wave your scarf above your head.' He turned to Sir Lucan. 'Come, Lucan, let us fill our lungs with fresh air. This atmosphere of sickness nauseates me.'

They moved slowly to the head of the train, then galloped off in a spray of clods of mud, Lucan almost at the King's side. They returned after a short while and James took his place beside the slowly progressing litter as Lucan rode beside Joanna Hampton. Sheer boredom prompted James to ride ahead again, this time alone. He was soon summoned by Lucan with a wave of his sword.

When he returned Lady Hampton and Lucan were already attending to the Queen. He leapt from his horse and rushed to the litter. Margaret suddenly leaned forward and vomited all over her rug and fur coverings. He yelled for water, then held Margaret's hot, clammy hands, removing the rings from her swollen fingers in case they restricted her circulation.

'God's blood, the stench is putrid!' he exclaimed. He turned to a nurse. 'She must be given air. Is it safe to remove her from the litter, mistress?'

'Your Grace, I . . . I . . . I –'

'Out of the way and stop your clucking,' he snapped impatiently. He pushed aside the tasselled blue and gold drapes, then flung the coverings out into the roadway. He instructed Lucan to order a groom to remove the saddle cloth from his horse.

He raised the Queen's head gently with his hand. 'Margaret, you need air. Can you bear to be moved?'

She nodded assent, but could utter no words. With Lucan's aid he lifted her on to the saddle cloth laid upon the roadside grass, with the lacquered yellow petals of lesser celandine sparkling all around it. He discarded his blue riding cloak and wrapped it across Margaret's slim, trembling shoulders. 'The air's cold, but anything is better than putrefying in that stench,' he assured her.

Lady Hampton hurriedly supervised the swilling out of the litter, but the horses stood champing at their bits and scraping their hooves on the pockmarked tracks. Those looking on flapped their arms and stamped their feet, for the rawness of the cold soon ate its way into inactive limbs.

At last, colour returned to Margaret's cheeks and James himself lifted her bodily back into the refreshed litter. The combination of effort and anxiety brought sweat to his brow, a clammy fear that he had made the wrong decision and the journey to Edinburgh might prove too much for the Queen. He sent messengers to gallop ahead, ordering physicians to ride out to meet them, fearing the child would arrive before they reached the capital. Once moving again, he hurried the train along as speedily as possible, remaining close to the litter, constantly checking that midwives, nurses and Lady Hampton were immediately at hand in the event of an emergency. The sight of the city of Edinburgh on the skyline never looked more welcome to him, nor to those who bore the brunt of his tension along the way.

Three days of agonised waiting followed. The Queen was confined to bed at Holyroodhouse, exhausted by the journey, so that James suffered the torment that his wish to travel to Edinburgh might yet cause the still-birth of his first legitimate heir. Throughout each day he alternated between stalking moodily about his own apartments and dashing through the palace to inquire of the Queen.

It was a merciful relief to the entire palace staff when news came of the birth of the baby Prince. Overjoyed, James immediately ordered wine for all and promised a great celebration. He visited Margaret and congratulated her, but near to exhaustion with labour, she barely recognised him. After being assured that rest would revive her, he held the infant Prince in his arms, then strode off to join the roisterers. With the Queen and most of her ladies absent, the rejoicing became increasingly hilarious and went on far into the night.

James was awakened by Sir Lucan, both of them bleary-eyed. 'I hear that the physicians have been called to the Queen during the night, Your Grace. I thought you would want to know at once.'

Leaping up immediately James asked, 'What's the matter with the Queen?'

'I've not yet found out, Your Grace. I came straight to you as soon as I heard.'

'I'll go to her and present my gift. That will cheer her Tudor heart.'

He gathered up a splendid silver cup in which he had heaped one hundred gold pieces. He took it to her bedchamber, but found her white-faced, fair hair damp with perspiration, eyes haggard as she writhed on the bed fitfully.

He held her hand and tried to calm her. 'Look what I've brought you, Margaret. My personal gift for the joy of having a rightful heir.'

Glancing up at the cup she groaned and said, 'The only gift I wish for, James, is to have a body free from pain.'

'That will come, my dear,' he replied solicitously.

'How do you know?' she demanded, eyes suffusing with tears.

A black-gowned cleric came to the bedside, indicating that he wished to speak to the King. James glanced at his wife with concern, wishing with all his heart that he could help her bear the pain, but the helplessness of his presence aggravated him.

The physician drew him beyond earshot of the large four-poster bed. 'The Queen must rest, Your Grace,' said Brother Dominic. 'She spends so much time upbraiding us and tormenting herself with thoughts of death that our potions are having no effect. She's preventing nature doing its recuperative work in sleep. Her condition causes us alarm, Your Grace.'

James patted his shoulder consolingly. 'It will pass, Brother Dominic. The Queen's overjoyed at presenting me with a baby Prince. Is that not natural?'

'It is, Your Grace. We all join in your felicity. But with the Queen, her excitement has become a fever coursing through her body.' He inclined his head respectfully, his large dark eyes imploring for understanding. 'If Your Grace would impress upon her the need of obeying what we prescribe.'

'That I will,' said James, returning to the bedside. A flash of inspiration occurred to him, a legitimate excuse for absenting himself from the sickly dolour of the days ahead. Again he held Margaret's moist, clammy hand. 'Madam, sweet Margaret, you're not looking well.'

Her eyes rolled as if she had difficulty in seeing him. 'I trust I've given you happiness, my lord. The physicians say that our son will live,' she whispered.

'Yes, lady, but Brother Dominic assures me that you can't recover fully until you relax into deep sleep.'

She jolted into wide-eyed wakefulness, and with an envenomed glare searched for the physician who had given this report to the King. Brother Dominic tactfully retreated towards the far wall. 'I feel so much pain, James, my whole body's wracked with it,' she complained.

'You will recover, Margaret, if you listen to the good friars. God has granted us the blessing of a son. He will also grant your recovery. Today I intend journeying to the shrine of St. Ninian on foot to pray for Our Blessed Lord's indulgence on your behalf.'

'No, my lord! Doubtless I need your good prayers, but your presence here would be more to my liking.'

'Your return to health is the first need, my lady. A pilgrimage to the gracious saint is the surest way of securing it.'

'But, my lord –' She broke off with an agonised cry, then slumped sideways, gripped by pain.

James beckoned Brother Dominic and hastily explained his intention. It met the friar's wholehearted approval and that settled the issue. To eliminate further objection, James withdrew to make arrangements for a pilgrimage walk to the Galloway coast and the shrine of his favourite saint.

The Court also approved of the King's action and assembled in the courtyard for his departure. Sir Lucan and four Italian minstrels were chosen to share the pedestrian penance. James set a hard pace from the start, and soon the minstrels were flagging, so James spurred them on when their music failed to enliven their pace.

As Bothwell and Argyll had predicted, Margaret had not failed in her duty and presented him with an heir, but he could not remain at her bedside whilst she prolonged recovery merely to keep him under observation. This pilgrimage and his prayers would serve as a mark of his gratitude towards her.

Upon arrival at the shrine the four minstrels were completely exhausted. James ordered Lucan to hire horses to despatch the blistered musicians back to Edinburgh, but they were so spent that they could barely keep themselves in the saddle.

James then went to the shrine and knelt at his prie-dieu. He offered up prayers with genuine devotion. In like manner, he made his Confession and rigidly observed his penance. This done, he fortuitously learnt that Lady Jane Kennedy was staying at a nearby tavern.

Withholding his true reasons, James summoned Lucan. 'I've a mind to tarry here longer, for I'm sure that through it the Queen's health will be favoured,' he said. 'Ride back to Her Grace and take my blessings. Return to me here when you can carry tidings good enough to permit my return.'

Not even Lucan suspected any other motive, for none could act more holy than the King when he chose. To dim Lucan's perception was the fair prospect of returning to Mistress Joanna Hampton, whom he had been courting recently. 'As you say, Your Grace,' he responded readily.

'The mission seems to suit you well, Lucan. Could it be that an English lass frets for your return.'

'I hope so, Your Grace. Though I made little progress last night. I fear there's another to be ousted before I can make real headway.'

James clapped him on the back and walked with him to the farrier who hired out horses. 'You should content yourself with a Scottish lass, Lucan. They take to the bed more easily than these cold English lasses.'

Lucan nodded without appreciation.

When they acquired horses, James said, 'Spur your horse to your lass, Lucan. If the feet of the Italian minstrels haven't healed, tell them to bathe their blisters in their own water.'

With a hearty laugh, James slapped the rump of the knight's horse and Lucan rode off with a suddenness that confused his respectful salute. James watched him right himself and break into an easy canter, then he too leapt exuberantly upon his horse and rode hard in the opposite direction.

Lady Jane received him in a small, garret room in which thick oak beams supported the sloping ceiling.

'Jane, what blessed coincidence brought you so close?' he asked, embracing her warmly.

The gleam of satisfaction in her blue-green eyes and the whimsicality of her smile apprised him that the coincidence had been contrived. He laughed out with relish. 'So my informant was your agent?'

He held her at arm's length, long enough to be fully stirred by her often tasted but still irresistible femininity. 'Jane! Jane! My sweet Jane!' he murmured, before crushing his mouth upon her cool, partially open lips.

She allowed his ardour full play, only easing him away when sure he would draw her back with renewed vigour. Her passionate responses were fired by the confident knowledge that in spite of an English Queen and a legal heir to the throne, part of the King of Scotland remained in her possession. It was the guarantee of her future.

Eventually, Lady Jane's diplomatic agent gave forewarning of Sir Lucan's approach, so James greeted his body knight at the shrine as if fresh from the devotions he had kept up during the day. The officiating priests at the shrine, however, were aware of his nocturnal absence from the devotee cell, but to charge their royal benefactor with misdemeanour would have meant the end of their mission.

James took Lucan into the frugal cell furnished only with an unpolished wooden chair, a small table and a hard austerity bed. 'Well, Lucan, what news do you bring of the Queen?'

Lucan unfastened his long jacket as he said, 'Good news, Your Grace. It's the belief of all that the crisis of the Queen's health passed with your arrival at this blessed shrine.'

James crossed himself as Lucan continued, 'Since then she's improved until there is no cause for alarm concerning mother and child. All in Edinburgh speak highly of the wisdom of your devotions.'

'As well they should,' confirmed James. After all, he had walked to St. Ninian's for the sole purpose of interceding for the Queen's health. Every day he had said prayers for her recovery, and now his prayers were answered, in spite of the way he had spent his nights.

'Yes,' murmured Lucan, then lapsed into reflective silence.

'How's your English lass? Have you bedded her yet?'

'No, my lord,' said Lucan disconsolately. 'It seems that some astrologer read her star courses and forecast misfortunes which have tormented her ever since. Now she has the notion that she wants to marry the man who's wooing her mother.'

'God's bones, Lucan, that sounds an unholy mess you'd do best to avoid!' cried James, flinging his riding cloak across his broad shoulders. 'Why don't you take my advice and find a Scottish lass?'

'Because I love this one, Your Grace, and want no other.'

They were simple words expressed with a sincerity that continued to ring in James's ears as they mounted their horses for the ride back to Edinburgh. With the passing of each mile he more clearly understood Lucan's uncomplicated devotion. A man could grasp at spurious relationships and seek relieving pleasures, but ultimately these counted for nothing compared with the real love a man could have for one woman.

Now memory of his sporting with Jane Kennedy became offensive, his return to the Queen a burden to be borne for the sake of his princely son. A solitary figure emerged as a mental image – the loving face beneath a blue marble stone at Dunblane Cathedral. Walking his horse to drink at a small burn, he gazed up at the brilliant stars enriching the deep indigo of the night sky, tears trickling down his cheeks, genuine tears for a lost love. He did not feel ashamed of them or try to brush them away. Not that it mattered, for Lucan was far too preoccupied with his own thoughts to notice them in the moonlight.

Even so, it bothered him that his faithful body knight should be so affected by an English lass. He could see no good coming of it, yet this was possibly because of his own experience. Lucan's love need not be tainted by the heritage of two royal families, and there were no vetoes on him following the dictates of his heart. His own royal marriage was different. He had an inborn rancour towards England, and his bride made it manifest in many ways that she too harboured a deep-seated distrust of anything Scottish.

THIRTEEN

During the autumn of 1507, James received overtures from King Louis XII of France to maintain the alliance between their two countries. The ambassador came shortly after the French apothecary Damien launched himself from a high parapet at Stirling castle, when attempting to fly to France. A large crowd from the castle and town gathered to watch the Frenchman clad in wings made from eagles' feathers make his leap from the castle wall. He fell to the ground and broke his thigh bone, complaining that too many hens' feathers had been put into the wings.

Back at Edinburgh several envoys came from King Henry to try and break the Scottish alliance with France, each one proclaiming that England had no dispute with France. Some of the Englishmen obviously imparted the purpose of their mission to the Queen, for she lost no opportunity of pressing her father's cause. Even so, James discerned the diplomacy, fully aware that both England and France had the powder smoke of war in their nostrils. This being the case, in spite of Margaret's dissuasions, he intended maintaining his alliance with France, at the same time ensuring that Scotland was not caught unprepared. Accordingly, he summoned the Earl of Bothwell and Sir Andrew Wood.

'Scotland must have more ships if we are to keep pace with the strength of the English fleet,' James told them, as they sat round the table of his Presence Chamber.

Sir Andrew Wood, ever an indefatigable servant of the Crown, had brought rolls of charts of coastal defences and plans for new ships. 'I agree, Your Grace, but our coasts are plagued by pirates interfering with our supplies of shipbuilding timber from France.'

'Then Scottish waters must be cleared of pirates,' flashed James. 'What do you suggest?'

'Employing the services of Robert and John Barton, as well as their brother Captain Andrew,' responded Sir Andrew at once. 'I've brought them to the palace with me, Your Grace. They seek a renewal of the letters of marque granted by your royal father against the Portuguese, for the plundering of their father's ship. They'll serve Scotland well in settling this family grudge, if you give your approval.'

'The letters of marque shall be renewed,' James declared, without hesitation. 'So, Patrick, pour some wine and let us see these three sailor brothers.'

Bothwell, whose eyes were darkened through recent illness, poured wine from a silver carafe, saying, 'They seek twelve thousand ducats compensation from the Portuguese. If the dagos refuse it, as no doubt they will, the Bartons have the skill and daring to exact that sum and more.'

'Excellent!' approved James, as the three tall, dark, bearded sailors were ushered in. They each had the bright, penetrating eyes of seamen and James greeted them warmly, particularly Captain Andrew.

'Sir Andrew Wood has spoken on your behalf and I know of your desire to catch pirates, Captain Andrew,' said James.

'My task will be made easier by renewing the letters of marque and having the support of my brothers, Your Grace.'

'That will be done, for you and your brothers, on condition that you keep our Scottish waters clear of pirates.'

Andrew turned to his two brothers and received their immediate approving nods. 'I made my own promise to you before, Your Grace, but now all three of us can concentrate on your mission. Sir Andrew tells me that he has a new ship nearly fitted for the purpose.'

'As soon as it's ready you shall take command of it,' James assured him. 'This is a mission that must be swift and successful.'

'You can depend upon us, Your Grace.'

James rose from his throne chair and looked at him fixedly. 'Yes, Captain Andrew, I think I can,' he said, with a hint of warning in his tone. His mood suddenly changed and he laughed out heartily. 'Now we'll drink to your success, gallant captains. May we soon see a token of it.'

'I'll despatch one to you direct, Your Grace,' promised Andrew Barton.

They drank a toast in an atmosphere of convivial confidence, then James bade farewell to the sailors with happy familiarity. Turning to Bothwell he said, 'I have a feeling we'll not regret our work this day, Patrick.'

'I'm sure we won't, Your Grace.' Bothwell hesitated, then tactfully added, 'A page has brought a message from the Queen.'

James heaved a sigh. Most of his communion with the Queen these days took the form of notes from her sick chamber. Still recuperating from childbirth, she always had some fresh ache, malady or whimpering plea to make on behalf of her father. After such an inspiring display of manliness, he felt disinclined to be drawn back into her valetudinarian nexus of pains and potions. She wanted to see him about the arrangements for her visit to the shrine of St. Ninian; a warning that her inquiries about the pilgrimage centre had elicited the name of Lady Jane Kennedy. This meant another long period of recrimination until she unearthed the truth, as she eventually would with the unerring instinct of a ferret. He smiled wryly. Only yesterday he had heard that most of her younger Scottish maids called her Madam Ferret, because nothing could be kept secret from her for long. It was a worthy title, and if he knew the lass who had so dubbed her, he would willingly have given her a gold piece. He read the note again, then bellowed for Lucan, his anger mounting when he could not be found.

'God's bones, Patrick, where's that whoreson churl? Of late he's taken to wenching by day as well as by night. Who is this English cat who has stuck her claws into him?'

Bothwell smiled tolerantly. 'The comely Mistress Joanna, so I am told.'

'No, not the chit who was bedded by your squire?'

'The very same, Your Grace.'

James shook his head incredulously. 'By thunder, the poor dolt's brains must be addled. Such a wench will be the ruin of him.' With a contemptuous snort, he stormed out of the chamber, yelling orders in all directions.

With innate cunning, Margaret had made her intention of visiting St. Ninian's shrine known throughout the Court, aware that any objection from the King would deny the blessings he had attributed to his own pilgrimage. It took seventeen pack mules to carry her baggage and James rode at their head full of foreboding.

His suspicions were confirmed upon arrival, when Margaret immediately revealed her unholy motives. 'I've not the strength to endure the devotions here, my lord, so I will leave you to carry them out on my behalf,' she informed him. 'Your last visit was so successful that I'm sure our cause will be in good hands. Please remember me in your prayers.'

What could he say? What could he do? The whole Court knew the reason for the pilgrimage and Margaret would have her women watch him like a hawk. He had Lucan with him so they could at least hunt and ride together during the day.

'Will you require me at night after you enter your devotee cell, Your Grace?' asked Lucan, soon after they arrived.

Ensnared himself he did not feel too sympathetic towards Lucan's obvious intentions. 'I suppose you want to go courting your English lass?'

'She's here with the Queen, Your Grace.'

'Perhaps, but if she has to tend the Queen's maladies, she'll not have much time for you,' observed James wryly.

Lucan smiled. Joanna Hampton had never complained to him of the Queen, but several of the Scottish attendants were not similarly reticent. 'She's devoted to the Queen, Your Grace. Evidently they were brought up together as children.'

'That may be, Lucan, but is she devoted to you?'

'Not as yet, Your Grace.'

They were in a stabling yard, having put away their horses. James rested his hand on Lucan's shoulder in a friendly manner. He looked genuinely puzzled as he asked, 'Then why do you torture yourself over her?'

'For the same reason I gave you before, when you asked a similar question – because I love her.'

'Yes, I remember,' said James. 'But if she doesn't love you, I can't see the sense in it.'

'It will all make sense when I win her, Your Grace, for that's what I intend to do.'

James turned towards the shrine, shaking his head. 'Then you have my blessings to do your courting, Lucan, while I spend my nights in one of these cells. I'll say a prayer or two for you as well, seems that I'm going to have little chance of doing anything else at night but sleep and pray. God's bones, I don't know why I should feel sorry for you!'

'Shall I go and see that a cell's ready for you, Your Grace?'

'No, I'll see the good father myself. You go to your lass. You'd better not tell her that the King thinks you're too good for her, but by all that's holy I can't imagine her making you happy, Lucan.'

The officiating priest greeted the King with an unction tinged with the awareness of the change of circumstances compared with the last visit. If he had not been a holy man, James would have cuffed the partially hidden smirk from his face.

So it went on for twenty days and nineteen barren nights, during most of which the queen avoided her husband, not only at night, but during the day as well. On the last day, as the pack mules were being loaded for the return to Edinburgh, James said to Lucan, 'I've had much time for fervent prayers, but they don't seem to have brought much in my favour. Have they done anything to further your cause, Sir Knight?'

Lucan turned from one of the mules and smiled wryly. 'I fear not, Your Grace. Mistress Joanna has the notion that her star courses don't include me in their reckoning.'

'God's bones, Lucan, you must be addle-headed! Why do you pursue such a lass? Surely there are others you could bed without having to bother about star courses?'

'No doubt there are, but none that inflames me as she does.'

'Inflame is right. She'd inflame me to the point that I'd skelp her. How does she report of the Queen's health?'

'Much improved, and she tells her ladies that it's on account of Your Grace's pious devotions here at the shrine.'

'Then thank God they've done somebody good and we can return to Edinburgh! It will be a long time before the holy shrine of St. Ninian sees me again.'

They continued assembling the mules as the Queen's baggage was fixed to them, but nothing happened to improve the King's temper.

Back at Edinburgh, James attended to what State affairs were necessary, then to escape the lacerations of the Queen's tongue concerning what she had learnt at the shrine, he sought the consolation of the cause of it all – Lady Jane Kennedy. Once again her receptivity brought oblivion to the true facts of his married life. Of course, the Queen found out about this interlude too, so further discord flared up between them.

It took the death of their son in February 1508 to reunite them in awareness of their royal duty. Margaret was distraught at the child's rapid deterioration, in spite of all her own efforts as a mother to save him. Her conscientiousness in this role wrung admiration from her husband, but not her reasoning as to the cause of the misfortunes that dogged their attempts to raise a family in which the thistle and the rose could flourish.

As he tried to comfort her at the supper table one night, Margaret confessed her innermost thoughts. 'I'm sure that what we're suffering is a punishment from Almighty God,' she said, looking at him beseechingly.

He saw her now as a fully grown woman, with attractions of her own, but as disillusioned with her life in Scotland as he was with his marriage. 'Why do you say that, Margaret?' he asked noncommittally.

'James, I must talk to you. We can't talk here privately. Can we go to my withdrawing chamber?'

'But, Margaret, you have not yet supped.'

'I've no stomach for food when my mind is so disturbed. I ask that you excuse me now, but when you've supped come to my chamber prepared to listen to me, not to lose your temper or rant against my father in England.'

James swallowed hard, but in fairness recognised that she had summarised the nature of most of their dealings with each other. 'All right, Margaret, I'll do what you say,' he conceded.

She rose saying, 'Thank you, my lord. I can promise that you will not regret your accession to my wishes.'

She summoned Mistress Hampton who came to her at once. James noticed her dark-featured comeliness, the firm swellings of her breasts and the trimness of her figure. He thought that he could not blame Lucan for wanting to bed with her, but then it seemed from past experience he should be aware that bed sporting was not to her liking, even though she had such a promising body. He watched them leave the Hall, wondering what was in store both for himself and for Lucan. He was soon to learn when he joined Margaret in her withdrawing chamber.

She offered him wine and attended to his comfort, then when they were both seated said, 'Through no fault of mine, James, we are again childless. I think we will remain childless unless you're prepared to alter your ways. My miscarriages and the early death of our children are your punishment from Almighty God.'

'My punishment for what?'

She looked at him intently. 'Remember your promise not to lose your temper, because I intend to speak frankly, since you feign not to know why you should be punished.'

James remained silent, chiefly because he had nothing reasonable to say.

'You're being punished for the way you ill-use our marriage and for your sacrilege.'

Enlightenment as to the way her mind was working now gleamed through, but he still kept silent.

'You went to the holy shrine of St. Ninian to give thanks for the birth of our royal Prince and pray for the return of my good health. Yet even whilst you were supposed to be on a pilgrimage you were lusting with that Kennedy whore. Don't you think that sacrilegious? Are you surprised that Almighty God should punish you?'

Put in this manner and appreciating her wifely humiliation he accepted what she said without comment.

'As you know I went to St. Ninian's myself because at first I could not believe the gossip. I know the spite of courtiers when it comes to gossip, but they were speaking the truth and relishing doing so within my hearing. Can you understand how that makes me feel?'

James rubbed at his beard agitatedly. It would have been so easy to have burst into a temper and escaped, but he had made a promise and her own calm discussion gave more weight to her complaint than shrill words. 'Yes, I can, Margaret, and I'm sorry for the distress I've caused you. I mean that most sincerely.'

Her eyes widened and mouth quivered as she said, 'But are you truly sorry, James? Haven't we said all this before? Yet you've been with that woman again since returning from the holy shrine, perhaps even since we lost our royal Prince. Lady Kennedy seems to have more command over you than your own wife.'

How could he answer that? 'You are my Queen, Margaret,' he mumbled inadequately.

'But not so delightsome in your bed as your leman!'

Again he kept his silence and temper in control, aware that Margaret was leading up to something.

'I came to you as a virgin bride, my lord, unversed in the ways of men. You can not expect me to be as adept as the whore who uses her body to gain possessions.'

Margaret paused, watched him, trying to determine the effect of her words. When he still remained silent she went on, 'Even, so, I have tried to be a good wife to you, James. Now I feel that if you really want a son, then you must spare me the humiliation of being the laughingstock of serving women who know where you seek your pleasure. My failing seems to be that I can't delight in bed, but my body has suffered much pain to try and bear you healthy sons. I am prepared to go on trying to produce an heir, but how can I when all the time haunted by the knowledge that your only enjoyment comes from bedding with that Kennedy whore? I think Almighty God agrees with me, and that is why we are now childless again,'

James had to smother an inner smile at her reasoning. He recognised it as the sort of guile he might use himself to gain his own way. 'You have always told me that it's your fervent wish to have a son who will one day become a king,' he reminded her.

'That is still my fervent wish, James, in spite of all the pain and suffering. But not if you continue to see that whore. I can't compose myself to motherhood with her lurking in the background all the time.'

Having had her say Margaret now remained silent. They stared at each other for a few moments each waiting for the other to speak.

'Well, my lord?' queried Margaret.

'I've listened to you, Margaret, and consider there's justification in all you have said.'

'So what are you going to do about it? This is not an affair of State in which you are constantly telling me not to meddle. This is about our private married life and concerns none but the two of us.'

'You're right, Margaret, and once again I apologise. I will ask Almighty God for forgiveness in my nightly prayers.'

Her eyes suddenly flashed anger, sensing that he was mocking her. He rose and moved across to her chair, kissed her on the cheek and said, 'You leave the affairs of State to me and I'll leave the motherhood to you.'

'And that Kennedy woman will be left to find others for her bed sporting?'

'I promise you that too.'

She put her arms round him and said, 'Then may Almighty God grant my womb the strength to conceive you a son mighty quick.'

'We must both pray for that,' he agreed.

He moved to leave, but she restrained him, saying, 'There is another matter to settle. Your body knight, Sir Lucan, wishes to marry my childhood companion Mistress Hampton.'

'Yes, but she'll have none of it, so he tells me.'

'It would seem that today she has agreed to marry him, if both you and I grant our permission.'

'Do you favour the match?'

'Joanna, like myself, has found life in Scotland much different from that in England. But I think she is now more settled and marriage to Sir Lucan could make her even more so.'

'Then I take it you are prepared to grant your permission?'

'If that meets with your approval, my lord.'

Inwardly James felt as if he were condemning Lucan to destruction, but he said, 'If it is their mutual wish, and you see no objection, then we will see them wed with our blessings.'

'Thank you, my lord. I'll tell Joanna straight away.'

'And I'll see Lucan.' He kissed her again, and they sealed a newly-found understanding with a clasp of each other's hands.

James sent for Lucan at once and saw him in his private chamber. 'The Queen tells me that Mistress Hampton has agreed to marry you, Lucan.'

Lucan smiled. 'If you and the Queen give us your blessings, Your Grace,'

'Sit down, Lucan, and talk to me as if I were not the King and your master. Do you really want this English lass?'

'With all my heart,' Lucan replied.

'After all the trouble you've had with her star courses and her fretting over her mother's suitors?'

'That's all over now, Your Grace. Joanna's talked with the Queen, and seemingly Her Grace has kindly recommended me as a suitable husband.'

'Does that mean that you wish me to do the same, even though all along I've advised you against it, and still do? I could forbid the match, Lucan.'

'On what grounds, Your Grace?'

'My regard for you as a faithful follower and friend. I don't want to see you linked with England as I've had to be because I am the King of Scotland. Be honest, Lucan, you've no more love for England than I have, but you're lucky, you have the choice of the whole of Scotland for a bride. I wish to God I had had the same choice. Is this lass pregnant?'

Lucan looked shocked and a little mystified by the King's sudden outburst. 'No, Your Grace. We have never bedded.'

'Then let it be your choice, Lucan. I'll approve whatever you wish.'

'I wish to marry Mistress Hampton and make her Lady Fairfax. I was made a knight in honour of her mistress's wedding, so ours should be a fitting match.'

James wagged his head almost unbelievingly. 'All right, I will see the Queen, Lucan. I only hope that this is something you will not live to regret.'

'You can be sure that we'll be happy,' Lucan declared confidently.

It was a confidence his master did not share, nonetheless he saw that Lucan was married in great style, presenting the couple with a handsome gift of silver plate and allocating them special quarters close to the royal apartments.

FOURTEEN

Whilst Lucan was away on honeymoon one of the King's most able advisers died, the astute Lord Home. The chief consolation was that the diminutive Alexander Home, so different in stature from the father whose title and estates he inherited, had already proved himself sufficiently accomplished to succeed to the office of Lord High Chamberlain.

As soon as Margaret heard of the possibility she came to James complaining, 'Alexander Home's been brought up on the borders, consequently nurses a grievance against England and anything English. Such an appointment won't please my royal father.'

James had no intention of arguing. 'Margaret, I've kept my part of our bargain. Now you must keep your part and leave me to conduct Scotland's affairs of State. That's final!'

She knew from his expression that this was so, but she clearly showed her dissatisfaction, then again when on the day of the appointment at the Palace of Holyroodhouse, James insisted that she attended the confirmation ceremony in his Presence Chamber.

The nobleman's blue eyes shone with determination, emphasising the smile of triumph on his flushed face. He bowed with deep respect to the King, shot a quick glance at the Queen, and paid similar reverence, adroitly managing to display his reluctance without being openly discourteous.

'Well, Lord High Chamberlain, your father would be proud of you,' said James, aware of the byplay being enacted.

'Indeed, he would, Your Grace. His life was devoted to the service of your royal person and that of Scotland. I thank you for this confirmation of office, and pledge that I'll strive to serve Scotland with my father's devotion.'

Margaret sensed the emphatic repetition of Scotland for her benefit. She searched for a cutting remark to strike at the nobleman's bombast, but as her wit was not keen enough for the occasion, maintained a haughty silence. After James signed the necessary documents and invited Home to be seated, she took her leave solely for the pleasure of making Home rise again to pay his respects. James's thoughts were too elevated to be bothered with his wife's petty concern about English reactions. He waved her off gladly and concentrated on Home. 'You come to office at a propitious time, my lord. The Holy Father, as you know, has seen fit to present me with a hat, gold hilted sword and scabbard, and bestowed upon me the title of Protector of the Christian Faith.'

Home stretched his dumpy, yellow hose clad legs and nodded. 'A fitting tribute to your ability as a Christian legislator and true son of Holy Mother the Church, Your Grace.'

'Perhaps,' murmured James, his dark brown eyes glinting with pleasure. 'And Scotland's courted by many foreign Princes, for our ships do well for us. We enjoy peace among our own folk, and we're on friendly terms with England.'

'Yet the possibility of war is not completely behind us,' observed Home.

'It never is, my lord. Doubtless there'll be comings and goings between King Louis and ourselves, but there is much for which we can give thanks.'

Home did not share the King's confidence, but deliberately concealed the fact, not wishing to jeopardise his new position by uttering inopportune words.

'Tonight, my lord, we'll celebrate,' said James. 'The palace needs enlivening with revelry. I'll display the gifts from His Holiness in the Great Hall. It will be a gathering for all Scotland to remember.' As he spoke he fingered the iron penance belt beneath his robe, warmed by the feeling that he had gone a long way towards fulfilling the pledge that his father's death should not be in vain. He smiled, then added, 'Now, my lord, I must prepare for the night's festivities. I invite you and your lady Agnes to sup at the royal table.'

Home rose and bowed in recognition of the honour, then retired as the King began summoning the palace staff with loud and boisterous orders.

At the High Table that evening, James, clad in magnificent cloth of gold robes, surveyed the scene with unrestrained satisfaction. His cousin, the Earl of Arran, sat on his right, the nostrils of his aquiline nose slightly distending each time good humour pulled at the corner of his mouth and animated the greyness of his eyes. 'Having returned victorious from Denmark, my lord, your next journey can be to France, to convince King Louis of our friendly intentions,' James informed him.

The flush on Arran's face was not wine-induced. A champion at arms, he kept himself physically fit, often preferring clear mountain water to some much-prized vintage. Those inclined to make jest of it were usually curbed by remembering the ferocity of his swordplay. 'I think King Louis will be more concerned about the military aid we can give him,' he countered.

James gesticulated with amused tolerance. 'No talk of that tonight, Jamie. The board is set for merriment, even the Queen sups with us. Be sure to tell King Louis of our fleet and the annoyance our sea captains cause the English, that will please him.'

At the mention of her countrymen Margaret eavesdropped avidly, but James cut the conversation short by inviting her to dance. At his command, the minstrels strummed a placid air and Margaret responded with more mental appreciation than bodily enjoyment. Pregnant again, still prone to sickness, she had no wish to take unnecessary risks. James performed with her dutifully until she tired, then chose a more spirited partner. As Margaret kept constant check on his movements, she tried to converse with the Earl of Arran, but he too sighted an unattached lady and excused himself. Lord Home lingered meaningly, but the new Lord High Chamberlain sat at the High Table against her wishes, so she pointedly ignored him.

In the middle of the dancing a steward rushed up to the King and bowed low. 'Your Grace, a gift has arrived from Captain Andrew Barton,' he announced. 'The sailor who accompanies it declares that the barrels must be opened only before the King of Scotland.'

'Then so it shall be,' responded James, bowing to his dapple-cheeked partner, who throughout the dance had never escaped the Queen's watchful eyes. 'Bring the fellow to me and have the barrels brought in, we can then open them with due ceremony. Perhaps Captain Andrew has won for us some particular vintage to befit the occasion.'

'I'm told it's neither wine nor ale, Your Grace.'

'Well, move, master, so that we may know what it is. The music has stopped and our curiosity whetted. Captain Andrew's no man for idle jesting. His barrels must have some import.'

As the steward hurried away, James returned to his table and the excited courtiers gathered in speculative groups.

'My lord, what's the cause of this babble?' asked Margaret, eyebrows arched in disapproval that the music should be stopped to give way to chatter. 'I'm tired and wish to go to my bed.'

'Surely not before you've seen Captain Barton's gift?' He knew her curiosity to be as keen as any other observer.

His secretary Patrick Panther appeared with a black-bearded sailor dressed in a long blue coat. Voices were cut short and the silence spread from group to group. Not a sound could be heard from the oak rafters to the stone-flagged floor as James turned to the sailor. 'You have a rascally grin on your face, master. What has Captain Barton prepared for us? I hope it is something worthy of the commotion we've had.'

The sailor pushed his hand through his short curly hair, unaccustomed to being the focus of so much attention. 'Captain Barton would think so, Your Grace. I'm sure of that,' he replied.

Another steward led in a group of house carls who trundled five large barrels into the centre of the cleared floor space. The barrels were black, damp and malodorous; sprays of floor rushes stuck to them as they were turned on their ends. The battens were removed and lids made ready to be raised as James walked from the High Table. He enjoyed the sense of drama aroused as everyone moved forward in expectancy.

Turning inquiringly to the sailor he asked, 'Well now, master, what's your message?'

The sailor drew himself to his full height, then bowed with unpractised ceremony. 'Captain Andrew Barton reminds Your Grace that his orders were to clear the Scottish coasts of pirates. The barrels contain proof that his mission has been accomplished.'

The sailor threw off the lid of the first barrel and it fell to the floor with a noisy clatter. Then, dramatically, he put his hand into the barrel and slowly drew out a bloody human head which he held by its matted hair.

'God's bones!' gasped James. His astonishment was echoed all around the Hall by shrieks and screams from the ladies, interspersed by gasps and hearty guffaws from the men.

With a sardonic grin the sailor drew a similarly gruesome head from the same barrel with his other hand. Swinging both in a sweeping movement round the other barrels he said proudly, 'Each barrel's likewise filled to the brim, Your Grace.'

Momentarily, James stood speechless, then realised that all eyes were upon him, awaiting his reaction before an expression of general horror or jubilation. Then Margaret sprang to her feet. 'My lord, are you going to condone such barbarism at your Court?' she demanded. 'Are we to become savages?'

James stared at the heads now dangling at the sailor's sides. 'Put them back, master,' he said softly. 'I would not have made such play of the barrels before the ladies had I known their content.'

Lord Home stepped forward. 'Are any of them English heads?' he asked.

'That I don't know, my lord,' replied the sailor. 'The King's orders were to seek out pirates; these I can vouch are pirates' heads.'

After a glance at the Queen, Home puffed out his chest to make up for his lack of height. 'Then Captain Barton's fulfilled his mission to the benefit of Scotland,' he declared, turning to the King. 'What do you say, Your Grace?'

It was the encouragement James needed. His mood suddenly changed and he cried out, 'Ay, that's right; let us drink to the gallant Barton brothers and the freedom of the seas for Scottish ships.'

House carls and servants scurried about serving wine and ale, but Margaret summoned Lady Hampton, and after an envenomed glare at Lord Home, swished her way out of the Hall with a rustle of her purple brocade gown.

Realising that he had tipped the balance with a timely interjection, Home followed her progress with his thick lips twisted in a satisfied smirk.

James also noted her departure and it broke down the last barrier of his restraint. He commanded the minstrels to play wild, skirling tunes of the Highlands, and soon there were dancers cavorting in gay manner round the barrels. As the wine flowed the revellers increased their tempo, until the prancing and yelling developed into an orgy of craving for the blood of all Scotland's enemies, but more especially those in England. Witnessing the scene would have confirmed the worst of the Queen's inborn fears.

A February frost had etched lacy patterns on the bare, scrawny limbs of the trees and covered Edinburgh and its countryside so thickly that it looked like a fall of snow. A tired horse and horseman with breath belching smokily from both their mouths arrived at Holyroodhouse with a message for the King. Immediately James read it he summoned Patrick Panther, Lord Home, the Earl of Bothwell, and finally, the Queen.

At a glance Margaret discerned the extent of her husband's anger. He expressed it in a voice high-pitched and threatening. 'Madam, your royal father has tried my patience yet again.'

'How so, my lord?' Outwardly she appeared calm, but a sense of crisis constricted within her.

James pounded heavy-footed round the long table of his Presence Chamber shouting, 'How so, how so! Only that he's imprisoned my own cousin and his brother upon their return from France.'

He watched with rising aggravation as Margaret sat and arranged the hemline of a crimson gown round her feet with deliberate time-wasting laboriousness. At last she looked up and said, 'They were travelling through England without a grant of safe conduct. Lord Home advised such a course.'

Home's protuberant eyes enlarged in their sockets, hostility towards the Queen cut into every fleshy feature. He leapt to his feet in objection. 'They would never have left Scotland had they waited for such a grant. The King of England likes not our dealings with our French ally. Only a highly suspicious mind could prompt such an unpardonable outrage.'

Margaret turned on him, lips trembling with anger. 'You are speaking of my royal father,' she reminded him icily.

James knew of the petty ill-will between his wife and chief minister, but this was a genuine grievance and a different matter. 'Your royal father's dishonoured our agreement. We are supposed to be sworn to peace. Do you consider it peaceful intent to imprison my own kinsman?'

'Your cousin will be treated as such,' assured Margaret.

'But detained from returning to his own King and country, nonetheless,' intervened Home.

'He violated my father's realm without authority. Largely at your bidding, Lord Home,' accused Margaret.

Home glanced at the King for support. James turned to his secretary. 'Get inkhorn and quill, Panther. Send a letter to His Grace the Queen's father expressing our strong disapproval of the detention of the Earl of Arran. Tell him we demand his instant release, together with that of his stepbrother, Sir Patrick Hamilton.'

'Perhaps I could intercede for their cause better,' suggested Margaret.

James cast a withering glance at her. 'This is a matter to be settled between kings, madam,' he declared.

Margaret rose with dignity. 'As you will, my lord. I know my father to be a peace-loving man.'

'He doesn't care for peace between Scotland and France,' Home emphasised.

'If I were a man you would not speak in that manner in my presence.' Bitter contempt rasped Margaret's tone as she moved towards Home, drew herself to her full height which exceeded him, then added, 'Nor would I have any scruple on account of so diminutive a figure.'

This derogatory reference to his stature brought blood rushing to Home's face. Dunbar had informed her of this weak link in the armour of his pomposity, its effect delighted her.

The letter to King Henry brought a visit from Thomas Wolsey, the royal chaplain. James refused to see him, so the Queen stormed into his private chamber demanding the reason. He controlled himself initially, but she persisted until her querulous voice irritated his flesh like a barber's itch.

'My father's ambassador brings an explanation of the detention of your kinsman.' It must have been the tenth time she had said it.

Blood afire he faced her yet again. 'The explanation is obvious. England doesn't want Scotland allied to France, and your father does all in his power to prevent it. I need no ambassador to explain what a child can understand.'

'But you must see his ambassador, he's my father's chaplain.'

'That doesn't make him my chaplain, madam.'

He stood glowering, trying to defy further talk. But she continued, 'He brings news of the Earl of Arran.'

James banged his clenched fist on the table. 'The only news I desire of the Earl of Arran is his release, which I'm denied. Now some fawning whelp comes to explain from behind the cover of a woman's kirtle. No, madam, I'll not be treated so, even by your royal father.'

'But you must see his ambassador.'

'You can make my apologies, madam. Tell him I am busy superintending the making of gunpowder, and that nothing he can say will affect my attitude towards France.'

Temporarily bested, she withdrew with her mouth clamped in a hard line of resolution. But the English rose had prickles too.

James flopped on the settle embroidered with the arms of Scotland. It was not long before the Queen returned to importune for her father's frothy mouthpiece. To secure a modicum of domestic peace, James eventually let the mealy-mouthed cleric have his faithless say, but immediately afterwards escaped without warning to the Galloway coast, leaving the Queen to deal with him as she pleased.

During his absence, Dr West visited Edinburgh to see if he could succeed where Wolsey had failed. He had several audiences with the Queen, who fretted over the King's neglect, knowing from her agents that Lady Jane Kennedy had also travelled to the Galloway coast. Sorely tried by her loyalties to two countries, and being well advanced in pregnancy, even normal tribulations assumed the proportions of disasters. In a fevered state of mind, she resolved that if that whore Jane Kennedy came to Court again, it would be the Queen she would have to deal with.

When James returned he refused to see Dr West. Hearing of this discourtesy to an ambassador of high repute, Margaret went unannounced along the stone-flagged passageway to the King's apartments. Newly-leafed branches brushed against the latticed windows and finches teetered on their slender footholds, songfully searching for nesting materials. Margaret was blind to signs of spring; the union between Scotland and England, and her marriage, had reached a crisis that required plain speaking. James had broken his word concerning that Kennedy woman, so he could not expect her to keep quiet any longer about the arguments with England.

Sensing her resolution, James remained prudently silent as she stood before him, arms akimbo, eyes fired by indignation. She prefaced her remarks, 'My lord, I'm determined to be heard.' She took a deep breath, then added, 'You may dishonour your word and deny me as a wife, but you'll not deny me as your Queen and the daughter of the King of England.'

He invited her to be seated, then said, 'State your complaints as daughter of the King of England.'

'You know them, my lord. It's the ill-treatment of my father's ambassadors.'

'They bring nothing but feeble excuses for the arrest of my kinsman.'

'His Grace my father is concerned by your league with France, knowing that a French embassy's on its way here.'

'Yes, and a right and mighty welcome it shall have,' confirmed James, with a grating laugh. 'Your royal father seems intent on managing the affairs of Europe to suit his own purpose. Has he not made himself ridiculous by seeking marriage alliances with your brother's widow Katharine, then the mad Juana of Castile and Margaret of Savoy?'

Margaret stiffened in her chair. 'My lord, I will not listen to you speaking of my royal father in such a manner.'

James waved his hand deprecatingly. 'I speak the truth, nonetheless,'

'Nor will I have his ambassadors treated so shamefully,' she went on, ignoring his attempts to convince her. 'I am well aware of how you make your bed more pleasurable. But, by God, my father of England won't have me so ill-treated of no avail. I demand that Dr West be allowed to state his mission.'

Bellowing with impatience, James jumped up and savagely pushed his chair backward. It clattered to the floor with a resounding splintering of wood.

Margaret rose swiftly and faced him. 'James, I've been humbled by your rage before, but not this time. Remember that your child is within me. Are you trying to cause the still-birth of the Prince you so desire?'

An expression compounded of annoyance and defeat twisted his features. No husband could fight against this weapon. 'What would you have me do?' he asked wearily.

'Not enter into any agreement before consulting my father.'

'Holy Mother of God!' exclaimed James, digging agitated fingers into his red beard. 'The whole nation of commons and nobles are in favour of renewing our alliance with France.'

'They take their lead from Lord Home. The Bishop of Moray is not of the same mind.'

'Because the fat bishop has interests in England.'

'Yet he is a man of peace,' said Margaret.

'And ambition,' countered James, walking across and staring at the splintered chair.

'But he's striving to maintain peace with England,' pressed Margaret, following his movement. 'Couldn't you send him to my father with the details of the French proposals when the embassy arrives?'

James sat on the table edge, scraping his buckled shoes among the floor rushes. 'He would do that willingly enough, glad of the opportunity of visiting England again.'

'So you'll send him?'

He sighed, sufficiently calmed to admire her tenacity. 'Yes, madam, if it pleases you.'

'Thank you, James. I'll arrange for Dr West to see you this morning.'

'Your loyalty to your royal father does you credit, Margaret.'

'It is no more than I would have for my royal husband, if he chose to inspire it,' she countered meaningly.

His expression softened as he put his hands on her waist and said, 'Then if it pleases God, I'll try to inspire it, Margaret. In spite of your royal father's devious ways, I acknowledge that you're a fitting mother for a future king.'

He meant it wholeheartedly, and her flush of pleasure moved him, a reminder that in their marriage, duty had to take precedence over delight. In this they were expected to be different from the flesh and blood of other mortals.

James had Edinburgh set out in great array for the welcoming of the French embassy led by his kinsman and internationally-renowned old warrior, Bernard Stuart d'Aubigny. Margaret played her part with good grace, armed with the knowledge that her father had granted the embassy a safe conduct through England.

James took part in the jousting staged in the Frenchmen's honour. Disguised in black armour with a white plume in his helmet, he presented himself in the lists, keeping his true identity unknown. The crowds cramming the stockades, together with those perched on all points of vantage beyond the brightly-canopied royal loge, were loud in bewailing the absence of their jousting champion, the Earl of Arran.

James intended giving them a new champion, remembering the time he participated in his own Margaret's honour at the jousts celebrating the arrival of Prince Richard. Today he would ride for her again, and in his mind's eye, the Tudor roses of the decorations became sleuth hound badges, and it was Meg who sat on the chair in the royal loge as Queen. Once the vital driving force of his whole life, he became obsessed with reliving it for one afternoon, just to show what he could have done with the right woman at his side.

During the first course he gave such an outstanding display in the finer points of the deeds of arms that all eyes were fixed upon him. Each time he reversed the French knights with well-aimed thrusts of the blunt tips of his lance, lusty cheers sounded in his favour; and each time he glanced through his visor at the royal loge, imagination furnished the image of the sweetest face he had ever known.

He remained last on horse, then, because the rules of the tourney stated that a mounted knight could not strike one on foot, he dismounted and plunged among the Frenchmen. With perspiration streaming down his face inside the visor, he fought on with obsessive fury, as if by conquering everything in his path, imagination could blossom into reality. His movements were so speedy and adroit that the marshals had difficulty in keeping an accurate tally of his score, but still he wielded his blunted sword relentlessly, prepared to bludgeon his way nearer to the impossible. Although blood pounded in his ears he knew that unaware of his identity the crowd had dubbed him the 'Wild Knight'. Each time he engaged a Frenchmen they yelled, 'Hurrah for the Wild Knight! Strength to the arm of the Wild Knight!' Their cheers rose to a crescendo as one after the other the Frenchmen were driven back against the stockade, forced to hold up their sword hilts as a sign of submission.

Long before the heralds proclaimed the result of the tourney the crowd cheered continuously for the Wild Knight, who had undoubtedly won the day for his side and aroused comparisons with the Earl of Arran. When the heralds' trumpets sounded to declare the worthiest knight of the conflict, the crowd announced it in thunderous unison. 'The Wild Knight! The Wild Knight! None other than the Wild Knight!'

Buntings, streamers, bonnets were flung in the air as James led his grey dappled destrier to the royal loge. This was the inevitable moment of clarity, the realisation that he had fought for a chimera queen, whose body rested beneath a blue marble burial stone. He kept his visor down to shield incipient tears, and with difficulty bowed low to his real Queen, indicating his display to be in her honour.

She rewarded him by tossing a rose from the bouquet presented to her by the Frenchmen. He caught it more by luck than dexterity, and the crowd demonstrated their delight by shouting, 'A rose for the Wild Knight! Long live the Wild Knight!'

The symbolism of the afternoon's enactment now weighed more heavily upon him than his armour. None other than himself knew the bitter irony of the Wild Knight's triumph. He left the arena quickly, anxious to escape explanations, or to let any observe the depth of emotion torturing him.

In the Great Hall that night, excitement hung over the feasting tables as the assembly discussed the prowess of the Wild Knight. Lord Home, who acted as chief marshal, sat with a golden goblet to be presented when the heralds called forth the worthiest knight of the day. The moment finally arrived and an unusual silence descended upon the lofty Hall on the first blast of the heralds' trumpets.

Lord Home rose and puffed out his barrel chest. He surveyed the gathering with a hard-eyed, arrogant glare, then called for the worthiest knight of the tournament. The lack of immediate response momentarily shocked the assembly, then heads began to look to and fro, puzzled that any knight should delay receiving such an honour. As looks gave rise to speculation, James stood up and called, 'It is I, my lord.'

A surge of surprise and pride brought Margaret to her feet, James felt most humble when she clapped her hands spontaneously and cried out, 'Bravo, my lord the King!'

Her words sparked off an outbreak of riotous appreciation which reverberated from the oaken rafters. James received it philosophically, having reasoned with himself since leaving the lists. His future achievements lay in forgetting the past and accepting what fate had decreed for him, which meant accepting Margaret Tudor as his Queen. He bowed and smiled, then after being presented with the golden goblet, turned and handed it to the Queen with full chivalric ceremony. The yells of approval gradually subsided as the heralds' trumpets blared out and stewards thumped the stone floor with staves.

Margaret looked at him wistfully. 'Did you fight with such daring solely in my honour, James?'

Filled with a sudden, genuine desire to keep her happy during her confinement time, he lied convincingly, saying, 'For none other, sweet Margaret.' Seeing her pleasure, remembering his already once broken promise to try and inspire her loyalty, and the splendour her father had made regarding the restoration of the blood of King Arthur to the throne of England, he added, 'Except perhaps for the child within your womb.'

With another spontaneous gesture she reached up and kissed him, while the courtiers cheered in a manner that required acknowledgement. James smilingly raised his hands, then said, 'If Almighty God grants us another boy to take the place of our much lamented Prince, he will be called Arthur, after the greatest of all kingly knights.'

A further outburst of cheering greeted this announcement. Swords were drawn and waved boisterously in the air; one knight attracted attention by balancing a silver goblet on his sword point raised at arm's length.

James raised Margaret from her seat and stood with his arm round her as he continued, 'If my conduct in the lists appeared inhospitable to our French visitors, then, as recompense, I invite them to a grand festival the like of which Scotland has never seen before, a festival which shall be known as the Round Table of King Arthur.'

This gave rise to a stampede nothing but exhaustion could quell. James led the Queen to her chamber, then returned to join the revelry, the noise of which travelled so far that it gave good cheer to the whole city of Edinburgh; and that night many a family in their cottages offered up prayers for the safe delivery of a son to their King and Queen.

On the following morning, James stood at the window of the State Chamber, listening to the song of two long-tailed tits courting among the sun-sprayed leafiness of a large beech tree. Having carried out their preliminaries, they performed a series of delightful acrobatics to announce their betrothal. Beyond the palace grounds, sunlight illumined the countryside, highlighting the subtle variations in foliage greenery, insignificant when isolated, but breathtakingly beautiful in Nature's broad canvas; an inspiring reminder of Almighty God's handiwork, untainted by the sins of man. To James it represented Scotland at her best, filling him with pride and appreciation. His ennobled thoughts were interrupted by the announcement of a French knight who burst into the chamber with tears streaming down his cheeks. 'God's bones, Sir, what ails thee?' queried James.

'Your Grace, our beloved Sieur d'Aubigny *est mort* – dead!'

'Dead?' repeated James, with a shocked expression of disbelief. 'How did it happen?'

The Frenchmen made the sign of the Cross. 'He passed away during the night. He was, how you say, age-old. The journey from France must have been too much for him.'

With slow, deliberate movements James also genuflected. 'May his soul rest in peace,' he murmured. 'The Queen will be as grieved as I am. Convey our deepest sympathy to your countrymen. Assure them that the gallant Sieur d'Aubigny will be mourned sorely in Scotland, for my people honoured his valour.'

He left the overwrought Frenchman to be tended by a squire, then went to the Queen's chamber himself, not trusting a servant to inform her of the news, fearful that in her condition it would be a disturbing shock.

The sudden and unexpected death of its leader completely destroyed the purpose of the French embassy. Celebrations ceased, funeral black took the place of pageantry, while burning of mourning incense silenced the fanfare of rejoicing.

To remove her from this grief so near to her critical time, James took Margaret to Lochmaben castle, birthplace of Robert Bruce. Here, when the Court looked forward to some relief from gloom, the Queen was delivered of a girl who barely outlived her birth. The planned celebrations never materialised, for owing to complications the Queen herself lingered for several days on the brink of death.

James stayed with her until legitimate State affairs demanded his return to Edinburgh. Sir Lucan accompanied him, but not with his former willingness, for Lady Joanna had requested to stay with the Queen. On their way, James once again heard Lucan's fears that his married life was being blighted by his wife's morbid fear of the warnings received from an astronomer. To add to the general depression, James learnt upon arrival that his close friend Patrick, Earl of Bothwell, had died that morning. These were sad, fated days to which there seemed to be no end, the passing of each proving to be the harbinger of yet another tragedy.

FIFTEEN

Soon after James conducted the Queen back to Edinburgh, Sir Patrick Hamilton appeared in the city, having escaped from England. Rumours quickly spread, concerning the English treatment of the Earl of Arran.

In spite of her wan condition, Margaret granted Sir Patrick a private audience, then defended her father's conduct among the rumour-mongers, assuring them that according to Sir Patrick, the Earl of Arran had no just cause for complaint.

The contradictions gave rise to a welter of bitter feeling, and Lord Home with characteristic bluntness brought matters to a head. He requested an audience with the King and immediately stated his case. 'Your Grace, Dr West is in Edinburgh with another crop of falsities about the continued detention of the Earl of Arran. Yet we have proof of your kinsmen's treatment, in spite of what the Queen maintains to be contrary.'

James fingered the cuffs of his crimson robe, aware that Margaret's denials must be stopped, but not through Home's promptings. 'You speak rashly, my lord,' he warned

The nobleman's pale blue eyes flared with alarm. 'Only what's in the minds of many, Your Grace.'

'It is not always wise to appoint yourself spokesman of many, my lord. I am arranging an audience with Dr West and Sir Patrick Hamilton.' With an enigmatic smile he added, 'The Queen will also attend. I can handle the matter unaided.'

Disappointment seeped into Home's face, realising that his importunity had excluded him from seeing the Queen humbled.

After arranging the meeting, James went to the stables, where he found Lucan checking his stirrup leathers, brow heavy and eyes sullen. 'Well, Sir Knight, what's your trouble? Your face looks as black as the Earl of Hell's riding boots.'

''Tis nothing, Your Grace.'

''Tis marriage, Lucan. You have never been the same man since you wed the English wench. But let us use this fine day to escape from kirtles and course a few deer.'

Lucan bellowed at a couple of grooms before turning to the King and saying, 'You're right, Your Grace, marriage is full of problems.'

''Tis nothing but problems, Lucan. I know that as well as you.' His courser ready, he leapt to the saddle and sent everybody scattering in the courtyard as he put it through its spirited paces.

Having ridden like a fiend through some of the Wild Knight's darkest moods, Lucan also mounted, prepared this day to match even the King's daring. With their riding cloaks billowing behind them, the two riders cantered towards the postern gate and were soon dark specks against the cloudless horizon.

Upon his return, it amused James to learn that the Queen had been seeking Dr West. Having foreseen the possibility of Margaret colluding with the ambassador, he had given orders for him to be conducted on a long tour of inspection.

When later Margaret was summoned to the Presence Chamber, Dr West faced the double gilt doors as she walked in. James watched in silent satisfaction as surprise halted her dignified approach. To her credit, she recovered quickly, but not without flashing him a look of awareness that he had outmanoeuvred her.

'Now, Dr West,' said James, when they were seated. 'Tell me the true purpose of your visit.'

West coughed discreetly to clear his throat, his bird-like eyes turning to his master's daughter as he too sensed the reason for the King's smug gaze.

'My lord King Henry is concerned about the outrages being committed on the borders, Your Grace.'

'By both countries,' emphasised James. 'But outrages on English subjects are not being committed in Edinburgh, as they are on my own kinsman in London.'

'My lord, we have Dr West's assurance that the Earl of Arran is being well-treated,' put in Margaret.

'Yes, we have, and many have been informed by you, madam, that Sir Patrick Hamilton confirms that view.'

'He gave me that information himself,' said Margaret, avoiding the intensity of her husband's gaze.

Momentarily, the Queen and the English ambassador were silent, staring awkwardly at each other, loath to commit themselves without previous agreement.

James reached out and pulled the blue and gold bell sash to summon his secretary. 'Panther, bring in Sir Patrick Hamilton,' he said, with a roguish smile.

Margaret gasped, made as if to protest, then checked herself. 'My lord, may I order wine for Dr West?' she asked, keeping her eyes downcast.

'Sir Patrick won't take long to discharge his business, then we can all have wine together,' replied James.

Margaret fussed unnecessarily at the seed pearl cauls of her hair. Dr West engaged in a similar nervous manipulation of the tasselled cord of his black habit. Sir Patrick Hamilton entered, tall and upright, then smiling sardonically bowed to the Queen.

'Now, Sir Patrick,' said James, motioning him to be seated. 'The Queen is in some confusion as to how the Earl of Arran and you fared in her royal father's hands.'

'How so, Your Grace?' queried the knight, turning to the Queen.

'I understood you to say that your brother and you were well-treated, Sir Patrick,' she murmured.

'God's nails, madam, that's a downright –' He broke off, bowed apologetically, then added, 'I have made it known everywhere that such was not the case.'

'Well, madam?' queried James, fingering his beard.

'I must have misunderstood Sir Patrick, my lord.'

'But you understand him now?'

She faced his impish expression with dignity. 'Perfectly, my lord.'

Enjoying the mastery of the situation, James turned to Dr West. 'And what does the good doctor say in view of his repeated assurances?'

Dr West gesticulated hopelessly. 'I can only repeat my orders, Your Grace.'

'Orders that are not in accord with the pact between our two countries,' observed James.

The ambassador could not argue.

'Then let this be an end to such guile,' said James determinedly. 'My royal father-in-law cannot complain of my friendliness to the French, if he has no regard for my own kinsman. Now we can take wine.'

As they left the chamber, James whispered to Margaret, 'You defend your royal father with more loyalty than discretion, madam. But let there be no more of it.'

Margaret for once considered it politic to remain silent.

Yule passed, followed by weeks of rain, winds and louring skies that lasted into April. Tired of looking from the windows at the black outlines of trees silhouetted against a watery veil of grey mist, James went coursing in the woods with Sir Lucan. They set off with manly vigour, as on so many occasions when frustration drove James into attempting prodigious feats of strength and endurance. But on this occasion he returned with Lucan's dead body slung across two pack mules. Arriving at the palace dazed and shocked, a groom greeted him with the news that the Queen had heard of her royal father's death at Richmond Palace.

James went to her immediately, still clad in a saturated riding jacket. She rose to greet him from the chair in which she had sat immobile all afternoon, stricken with grief. 'You've heard, James?'

'Yes, Margaret, and my heart bleeds for you. It is a bitter blow that comes in the wake of another ill. God's bones, it seems we cannot escape reminders of the grave!' He slumped down disconsolately on a richly upholstered chair, oblivious to the wetness of his clothes.

Margaret stood transfixed, face white and strained. 'What other ill, my lord?' she asked

'My body knight, Sir Lucan Fairfax. We were coursing hares on the east side of the city when he fell from his horse and cracked his neck.'

'Is he dead?'

'As dead as last year's mutton.'

Margaret clung to the table for support. 'Does Lady Fairfax know? Poor sweet Joanna, I must see her at once.'

James leapt to his feet with an angry bellow. 'Spare no sympathy on that churlish whore!' He began pacing the chamber, pounding one clenched fist into the palm of his other hand. 'God's bones, I can't understand it! Countless times he, and I like him, have fallen from our horses. Yes, and leapt up to mount again to prove superiority over the beast. Yet this time Lucan stayed in a twisted heap, dead by the time I could reach him. I believe he wanted to die, that whore-begat wench of yours having led him such a taunting caper.'

'My lord, you wrong one who is both servant and friend to me. She is still only a sensitive child.'

He spun round from an unseeing surveillance of the cherubs on the wall tapestry. 'I'll do her a mighty wrong if she's not kept from my sight. This is the second crop of mischief she's caused. Cosset her as you will, but one mite more trouble and she'll be banished from my kingdom.'

He stared out of the window until the climax of his temper subsided, then, remembering her deep affection for her father, turned sympathetically and said, 'I did not come to speak of that chit. The passing of your royal father causes me genuine grief, even though we've not found much to agree about. It comes at an ill time for you, Margaret. You must not let it affect you too greatly, for you know how quick you are to disorder when pregnant.'

Her lips trembled. 'Yes, I am aware of that, but I wish I could have seen him before the end.'

He helped her to a more comfortable chair saying, 'He led a full life and accomplished much. England mourns the passing of a great king. None can say, Margaret, that you have not upheld the high hopes he had for you, nor have you failed to defend him with exemplary family loyalty. Even though at times it has been against my wishes and Scotland's benefit.'

In the ensuing silence he sensed that his wife was thinking of the frequent occasions when her father had been the cause of contention between them. It made him realise the unenviable position into which she had been plunged by divided loyalties, yet her severest critic could not seriously fault her, either as Queen of Scotland or as daughter of the King of England.

'Your words bring me some consolation, James, and I thank you for them.'

He lightly put his hands on her shoulders as a gesture of assurance, then returned to the window view of the river. 'King Henry VIII now comes to the throne of England,' he said. A tentative remark, followed by further silence, awaiting her reaction.

'We must pray that peace is maintained between our two countries, my lord. That was the purpose of our marriage.'

He sighed, remembering his utter personal dejection when agreeing to the marriage. 'I think peace between our two countries would have been better maintained with your father, but now the future depends upon your royal brother. As you know, he's only eighteen years old, and my information is that he likes neither me nor Scotland. I have no idea why, but the way he expressed his opposition to our marriage indicates that he's quick-tempered and masterful. So we shall have to wait and see what politics develop!'

He paused, again awaiting any possible comment from his wife. When she maintained a diplomatic silence, he went on, 'I'll send the Bishop of Moray to congratulate him on his accession. If he desires peace he can return the Earl of Arran to his homeland. I can think of no better token of the new King's good faith.'

'You have every right to claim such a token, James,' she assured him

'I'm pleased to hear you say that, Margaret.'

She smiled tenderly; the loss of her father brought James closer to her. 'It has always been my wish to serve you well as wife and Queen, my lord.'

He held her close, trying to comfort her. Suddenly she said, 'There's something else your embassy could request of my brother Henry.'

'What's that?'

'The jewellery, plate and precious stones bequeathed to me by my dearest brother Arthur. Even if my father saw fit to hold this inheritance in safekeeping for me during his lifetime, surely Henry should now despatch it to its rightful owner?'

'Yes, most certainly so,' James agreed. He considered that any just demands he could make of the new sovereign would be an opportunity of testing his relationship with Scotland.

Margaret rested her hand upon his arm and became aware of his saturated riding jacket. 'James, you must change your robes, otherwise you'll catch a rheum.'

'I'll do that, and I'll instruct the tactful bishop to broach this matter of your inheritance. He's to have his journey to England, after all. So it will be to our advantage to commission him to an unpopular purpose to prevent him gaining more favour than is good for him.'

Margaret extended her hand and he held it for a moment. 'I think you act wisely, my lord,' she said, then reached up to kiss his cheek. 'Now you must change your robes. I'll go and console Lady Fairfax.'

'Don't forget to convey my warning words.' His tone had lost its earlier bitterness. He knew how much he would miss Lucan, but there was now so much more to occupy his mind, so many possibilities that could emerge from England's change of kingship.

June heralded news of King Henry's marriage to Princess Katharine, his eldest brother's widow. Any joy felt was quickly turned to sorrow by the death of the Queen's grandmother, the Countess of Richmond. This distressing news in the latter weeks of pregnancy caused anxiety concerning Margaret's health. The entire Court was aware of Scotland's desperate need of an heir, a healthy child to survive infancy and be trained as a future king.

On the night of the Queen's labour in October, James was informed that Lucan's widow, demented by the astronomer's words and her husband's tragic and unaccountable death, had slipped away from the palace and drowned herself in the Forth. As nothing could be done for the dead, he forbade the news to be conveyed to the Queen or Lady Hampton, knowing how much Margaret relied upon the comfort of her childhood governess.

Morning light brought better tidings, the Queen having given birth to a son who lived and was to be christened Arthur, Prince of Scotland and Lord of the Isles. The rejoicing increased with the news that the Earl of Arran had returned from England, having signed a peace treaty with the new King Henry.

James's delight with his royal Prince prompted Lady Jane Kennedy to remind him of their bastard son. As a result, the King appointed him Lord Chancellor and bestowed more lands upon Jane to prevent her creating mischief. When Margaret heard of this more trouble brewed, and she now had an ally in Lady Hampton, who took exception to the King withholding the news of her daughter's death until the Queen was out of danger. They both watched him with eyes as keen as any falcon. Nor as the months went by did the young King Henry send the treasure Margaret kept complaining about. In fact, thinking more of asserting his authority in Europe, he made a point of treating Scotland with a contempt only partially veiled.

When another empty-handed messenger arrived at Edinburgh, James went to the Queen's withdrawing chamber, determined to take definitive action against her recalcitrant brother.

Bowing stiffly, he said, 'I have had a messenger from England, madam.'

'With my brother's legacy?' she asked, her blue eyes agleam with hope.

'Not with this messenger, in spite of my repeated demands.'

Petulance pulled at the corners of her mouth as she leaned back in her chair. 'My brother has no right to hold my dues.'

'That King has no right to treat Scotland in the many shameful ways he chooses,' snapped James.

She invited him to sit, but he glanced contemptuously at the Tudor portcullis emblazoned on the upholstery and remained standing as he went on, 'Your royal brother's guided overmuch by his father-in-law of Aragon, who accepts him as an equal in statesmanship, but cares not a jot for his English kingdom.'

'Henry always loved flattery, even as a young child,' murmured Margaret reflectively. 'But surely war won't come of it, my lord? We have heard that Henry has concluded a peace treaty with France.'

James walked to the fire and kicked a straying holly log in place with his buckled shoe. 'A flimsy treaty, madam, you can be sure of that. One likely to cause more trouble than it purports to prevent. There are too many honeyed words covering preparations for war, and if it goes on, a single spark in the wrong direction could set the whole continent ablaze. It worries me, Margaret, so much so that I'm sending the Bishop of Moray to seek the Holy Father's aid in securing a genuine peace among Christian Princes. The Bishop will travel through England and France to make known his intentions. I believe such a Crusade could benefit all Christendom.'

'And my brother could show his good faith by sending my legacy.'

James nodded. 'He says that he withholds it through fear of it being used for war against him.'

'Have you informed him that is not so, my lord?'

'Countless times, lady. But Henry is guided by Ferdinand, not by love of his sister.'

'Will you renew the plea?'

'Of course, we ask for your dues, not a favour.'

'Yes, my dues,' she confirmed, clenching her small hands very tight.

To James the legacy had become more a matter of State than a personal concern. Henry had to learn to respect Scotland's wishes. 'It's late, Margaret, and you should be abed. You're still not fully recovered from the birth of our darling Prince.'

She reached forward and squeezed his hand. 'I feel better for knowing that you are aware of it, James.'

With a light nod he bent and kissed her brow, but his expression remained troubled.

In spite of the Bishop of Moray's efforts abroad the situation worsened. Clashes on both sides of the border became more frequent, initially stealing cattle and burning houses, then as tempers frayed, developing into barbarous killings. James recalled the ageing Lord Drummond to ambassadorial service, trying wisdom and experience where all else had failed. But Henry continued sending sweet-sounding excuses and empty promises to Scotland, and Margaret's jewels remained sealed in his coffers.

In an attempt to disperse the gathering clouds of impending gloom, James ordered a grand scale masque to be held at the palace. He danced dutifully with his wife until Patrick Panther appeared and attracted his attention. Not wishing to interrupt the merrymaking, James skilfully led the way across the Hall, dancing with no apparent urgency towards the small, wiry, jutting-jawed secretary. 'What is it, Panther?' he asked.

'Prince Arthur, Your Grace. His nurse came to my ante-room and interrupted my working on the documents of the wapenschaws. She complains that she can't stop his moans, and fears that his body burns with fever.'

Margaret's features tautened. 'I'll go to him, James. You summon a physician.'

'Yes, at once.' James glanced round at the revellers. 'But I'll not stop their capers. The way they perform is evidence of their need of it.'

Margaret hurried away with the secretary – dingy cleric robe and cloth of gold gown oddly contrasted, but both activated by the same concern and purpose. When they reached the Prince's bedchamber Lady Hampton was already there. 'Your chamberlain told me, madam, so I came at once,' she explained.

Margaret nodded, her eyes on the tiny pallid face lost in the vastness of the green and silver bed.

'I've cleaned and comforted him. I think he's asleep now,' Lady Hampton whispered.

The stench of sickness filled the room. 'What's wrong with him?' asked Margaret, advancing to the bedside.

'He's vomited freely and his bowels are squirting. I've sent for the King's physician, madam.'

'The King also seeks him,' murmured Margaret, gazing at the laboured puffing of the Prince's lips. His eyelids suddenly flickered open, revealing eyes glazed with infant lack of understanding. He started crying and Margaret took him from the bed to cradle him in her arms. Lady Hampton handed her the bed coverings to wrap round his fevered body.

James entered with a white-robed Cistercian friar, who examined the babyish-red body. Lady Hampton looked on, aware of the King's presence, casting envenomed glances she dare not frame into words.

'What's the matter with him, brother, is there any danger?' queried James anxiously.

As if to impress the urgency of his need, the baby Prince vomited all over the lower bed curtains. Margaret sent for hot water and bathed him herself, then, as women scuffled about cleansing the chamber, she wrapped him in clean clothes and held him to the comfort of her breast.

James saw the tears in her eyes, so walked round the bed and kissed the top of her head, then put his lips on the Prince's burning cheeks. 'I'll bring the posset and administer it myself,' he said, in a voice gruff with emotion.

Remembering her grandmother of Richmond's care of one of her infant brothers, Margaret stayed with the Prince throughout the night. The morning brought no change in his condition, so she had a cot for herself made up in his room. No possets or potions had any effect on the little Prince who could have grown to become a king. He wasted away daily before the eyes of his mother and father, until, after a week, the last hope of him wearing an earthly crown passed forever.

After a friar administered the Sacrament of Extreme Unction, Margaret clung to James. He stood with his strong arms supporting her, until they were alone with their dead child.

He looked at her with infinite tenderness, deeply moved, more than ever convinced that he should initiate a Crusade for peace. 'Once again we're childless, Margaret, and you, as gentle a mother as the Holy Virgin herself. You must go on a pilgrimage to the shrine of St. Ninian and rest. I'll escort you there myself and see you settled before I return to Edinburgh. The kingdom must still be ruled in spite of our tragedy.'

'Yes, my lord,' whispered Margaret. 'But I'll visit the shrine of St. Duthois of Ross.'

The flash of reproach in her eyes did not escape him. Through his association with Jane Kennedy he had prejudiced his wife against a holy saint. Could that really be the reason for Almighty God drawing his infant heirs to the protection of heaven? he asked himself.

At the end of summer 1511, in the Council Chamber at Edinburgh castle, James sat at the head of a long table. Opposite, Lord Home's face grimaced with rage. Around the table were the Earls of Huntly, Argyll, Arran, Lennox and Montrose, with Sir Andrew Wood in attendance as naval adviser. James stopped tapping the table top with his fingers, and glancing round said, 'My lords, I've summoned you because of another English outrage, this time against Admiral Andrew Barton.'

Home knew the details and considered them adequate reason for war. His feudal lieges were mustered for a march to the border, but in an earlier interview his speed of action had been reprimanded rather than approved.

'What's happened to Sir Andrew, Your Grace?' asked Arran, stroking a sword scar on his right cheek.

Home's hard eyes flashed with hope. Perhaps Arran's detention in England had embittered him sufficiently to press for war? A cousin and favourite of the King, his words could help sway the issue.

'The English had no just complaint against Admiral Barton,' James declared. 'Nonetheless, King Henry granted permission to Lord Thomas Howard, son of the Earl of Surrey, to fit out ships and capture him. They fell in with him as he passed through the Straits of Dover with our two ships, the *Lion* and the *Jenny Pirwin*. Evidently they surprised him with an unprovoked attack, then according to my intelligence, he fought a brilliant and desperate conflict before being shot through the heart by an English archer.'

The noblemen sat stunned. Sir Andrew Wood spoke first. 'His passing is a grievous loss to Scotland, Your Grace.'

'Yes, of a gallant sailor and his ships,' agreed James. 'The ships were captured and Barton's flagship, the *Lion*, made second man-of-war of the English navy.'

Despondency spread over Sir Andrew's weather-beaten face, for he had built the costly flagship. His one consolation was that he had almost completed an even bigger ship, the *Great Michael*. When it set sail it would be the largest ship in the world.

Home leapt to his feet. 'Don't you consider this act tantamount to a declaration of war, Your Grace?' he thundered, with wild protuberant eyes.

'Yes, I do, my lord,' replied James slowly. 'But I've also sent the Bishop of Moray to Europe in an attempt to bring about a Crusade for lasting peace. Success in that venture would please me greater than war.'

Home controlled the expression of his thoughts concerning the religious approach to peace.

'Have you demanded redress from King Henry?' asked Argyll.

James's face now matched the fury of his Lord High Chamberlain. 'That I have, Archibald, reminding him that our two countries have a league of peace, and that such an act violates our agreement. The reason I've summoned you is that I now have the King of England's answer.'

Their eyes turned to him expectantly. Even Home's rage simmered, for this was news to him. 'Well, Your Grace?' he queried, his thick-fingered hands clenching at the table, eyes fiercely demanding.

'I thought that question would come quickest from you, my lord. King Henry's words will add more gall to your restless spleen. He says that it does not become one king to charge another with breaking a league because justice has been done to a pirate and a thief. What do you make of that, my lords?'

Home spoke first again, rage now generated into the white heat of excessive control. 'That most surely is not only an insult to your person, but to the whole of the Scottish realm,' he thundered.

'What do you think, my lords'? asked James, flourishing his hand around the table.

Arran cleared his throat. 'Such a breach of confidence must be redressed, Your Grace.'

'It must, so I'll write to the Holy Father, informing him that since Henry of England has waged war upon my kingdom, both openly and secretly, I presume to be absolved from my oath to Holy Church. I will also make another demand for instant redress and the despatch of the Queen's legacy. You, my lords, can return to your lands and prepare for war by supervising the muster of your lieges. If Henry of England treats us coolly this time, then he'll rue the day he ruffled Scottish tempers.'

Home drew his sword and brandished it in the air. 'That he will, Your Grace, as long as there's strength in my arm to raise this on the battlefield.'

James smiled tolerantly, remembering the impetuosity that once marked his own actions, but still hoping to avoid bloodshed.

When the Queen returned to Holyroodhouse, James devised many amusements to divert her grief at the loss of their son. Sir David Lindsay, renowned as poet and soldier, took a principal part in the welcoming play and endeared himself to the royal couple in a manner assuring a successful future at Court. But at the height of the revelry in the Great Hall that night, Margaret caught sight of Lady Jane Kennedy dancing with a young nobleman.

James noticed his wife's pallid face turn even whiter, then following her gaze understood the reason. Momentarily, he considered summoning a page or squire to tell Jane to quit the Hall as unobtrusively as possible.

But Margaret reacted at once, and with eyes blazing hatred demanded, 'What is that whore doing at Court?'

James fingered his beard evasively. He had not known of her arrival, but realised the inadequacy of such an excuse. Margaret stood against the High Table, tight-lipped, small hands bunched and nostrils quivering like a hound catching the scent of a hare. 'I don't know, madam,' he said, keeping his voice deliberately low. 'She attends without my permission. I'll see that she retires.'

'That will not be necessary, my lord.' A glint of satisfaction lighted Margaret's eyes as she savoured full scent of her prey. 'I can manage this task unaided, in spite of my condition.'

He knew from experience that the direst sickness seldom shackled her tongue. This was the occasion Margaret had awaited, the opportunity for the wronged wife to strike back. Argyll sat at the table drinking, a mischievous smile of expectancy on his lips. James turned to Margaret in silent appeal.

The Queen made good any deficiency in articulation by declaring in a voice that no music could muffle, 'Her presence offends me, my lord. If she comes without your permission, then she must be dismissed.'

Dancers too now picked up the whiff of domestic battle. Their movements changed from flowing light-footed grace to inquisitive shuffling, and finally, to a standstill. The contagion of inertia affected the musicians, so that they lost their harmony and eventually put aside their instruments to gaze in the general direction of the disturbance. 'Play on, masters, play on!' yelled James, red-faced and desperate in the flourishing of his hands.

They obeyed in panic, producing a cacophony of strange sounds. It did not matter for the courtiers backed to each side of the Hall, opening up a causeway across which the Queen and Lady Kennedy flashed malevolent glances at each other. The musicians struggled discordantly, but finally submitted to the mounting tension and gaped with the rest. The whole assembly waited in breathless silence.

'Lady Kennedy, come forward!' Margaret's rasping voice shattered the stillness.

Jane's tall figure quivered like a yew bow, then her shoulders straightened, her head jerked erect and cold haughtiness suffused her features. Speculation ran high in a fever of earnest whispers, for as she walked calmly and slowly forward. Jane, in a purple gown trimmed with ermine, looked more than a match for the pallid Queen. James watched in agonised fascination, aware that the crisis had passed the stage of being graciously circumvented.

Jane curtsied low to him and smiled disarmingly. Never had she looked more desirably feminine, thought James. Her respect to the Queen came in a slight jerky movement, insolent in comparison, eliciting a titter from the ladies. This mockery added needle-point sharpness to Margaret's tongue as she imperiously rapped out, 'My Lady Kennedy, this assembly is gathered in my honour. Your presence here is thus offensive.'

The titters changed to gasps of astonishment, none expecting such forthrightness in public. Jane too visibly wavered. Then her blue-green eyes dilated, her sensual mouth quirked as in equally trenchant tones she replied, 'But His Grace the King ordered the celebrations. I think my presence not distasteful to him.'

The company looked on spellbound.

'Then you don't know my husband well,' countered Margaret.

'On the contrary, madam. I know the King very well, and did so while you were still in your nursery in England.'

'Lady Kennedy!' thundered James, in warning.

Margaret flashed a silencing glance at him.

With her eyes, Jane too beseeched the man who had so often shared her bed, but the virile man failed her and she saw him as a cur on a tether held by a cold and passionless Tudor. She turned to the Queen. 'What will you have me do, madam? I can retire, if you are so afraid of my influence.'

There were further gasps at her insolence, particularly as the barbed retaliation obviously struck its mark. Now the Queen's sharp features and small body tremored. But she remustered her spirit and snapped, 'It's the mutual wish of the King and myself that you return to your ill-gained lands.'

Jane spun round to the King. 'Is that your wish, Your Grace?'

All eyes flashed on him, trapped in the crossfire between wife and leman. Whatever he did or said could achieve no good. The Queen was his legal wife, even though she had behaved like a common fisherwoman. But she was a royal Princess; he could not shame her before the whole goggling-eyed, mouth-gaping Court. He bowed his head in defeat, murmuring, 'Yes, lady, and go quickly before more ill comes of it.'

Jane's eyes blazed at him, and for a moment he feared an unholy eruption of her feelings. Mercifully, she quelled the smouldering inner volcano, straightened her fine body, then walked away with a composure all but the Queen admired. Every pair of eyes followed her progress to the heavy drape over the large entrance doors. Her final glance at the Queen, her smile upon the entranced assembly and her contemptuous exit wrested victory from the ashes of defeat.

To emphasise her courage and his won freedom, James laughed out with a forced raucousness which the Court accepted as approbation. He then yelled for the musicians to strike up again, and feeling the need of vigorous movement to relieve his tension, grabbed a nearby lady, and defying the Queen's reproving glare, danced her through the bewildered groups until he galvanised them into noisy movement.

In disgust, Margaret left by the private door to the royal apartments. Noting her departure, James called for more wine and louder revels. He too still had some spirit left. Jane would most likely never forgive him and return to Angus, but that too had its financial compensations.

During the ensuing days, James avoided the Queen, not trusting his temper if the subject of Lady Kennedy was reopened. But when Seigneur de la Motte arrived in Edinburgh, the King commanded Margaret's presence at the reception. The French ambassador brought promises of money and munitions, including cannon. As a result, James let it be known to all that he intended renewing the 'auld alliance' with France, and the 'auld enemy' England could suffer any consequences that might ensue.

SIXTEEN

On Easter eve, 1512, Margaret gave birth to another Prince at Linlithgow. The relationship between Scotland and England now even more strained, the infant was baptised James, and proclaimed Prince of Scotland and Lord of the Isles, the same title given to the two infants who had not outlived their cradle. But this time the royal physicians unanimously declared the baby to be strong and healthy.

Whilst the Queen remained with the Prince at Linlithgow, James received King Henry's ambassadors, Dr West and Lord Dacre, in Edinburgh. He sat in his throne chair, watching with alert eyes as the Englishmen paid homage. His peace attempts unacknowledged, his promotion of the Crusade ignored, war with England now seemed inevitable. He had made up his mind that if Henry set foot in France, he in turn would march a Scottish army into England.

'Well, Dr West, what meaningless excuses do you bring from your honey-dribbling master?' he demanded.

The cleric ambassador's corpulent figure wobbled as he straightened up from kneeling. The King's tone suggested the likely course of the audience. 'My master desires peace with your kingdom, Your Grace,' he finally said.

'He could show it better by friendly actions rather than fatuous words. Have you brought Queen Margaret's jewels?'

'I have instructions regarding them, Your Grace.'

'That they'll be sent if I renounce my allegiance to France?'

'My master is so anxious for peace that he's offered to double Queen Margaret's legacy, if Your Grace will keep the agreed bond with England,' stated the ambassador.

'So that he can war with France without my intervention,' snapped James. 'Your King is no man of peace; he would not even grant the Bishop of Rieux an audience when he recently went to London to secure a peace settlement.'

'He sees no reason why this should involve him in war with Scotland, Your Grace.'

'And to prove his love for Scotland he withholds his sister's legacy, orders the murder of my Admiral, sends troops over the border to capture my subjects and chain them by their craigs.'

'Chain them by their craigs, Your Grace?'

'Yes, chain them by their necks,' said James, in mimicry and explanation. 'Is this treatment likely to persuade me to sever a traditional alliance?'

Up to this moment Lord Dacre had stood still, tall and soldier-like. He now moved forward and said, 'It's because of that alliance that we are here, Your Grace.'

'Well I know it,' snapped James, rising. 'But you can tell your master that he must change his tactics before he satisfies this King. He can no longer buy my promises with false offerings.'

'Is that your final word, Your Grace?' queried the doctor.

'On such terms, most final.'

West hesitated, but deciding against any fresh approach said, 'Then I request permission to withdraw, Your Grace.'

James nodded, but before they reached the door shouted for them to stop.

Dr West turned, a light of hope in his grey eyes. 'Your Grace?' he queried.

The change of expression did not escape James. 'Before you return to England, go to see the Queen and the young Prince at Linlithgow. She has tokens for the King her brother, Queen Katharine and Princess Mary her sister.' He added with a meaning smile. 'We are not niggardly in Scotland, my lords, and you can tell your master that in spite of the way he treats his own, Queen Margaret shall not suffer any loss.'

Disappointment seeped over Dr West's lined face as he bowed and mumbled his thanks.

The return visit of Seigneur de la Motte, with his handsome smile and shining white teeth, made many Court ladies favour the continuation of the French and Scottish alliance. Yet even after James accepted the French treaty, he remained prepared to listen to reason if Henry showed willing.

Margaret appreciated his open-mindedness until she heard that James had received a letter from the Queen of France, sending him a ring from her own finger. She appealed to him as her knight at least to set foot in

England, so helping the French kingdom and Queen in their time of need.

Margaret summoned Patrick Panther to try and confirm the rumour, but he proved glib-tongued and evasive. With James there always seemed to be a woman at the root of his motives. But he had chosen his secretary wisely, for the bright-eyed factotum could be as slippery as the seaweed covering the Scottish coastal rocks, and as tight-lipped about his master's affairs as the shellfish that fastened themselves to the rocks. The window mullions cut the strong sunlight into diamonds of heat as she wondered if James would answer her immediate summons.

He came more quickly than expected, clad in a riding jacket, brow furrowed.

She motioned him to be seated, but he preferred to stand. 'What now, lady?' he asked, with little tolerance. 'I'm about to ride off for consultation with Sir Andrew Wood.'

'Then you are still preparing for war?'

'Your royal brother leaves me no option.'

Watching his agitated pacing she said, 'My lord, will you please sit down while I speak. You're like a fretful charger at the lists.'

A heavy sigh indicated his impatience, but he obeyed. 'Then I show my feelings well, lady, for there is a limit to what I can tolerate from England.'

'I thought your forbearance was on account of our marriage; now I learn that you're influenced by another voice.'

He closed his eyes and pressed his feet hard on the floor. 'What do you mean by that?'

Margaret's eyes flashed at him accusatively. 'That your receiving a love letter from the Queen of France has made you agree to the French alliance.'

James chortled raucously. 'God's bones, madam, surely you jest?'

'This is not a matter for jesting,' she countered.

'But the Queen of France is old enough to be my mother.'

'She's a woman,' replied Margaret contemptuously. 'You were the Wild Knight in my honour. Now another commands you as her knight, and you prefer to listen to that lewd Queen who has been twice divorced than to your own loyal wife. Are you to war with England on her account?'

James rose slowly, taut with self-control. He stood over her, temporarily at a loss as to how to explain that although the French Queen had appealed to his sense of chivalry, it had in no way influenced him. At last he said, 'Madam, you sing a different tune since the visit of the French ambassador. Before that you lamented your brother's tardiness in despatching your jewels.'

'I still lament it.'

'Then why these baseless charges? Surely you know the Queen of France is near to dying of decline?'

'Yet you are preparing for war with England to please her.'

James's eyes dilated with rage. He began pacing again, not speaking, reasonable words seemed useless. But Margaret kept up her protestations. Unable to bear any more he came to a threatening stop in front of her. 'Madam, if you'll stop your prattling long enough for explanation, I'll give it,' he shouted. The raising of his voice coupled with his grim expression silenced her. 'Your endless dolour for the legacy of jewels and plate had no small part in my reckoning, and the alliance with France dates back to before both of us.' James went on, 'God knows that the Bishop of Moray has done all he can to bring about peace, but he writes from France telling me that all my honour in Europe will be lost if I don't support King Louis. Your royal brother is the faithless one, madam. Faithless to my kingdom, to France, and to you, his sister.'

He spoke forcibly enough to make her ponder on his words. 'Yes,' she murmured, after a pause. 'He has used my jewels for political purposes, when they should be adorning my person.'

'Then don't talk of romantic notions with one so near the grave,' warned James testily. 'There's enough trouble around us without making it from nothing.' He bowed with scant courtesy, then quickly withdrew.

Margaret hardly heeded him going. Her mind grappled with two main thoughts. The withholding of her legacy and the Queen of France. She could not decide which caused her the most prickling irritation.

Indicating that the alternative would be war, James sent King Henry a final demand for redress of the Barton outrage and despatch of the Queen's jewels. When he received the reply, he summoned Margaret, and in her haste, she arrived still fixing cauls in her hair. 'Well, my lord, what does my royal brother promise in the face of war?'

James looked up wearily, face sore from agitated fingers scratching at his beard. He nodded for her to sit down and said, 'I'll read you the message. Listen and judge its merit for yourself.'

He began reading in sarcastically mocking tones, expressing all the chagrin bubbling within him. 'My lord ambassador desires to have of me silver work, golden work, rings, chains, precious stones and other abuilzements pertaining to a Prince, left in legacy by my eldest brother Arthur, to my elder sister, Queen of Scotland. I grant thereto that she shall be well answered of the same and double thereof. And if the King of Scotland will promise faithfully to keep his word by me, I shall incontinent, with the consent of my nobles, make him Duke of York and Governor of England.'

'What do you make of it, James?' asked Margaret, her eyes suddenly brightening with its potentiality.

'It is faithless, Margaret, as you well know,' he snapped, both hands clenched before him on the table. 'Not a week has gone by during the past months without some ill-conceived promise from an English mouth or some outrage upon my subjects.'

He glowered at her, ready to stem any objection, but she passively fingered the gold work on the girdle of her gown.

'He refused a safe conduct to the Bishop of Moray, whose mission to France sought to secure a universal peace,' James continued. 'The Earl of Surrey has been put in command of the army in the north, yet Henry still prattles peace. His envoys come to my kingdom with fine words and nothing more, until Dr West's latest journey, when he brings a copy of the "bull executorial" confirming my excommunication if I attack England.'

'What are we to do then, James?'

James faced her determinedly. 'I stand by France. If it leads to war, then it is Henry's bidding.'

'And what of my jewels?'

'Rather than break my allegiance to King Louis, I will give you better jewels and richer abuilzements,' said James. Then with an enraged flick of his head, he thumped both hands on the table so hard that the silver candlesticks wavered and almost fell as he shouted, 'We've mouthed all this nonsense before, I want no further part in it.'

Margaret realised the futility of pursuing her accusation and rose to go, but a page entered announcing that Lord Home had come swift from Fastcastle with news from England.

Margaret moved to follow the page's withdrawal. 'Stay your body, madam,' commanded James. 'This latest information is likely to have some bearing on what we have been discussing.'

Lord Home entered breathlessly, face a mask of contorted rage. He bowed to the King, but made the minimum observance of the Queen's presence.

'Well, my lord, what comes new from England'?

'The final treacherous move, Your Grace. King Henry's sent twenty-eight ships to France. There can be but one thought in his mind, war against our ally.'

James stood white and silent for several moments, then turned to Margaret. 'Can you think of any other intention in your royal brother's mind, madam?'

Home's bedevilled eyes flashed upon the Queen, then back to the King. 'This is the last breach of faith. My lieges are mustered, Your Grace, ready to seek retribution for all the ill-treatment received on the borders.'

'Yes, my lord, they have suffered much,' agreed James. 'Neither have conditions been improved by the visits of Lord Drummond and Sir John Ramsay into England.'

'King Henry spoils for war,' charged Home, facing the Queen, prepared for any denial.

Margaret realised the gravity of the situation. 'Perhaps I have pressed overmuch for the despatch of my legacy,' she admitted. 'Surely no amount of jewels and plate should be the cause of two countries being set ablaze by war?'

James faced her grimly. 'It's too late now to start retracting your dolorous words, the mischief's done. Nor can an attack on France be so easily dismissed. This, madam, means war. My blood has been boiled to its limit.'

Margaret immediately burst into tears, but without heeding them, James issued orders to Home for a meeting of the Council.

Any hope of settlement became impossible after King Henry contemptuously replied to Scotland's formal declaration of war taken to him at Terouanne by the Lord Lion, Scotland's king-at-arms. James enumerated the causes as the chaining of Scottish subjects by their necks in prison, the slaughter of Admiral Sir Andrew Barton in a time of peace, and the withholding of the Queen's legacy. He demanded the withdrawal of the English troops from France, and since Henry openly refused, it left no option other than to attack England from the north as threatened in the final ultimatum.

James sent a fleet of ships to France under the command of the Earl of Arran, then sent heralds the length and breadth of the kingdom bidding his people prepare for war, and toured his own lands calling together his feudal musters. At the same time he started informing his nobles, the bravest and best of Scotland, to meet him with their armed men at Borough Muir of Edinburgh in three weeks' time.

The countryside was purple with heather and the air redolent with the scent of newly-mown hay, but even the most ardent peacemaker could not go on being provoked and humiliated without retaliation. So war clouds gathered, and the Wild Knight took charge of Scotland's preparations.

Margaret retired with their son to Linlithgow and James had promised to visit her there before the campaign started. He arrived at the Queen's private palace as the sun dipped behind the hills, firing the sky with crimson and saffron streaks. Hot and dust-covered from a long ride, not wholly satisfied by the musterings, his humour was as fatigued as his body.

To his relief Margaret did not renew her discussions concerning the coming expedition into England. His spirits revived as he delighted in the Prince's cooings and chucklings, and when he eventually retired with Margaret, he felt grateful for this unexpectedly docile homecoming.

In the middle of the night, Margaret began shrieking and screaming persistently. Roused from sleep, he lit the bedside candles. 'Margaret! My lady! Holy Mother of God! What ails you ? Are you in pain?'

Instead of answering, she took his head into her hands and pressed it against her bare breasts as she trembled. He succumbed until the twist of his body and the confusion of his legs with the bed curtains made him wriggle free.

'Margaret, what causes this fever of fear?'

Sobs still shuddered through her as haltingly she said. 'I've seen . . . seen a ghost . . . your ghost . . . yes, your ghost, James. I swear it!'

He drew back into the bed wraps and sighed heavily. This explained her earlier silent submission; all the time she had been planning this melodrama. She had no belief in ghosts, far from it; her guiding motions were essentially influenced by worldly acquisitions, and countless times she had scoffed at the supernatural.

'My lord, James, it was most real,' she persisted. 'And this is the second night I've dreamt of your death.'

He stretched out in the bed as if for sleep, but her voice went on, 'James, listen to what I say, for my dreams must be a warning against the war with England.'

He groaned, aware that if he did not listen she would prattle on throughout the night. 'Then speak, lady, so that we can sleep before dawn breaks.'

'Last night I saw you hurled down a great precipice, and as I gazed at your body crushed and mangled at the bottom, I lost the sight of one eye. Surely that means that no good can come out of this war?'

'It's the stuff of dreams, nothing else,' he countered.

But Margaret went on, 'Tonight I saw myself looking at my jewels, chains and coronets of diamonds. Suddenly a black cloud descended from the heavens. When it lifted, all my jewels had turned to pearls – the emblem of widowhood and tears. Is this double portent not sufficient warning to you, my lord?'

'Such dreams are the working of an uneasy mind,' he said, rolling over again.

'You don't listen because you would sooner please the Queen of France,' charged Margaret.

Realising that she now intended to repeat the entire gamut of her objections, he snatched the bed wraps and pulled them over his head.

She drew them away and continued, 'It is true that you honour that lewd Queen more than your own wife and mother of your Prince.'

With a bellow of impatience he jerked upright in bed. 'Margaret, you have spoken more than the say of a wise woman. Am I to seek a bed that contains no prattling? It would perhaps to be more to my delight than your purpose.'

This parry defeated her, for she sulkily covered herself with the wraps, and keeping as distant as the bed allowed, bade him extinguish the candles.

The following morning James went with his nobles to St. Katherine's Chapel to pray for the success of the expedition. Whilst at the pre-dieu a strange figure in blue gown belted with a roll of white linen came towards him. The stranger's head was bare, bald on top, with long yellow locks hanging on each side. He came forward until he almost touched the King, then bent down and in a voice as strange as his appearance said, 'Go not where you are purposed, or you will be confounded and brought to shame.'

The incident took James by surprise, and before he could think of a suitable answer, the stranger slipped behind the curtain concealing the private stairway leading to the upper part of the church. Sir David Lindsay, the prince's usher, went off in pursuit, reporting back that the figure had crossed the courtyard and entered the palace by a side window.

Sir David wanted to follow, but James restrained him. Smiling to himself he said, 'Go at once to the Queen, Sir David, and report this incident in all and every detail.'

James left the chapel, and after a rapid search of the palace, found the wearer of the false locks. With a dagger point at his throat, the astronomer Arfane confessed to being commissioned by the Queen.

When the Earl of Argyll arrived from Edinburgh, he told of an incident at Mercat Cross, where an unknown voice had called out a summons in parody of the King's requisition to his feudal militia. Instead of summoning them to do their bounden service for the usual forty days, the voice listed the names of those who would perish. Everything pointed to Margaret trying to render the attack upon England unpopular. James also knew that she had personally pleaded with Bishop Elphinstone and old Angus to raise their voices in protest.

Late that evening he went to the Queen's withdrawing chamber. Beneath his plain blue short jacket he kept his brightly aigletted shirt open in front, for the heat of the day remained within the palace. He felt tired, but satisfied that after searching thought he had reached the right conclusions, and he was cheered by the news that men were now coming from all parts of Scotland to join his army. After all his efforts he regarded it as a measure of their love and loyalty towards him, coupled, of course, with their hatred of the English.

Margaret ordered wine and devoted herself completely to his comfort. When they were alone she sat by his side at the carved table. 'Is there anything I can do to prevent this war with England?' she asked, with pleading eyes. He looked at her with probing closeness, trying to penetrate beneath any possible secrets. There were murmurings that her associations with old Angus came from a fondness for his grandson Archibald, who had recently lost his young wife in childbirth. Although most likely Court gossip, he had covered any such contingency in his will. 'The war's already started, Margaret,' he informed her. 'Over five hundred Scots were slain on Lord Home's raid into Northumberland.'

'Shouldn't that be a warning to you, James? In spite of Lord Home's braggart sword-waving his force has been severely used. The fleet under the command of the Earl of Arran has returned to Scotland without ever reaching France. The whole venture seems so ill-fated that it can only cause disaster. The Earl of Angus has said –'

James burst out, 'Margaret, I don't care a jot for the opinion of Angus. If the Doulases have hearts of slush, then they had best stay in Forfar. As for Home, his heart's in the right place, but his blood boils over and scalds his mind. It will be a different matter when the King of Scotland leads a Scottish army into England.'

'Your cousin of Arran has a great reputation as a soldier.'

Annoyance welled up within him, in spite of his intentions to control himself on what could be their last night together. 'Yes, but it would seem he is no sailor. It was a mistake to send him in command of the *Great Michael*.'

'Yet he refused to relinquish command to Sir Andrew Wood and has set sail again. Is that not another bad omen?' Margaret pressed.

'A grievous one for the Earl of Arran, and he will have to answer for it when he does return.'

'Then there's nothing I can say to penetrate the hardness of your resolve!'

'Nothing, Margaret, all has been said.' He gazed steadily at her, a bemused smile relaxing the tightness from his lips. 'Nor is there anything you can do, either by false dreams or false prophecies, and your hairy countenanced agent grovels in a dungeon in fear of his life. There will be no more ghostliness of his making.'

'It was all devised for your good, James.'

'That I reckoned, Margaret, and stayed the hands of those who would have not only pursued the astronomer with golden summer locks to his mistress, but also torn out his black liver.'

Her expression became more tender as she realised his protection. 'We were married to keep the peace between the realms of Scotland and England, James. Are you prepared to turn that agreement to nothing?'

He lightly put his hand over hers. 'Your royal brother has already turned it to nothing, Margaret. He can have little love for his sister, for nothing I have done justified the denial of your rights. For my part, I'm aware of your duty as a wife and intend to reward it. When I leave for England I confide to you in trust the subsidy of eighteen thousand crowns of the sun paid to me by King Louis, together with many other valuables. I've made my last testament and delivered it to Bishop Elphinstone. In the event of my death, you will be my heir and Queen Regent of Scotland, and have personal care of the infant King as long as you remain a widow. That, Margaret, is a token of the respect I have for you as my Queen.'

'James, if you will suffer me to accompany you, it may be that my countrymen will yield to a peace. I hear the Queen, my sister, is likely to be with the English army in her husband's absence. If we meet, who knows what God, by our means, might bring to pass?'

He smiled tolerantly. 'I know nothing of that, Margaret. But war is not a pursuit for the pregnant Queen of Scotland, even if it's thought expedient for the childless Queen of England. No, what's to be done is a matter for men. The feudal militia's assembling at Borough Muir. Tomorrow I join them, and when ready, we march for the border.' He lowered his lips and kissed the top of her head, then gently raised her to her feet. 'Say your good prayers for me, Margaret, and let Bishop Elphinstone be your guide if you're in any doubt.'

She clung to him tight and he felt the resurgence of their responsibilities as parents of a child who would one day be a king. Together they went to see the one-year-old healthy, sleeping Prince, then retired to her bedchamber. He had every wish to protect her from any trials ahead, respected her as a mother and Queen, but could feel no real love for her as a woman.

On the following morning, his thoughts were concentrated solely upon the war. As he rode away he noticed that the first flecks of autumn colours were beginning to tint the trees, the early flowering roses beside the lake had dark brown death crinkling at their edges, the brazen cuckoo no longer called for his mate, and ague would soon paralyse the gossamer wings of insects. But before the slow-moving cycle of autumnal death settled completely on the countryside, there was a battle to fight, and a victory to be won.

The Wild Knight who had beaten the Frenchmen in memory of his loved one now threw the gauntlet at a foe whose steel could penetrate the heart. This time it would be a fight in earnest, but the Wild Knight was ready to fight not only for his uncrowned Queen, but for the vengeance and the glory of the whole of Scotland. He was moving towards the destiny for which he had perhaps been born to fulfil.

SEVENTEEN

James left Edinburgh with the largest army ever mustered by a Scottish king. Estimates of its size varied from 80,000 to 100,000 men. They represented the whole of Scotland – clansmen from the highlands and farmers from the lowlands, more different from each other in dress and language than the lowlanders were from the English across the border. The towns had supplied burghers and tradesmen, and there were herdsmen from the southern uplands. These were the men who had gathered about his standard on the Borough Muir, carrying bows, long pikes, two-handed swords and round metal shields. Upon the strong arms and stout hearts of these men Scotland's future would depend.

James sensed the fervour of excitement at the prospect of striking a decisive and mortal blow at the 'auld enemy'. To support this mighty army were the cannon resulting from five years of experimentation. He had twenty-two now, and although it would take some four hundred oxen to pull them and thirty packhorses to carry the cannonballs in baskets on their backs, they would introduce a new element into warfare, something not yet fully tested. If successful, however, they could ensure a resounding victory. His Master Gunner, Sir Robert Borthwick, had every confidence in the artillery, and James respected his knowledge and ability. His troops too seemed full of confidence, as did all who cheered their way to the River Tweed on the eastern border. Everyone in Scotland, it appeared, thought of the imminent battle as having only one possible outcome – the complete routing of the English forces.

Once they crossed the Tweed they had reached English soil, and whatever the ultimate result, he had kept his word to the Queen of France. The weather soon made its mark on the campaign with heavy rain and strong winds. Horsemen and footmen, oxen dragging cannons, pack horses and baggage wagons all had to splash their way through endless pools of muddy water. Even so, the early signs were auspicious.

232

Whereas nearly twenty years ago Norham castle had proved impregnable, Scotland's artillery crumpled it after a six-day siege.

James held a war council at Twiselhaugh, resulting in unanimous approval to advance. The castles of Wark, Etal and Ford were taken with greater ease than Norham, increasing the jubilation of the troops, convincing them of their invincibility. After the fall of Ford, James established his force in a strongly fortified camp commanding the road which led north from Wooler, down the valley of the River Till. News came of Surrey's advancing army, but James arrived first to establish a formidable stronghold on Flodden Edge.

He then visited Ford castle with his natural son, the young Archbishop of St. Andrews. To his surprise a tall, raven-haired beauty with commanding dark eyes greeted him. She curtsied gracefully, and with a flickering of long lashes said, 'May I present my daughter, Your Grace. Both of us are your prisoners.'

James presented the Archbishop, then suggested that the gangling young lass acted as his guide for an inspection of the castle.

As the young couple departed he turned to Lady Heron, still drooped in obeisance, her blue and silver gown flounced out in a protective ring around her feet. Flushed with the exhilaration of victory, James's manliness rose turgid within him. He put out his hand and raised her to her feet. The hand was soft and white, essentially feminine, a rare prize for a battle-committed soldier.

'I understand your husband, the castellan of the castle, has been sent to Edinburgh as a prisoner of Scotland.'

'That is so, Your Grace.'

'You need have no fear of me, lady.'

She inclined her head slightly and smiled. 'I have heard that Your Grace is the most chivalrous of all knights.'

'Have you heard that in Scotland they call me the Wild Knight?'

Her coquettish display of alarm registered more encouragement than dismay, prompting him to become more adventurous. Long before the Archbishop returned, they had reached an understanding that the soldier need not return to camp that night.

The attraction of Lady Heron's embraces provided diversions no virile man could resist. He had always been motivated by a lusty appetite for sexuality. The women in his life would perhaps call it inordinate, but even now, with so much at stake, he knew that he would fight better for having recently enjoyed a woman. Amused by his title of the Wild

Knight, Lady Heron stimulated his wildness to a degree that elicited a resurgence of youth: a memory of Guelinda, coupled with the sexual agility of Jane Kennedy. It was a compound of delight he found irresistible under the enforced waiting circumstances, so he stayed to keep renewing the physical satisfaction only a sport-loving woman could provide.

When he finally returned to camp to check developments, Lord Home came to the point with typical asperity. The battle commanders were assembled in the King's tent and James sensed their unrest. 'The troops are eager to carry on their victorious way at all speed, Your Grace,' Home informed him. 'Many have deserted, either through lack of action after such early promise, or to return home with the booty from ransacking castles.'

James looked around at Argyll, Huntly, Lennox and Montrose, each clearly in accord with Home. Angus had arrived too, at the head of a large Douglas feudal muster. 'My lords, we occupy a good position here. I'm loath to leave it without first contacting the Earl of Surrey,' said James, staring hard at each in turn. 'Beside, we cannot move further south without leaving Berwick unmasked, thus affording Surrey an easy entry into Scotland should he choose not to engage us.'

There were a few agreeing nods, but the first voice came from Angus, who rose slowly to his feet. Although bent with age, he remained a massive, commanding figure, particularly in battle array. 'That's right, Your Grace, I agree concerning Berwick, but in this position the English could work round us.'

'Not the Earl of Surrey,' snapped James. 'He would not attack without issuing a knightly challenge.'

Angus's eyes smouldered in their deep sockets. 'You credit him with too much honour, Your Grace. Surrey marches towards us with thrice the size of army we expected, and he has a reinforcement fleet commanded by his son already under sail. This intelligence came to the camp this morning.'

'How does this affect Surrey's honour?' flashed James.

'It's not his numbers that dishonour him, but his methods, Your Grace. That pretty burde at Ford castle was doubtless under his orders to detain you while he gets gets his army into a favourable position.'

James leapt to his feet, eyes blazing fury. 'So the Earl of Angus pines for yet another wench his enfeebled bulk couldn't satisfy, is that the way of it?'

'Your Grace, I –'

'Stop your blather!' rapped James.

'We came to England to fight a war, not to wench,' burst out Angus, in a flood of anger. 'Your commanders agree that with a dwindling army we're ill-fitted to engage the approaching English. We now have less than half the army that crossed the Tweed. In the name of Scotland, your Queen and your heir, I entreat you to return home with the credit of the mischief already done to the English enemy; it more than redeems your pledge to the Queen of France.'

James stiffened with antagonism and resentment that Angus should dare to so address him. A heavy silence charged the tent, both men too overwrought for compromise. At last, James said, 'I came to fight the English, and if they have a hundred thousand more in numbers I shall stay and fight them. If the Earl of Angus has no stomach for such a battle he can return to Scotland. The King will retire when he's defeated the English or died in the attempt, not till then.' Red-faced his gaze swept over the assembled commanders. 'You, my lords, are free to act in accord with your wishes.'

Angus glanced round for support, but realised the commanders feared that deserting the King would prejudice their Court positions. Many of them, fools that they were, would follow the King to their deaths rather than let those back in Scotland think they had betrayed him. Angus turned to Home as the most likely to lead a revolt, but the diminutive nobleman, looking more like a jester in his chain mail and yellow jupon, wagged his head. Second to power, Home's next interest lay in fighting the English, and he now saw a long-awaited chance ahead.

'Well, Angus?' queried James, satisfied with the response from his noblemen.

'I shall retire, but only in protest against Your Grace's treatment of me. I leave my son George at the head of the Douglas muster to fight under the royal banner.'

'As you will,' snapped James finally.

They all watched the massive Earl quit the tent with head downcast. None enjoyed the situation, for it marked the beginning of disunity, a factor to be avoided by any army soon to enter battle.

James laughed out loud to show his unconcern. 'Well, my lords, that settles it. We maintain this position until we have closer news of my lord Surrey. I think our array will surprise him. Come, we'll make a tour of the camp.' He turned to Home, 'Alexander, summon my standard bearer. He can ride with us to let the troops see the emblem for which they fight.'

This inspired decision produced an instant flurry of activity. The King and his commanders mounted destriers fully trapped with battle trimmings. The standard bearer rode ahead of them, the red lion of Scotland glinting in the mellow sunlight shining from a watery blue sky. The sight of the King and the standard bearer during a break in the rain evoked sporadic cheers, which, as the progress continued, coalesced into a unified roar which reverberated across the hills and through the valleys, a full-throated expression of Scottish fervour. Its effect rid the atmosphere of the dolour of Angus's parting, and James remembered how the people of Edinburgh had sung with him when he led his young bride from England into the city.

He returned to his tent overprimed with memories. The wind blew refreshingly upon his face, and as he looked down the hillside of tussocky grass, his gaze concentrated on the widespread branches of a huge leafy oak. It was an old tree that had occupied its position long before his birth, and whatever the outcome of the battle to come, would remain there long after his passing.

Memory images flashed across his uncertain mind; his Queen – sister of the King of England. Coerced by his Council he had succumbed to their wishes, but only after realising that with Meg's death marriage could no longer provide him with any real affection or personal satisfaction. Yet his union with the English Princess had prevented outright war whilst her father lived, even though the marriage had never been more than a flimsy substitute for the joys of true love. The same sense of futility would now guide him back to Lady Heron, like Jane Kennedy, another substitute, a means of forgetfulness.

On the following Sunday news came to Ford castle that the Earl of Surrey had issued a knightly challenge from Alnwick castle. James returned to camp, summoned his commanders, then despatched a message that an Earl did not dictate terms to a King. The battle date he suggested as Friday the ninth of September, five days hence. The herald returned agreeing the date, but suggesting a different location for the battle. James reaffirmed the date, but refused to leave his advantageous position.

Speculation mounted with each successive day, contention gaining ground as, led by Lord Home, the Scottish noblemen expressed unrest. Further desertion occurred among the troops, whose eagerness to be looting among the enemy did not appreciate the finer points of knightly standards. Nevertheless, James insisted upon the correct knightly code being observed.

On Wednesday, two messengers brought news that Surrey was advancing towards their position. A Council meeting resulted in stormy scenes again led by Home.

The following day brought information that an advance column of the English army had crossed the Till and headed north-east. Home quickly assembled the battle commanders to confront the King. 'Your Grace, this means that the major part of the English army is likely to cross the river and defile within range of our cannons,' he pointed out. 'It's an opportunity of almost certain victory for Scotland if we open fire on them.'

'But it will not be the day fixed for the battle, my lord,' said James slowly, weighing the pressures upon his decision.

'Perhaps not, but such an advantage is not likely to be repeated,' countered Home. 'The Howards are fighters, Your Grace, they neither ask for nor give any quarter. If the advantage were with them, Surrey would not chew on it over long.'

Argyll's teeth protruded as he followed the exchanges with slightly open mouth. 'Well, Archibald, what do you make of it?' asked James.

'Home's argument cannot be gainsaid if tactics be the sole consideration, Your Grace.'

James nodded. He recognised this, also Home's remark about the advantage being the other way round. Surrey had a reputation for not always observing the knightly standards in battle. But when discussing campaigns at the time of his wedding, they had sworn to each other that any future contest between them in peace or war would suffer no infringement. It could not be regarded as an oath of honour, nonetheless James felt bound by it; fighting without mercy was not the same as starting with an unfair advantage. Yet listening to Home, it seemed a paltry reason on which to balance his life and the future of his kingdom. He could never make Home understand; brought up on the borders, accustomed to barbarity, he would not flinch from exploiting the enemy's weaknesses and pressing any possible advantage to its utmost.

'What would your decision be, Archibald?' asked James.

Argyll flourished his hands in a deprecatory gesture. 'Like you, Your Grace, I've always followed the standards of the tourney, but the responsibilities are not upon my head.'

'Responsibilities to the whole of Scotland,' Home interjected. 'If we let this army pass, they might invade Scotland by way of Berwick.'

'Or attack us from the north to offset the protection offered by our strong position on this southern slope,' said Argyll, stroking at his chin.

He acted very much the soldier now, no trace of his wine and women excesses.

'I realise that, my lords,' murmured James. 'Both are definite possibilities.'

'And both can be prevented by firing upon the English as they cross the Till,' pressed Home.

James hesitated, then with sudden decision announced, 'My knightly promise still stands. I will not break faith at this stage, the battle remains set for noon on Friday.'

Home's fleshy features wrinkled in disgust. 'Then I hope you are not given cause to rue that faith,' he snapped. 'I for one think it most likely that you will.'

James watched him bow stiffly, then stalk out of the tent almost blinded with rage. He too hoped that Surrey had not planned his course relying upon the honesty of a king's word spoken at a time of peace.

Throughout the next day, they lost touch of the English. Having fumed over the loss of their greatest opportunity, Home now pressed for a withdrawal by way of Coldstream, but the order to stand by the camp remained.

On the following day, when Admiral Lord Howard crossed Twizel Bridge, James absorbed the extent of the English deception: confirmation that Surrey had unscrupulously taken advantage of his good faith, exposing his troops solely to occupy a more favourable position. The rain again poured down upon the green and brown mélange of the country-side, autumn having moved nearer while the Scottish army stood still. James now felt as antagonistic as Home, especially as Lady Heron's sudden departure after sighting Surrey's force gave credence to Angus's accusation. It turned her lusty favours to insults, with Angus bound to go back to Scotland blabbing about it to justify his withdrawal.

James sounded an alert, then hurriedly conferred with his commanders, planning a quick change of strategy to recapture their lost advantage. He gave orders to fire all the camp litter at Flodden, and this provided a smoke screen for the Scottish army to move to Branxton Hill, about a mile to the north. As they took up their positions to make battle formations, they could see the Till winding its way through the countryside to join the Tweed. Beyond the Tweed were the moors and hills of Scotland, but between the Scots and Scotland now stood the English army.

Riding like a madman from one position to another, James urged his soldiers to their utmost, trying to inspire the blood and fire craving he had aroused after the failure of Prince Richard's proclamation. Events had multiplied in disaster around him. He had fallen victim to the temptations of a scheming whore, Surrey had taken advantage of his chivalric honour to deceive him, and he had told Angus that he would defeat the English or die in the attempt. Now the Wild Knight must prove his words. Towards this end he deployed the five Scottish formations across Branxton Hill. On the left flank, nearest to Scotland, were the Borderers and Highlanders commanded by Home and Huntly respectively. Between this force and his own centre formation was a contingent commanded by the Earls of Crawford and Montrose. The right flank was manned by a force commanded by Lennox and Argyll, with the new Earl of Bothwell commanding a division between them and the centre. Bothwell's men were to act as a reserve for the centre or right flank, wherever the need became greatest.

The rain kept falling in heavy showers. James noted with satisfaction that it was worse for the English, as it blew hard in their faces. Even so, all was not ready until four o'clock in the afternoon. He started the battle by ordering his cannons to open fire. The English had cannons too and returned the fire. It soon became apparent that neither side had the correct range of the other, so James ordered a cease-fire and signalled his left flank to advance. Almost immediately Huntly and Home's ten thousand strong pikemen swept down the hill in a solid phalanx.

Momentarily they seemed to engulf the English right wing led by Lord Edmund Howard, another of Surrey's sons. Seeing the disarray, the Earls of Crawford and Montrose bore down to press home this initial advantage.

James stood watching as the two contingents of Scots engaged two divisions of the English in fierce hand-to-hand fighting. When a wave of English horsemen swept forward to support their foot soldiers, James could no longer restrain his impatience to be at grips with the enemy. Without waiting for the rearguard to take up its planned position, he led his centre division madly downhill to plunge into the Earl of Surrey's centre division. Having left the top of the hill, they soon became aware that they were now exposed to the English cannon previously firing short of them.

'Forward!' James yelled, above the deafening din. 'Upon the English! Get upon them!'

The Scots followed their King to a man as the battle flared with the boom of cannon, clash of steel, pounding of hooves and the piercing cries of men with but one objective – to kill or be killed. Now the English archers obtained their range, and an air-displacing fury of arrows rained down upon the advancing Scottish centre. With the pick of the army behind him, James led the charge on foot into the English, never flinching for a moment.

Again the Scots followed their devil-crazed King. He killed five Englishmen with his long pike before it was broken by a blow from a halberd. He tossed the useless pieces to the muddy wet grass, drew his sword, brandished it forward, then once again plunged fearlessly into the fray. He struck all before him to the ground, remorselessly pushing on, supported by the combined forces of Lord Herries and Lord Maxwell. His sole object was to reach the Earl of Surrey's battle standard, then engage the man who had outmanoeuvred him by not observing the chivalric code expected from a knight of honour. Surrey should be made to pay for his deceit, but the way to him was barred by Sir Richard Harbottle, a renowned knight of huge bulk and strength. James took his sword in both hands and smote him on the shoulder with such force that the Englishman's body almost split in two down to the waist.

As the fighting grew fiercer near Pipers Hill, James summoned Bothwell to bring the rearguard to the front. At the same time he noted that the English left flank had pelted Lennox and Argyll's forces with so many arrows that their phalanx had broken in confusion. Now they too were coming down the hill to get at grips in hand-to-hand fighting.

James sensed the danger, that if some of the English could skirt round the side of Branxton Hill, they would be able to attack from behind. Realisation came too late, for at that moment Englishmen came pouring over the hill, and with their more easily manoeuvrable halberds caused havoc among the Scots, who could not easily turn around to make their long pikes effective.

The Scottish army was now hemmed in on all sides, but following the King's example, continued fighting furiously and with unyielding defiance. James had two divisions of English striking at his centre, but Surrey's standard remained in sight. If he could capture it, Scotland could still win the day. The thunderous noise from man, horse and weapons reverberated through the valley between the two hills. Once again James urged his men forward, hacking his way with his sword into wherever the battle was thickest.

Although underfoot the muddy wet grass was made even more slippery with blood, James continued to advance. If any man slipped he went down for good and was trampled under foot. Reaching Surrey was now the only hope of victory; it was still possible, the sort of challenge to which Lucan would have responded. Together they could have done it, shoulder to shoulder, closing the gap and removing all in their path. But Lucan was no longer with him. He had to achieve it alone, for Lucan's sake, for Meg's sake, for Scotland's sake.

Gathering all his strength, he let out a fierce yell and cast all caution aside. Here was the Wild Knight in full cry, no longer married to the wrong rose, but fighting again for the Queen of his own choice. Twenty years slipped away and gaining Surrey's standard symbolised the achievement of his heart's desire. He led a solid wedge of men who knew not how to yield other than to fall dead, or slump inert in an every-increasing pool of their own blood. Amidst this deadly close range fighting his own standard was cut down. Still James pressed on, then a shower of arrows fell upon them. He saw that someone had deliberately shielded him and died in the attempt.

The English halberds were proving far more deadly than the Scottish long pikes, but now they were looking into each other's eyes, fighting with swords, daggers, even their bare hands. Before him James saw Surrey's standard, casting a long shadow as the fiery sun moved gently to its cradle beneath the horizon. Time was running short.

Pressing forward once again, an arrow pierced into his unprotected groin and sent a searing shaft of pain down his right leg. He withdrew the arrow and flung it aside contemptuously and shouted. 'One more advance for the Wild Knight!'

The diminished group closed ranks and pushed forward yet again, driven solely by their King's unyielding impetus. Hot blood flowed down James's leg as the pain became more acute. An English halberd severed his left hand in two places. Bleeding profusely, he wielded his sword with his right hand alone, until, a mere spear's length from the enemy standard, another halberd struck him in the throat and blood sprayed all over his face. Flung to the ground, with more mutilated and dead falling around him, his blood gushed into the wet, dark earth.

As he clung to the last threads of sentient life, he realised this was the end, the Wild Knight's last tilt at success upon this earth. The Tudor rose of England Princess who had borne him a Prince would become ruling Queen of Scotland. His son, God have mercy upon the poor child, would perhaps one day honour his father by defeating the English.

A light airiness filled his head; a swift-moving phantasmagoria of the past flashed before him until one shimmering vision stood out with unmistakable clarity. Everything silent now, weightless, floating, even pleasant as clouds drifted by to the sound of a clavichord being strummed with a soothing gentleness.

In the final moment of consciousness failure became a triumph. The Wild Knight glided away on his last journey, and from beneath a blue marble stone at Dunblane emerged the image of his own truly chosen loved one to share what lay beyond the grave.